TO SAVE

A

KING

Endorsements for Rachel Hauck

TO LOVE A PRINCE

"Another compelling royal story by the master of princely tales!"
—Susan May Warren, *USA Today* bestselling,
RITA award–winning novelist

"*To Love a Prince* is breathtaking and enchanting! Rachel Hauck is the queen of inspirational royal romance."
—Teri Wilson, bestselling author of
Unleashing Mr. Darcy and *Christmas Charms*

"Hauck has taken elements we love from fairy tales and given them a fresh twist in a modern setting. A delightful read!"
—Becky Wade, bestselling and Christy Award winning author

THE FIFTH AVENUE STORY SOCIETY

"Hauck intertwines the stories of five New Yorkers who each receive a mysterious invitation to join a "story society" in this exhilarating inspirational… Hauck inspires and uplifts with this mix of tales. Readers who enjoy Karen Kingsbury will love this."
—Publishers Weekly

"Rachel Hauck's rich characterization and deft hand with plotting and setting had me enthralled until I turned the last page of this superb novel. *Fifth Avenue Story Society* is truly a masterpiece—a one-of-a-kind novel that lingers long after the last page is turned. This is one I'll reread often, and it should garner Hauck much well-deserved acclaim. This should be on everyone's shelf
—Colleen Coble, *USA Today* bestselling author

THE WEDDING SHOP

"I adored *The Wedding Shop*! Rachel Hauck has created a tender, nostalgic story, weaving together two pairs of star-crossed lovers from the present and the past with the magical space that connects them. So full of heart and heartache and redemption, this book is one you'll read long into the night, until the characters become your friends, and Heart's Bend, Tennessee, your second hometown."

—Beatriz Williams, *New York Times* bestselling author

THE WEDDING CHAPEL

"Hauck tells another gorgeously rendered story. The raw, hidden emotions of Taylor and Jack are incredibly realistic and will resonate with readers. The way the entire tale comes together with the image of the chapel as holding the heartbeat of God is breathtaking and complements the romance of the story."

—*RT Book Reviews*, 4.5 stars, TOP PICK!

THE WEDDING DRESS

"Hauck weaves an intricately beautiful story centering around a wedding dress passed down through the years. Taken at face value, the tale is superlative, but considering the spiritual message on the surface and between the lines, this novel is incredible. Readers will laugh, cry and treasure this book."

—RT Book Reviews, TOP PICK!

THE ROYAL WEDDING SERIES

"Perfect for Valentine's Day, Hauck's latest inspirational romance offers an uplifting and emotionally rewarding tale that will delight her growing fan base."

—Library Journal, starred review of *How To Catch A Prince*

"Hauck spins a surprisingly believable royal-meets-commoner love story. This is a modern and engaging tale with well-developed secondary characters that are entertaining and add a quirky touch. Hauck fans will find a gem of a tale."

—Publishers Weekly starred review of *Once Upon a Prince*

More by Rachel Hauck

Visit www.rachelhauck.com

True Blue Royal
To Love A Prince (Book One)
To Save A King (Book Two)

Georgia on Her Mind

Nashville Series
Nashville Dreams
Nashville Sweetheart

Lowcountry Series
Sweet Caroline
Love Starts with Elle
Dining with Joy

Songbird Novels with Sara Evans
The Sweet By and By
Softly and Tenderly
Love Lifted Me

The Wedding Collection
The Wedding Dress
The Wedding Chapel
The Wedding Shop
The Wedding Dress Christmas

The Royal Wedding Series
Once Upon a Prince
A March Bride (novella)
Princess Ever After
How to Catch a Prince
A Royal Christmas Wedding

Stand Alone
The Writing Desk
The Love Letter
The Memory House
The Fifth Avenue Story Society

Novellas
Hurricane Allie
A Brush with Love

TO SAVE
A
KING

RACHEL HAUCK

Cover Design: Kristen Ingebretson
Map Design: Penmagiccards
Interior Formatting: Author E.M.S.

To those who dare to believe

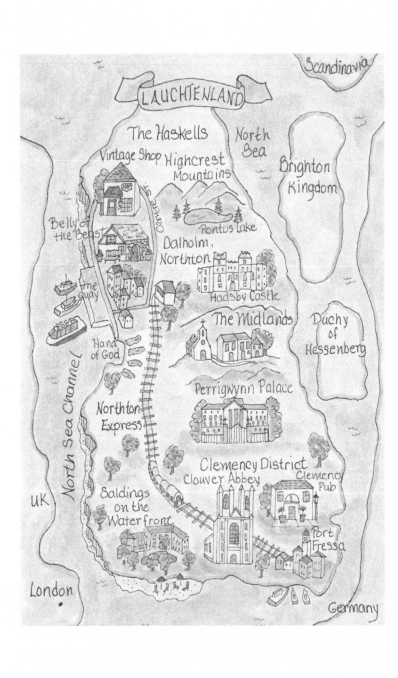

LET'S BEGIN HERE...

O*nce Upon a Time...*

… Prince John believed in fairy tales.

"Tell the fairy tale, Mum," he'd say on the nights his mum, the queen of Lauchtenland, tucked him and little brother Gus into bed, imagining the story's thick white feather, almost wishing it would appear before his eyes.

The Swan's Feather was as old as the House of Blue itself. When it began no one really knew, but for centuries the tale echoed in the halls of Hadsby Castle and Perrigwynn Palace.

On this particular night, Mum hurried ten-year-old John and eight-year-old Gus toward the gold and blue couch, the big skirt of her sparkling dress swishing. She'd told them frightfully grand men and women from around the world awaited her in the Great Hall.

"Quickly boys, I don't have long." Mum sat with a sighing smile.

"Tell *The Swan's Feather*, Mum." Though John was the oldest, if he didn't speak up, he'd not get his way.

"I hate that one." Gus leaned around Mum, making a face. "Tell the one about the knight who kills the dragon."

"We heard that one last time." Tonight, John was determined to win. After all, he was the crown prince and future king. If he couldn't rule his little brother, then who could he rule?

So the brotherly debate began over which fairy tale was the best and Mum, being a queen, settled it with swift diplomacy.

"We heard your story last time, Gus." She kissed her youngest prince on the head. "Tonight it's John's turn to choose."

John sneered at his brother then sat back. Mum was busy tonight and if they argued, there would be no story.

Being a queen was serious business and to be good at "queening"—as Dad liked to say—required a good deal of work.

"We're lucky men," he'd say. *"Mum loves us and her country with such devotion."*

However, Gus, being Gus, made a final appeal. *"The Swan's Feather* is about a girl. Blech." His protest came with a spew of biscuit crumbs.

"What's wrong with girls?" Mum said. "I'm a girl."

"No you're not. You're Mum and mums don't count."

"Be quiet," John said. "Mum can't be late to her dinner."

As for *The Swan's Feather* being about a girl? Well, that's *exactly* why John loved it.

"Here we go." Mum hugged both boys close. "The story of *The Swan's Feather*. Once upon a time, there was a young prince." Her voice was soft, almost a whisper, but full of an excitement John felt in his bones.

"That's me," he said, sitting up, gazing into his mother's beautiful face. "The prince."

"And me." Gus.

"Yes, it's both of you, but no more interruptions or it's straight to bed." John buttoned his lip and settled back. "Where were we? Oh yes, well, our young prince was destined to fall in love. He had no choice you see, for there was a writ, a law, that required all princes bound to be king—"

"I'm not going to be king." Gus again, declaring the obvious, and sounding disappointed. "But I can kill a dragon."

"Do you know what it means to be quiet?" John reached around his mother for a swing at Gus, but she caught his arm and held it in her lap.

"My little darlings, you must listen before you speak. Don't rob me of the pleasure of tucking you in before this dinner. Now, the young crown prince was all but commanded to find a wife or risk the right of the throne and lose the kingdom. But the prince wanted love as well as a wife. 'Love,' his father told him, 'is not a requirement, dear boy, but a luxury. Find a suitable bride is all we ask. Do your duty.'"

"But he wanted love, Mum." For some odd reason, John felt the pain of the fairy-tale prince every time. Why must he have a writ? Why must he marry without love? Even for the kingdom, it didn't seem right or fair.

"No talking." Gus, and who asked him?

"Alas," Mum went on, "in all the land, the crown prince found no fair maiden for his heart to love. He searched the high country, the low country, and along the mountain ridges and down by the seashore. Still, love could not be found."

"Did he look in the Heart of God?" John peered up at his mother. Surely, the prince would find love there. 'Tis where he'd look if he were bound by this writ, this law of love.

"That's not part of the story, dummy."

"Gus," Mum said. "Words."

He shrank back, shoving another cookie into his mouth from the endless pile in his hand.

"There was no Heart of God when the prince looked for love." Mum glanced toward the door where Dad leaned against the opening, smiling, hands in his tuxedo pockets.

No Heart of God for the fairy-tale prince? As far as John knew, the lights of the eight ancient cathedrals—which formed a heart—existed since the dawn of time.

John gazed from Dad to Mum then Dad again. Was that the look of love? Staring at one another with googly eyes—which made him squirm.

"Hurry, love," Dad said. "It's almost eight. Boys, listen to your mum's story then straight to bed. If you need anything, call Molly."

3

"Now you're the one interrupting." Mum shooed Dad with a flick of her hand. "I've lost my place again."

"The prince couldn't find a stupid girlfriend." Gus scooted to the edge of the couch and brushed his crumbs to the floor.

"You will clean that up, young man." Mum sounded irritated. *Thank you, Gus.* "Our poor prince is lost, looking for love. With no Heart of God to guide him, the prince had to do it all on his own. One day, his father, the king, sent him to faraway lands, braving stormy seas, to find a suitable princess. But again, none was found.

"Years passed and still no bride. What was he to do? A king without a bride in his kingdom was no king at all. Finally the king demanded the prince marry one of the beautiful maidens of his kingdom."

"This sounds like Cinderella. I hate Cinderella." Gus was kneeling on the plush carpet, gathering crumbs in his hand and dumping them into a china dish on the end table.

Mum frowned at the crumb deposits but pushed on with the tale. "But the prince insisted he must marry for love. He was so desperate he stayed behind in the abbey after vespers one day to say his own prayers. Did they avail anything? Was there any being to hear his plea? The prince had no idea, but he believed. Then it happened. The king announced a great ball and invited all the eligible maidens in the land."

"Cinderella," Gus muttered.

One more interruption, and John would sock him. Right in the nose. He balled his fist, ready to fire. They'd be sent to bed without the rest of the story, and maybe he'd even be grounded from his video games, but it'd be worth it.

"All the daughters of Lauchtenland, from high to low, purchased beautiful gowns from the shops in the Midlands, or sewed them at home, with their mums frantically supervising. They must be beautiful. They must impress the prince. A girl could do a lot of good being married to a future king. The night of the ball arrived, and the room was filled with women from every branch of society, their brightly colored gowns like the colors of the earth and sky. Red ones, blue ones, green ones. Purple, gold, black, and white. Sparkling bobbles on their ears and around their necks caught the light. The prince was both overwhelmed and overjoyed. Surely one woman in the room would steal his heart. The king agreed. Tonight, his son would find a bride. The fairest of them all would dance in his arms, and together they'd fall madly in love. By dawn's glorious light, the prince had danced with so many fair maidens his fine shoes were worn out. 'Well, son, did you find love?' the king asked. 'No father,' he said. 'Sadly, no.'"

"What a loser." Gus was back on the couch, half awake, half asleep, a cookie crumb clinging to his lower lip.

"'What are we to do?' the king asked of his queen. 'Believe,' she said. 'He will find love when the swans return to the garden pond.' But the swans returned every year, the king protested, and his son had yet to find love.

"The next day as the prince concluded his morning vespers, a thick white feather fell from the abbey's rafters. Picking up the large, perfect plume, the prince searched for the trespassing bird, most likely wounded and in need of rescue. Was he perched on a windowsill or on the flat surface of the wide rafters? He called for the gardener and the abbey caretaker. They searched along with the prince but no bird was found.

"Remembering the queen's prediction, the prince tucked the feather into his pocket, believing with all his heart this fine plume was a sign of his coming *true* love. Time passed and the king grew old. People feared there would be no new king because the crown prince had not found a bride and thus had not taken his oath to serve the people.

"'You must marry,' the king said, his voice weak with age. 'With or without love.' Alas, the prince agreed to marry a beautiful lady of noble stature and fine reputation. Everyone approved and the wedding date was set. Then. One day it happened." When Mum got to this part, she lowered her voice in a way that thundered, and a shiver always trickled down John's spine. "While on holiday with his mates, the prince saw the most marvelous girl. She was kind and sweet, very smart—"

"Like you, Mum," John whispered.

"—yet she seemed sad to him. Something troubled her. The prince wanted to be her friend. So he made her laugh and sing. Soon they were inseparable. And it happened. The prince experienced the powerful, moving sensation of love. It kept him awake at night. He thought of nothing but her. His friends chided him. 'She's not of noble birth,' they said. 'No one has ever heard of her,' they said. Was she worthy to be the bride of a future king? As much as the prince loved her, would she make a suitable queen? Would the people love her? He was already engaged to a fine woman the people admired. Sadly, the prince knew he must return to his homeland and never see the girl again. Their love came too late. Leaving his friends to enjoy their last day on holiday, he traveled to his love's modest home. While it was nothing like the palace where he lived, it was warm, cozy, and full of happiness. His heart swelled all the more with affection. He was served the most delicious tea and cakes. Her father regaled him with stories, even sang a few songs. They toured the family's modest barn and talked to the animals. At last the hour came for the prince to depart. As he was about to tell the girl of his upcoming nuptials, he spied a beautiful, thick, white swan's feather on the fireplace mantel.

"The prince could not speak. The moment was too sacred for words. At last he inquired, 'Where'd you get this?' He raised the shaft. 'I found it in our chapel, after my prayers,' she answered. Upon her confession, he embraced and kissed her sweetly, tenderly."

"Blech." Gus. Right on cue. Every time.

"The prince finally found love and proposed marriage, asking her to be his wife, his princess and future queen. To this very day, they are remembered for their deep love and affection. The girl who became a princess, then a queen, gave herself to charity and good works, to kindness and truth, and the kingdom prospered." Mum patted each of them on the back. "The end. Now, bedtime. I'm running late. Molly?"

Mum kissed each son on the head before their nanny shuffled

them off to bed—all while Gus proclaimed the story's stupidity and that his dragon would burn up *that swan* and its feathers.

John, however, even at his young age, believed all the more in the white feather and true love.

Lying in bed, staring through the dark at the faint light coming in from under the door, he understood he was the prince in the old Lauchten tale. Bound by a writ, a law, to marry for the crown, the House of Blue, and a thousand years of Lauchtenland history.

Marriage was a *must* for every crown royal in the House of Blue. However, love was not.

CHAPTER
ONE

JOHN

Whoever had penned his love story had a sordid sense of happily ever after. Even worse, the author had left him trapped between the inciting incident of Act One and the noble quest of Act Two.

Nearly a year after his wife's death, Crown Prince John of the House of Blue remained trapped by grief. It was impossible to go backward, but unimaginable to move forward—however much he'd begun to desire it.

Death. Sorrow. Pain. He wearied of those black clouds hovering over him. Surely sunshine would break through sooner or later. Yet if and when it did, he'd resent it. Of that he was sure.

Until then, he remained under the protective umbrella of his royal duties as a future king, a working member of Lauchtenland's "Family," the House of Blue, smiling for the public and doing good, all the while with a tornado twisting inside.

On this particular Friday morning the queen had summoned him to her office. His secretary, Briggs, scheduled the appointment without notes so the purpose of the meeting remained a mystery.

More than likely she just wanted to visit with her son and heir. They'd chat about life—okay, John's life—while sipping tea and savoring puffs. She called this sort of gathering "checking on things."

Leaving his apartment, John made his way down the Queen's Corridor toward Mum's office, passing through swaths of June sunlight and under portraits of his ancestors—monarchs who'd walked where he now trod. Literally and figuratively, mind you.

He paused under the twenty-foot painting of King Louis V— the royal Blue who inspired the famous—or was it infamous?— marriage writ by which all crown heirs of the House of Blue were bound.

You see, Louis enjoyed his bachelor life and found no need for a wife and child. He preferred his independence, his friendships, his dalliances, his sports, and books. No pleading with him to settle down, marry, and produce an heir came to fruition. So his father, King Louis IV, gave way to drastic measures and manufactured a way to march his son down the aisle.

John always suspected he gleaned his idea from the Family fairy tale, *The Swan's Feather*.

And so, it was decreed that if Crown Prince Louis desired to take his place as future king—thus taking the oath of office via the investiture ceremony—then he *must* marry.

However—and there's always a however—if he chose to carry on as a freewheeling bachelor, there would be no oath, no crown, no throne, no kingdom. He'd risk the monarchy and a constitutional crisis. And no Blue royal had *ever* risked either.

Marriage also, ole Louis IV claimed, ensured the posterity of the House of Blue throne. One of the oldest in Europe, fought for and won by the sweat and blood of their Blue ancestors and the men and women of the kingdom, the Family *and* legacy must continue.

This was all fine and dandy for the nineteenth century, but John lived in the twenty-first, for crying out loud. The writ was archaic and oppressive. As far as he was concerned, the time had arrived to nullify the old ways and methods and live in the new.

Some traditions were worthy of a modern nod, and others were not. Include the writ in the latter.

Besides, he'd found love. Once. He'd fulfilled his duty. Should he be punished because it was so cruelly taken away?

Surely the old writ didn't apply to him now. Though he'd not yet taken his sworn oath to serve and protect the people of Lauchtenland and be their king. Ah, it was a conundrum.

Meanwhile, as he mulled over the past and present in the red-carpeted hallway, the queen waited. He must get on.

Down the way, John greeted her secretary, Mason, who escorted him into her office.

"What's Hamish Fickle's scheme? Do you know?" Mum stood in front of the telly, sipping a cup of tea. "Ever since he was elected to parliament, he's a regular on the talk shows. You'd think he'd prefer to be a presenter instead of an MP."

John glanced at the large screen suspended above the fireplace. When Mum wasn't watching, she'd press a button and the telly would disappear magically into the ceiling.

"What's he going on about?" Hamish sat on the set of LTV-1's new mid-morning hit, *Tuppence Corbyn & Friends*.

"Your investiture and the plight of the Midlands clothing business."

"What?" John fixed a cup of tea and stirred in a drop of cream. "Turn it up."

Mum aimed the remote and Hamish Fickle's voice boomed into the room.

"One can't help but wonder why the crown prince hasn't taken his oath. Why hasn't the queen changed the writ? It's insane to expect a modern man to marry on demand. Is he unfit in some way? Has his wife's death taken the gusto from him?"

Tuppence, with her long dark hair and vivid blue eyes, gasped. "I think the prince is just fine. He's recovering. He was devastated when Princess Holland died."

"Of course, but he's more than an ordinary man," Hamish said, smiling as if he were choosing a word or number on a game show. "He lives not only for himself but for us. Should, and God forbid, anything happen to the queen and our crown prince has not sworn his oath, we could face political disaster."

"Goodness, you sound like a conspiracy theorist, Hamish."

The man chuckled and leaned toward his host. What a fraud. "I'm saying our monarchy, our very constitution and government, exists through the crown. Should misfortune happen to our beloved sovereign"—he lifted his palm as if to prevent any dastardly scheme from the gods—"and the crown prince has not been invested as our next king, we would literally be without a government, thus ensuring panic and chaos."

This bit of news appeared to rattle Tuppence, who flipped through her blue notecards, stammering, trying to move on. "Um, well, goodness, we, we... Clothes. Yes, we wanted to talk about the, the...the new clothing...manufacturer that has come into the Midlands. Hamish, as an MP, what do you think of our lovely boutique garment district? Will this large international company destroy our small businesses?"

"I do believe so, yes."

"He's a wealth of good news, isn't he?" John said, sipping his tea, listening as Hamish pontificated about Reingard Industries.

"This new manufacturer has killed the garment industry everywhere they've planted a new facility. They promise high wages but soon learn the locals do not know their equipment and thus cannot produce fast enough, so they lay everyone off and bring in their own people. Meanwhile, the manufacturers have suffered with costly production and reduced demand. The question I'm asking is how did this happen? On top of the fact, our own Eloise Ltd. was set to buy the land that Reingard Industries now sits on. And for half the price, I might add. It's rather a mystery, Tupp."

"He does raise valid questions," John said with no shortage of reluctance.

"I hope you get to the bottom of this soon, Hamish." Tuppence Corbyn seemed even more disturbed than before. "My own grandmother used to have a shop on Ribbon Avenue in the Midlands. It's gone now and so are the lovely clothes she used to make." Then, as if flipping a switch, she gathered herself and smiled for the camera. "More with MP Hamish Fickle after this word from Port Fressa Insurance."

John snatched up the remote and powered off the television. He felt some odd satisfaction as it, along with Hamish Fickle, disappeared into the ceiling.

"He's elected from one of County Northton's smallest regions. Midland Garden," he said. "Why is he on a national talk show? Shouldn't he be tending the needs of those who elected him?"

"He's charming," Mum said, moving to the cart to refresh her tea. "The shows love him. Though I find him a rather small man with a big mouth." She sat in her chair with a glance up at John. "How are you?"

"I know you didn't ask me here to inquire of my health." He sat in the chair opposite his mother. The one where she met with the prime minister, opposition opponents, and international leaders.

"Why not? I'm a mother. The welfare of her son is part of the job." She bit into a cinnamon-coated puff. "I saw LTV-1 has produced a documentary about our dear Holland and—"

"I know." He rather hoped she'd not bring this up. He'd been avoiding requests for interviews since January.

"Really? You never said. Did you take part? I'm surprised I wasn't asked."

"They made many requests but I declined." The life he'd shared with Holland, however short, was private, his personal treasure, and he'd not allow anyone to peer inside, disturb his memories.

"How's Briley?" Mum moved on.

"Fair." Briley, Holland's beloved horse, had broken his leg in the accident but the bone didn't heal well. He'd had a second surgery three months ago but still seemed hesitant to bear weight on the leg. "He's a fighter."

"Are you sure you're not keeping that poor creature alive to—"

"Mum, I would never." The question caused John to flinch. In the dark of night, he'd wondered the same thing. Was he keeping Briley alive because he was the last living thing Holland touched before she died?

"See to it you're not." Mum leveled a gaze at him from across the way. John never realized until now the large gap between the queen's chair and the guest chair.

"The veterinarian and groom are doing a brilliant job of his care. If either hinted at putting him down, I'd not hesitate." He'd not allow the ole boy to suffer. "So, what is this meeting about? Briggs left no notes. I feel unprepared."

"Briggs didn't tell you because I didn't tell him. This is a personal visit not Family business."

"Is everything all right?" John angled forward with a bit of trepidation. Mum *had* seemed rather out of sorts lately. Pale. Retiring early. Her voice and countenance lacked her usual steel.

"Yes, of course. I have several things to share. Private news." Mum retrieved a bound manuscript from her desk. "Your dear cousin Rachel's gone off and done a crazy thing."

Rachel was the daughter of Mum's sister, Princess Arabella.

"What's she done now?" And how did it involve him?

"She's published a book."

"Oh the horrors." John flipped through what appeared to be a picture story. "Shall we tie her to the stake? Send her to the tower?"

Last year dear cousin Rachel got caught in a tech company scam that nearly landed her in prison. To her good fortune, Mum and the Lauchtenland Investigative Service—the LIS—were onto the scheme well before her involvement. In the end, her innocence protected her.

"It's a fairy tale," Mum said. "Our fairy tale. The one I told you and Gus at bedtime."

"Funny, I don't see Rachel writing about shining knights and fire-breathing dragons." He paused to read some of the text.

"*...the young crown prince was all but commanded to find a wife or risk the right of the throne and lose the kingdom.*"

"*...king without a bride was no king at all.*"

"*The Swan's Feather*? She's stolen our story."

Perhaps it was the sentiment of his youth, or the realization he *was* a future king without a bride, that caused a rise of warm tears.

"She didn't steal it but nor did she ask my permission," Mum said. "But it's done and I see no reason to protest. After the mess last year with the tech scam, she needs a win. A career in capital investment was *not* her future."

"How can you let it go? The fairy tale was not hers to tell." It was theirs. His and Mum's. More specifically, his. He was the one who loved the tale as a child. The one who found a white feather in Clouver Abbey after his wife's funeral.

It'd been a sacred moment. As if she were still with him. His one true love.

"Isn't it? The story belongs to no one yet everyone. Especially to a Blue. I heard it from my grandmother who heard it from her grandmother. It's the Family's story and if Rachel profits from it, I've no quarrel. Perhaps she's found her calling."

"But you're the queen, the proprietor of the story. The crown heir who had to marry."

"Perhaps, but it's done. Arabella asked me not to make a thing of it and I won't. I'm really more concerned the publicity will bring up her faux pas from last year. I can see it now. On the set with some presenter. 'Great fairy tale, Princess Rachel, but do tell us how you became involved with Digital Light. Were you almost thrown in the dungeon?'"

"The onus of the media will fall on her publisher." John flipped through the story images, struck by how much the drawn prince resembled him.

"True, and Arabella claims they really believe in her and the book. She'll perform readings at schools and daycares, high-lighting the reading programs Arabella patrons. It's a win for all."

Mum excelled at supporting others, at believing in them. John used to attribute it to her position. Why not extol others from a queenly perch? After all, *she* was on top of the heap. But over the years he understood her generosity of spirit was more than duty. It was her nature. Her heart.

"I'll do what I can to support her." John returned the mock-up to his mother. "Why did we need a meeting about it? You could've told me over dinner."

"There's more than one purpose for our gathering." Mum scanned the pages of Rachel's book and smiled. "He looks like you. Didn't you always see yourself as the hero in this story?"

"When I was ten, perhaps." His eyes blurred again. He'd not confess it out loud, but that Family fairy tale had shaped his heart of love. "I found my princess without the journey of our hero. And she was *most* suitable. For me and the job."

Yet the fairy-tale prince had a happy ending. The real-life prince was a widower at thirty-one.

"You'll find a new love, John," Mum said with a comforting hope he couldn't quite accept. "You're young, intelligent, handsome, if I say so myself." She smiled her famous smile. The one Gus had inherited. "You *are* healing, aren't you?"

"There are days I feel normal, whatever that is, like I'm ready to move on. I've been through all the firsts—birthdays, holidays, wedding anniversary. All that remains is the memorial of her death." Almost two months away. At the end of August. "Other days I want to crawl into a hole. Twice this month, I started up North One to visit Briley but turned round at the first exit. I'm trapped, Mum, between my fairy tale"—he motioned to the manuscript—"and reality."

She set aside the book and crossed over to him, kneeling beside his chair. "What can I do to help?"

He kissed her forehead. "You're doing it. Listening. Loving me. Being patient." He offered her a hand as she tried to stand and stumbled. "Mum, are you okay?"

"The heel of my shoe caught. Don't fuss." Though she returned to her chair with a tired sigh. "There's another thing," she added. "I asked Gus to let me tell you."

By her tone and expression, he knew where this was going. "Daffy is pregnant?"

"Yes, but you can't be surprised," Mum said, low and tender, with a touch of pink excitement on her cheeks. Of course. This was her first grandchild. Well, not *technically*, but what did it matter now? "The baby's due in December."

"I'll be an uncle." Instead of a father. They'd announced

Holland's honeymoon pregnancy to the Family a month before the accident. John plastered on his best smile, downed the last of his tea, and set aside his cup and saucer. "The fun, eccentric one with a library of old books and a crow living on his shoulder."

Mum made a face. "You will be the uncle king who allows his nieces and nephews to play hide-n-seek in the throne room, who dons a red suit at Christmas to pass out their presents. John, look at me. You'll be the uncle who tucks in *his* children with Gus's during a wild, crazy summer sleepover. I know you lost more than a wife that day but—"

"Mum, please. Can we not discuss it?"

Her words, her vision of the future inspired more tears—which he found annoying. He'd cut off the waterworks six months ago. Crying wouldn't bring her back, or the baby she carried.

However all this talk of fairy tales, future children, the documentary, and the approaching one-year anniversary of Holland's death—where he'd place a wreath on her headstone... His tears had a will of their own.

"The thing is, Mum, I can't see my way clear. My future seems so...so gray and blank. I don't mean to sound ungrateful because I've more than most. I've a rare and privileged position. I know what and who I'll be ten years from now. Twenty. But I can't help wondering if God didn't mean for me to die on that day too. With them."

He was supposed to meet Holland for an afternoon of riding but investiture planning had waylaid him.

"Darling," Mum said. "You are here because you've a purpose. You will find your way. Have faith. A lovely future awaits you. I know this as sure as I'm queen of Lauchtenland." She left him no room to argue because Mum was most definitely the queen of Lauchtenland. "However, I urge you not to be passive about your future. Seek it. Ask. Don't assume your present situation is the model for your life. Death, as cruel as it can be, happens in the midst of life. Of living. Holland's journey ended. Yours did not. Not to sound trite or cliché, but she would want you to find happiness, marry, have children."

"What if my happiness doesn't include a wife and children? What if Holland was my only love? We've no promise on this earth of anything, clearly, lasting more than a day. If that even. We've no promises of a lifetime of love. Or living to a ripe old age. As a man, I can limp my way forward, fulfill my duties, and achieve some success, but as a future king, one *required* to marry… That is where I am most lost. I will not be forced into anything, Mum."

Besides, no woman came close to his Holland. Not one.

"No, no, of course not," Mum said. "But your father and Elias and I have been talking." Elias was Lauchtenland's prime minister who'd formed a government in the queen's name. She was his listening ear and adviser. He was her voice to and from the people. "We thought perhaps you could at least start dating."

"Mum, my queen, you and Elias run the country. Not me."

"Like it or not, John, as our future monarch, you *are* part of my duty. As well as the prime minister's."

"I'll do my duty for Lauchtenland and the Family, but I refuse to marry for the sake of a hundred-eighty-year-old writ. I'll abdicate and give the crown to Gus first."

Mum launched to her feet, rattling her chair. "A Blue has *never* abdicated. There is no reason to start now. Abdication in this modern age could mean death to the Family and a millennium of Lauchtenland history. Never mind a plain black eye on my legacy and leadership."

"I think the mark would be against me, not you. Mum, honestly, don't you think people would understand? If to keep our constitutional monarchy safe, we need a married and sworn-in prince, Gus is your man." Baby brother was married to the lovely Daffodil Caron, whom everyone adored, and now a father-to-be. "He'd make a splendid king."

"Gus doesn't want the job. Will you thrust it on him?"

"Why not? It's been thrust upon me. No one asked. Just first born, *boop*, here's your crown, laddo." John knocked the air over his head with a pass of his hand.

"I've trained you. Taught you. Invested in you as the next ruler.

Gus is thirty years behind the curve, John." Mum returned to her chair, smoothing her hand over her skirt, panic shaping her expression.

"You know the answer is right in front of you." John scooted to the edge of his chair with a bit of energy. "Change the writ. A crown prince or princess does *not* have to be married for the investiture ceremony. Remove the requirement to make a spouse part of the legal bargain. Allow future kings or queens to take their oath when they become of legal age. Twenty-one. It makes no sense to wait for marriage."

"Elias and I discussed that very thing, but we are both concerned changing the writ, at least at this current time, will draw fire from our opposition. They'll say we're changing the rules to accommodate my son. Playing favorites."

"Of course you are. I am your son. Why can't you change the rule? It's ours to change. Granddad Louis made it up to get what he wanted."

"True, but since then it's been codified by parliament."

"You can handle parliament, Mum." John smiled. "You've done it before."

"I also worry a change will have a negative impact on the future generations. Let them off the hook, so to speak." When she said "them" she really meant him, of course. "Marriage and family are the threads of our society and even more so, the monarchy. When I became queen, the Family was a hundred and twenty strong between my grandparents' siblings and their children. Twenty-five years later we're down to thirty." Her eyes glistened. "I've been to more funerals the last five years than weddings. Those of us who remain only had one or two children except Uncle George who had none and Millicent who bore three. We're not prospering, we're shrinking."

"It only takes *one* to maintain the throne."

"One *with* the Family, an army of Blues, surrounding him or her. How do you think we'll fare if you abdicate and Gus is put forward as the new crown prince? Do you think upstarts like Hamish Fickle and his RECO party will just doff their hats and bow? In the past year the move to be solely an elected republic has gained strength. More and more say the time of the monarchy has passed."

"An argument that has been going on since the American Revolution." Lauchtenland sided with their American cousins over their British family and neighbors during that conflict. For centuries, it had been a point of pride to have been on the winning side.

"I don't see why you can't simply invite someone to dinner," Mum said. "What about Lady Erin? She's well-born, educated, connected with charities. You've known her most of your life."

"Do not start, Mum. I'll not cull through a list of potential candidates. Besides, if I ask any lass to dinner, the media will have us engaged and down the aisle by week's end. No thanks."

Even worse, any consideration of moving on felt like a betrayal. *Yet...* Lately, when he was alone, reading, or sipping a good port before bed, acceptance whispered through him. Flash rays of sunshine broke through his clouds, and hope became a subtle prospect.

He'd not confess it here, but last month, he'd attended a dinner party at his mate Larrabee's place. He'd been seated next to Sydney Templeton, a distant acquaintance, and to his surprise, they talked for two hours, laughing, going on about anything and everything. He touched her arm. She touched his knee.

Afterwards, when he'd gone home and crawled into bed, he realized he'd not thought of Holland once, and the icy dread of forgetting her froze every ounce of the evening's joy.

Holland must be remembered. She must.

"Have you spoken to her parents?" Mum said as if reading his private thoughts.

"Not really. We've given each other space. We've not connected since we donated her clothes six months ago."

It was as if they wanted to forget he'd been a part of their family. He understood. He reminded them of their loss.

"Very well. There is one more item on my agenda. A special request. Please do not refuse me."

"I reserve the right, but what is it?"

"Will you go to Tennessee and make acquaintance with Scottie?"

He laughed. Truly. "You want me to meet with your long-lost daughter? I'm sorry, Mum, but Scottie O'Shay is your concern, not mine."

"She's your sister."

"Half sister but your full-blood daughter." John rose for the tea trolley. The puffs under the glass called to him. A moment like this needed a pastry. "Why is this my mission and not yours?"

"I'm the woman who abandoned her. Who she believed was dead."

"I'm the son of that woman." He returned to his chair with a plate of puffs, offering one to Mum who refused. "If you want a connection with Scottie O'Shay, invite her here. Or go there. Surely Dad would love a trip to America. Or Rachel. Even better, Aunt Arabella. Promise a shopping trip in Manhattan and she'd spend a day or two in small-town Hearts Bend, Tennessee."

"Or, you could go, spend time with Buck and JoJo. They've asked you over several times and you've yet to respond. Another delay and they might be offended."

"I hardly doubt— Mum, please tell me you didn't ring Buck." When John met the country music star on his European tour two years ago, their friendship was instant.

The entire Blue family loved Buck Mathews and his wife, JoJo. Mum invited them to Perrigwynn for New Year's last year. They attended John's wedding and met up with him and Holland on the end of their Riviera honeymoon. And last year, Buck left his world tour to attend her funeral.

"He's home for the summer, darling. You could go for a month. You could golf, fish, read, rest. I know from Briggs you've made no summer holiday plans."

"I don't care about golfing or fishing. I don't want to rest." Doing nothing made him remember what he wanted to forget. "Buck and JoJo hold Holland's memories for me. Past and future.

We talked about having children at the same time, spending holidays and vacations together."

Though they had yet to announce a Mathews offspring.

"You cannot abandon their friendship," Mum said with her kind wisdom. "Build new memories with Buck and Jo. When you find love again, you will bring her in to your relationships. You can still have children at the same time, arrange holidays together. In the meantime, help me bring healing to our family." Mum's eyes glistened. "To me, to Scottie."

John paced around the chairs, irritated that Mum's plea touched him. Even moved him enough to elicit a yes.

"Tell me again why you can't go?"

Mum rose up and moved to the window, gazing out over the palace grounds, over the lower tip of her kingdom. On the edge of the horizon were the bluish-green waters of the Port Fressa Bay and the spiral steeples of the ancient cathedrals. The ones that created the phenomenon, the Heart of God.

"You said you can't imagine your future? I can't imagine facing Scottie. I've run through every scenario a thousand times. Where we'd meet, what we would say. And it all ends in shambles with me sounding like a selfish shrew and Scottie cursing me, slamming the door on her way out."

"Give her some credit, Mum. She's an adult. She understands. You gave her to her father to raise because you had no choice. I'd think she'd be more miffed at her dad and grandparents for claiming you were dead."

"Yet they were the ones who stayed, raised her, loved her. I simply walked away. Let Trent raise her alone. I supported the lie that I was dead." Mum's tears were evident when she turned from the window. "Please, go. Talk to her. Get a feel for what *she* wants. Is she interested at all in meeting me? In being a part of our family?"

It was rare to see his mother so vulnerable. Scared.

"Maybe she can take my place," John said. "Become the crown princess. She is my *older* sister. I'm sure we can find some eligible, aristocratic chap to marry her. Lute is still single."

"Lute?" Mum grimaced as she dabbed her cheeks with a tissue. "He's charming, I'll give you, but please tell me we could do better than Amadeus Lute."

How well Mum knew his friends. "He'd give you no argument."

"As for Scottie, she's not my heir. I'm not even sure we'd make her a peer much less give her a title. But bringing her into the Family would be..." Mum's voice trailed. "Wonderful."

"I've never, *ever* seen you shrink from difficulty, Mum," John said. "You sank your teeth in when the finance minister wanted to raise interest rates. Again, when parliament wanted to enact a tax. And why not make her a peer with a title? You just said the Family was shrinking."

"Don't use my words against me. And yes, I sank my teeth in on those issues. It's my job to plead for the people. Those moments define me as a queen. If I'm praised or criticized, it's the job, not me. But in this, with Scottie, it's personal. It's about Catherine Blue. I'm a fifty-seven-year-old woman who's not seen her daughter since she was seven days old." Mum's tears overflowed again. "This entire ordeal returns me to that very scared twenty-one-year-old who fell in love and created a child she could not keep. The idea of meeting with Scottie and Trent feels like going to my father all over again with the news that I was pregnant. Then the agony of waiting to meet with the stern-faced members of his privy council. A third of them women, mind you."

Mum's request lingered in the air as the back-and-forth faded. A trip over the Atlantic might be an interesting distraction. He could stay for a month and return home in time for Holland's memorial with a new perspective. Though he doubted it.

Deep down, John was curious about Scottie. A year ago when Mum's tightly held secret burst onto the international scene, he exchanged a few private messages with his new-found sister, but it fizzled after a few weeks.

"What if she doesn't want to meet me?"

"Use your powers of persuasion to convince her."

"Am I to just show up as a surprise? Are you going to call her father, get him in on your plan?"

Mum's pinched expression was her answer.

"You can't expect me to just pop over to America and say, 'Here I am. Care to meet for tea?'"

"Why not? Besides, Trent's gone cold on me. I suppose he's getting me back for all the years I declined his requests to meet Scottie."

"Let me get this straight. My cover is a long holiday with my good friends Buck and JoJo, which, oh, look, how convenient my secret sister happens to live in the same town?"

"Rather fortuitous, don't you think?" Mum's wishful, hopeful expression made him laugh.

"You look like a kid begging for pudding when she's not finished her dinner." With each tick of the old grandfather clock, he warmed to the idea of a month in the American south. All that sun and heat... Might melt the ice that filled every part of him. "All right, I'll go. On one condition."

"Name it." Mum's smile reflected her relief. "Anything. Up to half my kingdom," she said.

Ah, that old joke. She never meant it. "Change the marriage writ." He sounded more confident than he felt. "I don't have to be married to take my oath. I'll hang out in Tennessee for a month, return for the memorial, and we can hold the investiture ceremony this fall. I'll be Lauchtenland's sworn and legal heir not just your anointed heir."

Mum's smile faded. "John, I can't—"

"Then lovely chatting with you." He started for the door.

"All right. I'll talk to Elias."

"Mum, this is *your* decision as leader of this family, as the sovereign. I don't care what parliament has codified. Besides, you and Elias can manage that lot. Whatever is your hesitation?"

"It's a solid, old writ that's served us well. Don't forget the investiture swears in the consort as well as the crown heir."

"When you tell me you've scheduled a meeting with Elias, I'll book my trip to America."

"All right, you win." Mum came toward him, hand extended. "You woo Scottie into the Family, I'll woo Elias and parliament about the writ."

Chapter Two

HEARTS BEND, TN

GEMMA

There comes a time in every girl's life when she must honestly answer the question "How'd you end up here?"

She, the one most-likely-to-succeed, a National Merit Scholar (she was good at taking tests), a beauty queen, had completely and utterly failed.

In a decade plus two, she'd sunk to a depth she'd never fathomed—lost in a black hole that still gripped her. But she battled her dark walls constantly. Willingly. Gratefully.

No one knew her *whole* story. Not her parents, her best friends Haley and JoJo, nor her foster daughter, Imani. As far as Gemma Stone was concerned, no one *ever* would.

Staring at her desk wedged into the nook of the old linoleum and paneled-wall kitchen, she was filled with gratitude. This run-down old place needed a major renovation, but it sat on the most glorious twenty acres west of Hearts Bend. She'd paid for it with cash. Every penny she'd managed to save, and perhaps, *maybe* a few she'd stolen—but *he* owed her—deposited on her one and only future.

With each sunrise and sunset, she managed to discover more of her own light and laughter. Lately, the black hole didn't seem as deep.

At the desk, Gemma shuffled through the pile of bills and sighed. Working one-and-a-half jobs didn't meet her needs. So far, her financial juggling act kept the lights on and a bit of food in the fridge and in the barn. If it weren't for a few generous donors here and there, depositing money for her at the feed store, she'd not be able to keep her small herd of rescues.

Still she slept well at night, knowing nothing could ever take her land. Not even her past.

Gemma pushed back the window's faded flowered curtain. Steam rose from the ground as the early-morning July dried the dew from last night's rain.

Looking farther, beyond the pond and giant, shading maple—where Daddy set up a homemade picnic table—her darlings grazed through the tall grass. Hercules, Whinny, and Silver.

The rescues that had rescued her.

"I can almost forgive you, Matt Biglow," she whispered. "But not quite."

This homestead, her surprise venture into animal rescue, and becoming the parent of a sixteen-year-old orphan, Imani, numbed the pain and disappointment birthed from the previous twelve years. Hollywood, she learned, was not always where dreams come true.

Looking toward the barn, she thought of her big plans for the house, the barn, the land. A total gut and remodel of the house. A new barn, though the one she had was in good shape. Better than the house.

She'd plant gardens. One for looking and one for eating. Then, eventually, build an outdoor living space with a pool and a She Shed.

But they were all pipe dreams until she recovered her losses—emotionally, physically, financially.

In the meantime, she worked at The Wedding Shop and assisted photographer Taylor Gillingham when needed. Gemma may not have achieved stardom in Hollywood, but she'd picked up skills like how to live on a shoestring, being organized while living with six roommates, set design, fashion, and makeup artistry.

Gemma checked her schedule and to-do list. Her days were fairly static. Wake up, feed the "herd"—three horses, five dogs, six cats, seven goats, two rabbits—muck out the stalls, haul food and hay, then spend her day managing the shop's accounts and inventory, occasionally working the sales floor, helping a bride find the perfect gown while her mother wanted another one.

But today was the Fourth of July and all work stopped. Nearly everyone in Hearts Bend and the surrounding cities flooded to the seventy acres by the Cumberland River to celebrate.

Thirty acres of this property were owned by the Castle family but everyone still called it the Scotts' Place. Since the '30s, as the town and the Fourth celebration grew, the city annexed another forty acres to host the growing crowds and expanded the games, entertainment, and a plethora of food stalls.

The Fourth was a big deal, and Gemma intended to indulge. One of her good friends, country superstar Buck Mathews, would take main stage after all the usual suspects—the local bands—and play a set or two.

So if she didn't get there early, there was a good chance she'd not get there at all. A free Buck Mathews concert...

The town may never be the same.

"Gemma, can I take the truck to the Castles'?" Imani, her foster daughter, a rescue of sorts who was also rescuing her, breezed into the kitchen, phone in hand. "Penny's already there waiting for Mrs. Castle's deep-fried cherry popovers."

"What about a cute boy named Justin?"

A slight pink painted Imani's caramel-colored cheeks. "He can get his own cherry popover." She reached for the keys on the hook by the door. "If I go now, I can get a good parking spot."

"I'll ride with you. I'm done here." Gemma closed her laptop, tucked her phone into her shorts pocket, and slung her red Prada tote to her shoulder. Another relic from her former life.

If she sold it, even used, she'd get enough for two months of groceries, feed, and utilities. But she couldn't bear to part with it. As much as it represented her mistakes, it also represented her success, however limited and short-lived.

"Can I drive separate in the truck? I may want to leave before you."

"Oh really? And go where?" Gemma pulled the keys to her BMW convertible from the hook by the door.

The car was another silver lining from La-La Land. As if silver linings mattered. If she sold it, she'd have enough for the next six months of groceries, feed, and utilities. But then what? Drive around in the beat-up '67 Ford Ranger that came with the house?

The leather interior was ripped and faded and smelled like a used wallet. The floorboards were worn. The passenger side window crank was a wrench. But the engine ran like a top, the old radio still hummed songs from the great Nashville stations, and the dinged-up and slightly rusted bed was perfect for hauling feed and hay. And Imani loved it.

"Just a bunch of us going over to Justin's for fireworks," Imani said, her hand on the doorknob. "His parents will be there."

"Fireworks? Hearts Bend puts on the best fireworks show in Tennessee. You know Buck is giving a concert, right?"

"So?" Imani shrugged. "We were at his house last week for a guitar pull."

Pardonez-moi. How ordinary to be friends with a country music great and his wife.

Gemma considered the request. "Be home by eleven. Remember second gear sticks so you have to double clutch."

"I know, I know. Pops showed me."

Pops wasn't technically Imani's grandfather, but since she had arrived on Gemma's doorstep two years ago, the teen had been more than embraced by the Stone family. "Can I stay out until midnight? I *am* sixteen and it's the Fourth of July."

"Oh, is there a special curfew dispensation for the Fourth?" Gemma's eyes met Imani's and in an instant, *she* was the teen begging her parents to extend her curfew.

"Please…"

With a sigh, Gemma agreed. "Stay in a group. If Justin's parents aren't home, you leave. I'm not kidding, Imani. If I find out they weren't there—"

"You're the best." The girl smacked a kiss on Gemma's cheek and shot out the door without a backward glance.

"Hey, don't worry about the chores and animals. I'll tend to them by myself." The passive-aggressive move didn't work. Imani was in the truck, windows down, radio blasting, heading down the driveway, the tires spewing dust and what remained of the gravel.

Oh to be young. Oh to know then what she knew now.

Closing up the house, she hopped off the low, rotting-board porch and headed for her car.

She should ask Mama for tips on how to wield "mother guilt." The woman was a master. Of course, she'd learned from the guru, the Yoda of the Guilt Force, Granny.

Down the long drive, she paused and glanced in the rearview mirror which framed the rambling farmhouse and red barn. A shallow satisfaction soothed her inner scars. Life was good, finally, and getting better.

This was the time to stop striving, bury old dreams and put down new roots, create a life from her rubble, and with time, forget she'd ever wanted to be a star. Forget she'd wanted to make a difference in the world. Forget she erroneously believed she was meant for something more.

To the herd, to Imani, Gemma was "something more."

She found her parents among the Fourth crowd, staked out at their usual spot under a moss-laden oak. Their circle of chairs surrounded a card table and a food table covered with a red, white, and blue cloth.

"I was beginning to think you weren't coming." Mama gave her a quick hug then scanned her empty arms. "Where's your chair? Your sunscreen, your hat, your sunglasses?"

"I left them on the kitchen table." Gemma sat in one of the *many* lawn chairs her parents provided.

"Where's Imani? Did you forget her too?" Mama reached for a plastic bag from Hearts Bend Apothecary. "I spotted this cute top at the drugstore for her." Mama pulled out a ghastly lime-green thing with a faux velvet green trim. "What do you think?"

"For a dust cloth?"

"Honestly, Gemma." Mama sighed and held up the shirt for inspection. "It's darling. She'll love it. Where is she?"

"She drove the truck. Wanted to hang with her friends." Gemma took the sack with the shirt and stuffed it in her Prada bag. "When she comes by, don't mention this to her in front of her friends. She'll say she likes it so she doesn't embarrass you."

"Maybe she will like it." Mama made a face.

"Probably. She adores you."

"I'm her granny, of course. Think of all she's been through. We're here to see she gets a good start in life."

"Not with that shirt." Gemma gazed toward the bandstand, listening as the first band tuned up.

At thirty, she had her life ahead of her, but when she slowed down for moments like this, she felt as if she'd lived three lifetimes. When she slowed down, the memories surfaced. The shame bit and stung.

The bluegrass band on stage started a beloved hymn in Hearts Bend about Jesus walking and talking with His own. But did He really?

While she worked to get her life back on track, there were moments when she wondered if the good Lord shouldn't have left her for dead when He had the chance.

"Don't miss our exclusive documentary on the life of Princess Holland."

— THE LIFE AND DEATH OF A PRINCESS,
LTV-1

"The Chamber Office announces Prince John going on July holiday. Destination unknown."

— THE NEWS LEADER

"Who's watching *The Life and Death of a Princess* next month? I'm in tears thinking about it."

— @ROYALFAN ON INSTAGRAM

"I don't know, do you think Prince John will ever move on, Hy? He was so in love with his wife. I'm a wee bit jealous. I always wanted that sort of love affair."

— MADDY FROM THE MADELINE &
HYACINTH LIVE!

"You're waking up to exciting news this July morning, Lauchtenland. A royal baby is on the way. The Chamber Office has announced the first grandchild for the queen and king consort. His and Her Royal Highnesses, Prince Augustus and Princess Daffy, are expecting their first child in early December. Everyone on the Morning Show wishes them all the best and a happy, safe pregnancy."

— *MELISSA FARIS, ROYAL REPORTER,
THE MORNING SHOW*

CHAPTER
THREE

JOHN

D ay four of his trip to Hearts Bend and he felt more like
himself than in the past year. The sweet, dewy air of the
South sparked a bit of life to his dried-up soul.

This morning he played a quick nine holes with Buck,
showered, breakfasted on eggs, bacon, and toast, stopped at the
local coffee shop, Java Jane's, for a cuppa cappuccino, and arrived
at the Fourth of July fairgrounds without having once thought of
her.

Standing by the bandstand in the rising morning heat, waiting
for Buck to finalize details for his concert, John's protection
officer, Gunner, shadowed his right shoulder. Scanning the crowded
fairgrounds, his attention landed on a woman with the same shiny
hair as his wife and nearly called her name. *Holland, darling!* But
a tall, lean chap caught her from behind and swung her round,
causing her to spike the air with laughter.

Of course, she wasn't Holland. No woman would ever be
Holland again. Nevertheless, what bothered him more than his
fairy-tale ending with no "to be continued" was the fact he had to
admit—he thought less and less of the love of his life. At least on
a conscious level.

He mused more over how to meet his long-lost sister—which
he had yet to do—than how to get on with living as a crown prince
widower.

"John." JoJo Mathews emerged from the throng of locals and tourists wandering in and around the food stalls, bounce houses, and carny games. "I need you."

"Shall I tell Buck you're throwing him over for a better man?" He glanced at Gunner who appeared to be sleeping where he stood. A former special forces commander, he excelled in strength and stealth. Gunner Ferguson was one of Lauchtenland's best.

"Very funny. I need you for a game." JoJo grabbed his hand and tugged him toward the crowd. Gunner pounced, breaking her grip with skilled precision. Then, "Sorry."

JoJo rubbed her arm. "What did I do wrong? Can't I touch you?"

"Yes, you can touch me." John aimed his reply at Gunner who'd reacted on reflex. While he'd been on the golf outings and lounged around the pool, Gunner stayed in the guesthouse, away from the familiarity John shared with JoJo—the brother-sister teasing, the nightly hugs.

Now that he thought about it, those moments provided healing and comfort more than anything.

"Good, because I need you to partner with someone in a three-legged race. Don't say no. Thanks." She eyed Gunner then grabbed John's arm again. "This way." She was back in JoJo Mathews form. "We're trying to win the trophy for The Wedding Shop. It's cheap and ugly, but Haley really wants to beat Pops Yer Uncle Ice Cream Palace. She says they win every year and it's time for a new sheriff in town. You'll be with Gemma. She's the perfect height for you."

"Who's Gemma?" John pulled his arm free and fell in step with JoJo, Gunner not far behind.

He'd won a three-legged race or two in his time. During his boyhood summers at Hadsby Castle.

"Our bookkeeper-slash-manager. With Haley being a mom and me hitting the road with Buck every year, Gemma keeps the lights on and the doors open. Hey, Gemstone, I found your partner."

Gemstone? Who was this gem... The crowd parted, as if by some ethereal force, and the most graceful, stunning woman emerged. She was tall and regal with generous curves and a mane of wild, chestnut hair falling about her shoulders. But it was her eyes that captured him. Deep and blue, intense, guarded, as if no one would ever peer into her soul.

"John, this is Gemma Stone, one of my best friends as well as the shop's manager. Gemma, this is Prince—"

"I know who he is." She offered her hand. "Welcome to Hearts Bend."

She held him with her gaze and it took a moment for him to move, to shake her hand. "Yes, thank you. Very lovely town. Reminds me of Dalholm in County Northton, only with a lot more sun and humidity."

"We bottle it and sell it at the local shops if you care to take some home with you."

"You what? You—" Her smile snapped him into reality. Of course, she was having him on, and when he laughed, it was weak and low. "I thought you Americans had come up with a secret the world had yet to discover."

"Y'all can chitchat later. Go sign up for our heat. It's next."

"JoJo, don't make this poor man run a race if he doesn't want to."

"Oh, he's running, aren't you?" JoJo leaned back to look at Gunner. "That's his protection officer, Gunner. You don't mind, do you?"

"He's free to do what he wants."

"All right you two, go see Hooley and sign up." *Hooley?* JoJo pressed Gemma toward the starting line where a man in a bright orange vest, visor, and bullhorn addressed a small gathering with a large, old-fashioned clipboard.

"Look, Prince," Gemma said. "You don't have to—"

"I'm in. When in Hearts Bend, do as Hearts Bendians."

Gemma peered at him and when their eyes met, *it* happened. The thing no man clinging to his first love wants to happen. His heart skipped a beat. *Steady, mate.*

Gemma started off, a slight hitch in her step. John watched her a moment or two.

"Excuse me, um, lass. Gemma. Are you sure you are able to manage a race?"

He stepped back as she whirled around with a bit of fire and brimstone in her eyes. "You worry about you and I'll worry about me, capeesh?"

"Capeesh." With that, he followed her to the sign-up station.

Meanwhile, Gunner redirected curious onlookers who recognized John and aimed their cameras.

"No photographs, please. The prince is on holiday."

However, John never minded a few candid shots. Made him seem more like an everyday chap.

Coming from a small North Sea island nation, he was used to some attention. Nothing like his British cousins, William and Harry, but enough. However between his baby brother, Gus, being left at the altar and his own wedding to Lady Holland Cunningham, the Lauchtenland royals landed on the global map.

Then Holland's funeral four months after their wedding sent the House of Blue into the stratosphere. There were entire books and movies about them. Coloring books. Toys. Souvenirs. All of which he avoided like the plague.

"Gemma Stone, howdy. You going to race?" Hooley looked her up and down. "With that hip, I don't know."

"Just sign us up for The Wedding Shop. This is my partner, John."

"John with a J?" Hooley tapped the clipboard waiting for John to answer.

"Yes, John with a J." He made a face at Gemma who fought a laugh. *How else would he spell it?*

"All righty-dighty, gotcha down. What's your team name?"

"The Winners." Gemma picked up a gunny sack and some rope.

Okay, John liked her more and more.

"Come on, Gemma. You can't use that name. Fleet from over at Pops Yer Uncle would have my visor and bullhorn. Haley and Cole are Wedding Shop One. Buck and Jo are Wedding Shop Two. What about Wedding Shop Three?"

"Boring. What do you think, Prince? Got a preference?" Gemma handed John the rope to tie their ankles. "Want to do the honors? I can't bend very well."

John studied the rope then her expression. Yeah, don't ask. "How about For The Wedding Shop?" He lined up next to Gemma, pressed his ankle against hers, and bent to knot the rope.

"Got it, Hooley?" Gemma said. "For The Wedding Shop. Prince, tie it around my left leg, please. And tie it with—"

"I know how to tie rope." John shifted to Gemma's other side. "Took a whole course on it when I was in the special forces."

Meanwhile, Hooley fussed over the team name. "For The Wedding Shop? Dang y'all, that's too long. Won't fit in the space on my printout. See?" He flipped the clipboard around for their inspection.

"Then write whatever you want." Gemma remained still as John tied her leg to his. "Special Forces Prince, not too tight or we won't be able to maneuver."

"Are you always this bossy?"

"When I need to be."

"I got it!" Hooley scribbled on his clipboard. "The Prince's Bride."

"Oh good grief, Hooley," Gemma said. "No. Just put WS3 or WSGJ. Wedding Shop Three or Wedding Shop Gemma and John. Will that fit in your box?"

"Too late, I done wrote Prince's Bride." He winked at John and showed him the paper. "You're a prince, right? I seen you on the magazines at the checkout stand."

"Then if you saw him at the checkout, you'd know he lost his wife a year ago. Have a heart, Hooley. Change the name. No Prince's Bride."

"Oh, beg pardon, Prince."

"It's fine." John stood, testing the knot. "No harm, no foul."

"Well, if'n you're sure. It's got a nice ring to it and my pencil don't have no eraser." He held up his baldheaded, chewed-on pencil before turning toward the racetrack—a strip of mowed field by the river—and raised his bullhorn, calling for the first heat.

"Sorry about that, Prince. My people don't know how to behave." Gemma hobbled, getting her balance. "We should practice."

"He's seems a nice chap." John held out the gunny sack. "Shall we give it a go?"

"He is nice, and by the way he acts, you'd never know he owns half the land southwest of town." Gemma fastened her arm about John's waist and leaned against him as they inserted their joint leg.

On instinct, he bolted upright, glancing round at her. No woman had touched him so intimately since, well, since...

"What?" she said.

"Nothing." His bland reply denounced the effect of her touch—pulsing adrenaline, drumming heartbeat.

"Well, let's do this. Wrap your arm around me or we'll hit the dirt out of the gate." Gemma butted her hip against his. "Hold tight, and no matter what, don't let go. If JoJo dragged us out here together, we might as well win."

"Right." His mouth was the Sahara, his thoughts tumbleweeds. This was ridiculous. He was a grown man. A crown prince, not to any exclusion of human emotions mind you, but come on, he was grasping at straws here. As this total stranger clung to him, all he could think, feel was how perfectly his palm rested on the curve of her waist.

"Let's practice." When she looked at him, he saw a new flare. A desire. She really wanted to win. But it was more than victory, it was some sort of comeuppance, a personal victory, proving herself. Perhaps something to do with her limp?

"On three," he said.

On the count, they started forward with a powerful kick, and Gemma stumbled into him.

"Geez, not that much, Prince."

"Sorry. I'm a bit competitive. But are you sure—"

She reared up tall and determined. "Don't ask me again if I'm sure. I'm in this for the win as much as you. If I have to, I'll carry *you* on my back across the finish line."

"Well, let's hope it doesn't come to that." He smiled. "Let's go again."

One…two…three, and they charged forward. This time without stumbling. The next practice run they launched on the one count to give them a good jump at the starting line. At last, they declared themselves ready and hobbled to the sideline to await their turn.

Standing among the racers, John watched the heat before theirs with enthusiasm, a bit of adrenaline flowing, realizing how much he wanted to win. How much he *needed* to win. To close out the year of Holland's death with a triumph. No matter how small. Something to remind him Blue blood flowed through his veins. And that there was more to life than death.

Even if it was a cheap, ugly trophy for The Wedding Shop.

Beside him, Gemma cheered on the couple in the lead. "Come on, Devon!" She looked at John. "She's my cousin."

"Then come on, Devon."

But Devon and her partner tumbled, rolling off the racetrack, laughing. After another two races, his and Gemma's heat was called.

Lining up at the starting line, Gemma baited JoJo. "You're going to eat my dust, Jo."

"*Whatevs*. Buck, did you hear that? She thinks they're going to win."

"A girl can dream but that don't make it real," Buck said with a glance at John.

So, the challenge was on. He leaned slightly forward, his arm taut around Gemma. She cinched her arm about him and gripped the side of his shirt.

"Y'all racers, ready?" The chap Hooley was at the starting line with his bullhorn. "On your mark, get set…"

A starter pistol sounded, and they were off. Out of the gate, three couples tripped, thus thinning the field. He and Gemma moved in perfect stride, their joined legs performing as one.

"We're going to win." She quickened their pace.

"Steady, don't rush it." They'd settled into a solid rhythm.

"Up ahead, up ahead," she said, nodding toward a couple who'd fallen. They hurdled them with ease.

"Good job, love," John said, leaning all the more into the race, into the win, each deep, humid gulp of Tennessee air clearing away a bit of his dullness.

To his left, Buck and JoJo raced with skill. To Gemma's right, Haley and Cole, whom he'd only just met, also seemed in command of their game. John urged Gemma forward, picking up the pace.

No longer a game, no longer about town pride, this race was John's life and he must triumph.

They neared the turnaround—a large tree—in first place. Splendid. He regretted ever doubting Gemma's ability.

"Watch out, Prince, more litter on the track." They leapt over another fallen couple and sidestepped a third.

But Buck and JoJo were closing in, yelling threats between fits of laughter.

"You can't win, you two. Buck, watch it, you're pulling too hard."

"Ready for another gear?" John said low into Gemma's ear.

Anticipating her yes, he looked over to see a slight hesitancy in her expression, but it was quickly consumed by a glint of steel determination. He increased his grip on the sack tighter and picked up the pace.

Together, they flew over the pitch and hurdled another downed, laughing couple tangled up in gunny sack and rope. The finish line was mere meters ahead. The win was theirs for the taking.

He pulled harder, dragging Gemma's tied leg with his. *Take that, death. Or life. Whichever. You cannot defeat me.*

"Hey, Prince, wait—"

"Come on, love."

He didn't see it—the divot in what appeared to be level ground—but his foot landed in it with such force he was thrown down, dragging Gemma with him.

Twisting. Tumbling. Falling. Yelling.

They landed with a thud, their faces and hands skidding across the surface. John felt his ankle twist in an unnatural direction and in his ear, he heard Gemma's cry of pain.

As he pushed up, trying to get a feel for their position—
entertaining the wild idea they'd skidded across the finish line—
Buck and JoJo sailed over them to win the heat.

John sighed and collapsed down to the ground. So typical. This
was his life, right? What made him think a silly carny game would
change anything? Because when a man loses in love, he loses in
everything.

CHAPTER FOUR

GEMMA

H her hip hurt as she rolled onto her side, waiting for the pain to subside. This better not set her back six months. After two years, she was finally healing.

"Are you okay?" The prince's handsome face appeared above hers and he offered his hand.

"Give me a minute." She pushed up, settling gently onto her backside, babying her right hip, reaching to untangle the rope and gunny sack.

The doctors had promised her hip bone would heal. Six months and she'd be back to her old self, they said. After all, she was young and healthy. But two years later, she still limped. Her hip ached when it rained or when the temperature dipped below a moderate fifty.

Gemma managed those things well enough. What bothered her most was how she wasn't "her old self." How each flare-up, or any question about her limp, brought up the night of her great humiliation. Even if she was the only one of her family and friends who knew, she'd never be the same.

At last she reached for the prince's hand. "What about you?" She stood, easing weight on her wounded side. "Are you okay?"

"Embarrassed but unharmed." He inspected her as if to ascertain the truth of her well-being. When his blue eyes looked too long into hers, she turned away. "I thought we had it."

"Me too." Gemma gazed toward the finish line. "But we can still finish."

"I don't see the point." John knocked a clump of grass and dirt from his skinned knee.

"Why not? Only quitters quit." She hooked her arm about him with a stubborn yank but buckled on her first step and fell against him. "Sorry. I'll be all right in a sec—"

"Steady on, lass. Lean on me." He slipped his arm about her and he angled forward, inspecting her weak side. "Are you sure—"

"Yes, dang it. I'm sure." She cupped her free hand about her mouth. "Let the world know, I'm sure. A limp is still a walk." She glanced at her partner. "Let's go. The finish is waiting." Gemma started off slowly, stretching, working out the kink, but her hip betrayed her again—as it was prone to do—and she stumbled into the prince. "Good grief. I feel like we're trapped in a cheesy, rom-com meet-cute. Small-town Southern girl falls into a prince's arms."

"My brother hit his wife in the head with a Frisbee. I think we're doing rather well in comparison."

She spewed a laugh, and this time when he looked into her eyes, she didn't turn away. She flirted. A little. For like five seconds. After all, that's what one did in a cheesy rom-com. She was, er, *used* to be an actress.

Meanwhile, a crowd had gathered, closing in and pressing against the protection dude, Gunner, as they snapped photos. Gemma charged toward the sideline ropes, straining against her aching hip.

"Get out of here. Shoo. Bunch of rednecks. Act like y'all been here before." She turned to John. "We have country music royalty all over the place, but let one *real* royal prince show up and they lose their heads."

His smile, *whoosh*, made her belly drop. "If anything happens to Gunner, I'm hiring you."

"I *do* know one judo move." That's when she got cocky. Tried the roundhouse kick she learned for a commercial—like ten years ago—and landed flat on her back.

"Gemma, are you all right?" Once again, John peered down at her, offering his hand.

"Does humiliated and in pain count as all right?" Gemma waved off his offer of help and pushed to her feet with a muffled moan.

"Hey! You two, finish." Buck. On the sideline. Holding up the trophy. "We get bonus points for every Wedding Shop team that finishes. Goes toward the final race."

"Give me a minute." Step, pain, step, pain. "Where's our sack and rope?"

"Forget the sack and rope," Buck hollered. "John, pick her up. Carry her."

"I can walk, thank you." Gemma pressed her hand over her hip and hobbled toward the finish line. Bath. Hot. Long. Tonight.

"That's it, we're doing this the easy way." In one hunky motion, the crown prince of Lauchtenland scooped Gemma into his arms. "I'd like to finish before midnight."

The rubberneckers and hoverers went wild, and team Prince's Bride faced a wall of smartphone cameras. Every moment, every move, captured.

Without once taking a labored breath, Prince John carried her across the finish line. Hooley announced their completion through his bullhorn.

"Team Prince's Bride. Last but not least."

No sooner had John set her down than Gunner appeared with a couple of local sheriff's deputies, dispersing the crowd.

"I should go," John said, backing toward Gunner. "I'm becoming a risk to myself and others."

"Wait, Prince." Gemma limped toward him. "Thanks. For back there."

"We had it, didn't we? The win." Again he smiled… She felt the hardness she'd been nurturing since leaving L.A. and Vegas give a little.

"We'll get them next time." Like there would ever be a next time. The prince offered a fist bump and when she responded, her eyes welled up. "See you around."

He disappeared about as quickly as he appeared in her life a few hours earlier, Buck and Gunner flanking him. Just before he disappeared around a set of bounce houses, Prince John glanced over his shoulder.

Gemma waved. *See ya, Prince.*

"Someone has a crush." JoJo bumped Gemma's sore hip.

"Careful, Jo." She started across the field toward her parents' camp where there was a plethora of chairs, food, and friends. As for a crush on the prince? Nothing doing. "*Someone* does not have a crush," she said to Jo. "We finished the race, end of story. You're the one who paired me with him. I'd have soon stayed behind eating barbecue."

"I saw you watching him. Say, do you want me to talk to him tonight? See if he likes you? You could write him a note and I'll pass it to him during dinner."

"Jo—" Gemma whirled toward her laughing, teasing friend. "I'm not on the market and I doubt he is either. So no, I don't want you to ask if he *likes* me. Girl, we don't even live in the same country. Need I remind you he's your friend, not mine."

"He *could* be your friend. I mean, he can't spend all of his time with Buck and me. He'd go crazy. As for love, he has to meet someone. He *has* to marry. It's a Lauchtenland law or something."

"Jo, just stop." The world stage was the one stage she never wanted to see.

"You have to find someone too."

"Who says?" Gemma wove through the crowd with JoJo at her side, a dull throb vibrating from her hip down her leg to her toes. "My romantic instincts are abysmal."

"Goodness, what happened to you?" Mama stood as Gemma approached, eyeing one of the reclining chairs.

"My partner and I fell in the three-legged race. I hurt my hip. Do you have any ibuprofen in your Mary Poppins' bag?"

"Betty," Mama said, motioning toward her bag, directing her longtime friend. "Look in my bag for my pillbox." She bent beside Gemma, dusting the grass from her knees, trying to rub the stain from her white shorts. "Is it your hip?"

"I'll be fine."

"You always say that but—"

"Because it's always true."

"I still wish you would tell me and Daddy what happened—"

"How about some barbecue, Mama, and a Diet Coke?" Gemma leaned forward and planted a kiss on her mother's forehead.

Mama's tight-lipped expression communicated her protest. She'd been asking Gemma for two years—ever since she returned home—why she limped. And for two years, she got bupkis.

About then Miss Betty returned with the ibuprofen. Mama hustled about filling a plate with barbecue and fries and grabbed a tall, cold, ice-dripping Diet Coke.

At last, all was right with the world again. Except for one small thing. She could still feel the prince's arms around her as he carried her over the finish line and how for a brief moment, all the pain had completely vanished.

Around five Imani found Gemma winning a game of Hearts.

"I'm going over to Justin's now, okay?"

"Who's going to be there?" Gemma counted her cards, happy to see she'd won the round.

"Justin's parents, if that's what you mean."

"You know me so well." Gemma excused herself from the table and faced her "daughter" of two years. Imani had arrived on her doorstep the day she'd signed the papers for the property and they'd moved in together.

"Am I wrong?" Imani snatched a carrot from the veggie platter on the food table.

"Miss Gemma, I promise my parents are going to be there." Justin looked like a scared rabbit, standing there with his ball cap crushed in his hands, not sure whether to look at Gemma or her father, the formidable Mac Stone, or Mama, the even more formidable Mauve Stone.

But the kid was a star. Smart and considerate, an excellent musician, and about the best-looking boy at Rock Mill High. "My dad is trying out his new smoker. Pork and chicken."

"Gemma, you won that round." This from Mama's other friend Betty—not to confuse things—who hated to lose at cards. "Are you playing again?"

"Go ahead without me." Gemma grabbed a bottle of water from the ice chest and chose a folding chair next to Daddy—who was inspecting Justin like he'd just confessed to breaking and entering.

Never mind he was good friends with the boy's father and played in a guitar circle with him once a month.

"He was bragging about that smoker last time I saw him," Daddy said with a side glance at Gemma. He tipped his head toward the waiting youngins with a look of, "*Let her go. He's a good kid.*"

"Don't you want to be here for the fireworks?" Gemma said. "Folks came from all over Tennessee and neighboring states to see our tiny town's display."

"Dad bought a bunch this year. Said he didn't want to fight the crowd." Justin emphasized his point by holding his hat in a death grip. "Going to have our own show tonight."

"Seems like a lot of effort." Gemma twisted the cap from her water bottle and took a long drink. "Be home by ten, Imani."

"Ten?" Her protest was quick and sure. "What happened to midnight? We're going to make S'mores after his dad's fireworks."

"Did I agree to midnight?"

"Sort of," Imani said. Which was the same as a "Yes" to every teenager on the planet.

"Can she stay, Miss Gemma?"

Justin asked so sweetly, so kindly, she had to relent. If for no other reason than to rescue his poor hat.

"Fine. But not a second after. Points if you come home before the clock strikes twelve." Gemma glanced at Justin. "She turns into a pumpkin, you know."

Justin started to laugh but Imani grabbed him by the hand and yanked him away.

"You're the best, Gemstone," she called over her shoulder.

Gemma watched as they dashed off—Justin setting his cap backwards on his head—and a piece of her heart went with Imani. Heaven help her but she'd do anything and everything to give that girl a life she deserved. To keep her from more hurt, from making the big mistakes. She owed it to Imani's parents. She owed it to herself. Imani was a future wonder woman and nothing was too good for her.

"You can't do it, Gemstone." She turned to Daddy as his subtle words landed with a resounding truth. "Can't keep her in a bubble. From mistakes. She's got to live her own life." He cut a slice of apple with his pocketknife and popped it into his mouth. "Let her learn while she's living under your roof so's you can guide her, help her."

"Who said I want to keep her in a bubble?"

"It's written all over your face."

"I just don't want her to be hurt. It's enough her parents are dead."

"I'd give my right arm for *you* not to be hurt. But you are and I still don't know why. That's your secret to tell or keep. Everything you're feeling for Imani, I felt. Pieces of my heart went with you every time you walked out the door." How did her kooky old man see through her? "But, Gemma, I wanted your dreams for you every bit as much as you." The knife cut through the apple again.

"I don't know how you and Mama did it. I was twice as fiery as Imani. Stubborn and strong-willed." She reached over and squeezed his hand.

"Because you raise your kids the best you can and let them fly. Imani has lots of good upbringing. Just so happens she's landed with you to get her the rest of her journey. You got two more years before college. Make them count. Just remember, you're not her savior. Not her redeemer."

"I know. Who said different?"

"That job belongs to Someone else."

"Again, I know."

"The One who died on that there cross—"

"Yes, Daddy, I've been to church."

"He's got a plan for her, for you too, far as that goes."

"Goodness, is it Sunday morning?" Gemma stood to move about and test her hip. "When did you become a preacher?"

"I have my moments." Daddy's cheek bulged with another slice of his apple.

"I love that you watch out for us." Gemma kissed her father's balding head and retrieved her Prada bag from one of the tables. "I should go, see to the herd."

"Come on back," Daddy said. "We'll be here 'til after the big show. I hear old Ted Taylor got some fancy new explosives. One of them even bursts into the American flag."

Maybe. Gemma made the rounds, saying goodbye to Mama and the group of friends clustered with her. She'd known most of them her whole life. They were the second parents, the honorary aunts and uncles. Hank and Betty. Al and Betty. Bill and Nancy. Ron and Deedee. Curt and Linda.

Her parents were hardworking, blue-collar folks who barely had two nickels to rub together but were rich in relationships.

Gemma had inherited Daddy's tendency to dream big. Like him, she'd failed. For most of her life, he lost his and Mama's paychecks, their savings over and over to get-rich-quick schemes.

"I can feel it, Gemstone. This is the one, and when I hit it big, I'm going to buy you a fancy sports car."

As she made her way to her parked car, Buck and his band were taking the stage for the first time, singing her home to his hit tune "When I Met You."

When I met you/everything changed/I'll never be the same/ Don't say goodbye

She was still humming the haunting melody when she pulled into the driveway. The dogs raced toward her, barking, clamoring around her legs as she stepped out.

Marcus, Barksy, Hal, Tweedy, and Blue led her to the kitchen and scampered straight for their bowls, looking at her with abandoned affection.

She scooped out kibbles for the collie, three pit bulls, and one aging bull dog. While they filled the house with the sound of crunching, she changed her sneakers for muck boots, thinking ahead to her chores.

Things went quickly when Imani helped, but tonight she'd go it alone, take her time, maybe have a contemplative moment with the goats. Miss Frances always seemed to enjoy a good heart-to-heart. As long as Gemma scratched around the old doe's hollow horns.

Reaching the kitchen door again, Gemma paused at her reflection in the cracked mirror tacked on the doorpost. It'd been left behind by the previous owners—whom she never met—and she had yet to take it down.

Leaning for a closer look—her hair knotted on her head and her T-shirt stained with grass—she wondered what he thought. You know, the prince.

Eyes drooping with bags and sadness she couldn't shake. Her lips were pale. Was that another line on her forehead? Taking a step back, Gemma rose up on her tiptoes to examine her breasts and waist. When she lived in L.A. and Vegas, she worked out six days a week, never touched junk food.

First week back home she went to Angelo's with the folks for a pepperoni pizza. First bite? Thought she'd died and gone to heaven. *Where have you been, my love?*

Worse than her so-called healthy Hollywood lifestyle was the one she fell into in Vegas. She'd been reduced to skin and bones. But since then, she'd put on a few pounds.

Still looking through the cracks in the mirror, Gemma pinched the skin on her side. How had she felt to the prince? Flabby? Heavy? Though he managed to carry her over the finish line without huffing and puffing.

He was no ninety-pound weakling though. Six-three, if he was an inch, and muscular. Like he worked at it.

She recalled how she'd locked her arms around his neck, and blushed. Wasn't every day a girl got cradled in the arms of a prince.

Gemma jerked away from the mirror. What was she doing?

"Come on, kids," she said to the dogs. "Let's feed the rest of the herd." The five of them moved on her whistle and darted toward the barn. They knew the routine.

She'd just opened the barn door when she heard tires popping over the gravel drive. A large black truck parked under the maple. Buck? Wasn't he on stage at the celebration? But it wasn't her friend and singer who stepped out from behind the wheel. It was the prince.

"I'm sorry," she called, feeling a bit more shaky than she liked. He seemed more handsome in the late afternoon shadows than when he carried her across the finish line. And she'd missed his graceful gait before. "We gave at the office."

Ha, ha, funny, right? And dumb. But what was he doing here? She tugged at her stained top and ran her hand over her hair, remembering her reflection. Then she glanced around, seeing her place as he might see it. A dump. At least it was *her* dump.

"Excuse me. Gemma? It's me, John." He hesitated as if deciding whether to turn back for the truck. His humble, self-deprecating demeanor gave her the same gushy, girly sensation from before. If she swooned, ole Blue better catch her.

"It's a joke. You know, what you say to telemarketers or door-to-door salesmen. 'We gave at the office.'" She walked toward him with the sentry of dogs. "Surely you've heard of it."

"Yes? No? Which answer will make me sound more impressive?"

"Too late." She stopped several feet away, observing, arms folded. He wanted to impress her? "So, how can I help you?" She leaned to one side, looking toward the passenger side of the truck. "Where's your Gunner?"

"He stayed behind. I, um, just want to see if you're all right." He pointed to the dogs. "Who have we here?"

When he bent down, Marcus, the old bull dog, and Tweedy, the mama collie, trotted forward as the welcoming committee. They loved people and would happily escort any would-be burglar into the house and straight to the Walmart-purchased dinnerware. Blue, however, hung back, taking a stand in front of Gemma.

"Marcus, Barksy, Hal, Tweedy, and Blue. All rescues."

Once Marcus and Tweedy survived the stranger, Hal and Barksy went in for a good neck ruffle and ear rub. Ole Blue, he waited, a small grumble in his throat.

"This is Blue, you say?" The prince knelt in front of the brown-and-white pit bull and slowly, gently offered his hand. "How are you, mate? I'm a Blue as well. House of Blue. Lauchtenland."

Blue looked up at Gemma. "He's safe. Go on."

Blue inched forward for a sniff. "Take your time, boy. I understand." John sat on his heels, barely breathing it seemed, surrendering to the sniffs and inspections of a former fighter. When Blue raised his snout to John's face, Gemma jumped in between.

"Blue, come here. It's okay."

But instead of doing what she feared, baring his teeth in warning, or worse, burying his teeth in John's cheek, he gave him an approving lick. Not one, but many.

"I can't believe it," she said. "He hates men and you've won him over in five minutes. Prince, I'm impressed."

Call it what you will, but if Ole Blue liked a man, he was the real deal.

"What's his story?" Blue fell against John as he ran his hands over his scars.

"A fighter. Barely survived his last one. Someone at the event rescued him and had the fortitude to call the authorities. The ring was busted a week later."

"I'll never understand human cruelty." Since Blue, Marcus, and Tweedy approved, the remaining two jostled for the prince's attention. He inspected each dog, ruffling their smooth coats again and again, and touched his nose to theirs.

"Barksy and Hal were also fighters. Rescued in the raid. When the sheriff's deputy brought them here, Blue went nuts, like it was old home week. Marcus, the bull dog, belonged to an old drunk who left the poor thing tied to a tree. Tweedy, the collie, was dropped off by a family who couldn't care for her anymore."

John rose up, surveying the house around to the barn and toward the back of the property where Gemma's equine rescues grazed under a tree by the pond. She wanted to raise her arms as if to "hide" what he saw—her run-down place—but it was too late.

"You run an animal rescue?"

"A small one. I started with the dogs and cats. Blue arrived first and he was a rough diamond. So wounded and scared. Seriously, I'm amazed he's taken to you. Took my daddy six months to walk past him without Blue growling and snapping."

"I suppose wounded souls know one another," he said, coming alongside Gemma and looking toward Hercules, Whinny, and Silver. He drew a long, deep breath, then exhaled. "Beautiful."

Beautiful? What was beautiful? As far as Gemma was concerned, *he* was beautiful. The most beautiful thing on the property at the moment. Including Whinny, who was a stunning, young thoroughbred.

This man, this prince, stood next to her as if they'd been *mates* all their lives.

Her brain said, *Get him out of here.* But her heart said, *Now hold on, give this half a sec.*

While he inspected her land, she took a moment to inspect him a bit closer. He wore his thick dark hair long on top but trimmed about the ears and neck. His blue eyes, evenly set in a Greek profile, sad and introspective.

Then, in the time it took for a puff of wind to cool her face, she and he were the same. Two wounded souls speared by disappointment, grief, and anger. He, the young, grieving widower and a future king. She, a desperate, humiliated actress, shame queening it over her.

"Buck said you were probably here, feeding your herd. Shall we get on? Where do we start?"

"Hey, Prince, seriously, you don't have to help me. You didn't come all the way from Lauchtenland to feed rabbits and goats."

"Why not? I've cleaned a few stalls in my time." The prince started for the barn and Gemma hurried to catch up. He shoved open the doors as if he'd been here a hundred times and stepped onto the barn's wide stone thoroughfare. Light from the opposite opening captured the golden hue of the limestone.

The barn was truly the nicest structure on the whole property.

"Our own yellow brick road." John spied the aprons on the hook and tied one on. Ole Blue decided this newcomer was his buddy and stayed just off his heels.

When he reached for the gloves, she conceded. Guess he was going to help. "We start with the rabbit cages, move to the goats, then the horse stalls. They stay out at night, but I leave the door open in case they want to come in. Silver hates thunderstorms."

She instructed and he followed, a natural with the bunnies, knowing how to hold them, talk to them. Then on to the goats, charming Miss Frances by the mere sound of his voice. By the time they'd fed the cats and cut up apples and carrots for the horses, they'd fallen into a natural rhythm.

Then he looked at her with a twinkle in his eye and Gemma felt the strange euphoria of hope, of desire, of being alive. But she bristled and pushed against it.

After tonight, he'd be off with whatever he came to Hearts Bend to do. Hang with Buck and what all. She'd never see him again. All she had to do was remember this moment, and one day, when she was an old woman who wore a scarf around her neck even in the summer, she'd tell the local children about the time a prince carried her across the finish line, then cleaned rabbit cages and fed the goats.

CHAPTER
FIVE

JOHN

He removed his apron and gloves, caught the water bottle Gemma tossed his way, and leaned against the open barn door.

"Is this place yours, Gemma?"

"Every square inch. Paid cash for it two years ago." She anchored against the opposite side and drank from her water bottle. "The barn is in good shape but the land and house need work."

What did he hear in her voice? Not much of a Southern accent, grant you. But was there a bit of embarrassment? Resignation? "Nothing money and hard work can't handle," he said.

She moved her hand through a blade of sunlight, and for a moment he believed she captured a few precious beams. "There's a fridge behind the last stall with water and soda. Help yourself if you want more."

He thanked her and drained his water, tossing the bottle to the bin marked Recycle. "Tell me about the horses." He thought of Briley, wondered how he was doing, catching the memories he carried with him, fighting the old sensations of sadness. He was content in this moment and refused to let it go.

"Here they come." Gemma turned toward the open back barn door. "Ask them yourself."

A warm spike of blue made her eyes wide and bright. She was a quagmire, this one. A blend of shadow and light. As if she didn't quite trust herself. Yet, there existed a natural, almost regal confidence. His stature, such as it was, seemed not to faze her at all.

A giant Clydesdale ambled under the barn opening, his head millimeters from the top. Beside him, a Shetland pony trotted, nose raised, bouncing as if he, or she, was the grandest horse of them all. The wee thing could've walked under the Clydesdale with room to spare.

Last but not least, an elegant, sleek, gleaming, and stunning thoroughbred. *Briley.* So much like Briley. His eyes glistened.

"Hey, Prince, you okay?" A few steps away, Gemma regarded him, looking close but not too close to his own veils and shadows. She *knew.* He felt it.

He cleared his throat, whispered he was fine, and moved toward the thoroughbred whose tender countenance tugged at him. Could he bury his head against that sleek neck and weep?

"Her name is Races to Win but I call her Whinny. Careful, she's like ole Blue and not too keen on men. To be honest she's not terribly fond of women either. Her owners, a greedy racing couple, ran her into the ground. Her father was a Kentucky Derby winner and her mother won races all over Florida and California. They thought they had a Triple Crown in her but chose cheap trainers and overzealous jockeys. I'm not sure how they got away with it for so long, but by the time the racing world caught onto them, they'd moved on to another horse and neglected Whinny. She lived in a barn not fit for any breathing beast. When she was rescued she suffered from rain rot and her bones stuck out from every angle. Her hooves were in horrid shape. Took me a year with lots of love and money to get her back to normal. Thank God her owners were banned from racing."

"There *is* justice in the world." John reached for an apple and stepped toward Whinny. She snorted and raised her head when he got too close. "Ole Blue, talk to her, tell her I'm a good lad."

Gemma took the apple from his hand, and Whinny stretched, sniffing, wiggling her lips to reach the piece without stepping any closer.

"Shh, it's all right, girl." John offered his hand but remained stationary. "Is this your dream, Gemma? To rescue animals?"

"Not really. When I bought this place, I, well…" Her voice faded as she retrieved another apple and some carrots. "I was in a different head space. Anyway, the dogs came and the rest is history. Now, this guy here." She offered the Clydesdale some apple. "He's my man. Hercules." She patted his thick jaw. "The grandson of an old farmer brought him to me. Once he arrived and I saw his sweet soul in his eyes, I knew. This ranch would be his forever home. All of them are home forever. They'll never have to worry about rain rot, starvation, abuse, fighting, or neglect again." She offered Hercules a carrot, which he took gently.

John loved the big guy immediately. He ran his hand down Hercules's neck and back and over his muscled rump. "You mentioned you'd been here two years. What engaged you before animal rescue?"

"Nothing to note." Clipped, crisp, with a lingering, non-spoken explanation. She moved onto the mini. "This little lady is Silver. The owners moved and thought they'd given her to a caring family, but they were too busy, and she was ignored. My name came up as a possible new home. She moved in and took charge six months ago. She's in love with Hercules." He snorted at the sound of his name then lowered his muzzle to Silver, who stretched toward him as high as she could. "Whinny tries to ignore her, but Silver's leadership rules the barn and the barnyard."

As they talked and admired the herd, an evening song began just beyond the open doors. A choir of pond frogs and crickets and night birds sang farewell to the day, bidding the reddish-orange July sunset good night and sweet dreams.

John made quick friends of Hercules and Silver with more apple and carrot treats, but Whinny remained skeptical and left the barn. Hercules and Silver soon followed. The dogs napped on the cool stone floor while the cats returned to their sleeping loft via a staircase of hay bales.

Standing next to Gemma, not quite ready to leave her company, he checked his watch. "The fireworks display begins soon. Are you returning?"

"I'm done for the day. Ranch life has turned me into an old lady. I'll stay here, warm up some leftover pizza." She brushed her hair away from her face, which became sweeter and more beautiful the longer he was with her. She possessed classic, timeless features. "Wait for Imani to come home."

"Imani? Your daughter?"

"Daughter of a friend. I'm her guardian."

"I see. Where is your friend?"

"She dropped dead of an aneurysm when she and Imani's dad, also my friend, were looking for a Manhattan apartment. I still remember the day she died. It rained so hard, like the heavens were weeping. Ethan died a few years later in a single-car crash." Gemma whistled for the dogs as she turned to go. They jumped up and darted ahead to the house. Except Blue, who paused by John with a wistful look in his brown eyes.

"Nice to meet you ole boy. But I'm shoving off." Though he was in no hurry to go.

"I have enough leftovers if you care to stay." Gemma drew the front barn doors closed then paused for his answer. By her tone he couldn't ascertain if the request was sincere or out of obligation. After all, he'd cleaned four rabbit cages and fed the goats.

"Thank you but I don't want to intrude."

"Please, you're not intruding. I can at least give you last night's—or was it the night before?—pizza and a glass of wine for your help. Unless you think Buck will miss you."

"He knows where I am."

"I apologize in advance for the house." She motioned for him to come along. "Like I said, it needs work."

"I find it rather charming. At least you own your own place. I live in a palace owned by my ancestors and now the Crown Trust of Lauchtenland."

Before she died, Holland brought up the notion of purchasing their own home. The family owned Hadsby Castle and their apartment there was three thousand square feet but still, she wanted a place of their own.

"For our children and grandchildren. Our own private retreat."

The screen door creaked as Gemma pulled it open. "Welcome to a '70s time capsule, Prince. Yellow linoleum, paneled walls, Formica counters and table, and shag carpet."

He followed her inside. The place was dated and dark but warm, cozy, and fragrant with cleaners, scented soaps, and perfume.

"If you want, we can watch the fireworks from the back deck. There's a perfect spot on the eastern edge. The deck is rotting, but I have two new deck chairs in a secure spot. Fit for a prince, if you dare."

"I accept your invitation to watch the fireworks and share a glass of wine, but please, let me spring for fresh pizza."

"Well you did make me fall..."

"Then we should order extra pepperonis."

While she dialed a place called Angelo's, John studied the kitchen and peered into the living room. Knock out a wall and she'd have a rather grand space. He chose not to venture down the long, dark hallway to the bedrooms. Too private. If any man understood privacy, it was the crown prince of Lauchtenland.

Back in the kitchen, Gemma cleared the glistening red Formica table of papers, a book bag, and leftover dishes, then poured two glasses of wine.

"Prince—"

"Or John."

"I'm really sorry about your wife. Not that my sympathy means anything, but I know what death feels like."

"Au contraire, your sympathy means a great deal. I take it to heart."

Their eyes met over the bottom of their wine glasses. So far, this evening, this moment, made his whole trip to Hearts Bend worthwhile. Scottie or no Scottie. In the '70s kitchen he wasn't an object of pity to anyone, most of all himself.

They sat on the deck, saying nothing except to comment on the lovely breeze until a horn sounded and Gemma pushed up, adjusted her stance, favoring her hip.

"Pizza's here."

John followed to pay then carried the large pepperoni to the deck and set up their dinner on the little table between the chairs. Gemma refilled their wine and as the last of the sunlight clung to summer leaves, John almost felt right with the world.

The pizza was hot and delicious, touching a hunger in John he didn't know he possessed. Or was it the brunette beauty next to him who touched his hunger?

As the twilight sky faded to black and they each reached for a third slice, Gemma said, "Prince, can I ask why you're visiting little Hearts Bend?"

"The queen asked me to come. Meet with Scottie O'Shay. You know that story, do you not?"

"How she's your long-lost sister?"

"Not so much lost as hidden."

"Why didn't your mother come?"

"Because she's a queen and made me her envoy. However, I arrived with no concrete plans—which is rather unsettling. The House of Blue does nothing without weeks, if not months and years, of planning and preparation, forming lists upon lists. But since this was more of a personal, family venture, Mum said, 'Off you go,' and here I am."

Gemma considered another piece of pizza but decided against it. "How can you tell when you're speaking to your mother or the queen? That'd be so weird."

"She's my mother. Always. But every now and then, she speaks as my queen. To be honest, Queen Catherine would've come to Hearts Bend in any other circumstance. The wife and mother, Kate, was terrified. But if you tell anyone I said that, I'll emphatically deny it."

As the words left his lips he realized he was confessing heart secrets to a stranger.

"You're safe with me, Prince. I'm not on social media and I loathe drama."

John took the pizza slice Gemma passed over. "What can you tell me about the O'Shays? Do you know them?"

"Not really. But they are kind of like Hearts Bend royalty. Wealthy, longtime citizens. Scottie's ancestors were founders."

Gemma closed her eyes and leaned into the breeze. It was fragrant with the aroma of land and open spaces. "I love the quiet out here."

A string of lights tacked along the deck rail popped on, and while they finished the wine, the first distant boom of gunpowder exploded a white, arching flame across the inky sky.

Blue whined and tucked in under John's chair while his mates hovered around Gemma. Another boom and Silver could be made out trotting into the barn.

John sat back, his legs stretched long. Explosion after explosion, the knots he'd been wrestling with for eleven months began to loosen, and muscle by muscle, he felt truly relaxed.

Holland, darling, you don't mind, do you?

He may have a new friend in this Gemma Stone, but he'd not forget his wife. His true love. After all, she'd delivered a white feather at his feet the day of her funeral and he knew. *She* would always be with him.

"Prince John saves a woman. More at 5:00 on LTV1 News."

"Swoon! Sign me up for whatever is happening here. Does anyone know where this was taken? Who's the lass?"

— *BRIGHTON KINGDOM'S MADELINE & HYACINTH LIVE!*

"Does anyone know the story?"

— *LOYAL ROYALS BLOG #PRINCESSBRIDE*

"Prince John is in America? Does he have a new love? Can't make out her face very well. Name? Details!"

— *#PRINCESSBRIDE #PRINCEJOHNSNEWLOVE*

"Late breaking news here on Cable News PF. Hamish Fickle, MP, is calling for federal investigation of Reingard Industries, a Grand Duchy of Hessenberg company, who purchased land in the Midlands. 'All I'm asking is for the Crown Investigation Bureau and Crown Justice to look into it.'"

— *CABLE NEWS PF @ 6:00*

CHAPTER
SIX

GEMMA

B y the time she arrived at The Wedding Shop Monday morning, Gemma was frustrated and hungry.

Note to self: go grocery shopping.

She sent Imani into town for a pre-basketball camp breakfast at Ella's Diner, so she had to handle the herd herself. While she was inspecting the rabbits, Taylor Gillingham called to confirm the wedding shoot at the wedding chapel on Wednesday.

"Do you have everything you need for Wednesday? This is a new client for me and if it goes well, I'm golden."

"Checked your storage locker last night. We're good. See you at 8:00 a.m."

Just when she was ready to head to work, she noticed a flood in the barnyard. A water pipe had burst. Mr. Sweet Pea, the Velveteen rabbit, gained lakefront property.

By the time she shut off the water, called Daddy for advice, and moved the rabbit cages, she was sweating and covered in mud.

In moments like these she found it hard to believe she'd ever aspired to greatness or ever lived in Tinseltown, consumed with her looks, her clothes, and her career.

If they could see me now.

Except Matt Biglow. Her life would be complete if she never clapped eyes on him again.

"Sorry I'm late." Gemma burst through The Wedding Shop's back door, grabbed a Haven's cinnamon bun and cup of coffee, and headed to her mezzanine office, pausing by Haley who worked a white gown over a headless mannequin. "A water pipe broke this morning. The whole barnyard was flooded. Mr. Sweet Pea was about to go swimming."

"Did you call Cole?" Haley bent to fluff out the voluminous skirt. "What do you think, Gemma? New from Elnora. Her designs get better every year."

"Nice. Pretty."

The brilliant white silk seemed to flow in the light coming through the large display window. The pearls seated on the seam of the V-waist radiated pops of color down the skirt. It was the sort of gown that would make any bride feel stunning.

"'Nice, pretty'? That's all you got?"

"It's beautiful." Gemma adjusted the strap of her bag and took a closer look, careful of her precariously perched pastry on her coffee cup. Careful of the cathedral train. "Fabulous really. I love it."

"That's better." Haley regarded her for a too-long second. "Gemstone, everything okay? I mean besides poor Mr. Sweet Pea going for a swim?"

Gemma sighed. What were friends for but to look beneath the surface and ask the real questions? In L.A., her friends mostly cared about her auditions, her callbacks, her party invitations, her workout routine and diet, and how in the world was she lucky enough to meet Matt Biglow.

"He's gorgeous."

"He's the hottest thing in L.A."

"What? You're going to Vegas to be on a Biglow reality show?"

"Yeah, I'm good. Just can't seem to get organized. Imani had to eat at Ella's this morning before camp. Why didn't I grocery shop yesterday? Aren't the weekends for cleaning, shopping, and binge-watching TV shows? What'd I do? Work. Researched designs for Taylor's shoot on Wednesday. Spent three hours in the storage locker organizing everything I needed. I'm a bad mom."

"If you mean you're showing Imani how to be a kind, caring, conscientious woman, who maybe isn't the best housekeeper in the world, then you're a great mom. You can't be good at everything."

"Feels like I should be. Especially for her. I want her to feel safe, you know, that she belongs with me. I want her to go into the kitchen, open the fridge or a cupboard to find it full of food and yell, 'There's nothing to eat. Can we order from the Fry Hut?'"

"She has all of that, Gemma. Well, except the full fridge." Haley embraced her with a laugh. "She knows she's safe and loved. When she first came to live with you, she never smiled. Now she glows. You've given her a life after so much death."

With those encouraging words in the air, Gemma's phone sounded. She set her breakfast down on the stairs and pulled the device from her pocket.

"It's Paula the Plumber," she said to Haley who waved off the call.

"Don't answer. She takes forever and then overcharges. Let me text Cole. He can have someone out there this afternoon." Haley's husband ran the fastest-growing construction company in middle Tennessee. "By the barn, you said?" She was already typing out her message.

"Hal, you don't have to do that. Paula maybe be slow and overcharge, but for sure I can't afford one of Cole's crew."

"For what I'm paying you, he can toss me some pro bono plumbing work."

Gemma teared up as she headed into the office. This was why she came home. Friends, family, support. This was why she'd never leave.

She launched the shop's email account and bookkeeping program, took a bite of her roll, then laughed when she spied the Fourth of July Three-Legged Race trophy on the file cabinet.

Pops Yer Uncle won the overall event, once again, but the shop took one heat from them. Next year, they'd take two if not the "whole blame thing." Haley was determined. Even mentioned something about starting to train in June.

"Cole's sending one of his guys to the farm after lunch," Haley said, leaning into the office. "They'll get it fixed. It's on the house too."

Since JoJo was off on Mondays, Gemma and Haley ran the shop in quiet camaraderie. In the afternoon when Gemma finished sorting a new shipment, Haley left to take her one-and-a-half-year-old daughter for a checkup.

She loved when she had the place to herself. The shop was peaceful, quiet, staged with symbols of love and commitment.

Gemma walked through the grand salon—which had an old Hollywood feel with a curved, gold sofa and two mid-century modern end tables—and glanced at the town from the picture window. When she turned back to the room, she noticed a layer of dust on the tables.

Grabbing a cloth from the supply closet, she worked her way around the shop, humming to herself, feeling rather, well, light-hearted.

When Imani came home Saturday night, she caught Gemma and the prince on the deck, in the dark, watching the stars, saying nothing.

When he left, Imani grilled her.

"W-what was he doing here? I didn't know he was so gorgeous. His eyes are like blue. Really blue."

Gemma recounted the three-legged race mishap, how he carried her over the finish line, and showed up later to check on her.

"He helped me with the herd because you abandoned me."

"Aren't you glad?"

"Then we ordered pizza. No big deal."

"No big deal? Gemma, he's a freaking prince."

"Tell me about your night at Justin's. Did his dad have good fireworks?"

She'd just finished with the shop dusting when a customer entered. A newly engaged woman with her mother.

"We drove up from Alabama. My grandmother bought her dress here in the forties when Miss Cora owned it." The young woman paced around the mannequins in the small salon where Haley staged the vintage gowns. "She said she donated it to the new owner when she reopened. I'd really love to find it and buy it back. Mom, do you see it?"

"If you don't find your grandmother's," Gemma said, "we'll try to find you one like it."

In the middle of helping them scout the older gowns, wondering what might be preserved in inventory, Gemma excused herself for her ringing phone.

Behind the counter, she gazed at the screen and sank slowly to the stool by the cash register. *Matt Biglow. You must be kidding.* What did he want?

"Miss, are there more vintage dresses? We can't seem to find my mother's." The bride's mother couldn't have been much older than Gemma's mom. She was pretty, with the countenance of success.

"Um, yes, forgive me. I'll go to the mezzanine and bring out the rest. Some of them are quite old so we preserve them."

The phone still buzzed in her hand as she took the stairs. The last time she communicated with her former boyfriend-slash-producer, it was with a string of hate-filled cuss words as she lay in the hospital, in post hip surgery pain, her head throbbing with a concussion.

She remembered every word she said but had convinced herself pain meds also played a part.

She let the call go to voicemail as she sorted through the vintage gowns, studying the pictures on the boxes, reading the details. She should ask the name of the grandmother. Haley labeled all the older, donated gowns with the donor's name and information.

But she couldn't concentrate. Matt Biglow had reached out. Why? She glanced at her phone to see he'd left a message.

Should she delete it? Listen to it and then delete it? The only reason she'd not removed him from her contacts was for a moment like this. If Matt texted or called, she wanted to know it. Just in case he was up to something. Legally he could do nothing with the reality show without her permission. But legalities never stopped him before.

In the dark, cool storeroom, Gemma gathered more vintage gowns and invited the women up.

"I do hope your grandmother's is among these. If you find it or one you like, I'll unbox it for you." She excused herself "for only a moment" and disappeared into the office.

Leaning against the closed door, she breathed deep and listened to his message. More than likely she was fretting over nothing. Of course. He called to say he's getting married. Or was getting out of show biz. *Please, let it be.*

"Gee Stone, long time no talk or text. Wow, you've gone up in the world. At least I think you have. Did I see you with Prince John?"

As if he knew she was listening, her phone buzzed with a text. On her phone screen was an image of her in Prince John's arms, laughing. Those redneck rubberneckers. They posted pictures?

"This thing has gone wild. So, is it you? Sure looks like you. Can't see your face really but I'd know that profile and those curves anywhere."

Her face was partially blocked by her arm and her laugh, but to friends and family, she must be recognizable.

"You're viral babe. #princessbride."

Viral? Gemma left Matt's text and searched the hashtag. Sure enough, there were pictures all over social media of her in Prince John's arms. And there were hundreds of questions.

Who is she?

Where was this taken?

Anyone know her?

There was even a video clip on something called the *Morning Show* with a reporter talking about this viral event.

There were hundreds of photos. Some before the fall. Some after. Some before the finish. Some after.

Even a video of Gemma charging the hoverers and calling them rednecks. This was a disaster. For the prince. For her. Because the one person, absolutely the one person who should not get ahold of this was Matt Biglow. Oh, he was seeing an opportunity here. And he would ruin her life all over again if he thought for a moment it would get him ahead.

CHAPTER
SEVEN

H e had a series of texts with his brother Monday morning in which he discovered scooping up Gemma to cross the finish line had reached the palace.

Spent the weekend at Hadsby. Came home to find you all over social media. What's with the woman in the IG post?

Just a friend of Buck and JoJo's. We were in a 3-legged race and fell. I carried her over the line. How's Daffy?

Nesting. Starting to think of nursery decorations. We didn't get to talk before you left. Are you okay with all this?

Please. I can handle my younger brother having a baby. Mum needs an heir, doesn't she?

I just don't want to make you remember...

That I lost a child as well as my wife? I'll always remember but I don't want to miss out on your joy.

Have you met Scottie yet?

On my way there today. Arranged things with her father Trent last night.

Keep us posted. And don't get caught up in
America. I know it's tempting after heartbreak but
you must come home. I'm not born to be a king.

I must be there for Holland's memorial and place the
one-year wreath on her headstone. For the record,
I'm not sure I'm fit to be king either."

He'd been with Buck and JoJo all day Sunday and off social
media. Not that he was on social media very much. Apparently
he'd missed an explosive post of him carrying Gemma. He could
kick himself in hindsight. What did he think would happen?
Carrying a beautiful woman in his arms was too much for people
to resist. And he'd seen the hordes of watchers holding up their
phones. The Lauchtenland media must be eating it up.

He would ring Gemma after his meeting, see how she fared.
Most people longed for a viral social media post, but he had a
sense she was not one of them.

However, the task at hand was meeting his sister. He'd arrived
at the modern O'Shay's Shirts home office, and as he walked into
the clean, white, almost-sterile lobby, with Gunner on his flank,
John collected his thoughts, arranged his expectations. Today he
was meeting his sister.

The woman at the receptionist desk glanced up from her
computer, then launched to her feet, toppling her chair.

"It's *you*." She yanked off her headset as she stumbled around
the desk and curtsied. "Prince John." She reached over the desk's
riser for her phone. "Can I get a selfie? Please?"

"Thank you but no," Gunner said, stepping in front of John.
Security details forbade posing for photos when out and about.

"Alena, leave the prince alone." A crisp, resonating voice
echoed through the cavernous lobby.

An elegant, well-built man in a pale blue button-down and
khakis ambled down the wood-and-steel floating staircase.

"Trent O'Shay," he said, greeting John with a firm handshake.
His bold manner was welcoming while broadcasting he was a man
of means. The king of an international enterprise. "Come on up."

John nodded to Gunner, who indicated he would wait in one of the modern, lime-green leather chairs.

"Alena, show his man to the cafeteria." Trent pointed to Gunner before heading to the second floor.

His man? Gunner would not like that much. He was a trained special forces officer serving in HMSD—Her Majesty's Security Detail.

"I trust you had no trouble finding us." At the top of the stairs, Trent led John down a row of glass-and-steel offices with a view toward the river, then down an L-shaped corridor where the offices doubled in size. Overhead, the mountainous ceiling brought in light from every angle.

"This is impressive," John said.

"After years and years of working in a dark, enclosed, '60s-era brick structure, we finally came into the twenty-first century." Trent's headquarters had a view of Hearts Bend from the river to the highway. "Come on in. Have a seat." He paused between his desk and a seating area where a rather grand leather couch faced two matching chairs and a designer center table. "Can I get you anything?" He pointed to the paneled wall where John imagined a hidden kitchenette. "Coffee, tea, water, soda, sports drink, juice."

"I'm fine, thank you." John started to sit but noticed the company's pictorial history on the walls.

Trent took a seat on the couch and John knew he was being inspected. Not as a prince but as his daughter's brother. As Catherine Blue's son.

"How do you like Hearts Bend? It's no Port Fressa but very sweet and inviting. We've got Nashville and Memphis for culture, should we feel the need."

"I'm enjoying it. Very peaceful." John scanned the pictorial avenue and moved down the wall to the beginning.

"Have you tried the Fry Hut yet? Best burger and fries anywhere."

"Not yet. But Buck has mentioned them."

"When I was in high school, my buddies and I ate at the Hut every night after football practice. Then went home for dinner and gobbled up whatever our folks made." His laugh was smooth and rich. John liked him.

"Founded in nineteen hundred." John read the brass plate tacked to the white oak frame. The history progressed from grainy black-and-white images to the high tech, brilliant colors of the present.

"My great-grandfather started out with a seamstress and a bolt of cloth. He was sixteen."

"Quite the entrepreneur." John spotted a young Trent by an industrial loom. His expression bore the same confidence and swagger he displayed in the few photos he'd shared with Mum, which she'd finally shown the family. "I'm sure he'd be impressed with what you've done with the business."

"Maybe. I sometimes think he wonders why we work so hard. He was ambitious, no doubt, and wanted to live well, but he was a family man. And he loved his travels. I've not left the office for more than a long weekend fishing trip in seven years."

"Then you must schedule time away." John paused at the final photo. It was taken at what appeared to be a new plant with Trent and the striking brunette that was his half sister.

"With all of our construction finished, I'm inclined to agree with you, but I can't seem to break away."

John inquired of the revenue—not specifics—the number of employees and the company's charitable work. Trent answered with open ease and handed John a pamphlet of the shirts they manufactured for the homeless and men in recovery programs.

"We have a Fresh Shirt Foundation, and a Back to Work program provides training and clothing for men ready to reenter the marketplace. We've actually hired quite a few of our graduates to work for O'Shay's."

"Nothing for the ladies?" By the look of Scottie, he'd have thought she would've championed a women's division long ago.

"We've researched a possible women's market but it's vibrant with companies doing a stellar job. Though we do partner with charities that help women return to the workplace. In the end, we decided to stick with what we know, our expertise, and uniqueness. But you didn't come to talk about O'Shay's Shirts, did you?"

"No, I suppose not." Taking a seat opposite Trent, John noticed a large backpack in the corner. The kind he'd used the year he trekked across Europe then North America. "Is she—"

A feminine voice echoed in the hall. A door clicked. "Okay, Dad, I'm going home and—"

John stood as Scottie walked in. She was the image of Mum. Piercing blue eyes peering out from a regal, sculpted face, the embodiment of the glass-and-steel structure surrounding them.

Her brunette hair was dyed a white blonde, worn short and neat. Dressed in hiking trousers and boots, she appeared to be on her way somewhere. Or perhaps returning.

"What's going on?" She glanced from John to her father.

"Why don't you sit down?" Trent motioned for Scottie to join him on the sofa.

"What for?" That was intended for John, he knew. "I don't mean to be rude, but I'm hungry and desperate for a long, hot bath." She reached for the corner backpack.

"Alena can bring you something from the cafeteria, Scottie, and you can wait ten minutes to clean up." Trent turned to John. "Scottie has been in Guatemala for six weeks." He ordered a sandwich lunch box with fruit, chips, and milk via the smart device on the center table. Then one more time admonished Scottie to sit down.

"I don't know what you're up to, Dad, but today is not the day." She hoisted her gear onto her shoulders. "Sorry, Prince John, I know you've come a long way but I hope your purpose was for something more than meeting me."

"Scottie, sit down." Trent didn't bother to disguise his exasperation.

"Why? So I can hear the queen's excuses along with yours? Even more from her son. Yet none from her own lips. I'm not in the mood." She turned to John. "I suppose they lied to you too."

"We didn't know you existed."

"Better than being told a bald-faced lie. For thirty-four years I

74

think my mother died but turns out she's not only alive but a queen. A queen!"

"Scottie, I know you're tired," Trent said, "but please act like we raised you right." He angled forward, arms on his legs, fingers loosely laced. "Her grandmother, my mother, Shug, and my father, Fritz, wanted to shelter her. So we told her, well, the *big lie*. Plus, I think Mom secretly wanted a daughter and this was her chance to mold someone into her mini-me."

"Don't blame them, Dad." With a sigh, Scottie unloaded her backpack and dropped into the nearest chair. "You could've told me the truth at any time."

"I'm afraid the queen didn't want him to, Scottie." John wasn't defending his mother or Scottie's father, just interjecting the facts, the complications. "Even in nineteen eighty-five, a pregnant crown princess without a husband was scandalous."

"She knows," Trent said. "I've told her everything."

"So everyone looked out for themselves with no regard for me." Scottie stood and squared off in front of John. "Why are you here?" She was way more steel than glass.

"Well…" He'd prepared a speech but with her staring him down, he couldn't recall a single word. "First, it's nice to meet you."

Her tense posture broke with a smile. "Yes, of course, it's nice to meet you too. It's weird, I guess, to have a brother."

"Two brothers. And it's weird for Gus and me as well. We've a big sister."

"Watch her, Prince John, she's bossy."

"Please, call me John. Both of you." Ah, he remembered his speech. "Scottie, on behalf of the queen and the royal House of Blue, I welcome you to the family."

That was ghastly. Sounded like he was offering her a palace job.

"Thank you, but can I be clear? You can tell your mother and the Blues I am not a member of your family." She stated her truth without guile or resentment. "I'm an O'Shay. Princess of a different kingdom. One that makes and sells one of the best men's clothing lines. I'm happy my mother is alive, and it's interesting, if not awkward, to know I have blood siblings, but let's not try to mend fences or create some sort of happily blended family. We're from very different worlds, John. I have no interest in yours and you certainly have no interest in mine."

"My daughter doesn't mince words," Trent said.

Scottie's box lunch arrived but she didn't reach for it. "I hope you didn't come all the way to Hearts Bend just to meet me." Retrieving her backpack once again, she hooked it over her shoulders with ease.

"I'm afraid I did. At the behest of the queen."

"You're her olive branch?"

"She sends her greetings." Should he relay any of her private musings? How the woman, not the queen, felt vulnerable to rejection? How she knew she'd done her daughter a disservice. John stood to meet his sister's kind but hard gaze. "My mother, our mother, wears a crown as well as any queen. She's strong and stable, wise, just, and kind. She listens. She tries all sides. But when the crown comes off, she's just a wife and a mum, a woman with flaws and failings, struggles. For what it's worth, Scottie, she hurts over this situation as much as you, probably more. Because she knew you, carried you in her arms, kissed your wee forehead and handed you over to your father knowing she could never look back."

He stopped, restraining any farther emotional soliloquy. Scottie's eyes glistened and he felt a bit of a teary burn himself.

"Does it matter how I feel? Everything seems to be about her and her position as queen."

"I understand, believe me. It's complicated. But she's reaching out to—"

"Reaching out? Why now? Our story broke over a year ago and I've heard very little from your family. What's so important that I have to accept her olive branch?"

"That I cannot tell you, but here we are. To be fair, after the news broke, she did, I believe, send an inquiry?"

"Her secretary wrote to Dad. That's not a mother reaching out to the daughter she abandoned." Scottie adjusted the backpack, holding onto the strap with her hands. "It's too late. I'm sorry. I'm thirty-five, not a child."

"It's too late for your childhood but not for the rest of your life, Scottie." Trent's fatherly wisdom turned her tears to ire.

"Don't think I've forgotten your part in this."

"Scottie, my hands were tied. Come on, let it go. Or try to understand."

"You could've at least told me she was alive. Know what? Forget it. I'm not going to rehash this. John, enjoy your time in Hearts Bend." She stuck out her hand. "Nice to meet you. Give my regards to your mom, brother, dad, aunts, cousins, whoever."

"And if I'd told you, Scottie, then what?" Trent wove his question in between her flippant salutation. "You'd have started asking to meet her. Wondering where she lived, what she did with her life, why she left."

But Scottie was already at the door. With the soft click, John was alone with Trent.

"She's bullheaded."

"Like mother like daughter."

"She and I are having dinner tonight. Join us. She'll be more affable after a bath, a bit of food, and a nap."

"Are you sure?" Gemma came to mind. If he agreed to dinner, he'd like an ally at the table. But was she an ally? "She seems resolved to her position."

"I'll text you the address." Trent retrieved his phone from his desk. "Bring a guest if you'd like. Do you know anyone in town besides Buck and JoJo?"

"I've made a recent acquaintance, yes."

"The girl from the Fourth of July three-legged race? Alena showed me a plethora of social media posts when I came in on Monday."

Plethora? Understatement of the year.

"Gemma Stone. Do you know her?" John's phone pinged with a text from Trent. He tapped the screen to find a map to the man's home.

"Not personally. I know *of* her. After Scottie graduated from Rock Mill High, Gemma became the school's new darling, being voted prom and homecoming queen. You know, those crazy All-American traditions we both love and loathe. I'm sure you have similar ones in Lauchtenland. Anyway, I believe she even won a local beauty contest and then bugged out to Hollywood. I didn't know she was back in town."

So it was Trent O'Shay who peeled back the first layer of Gemma Stone.

"Apparently. I don't know much of her except she can't weigh more than nine or ten stone. We were paired in the race by Jo who wanted to win a trophy for her wedding shop."

Trent laughed. "Everyone wants to take down Pops Yer Uncle. They win every year. So, yes, bring Gemma. Buck and JoJo too. Scottie knows them. Friendly faces might defuse some of the tension."

"Buck's playing the Ryman tonight but I'll bring Gemma if she's available."

"Seven o'clock." By Trent's manner, John could tell he wanted to return to work so he said goodbye.

On his way to the truck with Gunner, John texted his brother.

I met her. Tough but tender. Reminds me of Mum and Great-granny.

She's a Blue then.

In her DNA but otherwise she's an O'Shay.

Does she want to meet us?

Not really but having dinner tonight.

Have you informed Mum?

Let's see how things progress. How is she by the way?

Good, I think. She and Dad are at Hadsby for holiday. Give sis my regards.

John smiled.

Will do. She sent hers, btw.

Driving the quiet Tennessee roads—with Gunner riding silently beside him—John sorted and categorized the meeting, wondering all the more why Mum wanted to meet Scottie now.

Her challenge was spot-on. It'd been a year since the truth came out. So why ask to meet this summer? And if one wanted to be technical, the truth had been alive for Mum and Trent for thirty-five years.

Well, he'd done his bit. Met his sister. After dinner tonight, he'd enjoy the rest of his holiday before returning home to face reality. The anniversary of Holland's funeral and the memorial service when he'd lay the final wreath. Then on to his investiture ceremony. Would Mum indeed change the old writ?

But for now, he'd shove all that aside and extend a dinner invitation to Gemma. His rather lovely plus-one, if she'd do him the honor.

"Eloise Ltd. is claiming something afoul with the sale of a Midlands tract of land to Hessenberg manufacturer Reingard Industries. 'Three months ago we were denied the purchase of the north Midlands tract. Today we learned Reingard Industries is breaking ground for a massive plant. We are asking for an investigation.'"

– CLARK WILSON, THE NEWS LEADER

"Cecily and I were wondering whatever happened to the portrait of Princess Holland? Was it completed? Will it ever be revealed? We think it should be, don't you?"

– LOYAL ROYALS BLOG

"The queen and king consort are on holiday for the month of July, enjoying Hadsby Castle in the Old Hamlet part of Dalholm. Here's our royal reporter Melissa Faris on what it might be like to live in the ancient castle."

– STONE BRUBAKER, THE MORNING SHOW

"Can anyone tell us what's going on with Prince John and the mysterious woman in his arms?"

– @STEFWITHANF ON INSTAGRAM

CHAPTER
EIGHT

GEMMA

O kay, life was getting weird. First the call from Matt Biglow. Which she did not answer.

Now, on this Monday afternoon, as she helped a customer with her dress, Prince John peeked into the grand salon.

"May I speak with you?"

The bride and her maid of honor gasped and collapsed together onto the gold couch as Gemma excused herself and motioned for John to follow her to the butler's pantry.

"Will you join me tonight for dinner at the O'Shays'?"

"Are you serious?" Dinner at the O'Shays' with the prince?

She fired off a series of questions. What for? Who else was going to be there? Was it dress-up or casual? Did they know she was coming? Was he sure? She must've asked that ten times.

In the end, he wanted a friend—was she his friend?—at the table. And yes, he was sure. Even Trent O'Shay said to invite her. He had no idea if the evening was dress or casual. He guessed casual.

"Scottie has just returned from Guatemala," he said.

"I-I guess." Gemma looked at her phone as if to check her calendar but she knew full well her evening was free. "If you're sure."

"I'll pick you up at six forty-five. Dinner is at seven."

Well that exchange blew her concentration for the afternoon. Even the bride and her maid of honor couldn't seem to focus.

They left without purchasing dresses but promised to return.

When Marla, the part-time sales staff, arrived at four, Gemma scooted over to Roseanne's Vintage. She had about thirty bucks to dress for a date with a prince and the titans of men's clothing.

She arrived home a little after five and dropped her packages on the crowded kitchen table. Seriously, she needed to deal with the clutter. But there was no space. No storage.

"Gemma, ooh la la." Imani entered from the hallway with a basketball anchored on her hip. "What'd you get at Roseanne's?" She peered inside the pink sack marked with an interlinking R and V.

"A dress and pair of shoes."

Every once in a while, Roseanne hit the jackpot with Nashville celebs and Music Row executives. Gemma had walked in just as she'd finished staging her latest haul. Half the clothes still had the tags on them. She spent a little more than her thirty-dollar budget but she didn't care. The dress was a McQueen and shoes Jimmy Choo. And barely affordable at Roseanne's Vintage prices.

"A dress?" Imani curled her lip. "For what?"

"To wear, why else?" Gemma opened the dishwasher from 1980, catching the door with her knee before it knocked against the floor, and collected the clean dishes from the counter and loaded them onto the bottom rack.

Oh yeah, the blame thing didn't work. It held their everyday dishes ever since Gemma opened one of the cabinets last year to find a community of cockroaches.

She bug-bombed the place, but so far the dishwasher was the only safe compartment.

"Where? The barn? I mean, Hercules loves you, but I don't think he knows the difference between muck boots and designer clothes." Imani pulled the pink paisley with the silver chain belt out of the bag. "Gemma...oh my gosh... Chanel. Can I have this?"

Gemma snatched the dress from her. "Do your homework."

"Funny. School doesn't start for another month. Whoa." Imani found the shoes. Pristine, never worn Jimmy Choo leather wedges. "These are..." She looked at Gemma with kid-at-Christmas eyes.

"I have to have them." She hugged the wedges to her chest. "Can I wear these on the first day of school? Please? I promise to take really good care of them. I'll do extra chores, cook breakfast every morning for a month—if you buy food—and—"

"You done yet?" Gemma feigned a sternness she didn't possess. "You do chores because you are a member of this family."

Imani stared back. "I am?"

"Of course you are—" Imani dropped the shoes and launched into Gemma's arms and squeezed tight. "Hey, what's all this? You know you're family. This home is *our* home. You're my girl. Mac and Mauve are your Pops and Memaw."

"I know we say that but I didn't know it was real. I mean, I'm not officially family. You're my guardian, not my mom. I have grandparents. One anyway. She doesn't want me."

"What brought this on?" Gemma moved Imani back so she could see her face, sensing this conversation had been brewing. Every once in a while, Imani referred to her parents and grandparents, but it'd been months.

"The kids were talking about their parents coming to the games. It hit me that my family isn't really my family. I mean, it's stupid but—"

"It's not stupid. You're allowed to mourn. You lost parents and grandparents in a short amount of time. But we are your family. You can always talk to me. It's okay to miss them."

Tears washed to the corners of Imani's eyes. "More and more I can't even remember my mom. I try, you know, but she gets further away. Then sometimes at basketball practice, Coach calls my name and I'm sure it's Dad. I jerk around to see him, my heart pounding, but it's not him. Then Grandpa and Grandma Cook passed, and Grandpa Shumaker. Gigi Shumaker couldn't stand the sight of me. Am I cursed?'"

"What? No! Imani, you are not cursed. I know it seems you've been dealt death too many times but—"

"Yeah, like what if something happens to you? Or Pops and Memaw? What then?"

"First, I'm not going anywhere. You're stuck with me. Second, your Gigi Shumaker loves you. She sends gifts and money. She calls." Once in a while, okay, not a lot. "Losing your mama and daddy did everyone in. Then your Cook grandparents died. And suddenly Grandpa Shumaker... I think your gigi just broke. You reminded her of everything she'd lost. Her daughter-in-law, her son, her husband, her friends and in-laws."

"But wouldn't that make her want me all the more?"

"Pain has a strange effect on people." Gemma brushed her hand over Imani's cheek. "Give her time."

"I'll be eighteen in two years. She and that stupid new husband of hers may never see me play."

"I'll talk to her. I'll be there. Pops and Memaw will be there. And that rowdy bunch of their friends."

"Do you think they're watching? From heaven? Mama and Dad, Granny and Gramps Cook, Grandpa Shumaker?"

"Absolutely, and I know they're so proud of you. Your dad's telling all the old basketball players in heaven, 'That's my girl, fellas, she's a star.'"

"You're so *stoopid*." Imani smiled as she brushed away her tears and reached down for the shoes, hugging them to her chest again. "Since I'm a star, I think I need to wear these the first day of school."

Gemma laughed. "We'll see. But for now, you have rabbit cages to clean."

"Yes, *Mother*." Imani elongated the word as if trying it on for size. She'd never called Gemma Mom or Mama or even referred to her as her mother. She'd said "guardian" and "person I live with," even "protector," but never Mother. Gemma liked the feel of it.

"I'll be out tonight, *Daughter*." Hey, that felt pretty good. "Dinner at the O'Shays'."

"The O'Shays'?" Imani looked up from where she'd kicked off her sneakers for work boots. "With the prince? Is he meeting his sister?"

"Yes and Trent told him to bring a friend. Guess that's me."

"You're friends?" Imani made a face. "With Prince John of Lauchtenland?"

"Acquaintances. He'll be gone in a month so don't go getting ideas." Gemma finished with the dishes and closed the dishwasher door. "There's nothing for dinner, so order pizza."

"A bunch of us have the fundraiser meeting for new uniforms with Coach March at Ella's. Is there anything we can donate to a rummage sale?"

"This whole house is a rummage sale." But it was her rummage. And she was grateful. Gemma started for the hallway to the bedrooms. "Come home after the meeting."

"Can Penny come back with me? Watch a movie?"

"If she comes, Justin won't be far behind." The three of them had been friends since grade school.

"So? All we do is hang out, eat, talk basketball, music, and watch shows."

"What if Penny can't come?"

"Then it'll be Justin and me." Imani shrugged like it was no big deal but averted her gaze, finding the trash bag by the door very interesting.

"Do you like Justin? As more than a friend?" A rose blush hit the teen's brown cheeks. "Yeah, that's what I thought," Gemma said. "We can talk about this later. I have to get ready."

"He's a good guy, Gemma. You can trust us."

"I said the same thing to my parents. And it was true until I climbed into the back of Dash Stapleton's truck and started making out."

"I've never been in the back of Justin's truck. Not alone anyway."

"Not yet." Gemma kissed Imani on the forehead. "I love you, you know that, right? I'm going to do my best by you for your sake, your parents', and grandparents'."

"I know and I'm glad but why does that mean you can't trust me?"

The plea in Imani's eyes and voice echoed with the one Gemma made when she was sixteen. She'd had every good intention. But one kiss, one touch, and every boundary line she'd established started to move. By the time she hit L.A., it was almost anything goes. And that, dear friends, led her to Vegas.

But tonight was not for reminiscing. Nor comparing her sixteen-year-old self with Imani. She had a date, no, not a date, an appointment, with a prince.

"We'll talk later, okay? But no Justin alone. Hey, take the trash out when you go."

In her room, door closed, Gemma sank to the edge of the bed. She'd hurdled her first talk with her girl about boys and life. One down, a million to go.

JOHN

Being a good prince who'd trained in the military and the law, he considered himself a capable conversationalist. As he dressed for the evening, he aligned possible topics for dinner. Ways to bring up the House of Blue, Mum, and how the scenario with Scottie could have a happy ending for all.

Even though he was pretty sure happy endings didn't exist.

The main thing to remember was Scottie was not the enemy. She was Mum's daughter. His sister.

Dad texted just before John left to collect Gemma, asking for an update on Scottie.

> Seeing her tonight.

> Good, let me know how it goes.

> Dad, are you Mum's envoy as well? Sooner or later she's going to have to make her own overtures.

> She knows but she felt a bit tired after our walk today. We went too far. She took a long soak and headed to bed.

Hmm. Didn't sound like Mum, the woman, the queen of boundless energy. She worked tirelessly. Even on holidays she insisted on gardening or taking long walks.

Arriving at Gemma's, John parked beside her BMW and stepped from behind the wheel. Gunner waited in his idling motor.

Of all his musings this afternoon and evening, he'd not planned for Gemma herself. He was halfway to her door when she came out and completely stunned him. He stutter-stepped and caught his breath. Was she always this beautiful?

Wearing a pink dress cinched at the waist with a shiny silver belt, and her hair bouncing over her shoulders in long, shiny waves, she moved toward him with an easy smile, her hips in a soft sway.

"You look nice," she said.

John glanced down at his khakis and suede Bruno Magli shoes. He should go home and change. Put on nice slacks. Change his shirt.

"Prince? Isn't this where you say, 'Thank you, so do you'?"

"You," he said, reaching for her arm and escorting her to the truck's passenger side, "look amazing."

Their eyes met in one of those *Oh no, am I going to kiss her?* moments, but she reached for the handle and popped open the door.

"You don't think I'm overdressed, do you?"

"You're perfect."

Perfect? Was she? Why did he choose that word? It sounded so head-over-heels-I-can't-think. Which was not true. Being out of Lauchtenland had a strange effect on him. Tempted him to move on with his life, perhaps fall in love again.

Thankfully, gratefully, he'd return home in a month, back to his widower apartment where he belonged. If Holland couldn't live, then neither should he.

Trent O'Shay's place was a mid-century modern built with the same glass-and-steel design as the office. Gemma said nothing as they walked up the concrete stairs to the long, wide porch. John smiled at her as he rang the bell.

"Thanks for coming with me."

"Gave me an excuse to go shopping."

Scottie answered the door in her bare feet, wearing a T-shirt and shorts, her appearance like one who'd been bathed, fed, and rested.

"Can I get you a glass of wine?" was her only greeting.

After John made introductions, he and Gemma snacked on hors d'oeuvres while making small talk with Scottie and Trent until a cook announced dinner.

Scottie gave Gemma most of her attention, asking about her years at their high school, time in L.A., and if she knew anyone famous.

"Um, yes, a few people. I was in the Gonda film with Chloe Daschle. *Bound by Love.*"

"Really, I loved that film. What part did you play?"

"That part that hit the cutting room floor."

"Oh no, really? I hear that happens a lot. I hope it didn't make you give up. Is that why you came home?"

"No."

John paused his sip of wine, waiting. *No* and... But Gemma didn't expound and a bit of the shadow she carried flickered through her eyes. Scottie didn't press for more but passed around the hors d'oeuvres instead and John asked about her trip to Guatemala.

Dinner was steaks on the grill, baked potatoes, salad, and apple pie made by the grandmother, Shug.

"She wanted to come but I said no." Scottie passed John a healthy slice of pie.

"Who is Shug again?" Gemma asked.

"Dad's mom. She raised me."

The elephant in the room—Scottie being a Blue—never sat up to the table. They talked about her travels—Trent wanted her to experience all she could before the business claimed her time—and her role at O'Shay's Shirts as vice president of development.

"But I've worked in every O'Shay department from the reception desk to shipping to production inspection. I know this business."

The post-dinner coffee in the living room where a large plate glass window faced the river. Suddenly the conversation fell flat. The elephant, however, doubled in size.

"All right, Dad," Scottie said, setting her coffee aside. "You called this meeting. Go."

"Meeting? This is dinner. You're getting to know your brother."

John sat forward. "May I speak?" He'd waited long enough. "Scottie, the queen, Mum, would like very much to meet you."

"Then why are you here and she is not?"

If he was going to get anywhere with this mission, Scottie had to stop asking the obvious.

"Now it's my turn to speak." Trent sat on the edge of his seat, coffee cup in hand. "You two should spend time together, get to know each other. Scottie, I'm not going to be around forever, and I'd like to think you had family around you. Siblings. Nieces and nephews."

"I'll be an old, crotchety lady by the time you depart this earth. Don't worry about me. And if you wanted me to have siblings, you should've married and had more children."

"That's another story." Trent peered at John and Gemma. "I'm going to treat you two like trusted friends here so don't let me down."

"Of course," John said.

"I was never here." Gemma.

"I'm fifty-nine," Trent said more to Scottie than John and Gemma. "As you noted, I never married, never gave you siblings. I was consumed with work and raising you. There was a part of me that wondered if, maybe hoped, Catherine would come around one day and want to see you. If so, I didn't see a wife and children fitting into a semi-royal life. I didn't want a stepmom to claim any of your affections."

Was Trent still in love with his mother? Oh the human heart. So beguiling, so bewitching, so betraying.

"So you want John to be my brother? And the other guy. What's his name?"

"Gus," John answered softly, but he felt quite sure Scottie knew every name in the Blue family.

"That's right, Gus. Coral Winthrop, the cosmetic heiress, left him at the altar." Scottie scooted off the couch, setting her coffee cup on a tea trolly. "I'm sorry you regret your choices, Dad, but don't put it on me to ease your guilt. Gemma, it was really nice to meet the girl who replaced me at Rock Mill High." Her laugh was warm and soft. "I'd love to hear more about your time in Hollywood. We've provided clothes for movies over the years and I love being on set. I'm good friends with the Gondas."

"I'm sure Jeremiah Gonda doesn't remember me." Gemma's answer was crisp but not rude. By her posture and tone, Holly-wood was not a favorite topic.

"John." Scottie offered John her hand. "It's been a pleasure." She kissed her father's cheek, grabbed her shoes and bag. "Dad, I've a hair appointment in the morning but I'll be in for the staff meeting." Then she turned to John. "I meant to tell you I am really sorry about your wife. She seemed like an amazing woman. I'm sorry I never met her."

"Thank you." Just when he thought his report about Scottie would be a no go, she came around with surprising tenderness. "She was more than amazing."

With that, Scottie bid them all goodnight.

"See," Trent said as the door closed behind his daughter. "I told you she'd be more affable by dinner. And before you go, let me send you home with some pie. If not, I'll eat the whole thing and I'm too old for that sort of indulgence." He patted his flat abdomen and headed to the kitchen.

A few minutes later with pie slices in glass containers, John and Gemma walked down Trent's long driveway in silence.

At the truck John opened Gemma's door. "You made the evening so much more enjoyable. Scottie liked you."

"More like she wanted to know the girl who usurped her reputation in high school."

"Trent told me you were a beauty queen."

"In a very, very small pageant. But I'm not that girl anymore." Gemma climbed into her seat and the hem of the pink dress slid down her smooth thigh. He stared for a second, then collected himself and slid behind the wheel. Behind him, the lights of Gunner's motor flashed through the dark.

"Scottie commanded the night, didn't she?" Gemma said more to herself than John. "She's pretty, well, cool. I always wanted to meet her."

"You just saw a glimpse of Queen Catherine II only with an American accent. She looks like her, acts like her, has her fortitude. But underneath, the woman is mush. She cares about everything and everyone. If she's like Mum at all, she'll go home tonight and cry."

"Now you know why neither one of them want to meet."

Well that put a different light on things. "Of course, you're right." Why hadn't he considered that as well? Bravo, Gemma.

"I have to admit, I thought you'd say more tonight, you know, be all princely and—" From the corner of his eye, he saw her spear the air with her finger. "'You're commanded to see the queen.'"

"It's the twenty-first century, Gemma, not the first. We can't make her. As for dinner, I'm an observer. I like to get to know someone before I move in." The headlights cut through the darkness, highlighting the two-lane road. He was tired and wanted to think through the evening but he wasn't ready to say goodnight to Gemma.

"Want my advice? And please, feel free to say no." He glanced over at her, waiting. The question was rhetorical. "Give her time. She lived her whole life thinking her mother was dead. She was raised by Shug O'Shay, who is nothing short of a Southern hurricane. My granny served with her on a church committee and the only time I ever heard her swear was when she collided with Miss Shug."

"Seems like solid advice. I'll ring her for coffee later in the week. Java Jane's. I've been enjoying their lattes." Now it was his turn. "Can I ask *you* something?" Gemma waited, silent. "What happened in Hollywood?"

She shifted away and stared out her window. "What makes you think something happened?"

"You changed when Scottie brought it up. When she said she wanted to hear more." He stopped at the intersection of Ox Bottom Parkway and River Road, then continued on.

"Would you care for a cup of coffee at my place?" Gemma said. "Eat this pie? Leftover is never as good as fresh."

"Stellar point, my friend. Besides, Buck's on some low carb, no sugar diet. What sort of guest would I be if I stored temptation in his refrigerator?"

"Exactly. But first, turn here." She pointed to a little convenience store sitting like a beacon of hope on a dark corner. "I'll need to get some coffee and cream."

CHAPTER NINE

QUEEN CATHERINE

Another sleepless night combined with her medication made her restless and irritable. After a week at Hadsby, she had asked Edric to take her home. The old familiar castle wasn't proving to be as cozy and restful as she'd hoped.

Besides, she wanted to work. To get busy, take her mind off how weak she felt. After all, she was the queen.

In her office, she prepared for her meeting with Elias, the prime minister. But her feet and hands burned with a pin-sharp sensation.

The clock struck eight and Mason entered. "The prime minister, ma'am."

"Elias, good morning." She fought the pain and shook his hand, then sat in her regular chair. Oh, how she wanted to kick off her shoes and rub the pain from her feet.

"Your Majesty." Elias sat, crossing his legs, ready to give his report. "How are you? You're supposed to be on holiday this month."

"I'm irritated, if you must know. I seem to have some sort of virus or flu that insists on plaguing me."

"Vitamin C, my wife says."

"Any more vitamin C and I'll turn into an orange."

His cordial laugh led them straight into work. Elias reported nothing out of the ordinary. Taxes, businesses, spending, and oddly, the recent hullabaloo over the Midlands land sale to Reingard Industries.

"MP Fickle is a dog with a bone, ma'am. He believes something underhanded has gone on and he's determined to dig it up."

"What sort of underhanded? I read the sale was perfectly legitimate."

"As did I. I even spoke to the local authorities and environmental ministry. Eloise Ltd. paid for all the testing on the land but in the end, failed to come up with the finances to make the purchase. Reingard swooped in."

"That's unfortunate for Eloise, but perfectly within Reingard's rights," the queen said. "What do you make of Hamish?"

"He's ambitious, smart, intelligent, charming. He's a uniter."

"Uniter? More of an instigator from where I sit. Stirring up trouble. You don't think he'll steal the affection of the people, do you?"

"From who? The Family? From Prince John? A young, handsome widower who patrons seventy charities and champions everyday people? I think not."

"It's important for Prince John to get it right going forward. My father made sure I was the crown princess of the people, not just the House of Blue."

"Which is why he would not let you marry your American. Nor keep your child."

"We all must make sacrifices." She shifted in her seat, combating the waves of prickly pain in her hands and feet. On top of which she felt so weary, as if she might fold and slip right down to the floor.

"You look tired, Your Majesty. I should go. Let you rest."

She wanted to refute his observation, but felt suddenly weary with no more energy for conversation. When Elias had gone, she told Mason she was not to be disturbed. Fixing a cup of tea, she returned to her desk but could barely hold up her head. She had no time for this nonsense.

Being ill did not suit her at all.

From the window of her high and lofty third floor Perrigwynn Palace office, she could see the realm of her ancestors. The capital city of Port Fressa was alive and vibrant as any in the world.

Modern skyscrapers shadowed ancient shops and homes, cathedrals.

And much like New York, Port Fressa never slept. At night the glow of streetlamps haloed the Clemency district like a tiara woven through a head of silky black hair.

If she pressed her cheek against the thick glass, she could just make out the radiant lights of the Heart of God. In the daytime, the steeple lights paled, but at night, they owned the darkness and formed a heart.

No one knew the phenomenon of lights had been created until the first structure over six stories was erected. The eight cathedrals in the city centre were so set that they formed a perfectly shaped heart. It was magical if not miraculous.

She'd shared her fist kiss there. With Trent O'Shay. What choice did she have but to fall in love? She'd arrived late to the love game, being sheltered in the palace, then at a girls' school, being followed by protection officers and governesses. Even her time at Haxton University was chaste and conventional.

"Darling?" Edric, her handsome, solid-as-a-rock king consort, leaned over her desk and kissed her forehead, drawing her from her memory. "You're warm. Do you have a fever?"

"What does it matter? I've work to do." Catherine patted his chest and returned to her computer screen. "Have you heard from John? Has he met Scottie?"

"Yes, but he's given no details. What do you make of the social media posts? William Clark mentioned them to me today during the Development Ministry meeting. Said everyone speculated John had a new love."

"Then they don't know John. I want him to move on, but I'm quite sure he's not met a new love after a week in Tennessee. Besides, as much as we all love our American friends, he'd not be foolish enough to fall for an American, no matter how lovely." For once she was glad her son was still very much in love with his wife. "After what Gus went through with Coral Winthrop, being left at the altar, he'd steer clear of any sort of repeat." Catherine shuddered. What a nightmare. "As a future king, he knows to marry someone who loves Lauchtenland as much as he does."

"You sound as if one can easily steer the human heart. And we know now why Coral left Gus. She'd known they weren't right. She'd encountered God. Surely you know what that's about, Kate."

"Don't use my experiences against me." She smiled softly. Edric was her rock. He knew her better than anyone. "As for steering hearts... I was in love with Trent O'Shay, but when I realized our relationship could not go forward, I let it go. Then I found you." She reached for his hand. "Best decision I ever made was to marry you."

"Is Trent part of the reason you wouldn't go to Scottie yourself?" Edric released her hand as he perched on the edge of her desk and gazed down at her with nothing but tenderness in his gray-blue eyes.

"I don't think so, no. Trent I could handle. But Scottie, after all these years, rejecting me as I deserved, would still be crushing. Besides, I want to beat this cold or virus, whatever seems to be plaguing me."

"Darling, go to bed. I'll tell Mason to clear your diary."

She was too weary to fight him. Leaning on his arm, she returned to apartment 1A. "Can you ask Pablo for some tea?"

Edric rang for the butler, giving him instructions, then returned to Catherine. "I want to call the doctor. This has gone on too long."

When she reclined on the couch, he slipped off her shoes and rubbed her feet. She winced with each touch, but it seemed to relieve the prickly pain.

"Thank you," she whispered. But her gratitude was about more than his foot massage.

It was for loving her.

For over thirty years she hid the fact she'd had a daughter. After Trent, and well, the whole ordeal, she was so broken she thought she'd never love again. Then she met Edric at a small garden party and he made falling in love easy. Fun. And when she handed him her heart, she wanted his love and trust in return. To appear as the woman of integrity she purported to be.

What if confessing everything about Trent and Scottie made her look less in his vivid eyes? So she never told him about her daughter.

"Pablo will tend you, darling, I must be off. I've another meeting this morning. See you at dinner." Edric kissed her cheek and on his way out asked Pablo to attend Her Majesty carefully.

Catherine tried to nap after her tea but almost felt too weak to sleep. The July sunlight warming the window cheered her so she kicked off the covers and traipsed slowly to the window and glanced down at the palace gardens.

They were a beautiful array of colorful flowers blooming from beds of dark dirt all hemmed in by fastidiously trimmed green grass. She ached to go for a walk, to be out of doors.

In the distance, movement caught her eye. She squinted through a bit of sunlight to see a man in a long, woolen anorak and a wide-brimmed hat under the shade of the King's tree. A woolen coat? In this summer heat? Catherine pressed for a closer look then jerked back. What was *he* doing here?

Emmanuel.

Chapter
Ten

Gemma

While the coffee brewed, Gemma cleared the kitchen table, not bothering to make excuses of her mess—what was the point?—and exposed the poppy red Formica and chrome, a tribute to days gone by.

"When I was at uni, my mates and I frequented a pub that had blue Formica tables along the wall. The rest was plaster and wood from the eighteenth century, but those tables were a tip to the modern era." He stooped down, looking underneath. "Where'd you get this?"

"Came with the house. If you're looking for gum, I have never-been-chewed pieces in my bag."

John raised up with an expression that made her laugh. "I was checking out the maker."

"Give me a sec to wipe down the table." Gemma snatched a paper towel from the roll on the wall and the Formula 409 from under the sink to wipe the table. "This place just has no storage."

"You should've seen Gus's room when we were growing up. Clothes and toys everywhere. No sooner would a maid clean and straighten, he'd have it all out again."

"Did you have a lot of maids and nannies growing up?" Gemma tossed away the paper towels, stored the cleaner under the sink, then searched the cupboards for Granny's china.

"Two nannies before school. Maids worked for the palace, so they didn't impact my world as much. My parents were involved, not leaving all our care to others. We ate breakfast and dinner together. Tuesday and Thursday nights were family night unless there was some state function. We traveled with them every summer. They both took off work during the holidays. It was quite normal, I think."

"For living in a palace and wearing a crown, having protection officers." He'd sent Gunner home once they arrived here. A command the man didn't seem to like. Now, where are those cups?

"We all have our burdens to bear," John said with a bit of sarcasm. "What about your parents?"

"Ah, Mac and Mauve. Where to begin?" Found them. Only two cups and saucers remained after a fire several decades ago. Granny gave these remnants to Gemma when she moved into the house.

"It was Grandpa's and my wedding china."

Gemma set the table with the cups and saucers, a fork and spoon, then sniffed the milk in the fridge—still good—and collected a couple of napkins. "I don't believe I have any sugar."

"Cream is fine." The prince spread out his napkin, neatly removed his container's lid, and picked up his fork.

When she'd poured the coffee, she sat and raised her fork. "Bon appétit."

"Bon appétit." John creamed his coffee then took a bite of pie. "This is so good I don't care I'm having a second piece."

"I pretend to work off extra calories in the barn. But I know it's not true."

"So, what about your parents? I feel at a disadvantage. You know about mine, but I don't know about yours."

"They are the salt-of-the-earth type. Hard workers, honest, decent. Raised me right."

"You're an only child?"

"Not on purpose. She couldn't have more after me."

"Were you spoiled?"

"Do I seem spoiled? I didn't have to share with siblings if that's what you mean. But we never had a lot of money. Most of the time we were broke. Dad's a dreamer, always looking for a way to turn one dollar into a thousand. In the summer, we'd sit in the lawn chairs, listening to the crickets, watching the stars, and dreaming. I wanted to be a, well..." She took a bite of pie. *Don't tell him.* It would only lead to more questions. "Daddy used to go on and on about all the things he was going to buy Mama and me one day. But for every dollar he invested in some scheme, he lost two." Gemma set down her fork for a sip of coffee.

"But you had everything you needed?"

He sounded concerned and it touched her. Her years in Hollywood, combined with her relationship with Matt, had made her hard. Guarded. She saw displays of tenderness and caring as a way for others to gain advantage over her.

"Daddy drives a delivery truck and Mama is the head house-keeper at Hearts Bend Inn." Might as well paint the whole picture. Be up front and honest about her very humble roots. Not that it really mattered but since he asked.

"I grew up in a double-wide trailer on a tract of land my grandfather gave to us. We had a gravel driveway that washed away every spring and iced over every winter. There were rust stains in the sinks from the well water. When I learned to drive, I'd go to town to do my laundry because Daddy was forever forgetting to buy water softener. I had clothes, food, education, even dance lessons. My parents run around with a tight group of friends with whom they play cards several nights a week, drink on Saturday night, but just enough to get them dancing to oldies. On Sunday mornings, they're up early and on their way to church to repent."

When the prince didn't respond, Gemma fought a sting of embarrassment. She'd said too much. But it was all true. In a good way. Did he think she threw her folks under the bus? Or that they were a bunch of hick rednecks?

She finished her last bite of pie. "This would've been perfect with a scoop of ice cream."

"What you just said—" The prince shoved his container forward. "About your parents, your honesty. It took Holland almost until we were married to speak so freely. I knew her parents, Lord and Lady Cunningham, so there was no real mystery about her upbringing, but she never talked about them or her childhood. It was like she feared something would put me off or turn me away."

"Love makes us do strange or unusual things."

"Did love make you do strange things?" John collected their dishes, carried them to the sink, rinsed them, then opened the dishwasher.

"Doesn't work," Gemma said with a low laugh. "I use it for storage. Just leave the dishes for later. So, did Holland eventually share more of her life?"

Funny how he focused on how love made one do strange, unusual things. She said it as a toss-away line but John seemed to think it meant something more.

"She did." John stared out the kitchen window over the sink. "Seemed like we were just getting started when she died."

She was about to ask about the accident when the door flew open. Imani and Penny entered with the dogs, their claws scratching and clicking on the linoleum.

John turned from the window and gave each girl a nod. "Ladies."

"John, you remember Imani. This is her friend, Penny. Girls, curtsy, this is Prince John."

"Hello," Imani said, offering her hand, but seemed locked in a dream-like trance. Next to her, Penny, the six-foot center for the Rock Mills girls' basketball team, giggled and blushed.

Imani suddenly found her voice. "Oh my gosh. W-what are you doing in dumpy Hearts Bend?"

"Having a bit of a holiday. Your town reminds me of some of my favorite places in Lauchtenland." He went on to describe the Midlands and Dalholm, even the north country of The Haskells. The girls asked intelligent questions, recalling their history and geography. Gemma was quite proud. And just like that, the prince became a real man and stole their hearts. The girls', of course, not hers.

Then Imani got to the important topic. Pop popcorn and a movie. "Can Penny stay over, Gemma?"

"Don't see why not. But you have chores in the morning before basketball camp." She glanced at the prince, who smirked like he enjoyed her role of mother. "Speaking of, how was the fundraiser?"

"Good. We're going to hold the rummage sale at the end of the month. I'm going to go through all those boxes in the attic. Maybe the former owners left some treasure."

"More than likely you'll be throwing all the stuff away." But Gemma could check "clean out the attic" off her long to-do list.

"Oh, and I got a job," Imani said, searching the cupboards for popcorn. "Ella's Diner. Tina needed someone a couple nights a week. It's okay, isn't it? I'll try to work around feeding the herd."

"I can help." Everyone turned to the prince. "I mean, if you need any."

"Wow, really?" Imani threw her arms around him as if she'd known him her whole life. Penny, still giggling, hunched her shoulders, shrinking as low as she could. Tall-girl syndrome.

Then it was discovered there was no popcorn, so the girls decided to run to the corner store for snacks.

"She's lovely, Gemma," John said when they were alone again. "What's her story?"

"Too long and sad for someone her age. And, Prince, you don't have to help me with the chores. You didn't come all the way—"

The back door rattled with a knock, then opened. She expected to see Justin—he was never far behind the girls, especially Imani—but Doc Goodwin, the old town vet, stepped inside.

"Can I interrupt?"

"Certainly. Come in." Gemma hopped up, pulled out a chair for him to sit, and offered him a cup of coffee, which he gladly accepted. "What can I do for you?"

She squirted some dish soap on a cloth and washed one of the china cups.

"I need you on the porch." He peered over the rim of his wire glasses, his tattered straw hat listing left atop his thinning, gray hair. Around his middle, a worn leather belt cinched a pair of stained, threadbare trousers. "The Cranes' collie retriever was hit by a car. A beautiful dog. Such a tragedy. I'm not sure they'll get over it. Can't figure for the life of me why a new mama would be out wandering around except to do her business. My guess is Rolf hit her when he came home last night from billiards. I told him a hundred times he's blind as a bat on top of the fact he can barely see over the dash of that big car of his. Of course, I didn't say any of this to them. They were heartbroken enough." He finally noticed the prince. "How do? Doc Goodwin. I'd shake your hand but mine ain't clean."

"No worry, mate." The prince offered his hand and after a moment, the doc took it. "John Blue."

"John Blue, eh? I know who you are, and far be it from an old coot like me to pass up a handshake with a real prince. I'll be." He chuckled as he reached for his coffee. "Maggie left six puppies behind. Three days old and orphaned. Eyes ain't even open. Come, Lord Jesus."

"Six...oh, Doc."

"I told Rolf and Shelia to get her fixed, but they insisted Maggie was safe, never wandered off the property." The doc took a gulp from the cup and motioned for Gemma to step outside. "Flip on the light, will you?"

In a large box, six black-brown-and-white collie-mix puppies squeaked and squirmed. "I brought formula and a list of what you got to do. It'll be all hands to the pump for a few weeks, but ain't they the sweetest things?"

"All hands to the pump? What? Doc, I can't take these puppies. I don't know anything about caring for them. And I have a job."

"True enough." He reached around to his back pocket and produced a folded paper. "Here's the list. Just do what it tells you. It'll be tough at first because they'll need watching twenty-four seven. But things will ease up in a few weeks."

"Doc, you heard me. I have a *job*. In fact, one-and-a-half jobs. Can't the Cranes take care of them? They lost Maggie but gained six of her puppies."

"Did you hear what I said? I think Rolf ran Maggie over. I can't trust them with these precious ones." Doc grunted as he pushed his hat back. "Rolf is eighty-five going on a hundred, and

Shelia can't bend down to tie her shoelaces. Now, the heat lamp, bottles, and formula are in my car. Where are you going to keep the pups? I think the barn is good. Set up a nice bed of hay and blankets in one of the stalls. You think your pack of five will be okay?" He reached down to tap Blue on the head. "How do, sir?"

"Yeah, I think so. But Doc, I can't..."

He set his cup on the narrow porch railing and headed for his car. Gemma grabbed the cup—the railing was too precarious—and ran after him.

"I'm serious. You can't leave them here. I'm putting my foot down."

Meanwhile, the prince cradled one of the puppies against his chest. Not helping.

"You're my last hope, Gemma. I called several other places but I didn't like the sound of their voices."

"Who cares about the sound of their voice if they have the heart and people to do the job."

"You can tell a lot by a voice. Take the prince here. Just in his hello I knew he was a decent, stand-up fella. I'm convinced you're the one to mother these babies. I may be an old country vet, but I have a gut feeling about these things. Something, or *Someone*, told me to bring these babies to you. So here I am."

A tender puppy-cry rose from the box and Gemma glanced back, feeling herself crumble. *I don't have time for this.*

Then John changed everything. "I'll do it. Gus and I took care of newborns one summer at Hadsby. The gardener's dog birthed her whelps in one of the mews' stalls."

"John, no, you're on holiday. I'm sure I can get on the phone and find folks to help."

"What sort of prince would I be if I left my friend and her new charges to flounder when I've nowhere to be and nothing to do." John picked up the box. "Worry not, loves, I'll take care of you. Shall we?" He stepped off the porch and paused by Gemma. "The sooner we get them settled and fed the better."

"Look there, you got an expert," Doc said. "I'll carry the heat lamp. Gemma, you get the formula."

Imani and Penny returned, jumping from the car, curious as to the contents in the box, squealing to see the puppies. Well that was it. Gemma would never rid herself of this chore now.

They were very sweet and so helpless, but she had a job. Not to mention, very limited funds.

Since there was no use fighting it, Gemma launched into director mode—her endgame in Hollywood was to direct. Act for fifteen or twenty years all the while slowly move behind the camera.

"Imani, Penny," she said. "Help Doc and carry the formula while John and I set up one of the stalls."

The commotion alerted the rest of the dogs and they charged out of the house. When the screen door didn't close all the way, Barksy knew how to push it open.

"Last stall on the left, Prince." The other three belonged to Herc, Whinny, and Silver, even though they lived outside most of the time.

She went to the loft for hay and the old quilts folded in the corner. She'd just decided to get rid of them last week but now they were perfect for her new rescues.

When the puppy bed had been made and lined with the soft, worn cotton of the quilts, Doc clapped John on the shoulder.

"I'll leave it to you, Your Highness. Much obliged. Feed them and keep them warm," Doc said as he exited the barn. "That's all you got to do. Oh, and wash their privates to get that business going. And weigh them every day. Make sure they're gaining weight. You got a scale? Yeah, you do, I see it. I'll check on you in a couple of days. Call if you need me."

With that, everyone got to work. Positioning the heat lamp, making the formula, keeping the puppies warm.

Blue and Tweedy insisted on inspecting the babies, but Gemma had Imani take all of the dogs back to the house. They were sweet, but three had been fighters. Best to introduce new dogs gradually. Now Tweedy, being a collie, an old collie but still a collie, might step up as a surrogate mama.

Sitting against the wall, she and John cradled the puppies until

Imani and Penny arrived with the bottles. Then the little beggars slurped and drank, pushing their wee paws against the bottles and the hands that fed them.

Then, miraculously, they slept.

"Let's cuddle them in the center of the bed," John said. "They can keep each other warm, but we'll need to stay with them."

When the puppies were settled, the girls excused themselves to their movie.

"Now what?" Gemma said, lying on her side, her hand over three of the little guys. "Are you sure you want to do this, Prince?"

"I don't have to be anywhere." His voice was gentle and the light in his eyes sincere. "We'll need to feed them in a few hours. Let's talk about a schedule."

Gemma got up for the doc's printout and found her old carpenter's pencil on the workbench.

"What time do you have to be at work?" he said.

"It's flexible but I like to be there by nine. Wednesday I have to be at the wedding chapel at eight for a photo shoot."

The prince looked at his watch. "It's almost midnight now. Let's set up a three-hour feeding schedule. Midnight, three, six, nine, noon, three, six, nine, midnight."

"We can take shifts. Between you, me and Imani, and maybe Penny, we can care for six newborns, right?"

Whinny peered around the open stall, raised her nose, and pawed the stone floor once.

"We'll take care of them, Whinny," Gemma said. "Don't worry."

With a short snicker, the thoroughbred left the barn, and Gemma heard her hoofs striking the summer ground as she galloped away.

"Remind me of that moment when I'm cranky and tired." Gemma returned the pencil and schedule to the worktable, then went back to the puppy bed.

"All right, I will." His tone gave her pause. There was no contradiction. No hesitation. No "Ha ha, I won't know you when you're old." And the desire to know him gripped her. But she fought it because longing for the impossible was a weakness of dreamers. "You've given Whinny freedom, Gemma. Restored her spirit."

"I'm not sure I have that kind of power, but one thing I do know, they've restored me."

"Are there any more blankets?" John said. "The hay isn't the softest bed."

"Plenty. Whoever lived here before left almost everything behind." Gemma texted Imani to bring out more blankets and pillows. The prince made a bed on the right side of the sleeping dogs and Gemma the left.

She set an alarm for midnight while John texted Gunner, who'd gone back to the guest house, and Buck, letting them know his plan for the evening. Gunner replied he was on his way. He'd sleep in the car.

"He can sleep in the house if he wants. Or in here. The car doesn't sound comfy."

"He's former special services. He can sleep anywhere. The car will suit. Gunner's a good PO, he gives me my space and privacy. Though he was really nervous when I sent him home while you were in the convenience store."

"I understand he's not really a friend or companion, but isn't it nice to know someone has your back?"

"Do you want someone to have your back, Gemma?"

There, he did it again. Keyed in on what she thought was a throwaway comment. "I thought I did once. But turns out he didn't."

"You have your family, your friends. Buck and JoJo, Haley."

"You're right, of course, yes, and that's why I'll spend the rest of my life in Hearts Bend."

"You could do worse," John said with a fun lilt in his voice, stretching out, hands locked behind his head.

"Yes, I could do worse." Much worse. She knew because she'd already been down that road and somehow managed to live to tell.

"Prince Gus and Princess Daffy on a walking tour of The Haskells winery. The princess showed off her baby bump while sipping sparkling water."

— *LOYAL ROYALS BLOG*

Remembering Princess Holland documentary to air the evening of her memorial, August 31st, 8:00 p.m. on LTV-1.

— *PRINCESS HOLLAND BLOG*

"Hamish Fickle joins us tomorrow morning to discuss the sale of the Midlands property and to talk about the prince's investiture. Should he have to marry to take his oath? Plus, we'll challenge the young MP to a game of Lauchtenland trivia."

— *MELISSA FARIS, ROYAL REPORTER,*
THE MORNING SHOW

"The Chamber Office confirmed Dr. Ritter's visit to the palace. 'She's had a touch of the flu. She'll be fighting fit in a day or two,' he said. We're looking forward to seeing her at the Yacht Races during the August Renaissance. Back to you, Estelle."

— *PERRY COPPERFIELD, CABLE NEWS PF*

Any update on Prince John and the girl he was carrying? My sources tell me it was nothing. A fair in some country. Maybe America?

– @ROYALFAN ON INSTAGRAM

CHAPTER
ELEVEN

JOHN

H
is phone startled him awake, ringing and rudely pulling
him away from Holland with whom he snuggled, his arm
wrapped about her waist, the feel and fragrance of her skin
filling his senses.

He wanted to stay asleep, spooned with his wife, but his phone
rudely beckoned. Fumbling through his bedding and bits of
straw—*straw?*—he answered with a guttural, whispered, "What
is it?"

He ran his hand over his rumpled hair and caught a piece of
straw. Why did he have straw in his hair?

"Son? John?"

"Dad, hello." His father's voice startled him and awoke him
into the present. On his feet now, John squinted through the
morning sun beaming through a high, square barn window.

The barn. Hearts Bend. Puppies. Gemma. His heart plummeted.
He wasn't at home with Holland. She was still dead and he, very
much alive, hugging an armload of hay wrapped in an old quilt.

"Did I wake you?" Dad said. "I tried not to call too early.
How's your holiday?"

"No, I'm awake." Now. "Is everything all right?" John stepped
from the puppy stall into the much cooler center aisle and pulled
his sweat-dampened T-shirt from his warm skin.

"Well, I wanted to let you know before you read it online.
Mum's in the hospital for a few days. She went in yesterday but

Dr. Ritter wants to hold her for testing. She protested, but her royal powers did not prevail."

"Testing? Why? What's the matter? Should I come?" Mum, the queen, never fell ill. She claimed no sickness or disease would dare. A cough or sniffle, headache, or any sort of ache was dismissed as "nothing."

"No, stay. It cheers her to know you're away, enjoying yourself, meeting Scottie. I'll keep you informed. She is rather eager for an update however."

"What is her illness? I thought she had a cold."

"They thought it was the flu, but she's very weak in her limbs, and tired. This morning she was having trouble breathing."

"Are you sure I shouldn't be there?" John tried to picture his mother in a hospital bed but the image was incongruent with every memory he held dear. As for protesting? She must be frustrated to find her skilled, articulate objections were like boxing the air.

"No, stay."

"Give her my love."

"I will. How did it go with Scottie?"

"Well enough. She's as formidable as Mum."

"I'm not surprised. Is she agreeable to a meeting?"

"Not really. She claims she's an O'Shay and while she appreciates knowing the truth, she's not very keen to meet Mum. Or any of us. I'm ringing her for coffee later in the week so perhaps she'll sing a different tune now she's had time to think on it. She'd just arrived from Guatemala when we met, and my guess is she felt ambushed." The sunlight filling and warming the barn, and flooding the floor beneath John's feet, faded behind a cloud. "In all truth, Mum may have to come here. Make the first move."

"I've told her this several times. She's convinced Scottie will reject her, I think."

"Even a queen must battle human fears. Anyway, I'm here for a few more weeks. I'll keep trying."

"One more thing. I assume you've seen the viral posts? With the lass in your arms? Who is she?"

John glanced down at Gemma still sleeping on a bed of hay

clutching her pillow, her cover tossed aside, a light perspiration glistening on her face. Her left hand rested on three of the puppies. "A friend."

"Does she have a name?"

"You mean you don't know?" HMSD usually knew everything about a newcomer to the royal Family before they did. "Gemma Stone. JoJo paired us in a three-legged race during the Fourth of July celebration. We tripped, fell, lost the race, but decided to finish anyway."

"You'd tell me if there was anything more, wouldn't you? If not me, your brother?"

"Like what? Dad, I've known her all of a week. Ten days. What's to know? That I'm falling in love? I've no plans to move on with anyone for a very long time. Holland is a very difficult act to follow."

For the first time since he'd met her, he felt as if he were merely willing his comment to be true.

"But not impossible." Dad's admonition irritated him.

"Easy to say when you're on the outside."

"Don't use pain as a fortress, John. Don't think no one knows what you're going through and that you're some sort of romantic martyr."

"I'll manage my grief and my life my way. I'm not a child." John moved toward the open barn door, his bare feet brushing over the dirty stone. Whether it was Mum's illness or the barrier of the phone, Dad chose this moment to boldly cross a line. "Gemma is a nice woman. Been kind to me. Makes me feel normal. Like I'm not an object of pity to the world. But that's all."

"You will always be my child, so you must accept my advice." Dad's voice broke with emotion. "All I ask is for you not to become bitter, John. Your mother chose me after Trent and giving up her daughter. She never thought she'd love anyone like Trent, but she did."

"She wasn't married to him. Besides, she had no choice but to give up Trent and Scottie. No freedom not to marry. She was the crown princess, bound by the marriage writ."

"And you are the crown prince bound by the same."

"As if I could forget. Has Mum fulfilled her promise? To change the writ?"

He turned at the sound of a thud, which was followed by a low, harsh mumbling. Gemma emerged from the stall, hopping down the stone thoroughfare, wiggling her feet into a pair of flip-flops.

"Dad, I'll ring you later."

"I'm late." She breezed by John as he ended the call. "I'll see if Daddy can help with the nine o'clock feeding. His truck route goes by here." She stopped in the doorway, ran her hand through her wild mane, and looked back at John as if struggling to orient herself. "But you can't stay here all day, can you? Um, I'll, I'll— Imani, yes, she'll have to miss basketball camp." Gemma motioned to where an old Ford truck sat the night before. "Rats, she's gone. I'll tell her to come straight home after practice. I've got to go. I'm so late."

"Gemma, I can manage. Gunner is good for more than being my shadow and sleeping in the car."

"There's no food to be had." She patted her pockets, still looking dazed and half awake. They'd awoken every three hours to feed the puppies, and every time the alarm sounded, John rolled over to see Gemma watching the puppies. If she slept a solid two, three hours, he'd be surprised. "I'll give you my credit card. You can order from Ella's or Angelo's. Haven's bakery delivers too. Oh, they have really great ham sandwiches. Use my shower if you want and I'll be back as soon as I can. I'm so sorry about this." She smiled, which he felt from his head to his toes. "You really are a prince charming."

"And you really are late, lass. Go. I've got this. I volunteered to help, remember?"

She dashed into the house, and John roused Gunner from the car, where he slept reclined in the passenger seat, his arms folded across his chest.

They sketched a plan for showers, clean clothes, food, and feedings. A few minutes later Gemma dashed from the house to her BMW, a large tote over her shoulder. She wore a pair of shorts, and as she walked, her skin flexed with long, toned muscles. Her damp hair was knotted on her head.

He admired her for an extra moment—beauty demanded admiration—then looked away. Far too many times these past few days she stirred a desire in him he preferred to leave dormant.

"By the way, Prince, I was thinking in the shower—"

"Where all great ideas are born."

"We could name the puppies after the cast of *Friends*. Ross, Joey, Monica, Rachel, Phoebe, and Chandler."

"*Friends* it is."

She was about to duck into her motor when the veterinarian's oversized Cadillac bounced down the gravel.

"Well kids, I see y'all are still standing. How are they doing?" Doc handed John another batch of puppy formula, then as an afterthought, bowed. "I tried to get over yesterday but the Moore's cow was having a hard birth."

"To think I didn't want them and now I can't imagine letting even one of them go." Gemma backed toward her car. "I'd love to stay, Doc, but I've got to run. The prince will fill you in." She smiled and waved at John, then mouthed a "thank you," which hit him with the strange urge to kiss her. As if to say, "Goodbye, darling, have a great day."

What on earth?

Still, he watched her go then found doc in the stall, examining the pups, mumbling to himself, mumbling to them, at last giving John a nod of approval.

"You two know what you're about. I'll be back in a few days. Remember to do everything on the sheet. Call me if anything seems amiss."

With Gunner running errands, John fixed the nine o'clock bottles, weighed the puppies, then fed them one by one. In hindsight, perhaps he shouldn't have sent Gunner for clean clothes and breakfast before the feeding. The last one slurped his breakfast down as if he were about to starve. Poor darling.

He and Gemma had cared for the rest of the herd after the 6:00 a.m. feeding so everyone was set. Hercules, Whinny, and Silver were out grazing, the cats napping, the goats staring and occasionally headbutting, and the rabbits, well, rabbiting.

The dogs appeared in the barn every now and then. Blue and Tweedy had spotted him from the barnyard and trotted over.

"Want to meet the babies?" John led them to the "nursery" and watched as they sniffed the puppies—if he heard so much as one growl, he'd pounce—but then a wondrous thing occurred.

Tweedy eased down into the sleeping huddle while scarred ole Blue pawed a spot for himself in the hay on the other side.

Well, well, Mama and Papa had arrived. Rescues loving on rescues.

The puppies wiggled and squeaked and rooted against Tweedy's belly, who didn't seem to mind she had nothing to give. She nuzzled them and licked their bums in the manner God and nature instilled in her. Blue supervised the operation while sniffing the pile as if to ascertain their DNA. When he'd satisfied his curiosity and approved, he rested his chin on his crossed paws.

John washed out the bottles and lined them up for the noon feeding. Checking his watch, he gazed toward the road for a sign of Gunner. But he'd be a while, what with his own showering, gathering clothes for himself and John, stopping for a latte at Java Jane's and breakfast takeaway from Ella's.

He settled in the hay next to Blue. "What do you think, mate, shall we keep them?"

In the quiet, a muffled sound came from beneath the matted hay of Gemma's bed. John perked up listening. Was that a Buck tune? A flash of light drew his attention. Stretching, he dug around Gemma's bed until he found her buried phone. The name on the screen simply read "Matt."

Should he answer? Was it important?

"Gemma's phone," he answered.

"Who's this?" a male voice boomed in his ear.

"May I inquire of you first?"

"Her boyfriend."

"I see. She's not here now. Can I give her a message?"

"Look, dude with the accent, why do you have her phone?

Why did you answer? Are you sleeping with her?"

John glanced at Gemma's empty pallet. "Not at the moment. She's gone to work." Who was this arrogant chap? Gemma never mentioned a boyfriend. John didn't like him. Surely she had better taste.

The man called John a name he knew to be untrue and ended the call. Then he stared at the screen before tucking the phone in his pocket. *Well, Matt with no last name, you've raised my curiosity.*

How did Gemma get away without her phone? Was she in need of it? He'd take it to her if he knew where she'd gone. He had his truck since Gunner was off in the rental car.

A squeaking drew his eyes to the puppy pile. The small chap, whom he already named Chandler, was away from his siblings, blind and lost.

"I know the feeling, little guy." John cradled Chandler on his chest as he rooted around, sniffing his shirt, his skin.

Tweedy placed her paw on his foot as if to say *Be careful*, while Blue watched with steely, dog-fighting eyes.

According to Doc's sheet, the puppies should weigh about a pound, but wee Chandler had clocked in at twelve ounces.

"Maybe a little extra for you at noon."

He'd just returned Chandler to Tweedy and the pile when Gemma's phone buzzed from his back pocket. This call said it came from Taylor Gillingham. Ah, Gemma's friend. From the footrace.

"Hey, it's me. Did I leave my phone in the barn?"

"You did." He felt oddly delighted to hear Gemma's voice and the casual way she addressed him. *"It's me."*

"I can't believe I forgot. The phone has all my notes for the shoot. Is Imani there by chance? She could bring it to me."

"She is not."

"Shoot. I'd leave but at the moment, I'm about to string Christmas wedding lights through a set of rafters. And Taylor is frantic. Her model isn't here. If I leave, she might lose it."

"I'll come round when Gunner returns. Text me the address. By the way, Chandler and I spent some time cuddling. We'll have to take care with him though. He doesn't weigh a pound."

"Chandler? So you've assigned the names?"

"Not all. Just the Chan-Chan man."

Her laugh kissed his morning. "Save Monica for me. She and I are kindred spirits. And sorry about the phone. I really appreciate you bringing it to me. I guess there's no rush since the model is late but I'd like to be ready whenever she does show."

Gemma gave him quick, verbal directions to the chapel. It wasn't far. Just down River Road a few miles. He considered Matt's call. Should he mention it?

"Um, Gemma, you had a call. I answered it which I shouldn't have. So my apologies. It was from Matt. He said he was your boyfriend."

This elicited a colorful response. "He's such a liar. What did he say?"

"Just that he was your boyfriend and inquired if I was sleeping with you."

"Oh, Prince, I'm so sorry. He's an idiot."

"Well, I had some fun with him. I was staring at our hay beds when he inquired of our relationship so I told him I wasn't sleeping with you at the moment. Which he did not find amusing."

Gemma, however, laughed a robust and rich laugh, which made the sun rise a little higher over John's valleys and shadows.

It was going to be a good day. Maybe even a good week. The awkward mission for the queen aside, he was glad he'd traveled to Hearts Bend.

GEMMA

The chapel was silent except for the hiss of steam coming off Taylor. It was after ten and the model had not arrived and the agency had no answers.

Gemma sat on the altar steps amid her boxes, wondering what to say if anything at all. Poor Taylor.

It'd taken everything Gemma had to string the lights from the rafters. Crawling across the beams, she felt both lightheaded and heavy. There were moments when she couldn't breathe, and she was back in Vegas, in the dark hole, slipping and falling.

But this time she paid attention to her moves, stayed alert and aware of her surroundings.

You won't fall. You won't. All the while her thudding heart said, *Oh yes you will.*

Because she had fallen, hadn't she? In more ways than one. Then she heard his voice, Prince's, telling her about Chandler. She smiled, picturing the big man with thick arms and a mop of rich dark hair cradling the tiniest pup in the litter. Suddenly all was right in her world. She filled herself with a long, cool inhale and finished the job.

Now she sat, staring down the aisle where she'd scattered faux spring flower petals. No use finishing the staging if there was no bride.

"Well, Gemma, I'm sorry." Taylor's voice echoed in the stone and beam space with the high ceilings.

"It's okay, not your fault." She grabbed one of the boxes to start tearing down. "Let me know if and when you resch—"

"You're going to have to do it."

She looked up. "What?"

"You're my model." Taylor pulled out her phone and tap-tapped on the screen. "I'm not letting this opportunity go because of some lame modeling agency—I *knew* I shouldn't have used them—they've done this to me before."

"Me? No. Taylor, I can't be your...*your* bride."

"Why not? You're drop-dead gorgeous and the camera loves you."

"I'm not dressed."

"Well no, but there are the dresses." Taylor pointed to the rack with a smirk and dialed someone on her phone. "Come on, it'll be fun."

"My hair is a mess. I don't have any makeup."

"Hey, Mia, Taylor Gillingham... Good, good, listen, I have a *huge* favor."

Mia was the new hairstylist in town. When she purchased Miss Orla's Cut & Curl last year (she retired) and changed the name to Mia's and hired stylists from Nashville, everyone in town—from the old men who played checkers in Gardenia Park to the Friday night guitar circles to the Ladies Auxiliary to the teens eating burgers at Ella's lunch counter—wanted to sit in a Mia's chair.

"Mia's on her way," Taylor said, pointing to the dresses. "Start with whichever one you want. We'll knock them off one at a time."

"What about the staging?" Gemma didn't *really* care about the set, she cared about *not* doing this. When she left show biz, she meant it. Even a local modeling project was off the grid. She'd vowed, pledged, promised to never, ever put herself out there again.

And now that Matt was calling, telling John he was her boyfriend... She couldn't think about it. She couldn't. Otherwise she'd pack up Imani and run away to where no one would find her.

Taylor peered inside the staging boxes. "I'll decorate the pews. We can use the chapel's candelabras. And you know, it's a gorgeous day. Let's shoot outside. Jack is always telling me, 'Think outside the box, darling.' He's an ad man through and through."

"Taylor, really I can't—"

"I'll pay you the model's rate." She wagged her finger at Gemma, winking. "You drive a hard bargain."

"I'm not bargaining."

"I know it's not supermodel money but—" Taylor rattled off the fee. Gemma actually gulped.

"That's two months' salary at The Wedding Shop."

"I'll get some light readings." Taylor started down the aisle and out the door. "Get changed."

Two months' salary? Bump her vow and pledge. Gemma was a model today. Really, why was she worried? None of her former friends and colleagues could give a flying fig. And Matt Biglow would take a bullet before ever picking up a bridal magazine— even if Gemma miraculously made the cover. Marriage and commitment were striking vipers to him.

But there was more, wasn't there? Gemma in a white wedding gown… It was darn near sacrilegious.

Still, an hour later she stood on a dirt-and-leaf path under a canopy of shading oaks when a truck door slammed.

Mia had styled her hair in long waves and clipped a steel rose at her temple. *Oh to actually be a steel rose.* Then she made up her face, complimenting her complexion and bone structure until Gemma blushed.

"Your cheekbones are perfect."

Hardly. And nothing on the inside came close to perfect. Not at all.

The gown she modeled was off-white with sheer sleeves and a long, flowing skirt of airy silk and organza. The back was cut in a V and flowers embroidered the chapel train. The bride who chose this dress would be beautiful.

"Gemma, raise your chin," Taylor said. "Perfect. Now lift your arm. Give me a whimsical 'I am stunningly beautiful' pose."

Gemma hooked her upper lip, making a face.

"Yeah, like that." Taylor laughed as the shutter whirred and clicked.

Then Gemma relaxed and fell into a soft, elegant pose that defied everything she felt inside. Everything she was. If she could be free, escape the darkness that echoed through her, this, *this* was how she'd choose to be.

JOHN

He stepped onto the edge of the shoot, scanning the scene for Gemma, her phone in his hand. The photographer, Taylor, circled the model, gently giving instructions.

A soft breeze kicked at the woman's hair then picked up the hem of the skirt so it became a wing, flying.

With her chin raised and her hand poised so delicately, she looked like one of the goddesses the ancients painted and hung in galleries around the world. Beautiful and statuesque.

But he didn't come here to admire a wedding gown model. He came to find Gemma. Not seeing her, he started for the chapel.

"Prince, hey."

He turned to discover the beauty in the gown was Gemma. "Sorry, lass, didn't... You never said you were the model."

"The one Taylor booked didn't show, so she forced me."

"I hired you."

"She told me the fee." Gemma flashed a genuine, bright smile. "Then I pushed her down and raced to the dresses."

He laughed, which felt like bubbles in his chest, stepped back and worked up a proper, friend-like compliment. "You look very lovely."

"It's the dress." She strutted around, batting the air with her hand, which stirred the annoying flutter in his chest. "The bride who wears this dress is a kick-butt-and-take-names kind of woman. Like, yeah, that's right, I'm the bride, look at me."

"Beauty demands admiration," he said with his heart and not his head, and the atmosphere suddenly changed.

She swung around and pinned him with an intense, level gaze. "What?"

"Um, I said..." If he said it again, he feared actual sparks might snap in the air. "The dress... It's beautiful."

He felt hot, more than the July heat warranted. *Steady, mate, you are still in love with your gorgeous, talented, amazing wife.* Nevertheless, he was also a man—and not a stupid one.

"Ah, your phone." He handed over her device. "Sorry it took so long to get here but Gunner took a while with his errands."

"Turns out I didn't need it." She unlocked her phone and checked her messages, sighing as if relieved. "He didn't call again, did he?"

He? The boyfriend. The reality of her past as well as his doused a bit of reality over his romantic sensations. "He did not."

She exhaled and handed back her phone. "Can you put it on the chapel steps?"

"Don't just stand there, Prince John, move in, look like a man in love." Taylor circled, aiming her camera.

"I couldn't possibly."

"Taylor, stop," Gemma said. "Leave him alone."

"I'm far too common to be in the photo with Gemma." John motioned to his shorts and T-shirt. But oh, he was anything but common.

"Click-click with my editing software and you're wearing an Armani tux."

"I can't," John said, though a part of him wanted a picture with this beautiful woman. "Too risky. If it went public—"

"Your Royal Highness, I understand your position." Taylor came behind him and shifted his position and raised his chin. "If these get out, the press will have you engaged and down the aisle before you know it."

"Yes. Fueled by the pressure to take my future king oath, which requires me to be married—"

"I get it. Trust me. These are for me."

"You can trust her, Prince, but you don't have to do this." Gemma leaned toward her friend. "Does he, Taylor?"

"I can't resist shooting a stunningly gorgeous couple. It's against my photographer's oath. Besides, when am I going to get a chance to capture a crown prince on film again?"

"I'll hire you to come to Lauchtenland."

Taylor continued circling, snapping pictures, giving small commands that they each obeyed with puzzling curiosity.

"Taylor, stop, give him a chance to walk away." Gemma held up her hand to block the next shot.

"If you want out, move, sir," Taylor said, all the while circling, capturing everything with her lens, and John, whether by want or reflex, posed and smiled.

When she was satisfied, she asked Gemma to break away so the prince could pose on his own.

Taylor promised a thumb drive so he could use them for

himself. John agreed a photo of him alone might make a good gift for Mum. Most of the photographs of him on the Family mantel were with Holland.

Meanwhile, Gemma walked off toward her ringing phone. When she answered, her speech spiked the fragrant air.

"Never… You heard me. Matt…not your business."

John had one ear on Taylor and the other on Gemma.

"Put your hands in your pockets…now take them out…good… walk away…come toward me…raise your chin just…perfect. One more…look at me."

Meanwhile, Gemma gazed off toward the shadows of the shading trees. She seemed so frail. The call demolished the confidence she exuded a few moments ago, the confidence he saw the day they met.

"Everything all right?" he asked. *Win this one, Gemma. Fight on.*

"Absolutely." She masked whatever emotions she battled as she walked toward him. "Hey, you're a pretty hot model, Prince. If the royal thing doesn't work out—"

He laughed, which made her laugh, and suddenly everything seemed right. With her. With him. With their mutual shadows. But he knew it wasn't.

If he could, he'd take on this Matt fellow for her, but since she'd said nothing about him really, John decided to leave it alone. Besides, he'd return home in a few weeks, back to his life, the investiture ceremony—if Mum changed the writ—placing the final memorial wreath on Holland's grave, finding a way to carve out the rest of his life.

However, for his remaining time in Hearts Bend, he'd do everything in his power to shine some light in Gemma's life, and in doing so, seek some for himself. He was sure Holland wouldn't mind. She'd always been generous of spirit. So befriending Gemma was in fact honoring his dead wife's legacy. A worthy, worthy endeavor.

"The Chamber Office announced more cancellations from the queen's diary. Her Majesty will not attend the opening of the Royal Symphony. Princess Arabella will represent the Family. This is the third event the queen has missed in a week, and the Office confirms the queen is 'under the weather.'"

– SYDNEY FRITZ, NEWS AT SIX, LTV-1

"Hamish Fickle is so hot. Anyone have a fan account on him yet? Saw him on *Afternoons with Ari* talking about the investiture and how Prince John has to be married. Such an antiquated rule. Anyone else with me on that? Still, I love HamFick!"

– @STEFWITHANF ON INSTAGRAM

"A lower court of the Justice Ministry heard arguments today in the case of Eloise Ltd. versus the Reingard Industries. Reingard snapped up the Midlands property just after the land was cleared for development leaving Eloise out of pocket for the environmental study fees but no land."

– PERRY COPPERFIELD, CABLE NEWS PF

CHAPTER
TWELVE

GEMMA

A s the sun moved west over Hearts Bend, she finished the shop's inventory and started to clean her desk, which was lined with coffee-stained cups.

"Are you coming tonight?" JoJo offered Gemma a cheese snack. "It'll be fun. Buck's tricked out his truck with everything but the kitchen sink."

"I don't know." She peeled the wrapper from a turkey stick and took a bite. Lunch. "Imani's manning the puppies this afternoon but she has a shift at Ella's tonight. Thursday night is one of their busiest. We've trained Justin and Penny to help out if needed but they also have jobs and responsibilities with their families."

In the past week and a half she'd become a mother hen over those sweet puppies. Feeding them, weighing them, sleeping beside them. Tweedy and Blue also took ownership, sleeping by them and washing them, observing very closely as they were fed and weighed.

"You have to come. A late showing of *Casablanca* at the drive-in. Nine forty-five. Seriously, you should see Buck's truck. It's ridiculous. He had custom seats made for the bed. It's a rolling living room, I tell you. He purchased a professional-grade popcorn machine. I can't believe the theater owner is letting him bring it in, but apparently the drive-in machine is on the fritz. We'll be serving popcorn to moviegoers all night."

"How's he going to pop popcorn at a drive-in?"

"With a mini generator. Word to the wise, when you see his setup, do not ask how any of it works. You'll miss the movie."

"I guess I could make it by nine forty-five. Let me see if Justin and Penny can puppy sit. Or my parents. But they play cards Thursday nights. The diner closes at eleven so Imani might be home before the midnight feeding." Sweet JoJo feigned interest as Gemma worked out her schedule verbally.

However, feeding the puppies had become the highlight of her days. Their little personalities were starting to show. Joey liked to eat on his back, resting in her palm. Rachel preferred to be flat on her wee belly. Gemma loved the sweet, eager slurping sounds of breakfast, lunch, and dinner, and every meal in between.

She bonded with them over their helplessness. She would be their champion.

"Buck said Prince John was coming." JoJo acted all casual, moving about the office, but there was a hint of something, a feeling, like a bomb going off.

"The prince? Oh, well, good for him." He never said. And he'd been with her last night, helping with the puppies.

The first week he stayed in the barn every night. Then they worked out a schedule for him to split his nights with Imani. Now that basketball camp was over, Gemma didn't mind Imani sleeping on a bed of hay. John and Gunner took day shifts when Gemma worked. Most of the time John stayed to help with the evening feedings as well.

How easily they'd fallen into a comfortable routine. When feeding and weighing the puppies, or tending the rest of the herd, they worked in a synchronized tandem, choosing opposite chores without discussion. They chatted about movies and television, music, sports, education, his time in the military, her family, his family. She even braved a few Hollywood stories. Like being in a Super Bowl commercial and her small part in the movie *Bound By Love*.

But they did not talk about Holland. And definitely not about Matt Biglow.

"'Good for him'?" JoJo said. "Come on, dish. What's going on between you two?" She shoved aside the mugs and perched on the edge of the desk. "That gorgeous hunk of a prince spends so much time with you I think Buck is jealous."

"He's simply helping with the puppies. Nothing more. Well, he helps with the herd too. It's rather sweet and to be honest, I don't know what I'd have done without him."

"Have you two ever, you know, gotten *romantic*?"

"What? No. Geez, Jo. He's still in love with his wife. And I'm not in the market for *romance*."

"You do know he's turned down Buck for golf. A game he loves. He's not gone riding or to the shooting range." JoJo tapped Gemma's shoulder as if to really get her attention. "We invited him to the Vegas concert, a city on his bucket list, and he *respectfully* declined."

"Good, he's not missing anything."

"I think he's in love."

"If you're going to talk crazy, I'm leaving." Gemma collected the dirty mugs and headed for the door downstairs, her hip bothering her more today than in the past. She blamed sleeping in the barn but until the puppies were strong enough to be on their own, she'd deal with it.

"You mean to tell me two gorgeous, kind, intelligent people are hanging out together all day and sometimes all night and there's no chemistry?"

"I never said we didn't have chemistry." Gemma continued down the stairs, wishing back her words. But JoJo caught them.

"I knew it! I told Buck, 'They'd make such a good couple.'"

"We are not a couple. Now or ever. Jo, he's a prince. Get your head on straight." In the butler's pantry, Gemma filled the sink with hot sudsy water and sank the mugs. "Don't make something of nothing. We're friends and we get along, but that's the end of it. To be honest, I think we remind each other there is good in the world. Hope."

"Gemma," JoJo said with a bit of a sigh as she reached below the sink for the dish drainer. "Your limp... What happened in

Hollywood? Why won't you tell us? I can't help but feel it's holding you back somehow."

"I've told you. I got tired of the rat race."

Every once in a while, JoJo or Haley butted into her business. As good friends do. Gemma didn't blame them. She knew they cared. One rarely limps home after twelve years without ever speaking of it.

"And your hip?"

"Told you that too. There I was on the Great Wall of China for a photo shoot when a spaceship burst through the clouds." She raised her voice for dramatic effect. "We were all terrified, as you can only imagine, and we were frozen with fear. Then bam! Chaos, scrambling, running, screaming, every man for himself. I started—"

"Fine. Don't tell me."

"Just because you don't believe me doesn't mean it's not true."

"Is it true?"

The shop chimes told them someone had walked in. Jo stuck her head out of the pantry and called, "Be right there," then offered a final word to Gemma. "You know we love you no matter what, right?"

Gemma resented how the conversation stirred her tears. "Yeah, I know. Go, greet the customer."

She was confronted with the fact she'd not fooled her friends as well as she'd thought. They didn't know the details of her sordid story, but they *knew.*

So tell them.

Gemma rehearsed her story as she washed the mugs and set them in the drainer. How she'd begin, which details she'd share, which ones she'd omit, but when she imagined their faces, she felt sick. No, she'd never tell. Ever.

She'd just emptied the sink when her phone pinged. Gemma pulled it from her pocket to see she had a message.

The male voice was deep and craggy, from a man named B. A. Carpenter, Attorney at Law. Said he needed to talk to her.

But she didn't know B. A. Carpenter or why he'd be calling

her. Probably a scam. Once in L.A., at some swanky party with too much booze and drugs, she sat next to a man who spent his life developing email and telephone scams. All quite illegal but he boasted as if he'd won an Oscar.

Gemma deleted B. A. Carpenter's message and finished cleaning up the kitchen. Truth was, she'd tried to tell her story once. During her hospital stay when a compassionate nurse found her crying. But the moment she started speaking, only sobs came out.

The pain she battled was more than physical, more than healing from a broken hip. The pain was soul piercing and hidden in a place no bandages or medicine could reach.

Yet it was in that moment with the nurse she'd surrendered. She'd go home. Give up the dream of "being somebody." Even the prodigal son was wise enough to realize returning home after his life of foolishness was better than living with pigs.

And for Gemma, home meant her journey of a thousand bad decisions would end.

Chapter
Thirteen

John

Scottie greeted him as he entered her office by handing him a deep blue, glossy shirt box tied with a yellow ribbon. "Dad had these made for you. The House of Blue crest is sewn over the pocket. If you want a couple for your brother, let us know."

"How did you know my size?"

"Forty-four regular." She slid open a part of a wood-paneled wall to reveal a kitchenette. "A bit wider in the shoulders and tapered at the waist. Does someone tailor your shirts in Port Fressa?"

"Depends on the shirt. How'd you do that?" John set the box on a live edge, polished table positioned in front of a modern, deep-green couch with a low back and wood frame.

"It's my superpower. Coffee? Tea?"

"Tea if I'm staying long enough?"

"I'm sorry we've not connected before now. My trip to New York last week was unexpected." She set out two mugs bearing the O'Shay logo then activated an electric kettle.

"No worry. You've a business to run and I've been helping with newborn puppies."

"Puppies? How'd you get roped into that?" She held up a carton of cream and he nodded.

"The night I had dinner with you and Trent, Gemma invited me in to finish our carry-away desserts. We'd just finished when Doc

Goodwin dropped off six two-day-old puppies. Since they need feeding around the clock, we banded together to keep the wee things alive."

"I didn't peg you for the rescue type but now that you mention it…" Scottie held up a familiar tin of tea. "Lauchtenland's Titus blend. Is that okay?"

"You've a Titus blend?" Hands locked behind his back, he approached his sister as he might approach the skittish Whinny. "I'm surprised you have anything from Lauchtenland."

"You make me sound like a bigot," she said. "I'm stubborn but not unreasonable. I thought why not start with their famous tea?"

"Fair enough." He stepped a bit closer. "And?"

"I have a cup every morning." Her confession was slightly bent with humor and the long drawl of the American south.

"Shall I take it you are warming to my homeland? More specifically, the House of Blue?"

Her laugh carried the same resonance as Mum's. "It will take more than a cup of tea, I'm afraid."

She handed John a steaming mug, talking all the while about how they designed and made his shirts, leading him to a small seating area by the window.

"What shall we talk about?" she said. "Our childhoods? Our likes and dislikes? Why you grew up with our mama and I didn't?"

"I'm sorry you got the short end of the stick."

"Maybe, but I had Shug, so it wasn't a total loss."

"Why do you call her Shug?"

"Shug is short for sugar. And it's what she wanted. The first time Dad referred to her as 'grandma' she had a coronary. Hyperbolically speaking, of course. She said her grandmother was Grandma and a nastier woman never drew a breath. So she wanted something sweet."

"Like sugar," he said.

"Exactly. Then Fritz claimed he wanted a unique name as well. He called his grandfather Fritz, and apparently a *sweeter* man never drew a breath, so he claimed the name."

"What are they like? Shug and Fritz?"

"She's queen of the O'Shays, trying to run our private lives while Dad and Fritz run the business. Fritz is semi-retired but he comes into the office a few days a week. Shug also tries to boss around Hearts Bend without ever running for election. If there's a committee for improving the town, she's on it. Chairs most of them. It's a full-time job. But when it came to me, Shug cared for and loved me like no one's business."

"You may have had it better than Gus and me, Scottie. Growing up normal, if I'm allowed to use that word. Not having the press spying on you twenty-four seven."

"Maybe. O'Shay's Shirts exploded in the mid-90s and suddenly, thanks to the internet, I became small-town royalty. Which comes with its own set of issues. You actually know the people who say mean things. I was a teenager when Dad and Shug and Fritz built their dream homes. Mini mansions with gourmet kitchens, pools, tennis courts, and for Dad, a putting green. People actually accused them of fraud and laundering money. Never occurred to them how hard Dad, Fritz, and Shug worked. The music industry hadn't started moving into HB yet so anything more than a three- or four-bedroom ranch was a mansion. Then Dad bought his dream sports car. Suddenly people who paid me no mind wanted to be my friend. But I still had a really good group of friends and high school was a blast. When the business was featured in *Forbes*, some folks started the gossip mill again. Then actor Jesse Gates was seen in an O'Shay shirt and boom, everyone wanted an O'Shay. I'd just graduated but man, it was hard. Not the success, but how everyone treated us. It was like we didn't belong anymore. Like we'd somehow betrayed the small town code. I think that's why Shug is so involved. She wants to give back, prove money and some acclaim didn't change us."

"So then you know some of what life as a Blue is like. Maybe life, or even God, has prepared you to join our family."

"Don't like where you're heading, little brother." There was little affection in her term of endearment. But some. A dollop.

"Sorry, but my mission is to woo you into our fold." John sipped his tea before it got cold. "Now that you know, aren't you curious about Mum?"

"Maybe. Some. Yes. But I'm not sure I'm ready. I like my life. I like my travels. I like doing mission work I believe in. I like representing O'Shay's Shirts and our foundations. You love your heritage, I love mine."

"Yes, but you're ignoring half of your heritage."

"Am I? Seems my heritage ignored me."

Well, she had him there. "So, you're firm on not joining our family?"

"John, I have a family. I'm firm on one thing—my future with O'Shay's. I will say now that I know more of my heritage, I understand myself a bit more." She grinned as she raised her teacup. "It's a wonder I've not imploded. All that Blue blood mixing with Irish green."

John laughed, spewing a bit of his tea, and reached for a napkin. She was a hundred percent spot on.

"What about you?" Scottie said, her tone becoming more intimate. "How is your life after losing someone you love? Isn't there some rule that you have to be married to be king?"

"Yes, but I made a deal with the queen. I'd come here and meet you, if she'd change the writ."

"An ulterior motive. Should've known."

"I'm glad I came, if you must know."

"For the puppies and their beautiful rescuer?"

Yes. But no. "To meet you. I like you, if it matters."

She regarded him for a moment. "It matters. I like you too."

Good. They'd reached another level of common ground. "I'm not sure she'd want this known," John said. "But the queen hasn't been well. She spent a few days in the hospital. She's home now, recovering I believe, but if you have wanted an ulterior motive to meet your mother, realize life is short, Scottie."

Scottie stood and looked out the window where a pack of midday blustery clouds promised rain.

"Is her condition serious?"

"I don't think so. Probably just complications from some bug or virus."

She looked back at John. "It's easy for you to come here because nothing really changes for you. So you have a thirty-five-year-old big sister. But I have a mother I never knew existed. I have brothers and a stepfather. It changes everything for me. I'm not sure... I don't know... I should jump at this chance, right? What kid doesn't want to meet her once-dead mama? But I'm not a girl. Or a teen. Or some unloved, abandoned woman. I had a great childhood. I have a great family. I know this life. I don't know yours. And if I open up the door to meet her, what dominoes will fall? What will change? I'm a planner, John."

"I understand. All I ask is you don't close all the doors and windows to Mum. Keep one cracked open for a chance to meet one day."

An employee knocked and entered. Scottie answered the man's questions about a marketing proposal as John finished his tea and set the mug on the table.

"I should go. You have work to do."

"I promise to think about it." Scottie retrieved his box of shirts. "These come with a money-back guarantee."

He laughed softly. "Can I say one more thing? And I'm not trying to push or manipulate but I think Mum would want you to know she did what she thought best. Saving you from being the queen's illegitimate daughter. From being ridiculed. From being divided between families and nations. If you knew my mother, she would've gladly braved all of those things and guided you through them, but she was a crown princess and some decisions were simply not in her command."

"Do you think I was ever really taken into consideration?"

"Yes, I do. But the question you have to ask yourself is, 'What now?' Can't change the past, Scottie. What's done is done. But you can change the future with the information you have, and if you don't, that's on you."

"And if I engaged in a relationship with the Family now, do you think I'll avoid any firestorm or gossip?"

"Probably not but as you said earlier, you've had some experience with being in the public eye. We'll do our best, I'm sure. But again, you've a chance to meet your mother. So what if the press mocks you. There will always be cruel people in the world."

Scottie walked with him to the door. "At the end of it all, your mama and my dad decided where I should be raised and by who. In doing so I became the heir to O'Shay's Shirts. You feel an obligation and loyalty to the House of Blue? I feel one to the House of O'Shay. My great-great-grandfather started this company and I intend to carry on the traditions the same way you intend to carry on yours. You serve the people of your nation, I serve the people associated with our business, giving them jobs by which they support their families. My kingdom is just smaller and less known than yours." She delivered her speech with a tangible passion. "But begging your pardon, every bit as important."

"No one ever said otherwise, Scottie. Don't think that's how we see you and this family." John nodded his goodbye then came back for a final word. "One last word in Mum's defense. She doesn't go to people. People come to her."

"I'm not just any people, am I?"

"No, you're not."

Scottie's assistant came round, reminding her of a meeting.

"John," Scottie said, walking with him down the hallway to the stairs. "You're a good son and brother...a good...brother."

"I'm trying." He started down the stairs then had a thought. "Some of us are going to the drive-in tonight. *Casablanca*. Buck's bringing his own popcorn machine. You should come."

"Already have my ticket."

"Then I'll see you there. Follow the smell of popcorn."

"And the crowd of people wanting a close look at a country music great and a royal prince."

"Buck will be the one wearing the crown."

Down the long stairs and through the marble lobby, John was grateful he came. Whether or not Mum reversed the writ. He had a sister. He liked her and he wanted to know her more.

As he headed home to Buck and Jo's, he almost detoured toward Gemma's place. He was off puppy duty but he missed the little rascals. Maybe he should invite Gemma to the movie. Yet they already spent an inordinate amount of time together. Lately, he thought less and less of Holland and more of the woman who rescued horses, goats, and puppies. Of the woman who was perhaps rescuing him.

CATHERINE

"What are you up to today, darling?" Edric entered the office from a private hallway, asking what he always asked. At her desk, he bent to kiss her cheek. "You were up early."

"Couldn't sleep."

"The burning sensation again?" He paused at the service table for a cup of coffee. "Have you had breakfast?"

"No, I was waiting for you. Yes, the burning in my hands and feet. But I'm better now." She'd not mention the labored breathing and a rapid heartbeat. Last time she did he carted her off to hospital.

She'd been home from the hospital over a week and so far, all the tests, the drawing of blood, the scans concluded nothing.

"I slept like a rock," Edric said, taking a long sip of coffee.

"You always sleep like a rock."

"Don't be jealous, Kate. You have your superpowers too."

She laughed. "Like what? And don't say being queen."

"Your intuition is very keen. And I've always envied your spirituality, your second sight. I think John has that quality as well, though he'd never admit it."

"And Gus."

"Right. I'd forgotten his encounter with Emmanuel. Do you think I've done something to offend him? He never appears to me." Edric sat in the chair opposite Catherine's desk, legs crossed, spoon tapping the rim of his cup as he stirred.

"You don't need it. Your faith is different. More rooted than ours in some ways. You don't question what you believe."

"True, but still, I'd love a peek beyond the veil, as they say."

"Why? It only makes you all the more accountable." Catherine moved to the window. She had no right to doubt the supernatural when she saw it firsthand. "How'd we get on this?"

"You brought up superpowers. So, have you seen *him* again?"

"No." She'd informed Edric about seeing Emmanuel a few weeks ago, sitting below her window on the iron bench. But by the time she got down to him, he'd gone.

While it made her curious, she didn't find it out of the ordinary. Last year she'd found three secret diaries of her grandfather who journaled of visits from Emmanuel.

Then, she had a mysterious message this morning, sitting on the table by her chair. Pablo didn't know where it came from, nor the maids when asked. She drilled Mason and the footman. But no one claimed responsibility.

Meet me by the First Gate.

The First Gate was an old stone gate on the northeast corner by the sea and built by King Rein the First in 1520.

"Did you hear about Hamish Fickle on the *Samm Mann* show?" Edric said.

"What's he done now?"

"More of the same. Time for change, abolish the monarchy, come into the twenty-first century, why do we need a royal family, et cetera. And he's offering his unwise take on the legal case between Eloise and Reingard."

"Anything to make people like him. Did I read right that he gathered a large crowd on Hax Square?" The main thoroughfare of Haxton University. The site of the original campus.

"Yes. You'd think he was running for parliament instead of being an elected member already. He has an angle, that's for sure. He's charming, good-looking, a light for all the moths." Edric turned to Pablo and ordered breakfast. Catherine wasn't hungry but she agreed to eat. Otherwise, he'd fuss.

She was too tired, and in too much pain to eat.

"We'll dine here, in the sitting room." Edric gave the final instructions to Pablo who left the room with a curt bow to each of them.

"John is charming and good-looking," Catherine said after a moment. "Why can't he be the light, as you say, for the *moths*."

"You know why. He's establishment. The member of the *old* guard. This generation feels they have better ideas. They know it all."

"We thought we knew it all." Certainly, she did. At twenty-one, taking up with Trent O'Shay, believing true love conquered all obstacles such as distance, nationalities, protocols, and an ancient royal house.

"They are more confident in that assumption than we were, darling. They want something new, something better. Except when they arrive at their destination, they'll find it's more of the same. Or most likely, worse."

"I see no need for alarm. We've weathered the Hamish Fickles of the past, we'll weather this one too."

Every two hundred and fifty years or so, a man, or woman, challenged the establishment. Not to make it better. Not because it was oppressive and unjust, though at times it was, but merely because they wanted something *else*. Something of their invention.

"I wish John were here. I know he's on an errand for you but if he came home, he could get to work, back to his duty, outshine that wee little man, Hamish."

"Be kind, Edric."

"You're right, darling, I stand corrected."

"Ma'am." Mason entered the office. "It's nine o'clock. You asked for a reminder."

She regarded him for a moment. Yes, Emmanuel. She collected her phone and rose from her chair. "I forgot, I've an errand, Edric. I'll breakfast when I return. I'll see you at lunch. Or are you busy?"

"What errand?" He kissed her goodbye. "Can't someone else go?"

"A silly meeting." She wasn't sure why she hid the fact Emmanuel had beckoned her. At least she thought it was him.

Who else would leave such a note? Hamish Fickle?

Besides, she wanted to meet with the holy man alone. If she told Edric, he'd want to tag along, see him for himself.

He made a face. "The queen never attends a silly meeting. I can see you don't want to tell me so do fill me in later if you can. Meanwhile, I'm going to ring John, see if I can't get him home."

"No, Edric, leave him alone. He'll be back soon enough, in the public eye when he places the wreath on Holland's grave. The news and social media will be all about her death and how sad he must be. Let him be someone else for a few more weeks."

"Speaking of being someone else, will you change the writ so he can swear his oath of allegiance to Lauchtenland and the monarchy without being married?"

"I really must run. I don't want to be late." She kissed his cheeks and used every ounce of energy to escape the room.

"Kate, darling…"

She'd underestimated her weakness as she climbed the steep incline to reach the First Gate. Her low heel pumps slid against her stockinged feet and after stumbling twice, she removed them, straining to make her destination.

At last, she was above the city with the North Sea well below, its churning waters crashing against the craggy rocks.

There was little to no beach on this side of the shore, and in the days of ship warfare, Lauchtens gained a huge advantage from this position.

In recent decades, windsurfers found the height and churning atmosphere ideal for their sport. And climbers saw the sheer cliff face as a challenge.

But she wasn't here to muse about land, sea, or history. A little farther and she'd arrive at the bench. Drawing on the last of her strength, Catherine pushed up the steep pathway.

Arriving at the pinnacle, she saw him. Emmanuel. Sitting tall on a bench, broad shoulders covered with a heavy anorak, his hat squarely on his head and his chestnut hair tucked into his collar.

When he turned her way, his eyes were like the stars, and stole the last of her strength. He was beautiful, regal, and silent.

Without a word, she sat on the opposite side of the gate's bench, the wind whipping her hair about until she thought she might lift off the ground. But it felt so freeing to be out of doors and sitting above the earth.

She glanced at him. Should she speak first? Or wait? He'd called this meeting, such as it was, and as the senior royal, he would conduct the meeting.

"How are you?" he said after a moment.

"Not very well. But I assume you know."

"Isn't it beautiful here?" He raised his hand to the wind, and Catherine half expected it to change elements and materialize in his hand.

"Very beautiful. One of my favorite places in all of Lauchtenland."

"Are you worried, Catherine?"

"No more than usual. Is that why you've come? To tell me I worry too much? I'm a mother as well as a queen."

"One day, you will feel silly for all the times you've fretted and worried for nothing."

She tried to hold her laugh, but a small sound escaped. "Well said."

A thousand questions flared at once and while she sat next to him, trying to discern her own feelings, trying to figure out what she wanted, he said nothing.

Are you here about John? Will he be all right? Will he converse with you one day? Has he already? What shall I do about Hamish Fickle? Am I going to be all right? What is going on with me? I'm so weak.

But when she opened her mouth, no words came. It was enough to sit in his presence and rest. To be completely, utterly at peace.

CHAPTER
FOURTEEN

GEMMA

"Imani, I'm going." Gemma grabbed her bag with one last look in her bedroom mirror. She'd made a bit of an effort with her appearance even though she was only going to the drive-in.

Even at 9:30, the air was warm and muggy. Her hair would be flat by 9:45. Prince John was going to be there—not that she was trying to snag his attention or anything—but he admired her last effort when she dined with him at the O'Shays'.

Then there was the look he gave her at the wedding dress shoot. What girl didn't like a smoldering look from a good-looking dude now and then? She didn't have to be in the market for love and romance to appreciate being appreciated.

She paused by Imani's door. "Hey, did you hear me? Child o-mine, I'm leaving." Gemma cocked her head to one side when she heard a bump followed by a slamming closet door. "Imani?"

"Hey." The door swung open, a breathless Imani on the other side, her black hair disheveled and her T-shirt a bit twisted and off the shoulder. "You leaving? Have fun. I hear *Casablanca* is a classic."

"What were you doing in here?" Gemma smoothed her hand over the girl's head of corkscrew mayhem and peered into her room.

"Homework. I mean, exercises, sit-ups and push-ups, for basketball. Coach set out a routine for us to follow now that camp is over."

"Does it require you to slam a door?"

"Oh, that, um." Imani tugged at the hem of her T-shirt. "I fell against it when I stood up."

Gemma regarded her for a second, fully remembering her own shenanigans at sixteen. She was both wise and stupid, careful and reckless, independent, obeying her parents while also being rebellious and arrogant—which meant sneaking her boyfriend in through her bedroom window after Mac and Mauve had gone to bed.

"Be more careful then. So, the puppies...you're in charge. Please check them in a few minutes. Blue and Tweedy are on duty but Chandler and Phoebe were shivering earlier. Keep them warm."

"I'm on it." Imani folded her arms and leaned against the doorjamb. "Good thing Tina let me go early. The diner was dead. Everyone was going to the drive-in." Imani walked with her down the hall. "Justin and Penny will be here to help."

"Justin?"

"He wants to help."

"He wants to be with you."

"Is that so horrible?"

"No, but I'll worry."

"About what?" Imani leaned against the kitchen wall with the '70s wallpaper, arms folded.

"You. Being sixteen with a hormone-infested sixteen-year-old boy."

"Ooo, come on. That's not fair. Gemma, you can trust me. I promise."

Gemma peered into the hazel beauty of Imani's eyes. "Can I?" Her parents thought they could trust her at sixteen.

"What do you think we're going to do? Leave Penny and go make out in the loft?"

"Yes." Gemma's friend Susie used to get so mad at her for leaving with Dash to make out, leaving her alone with Dash's geeky friends.

Imani turned Gemma toward the door. "Go, have fun. You deserve it."

"Am I being a nag?"

"A little."

Well then, she'd be off. Not going to lie, she looked for Justin's truck parked behind a tree or off some side road as she headed for the drive-in—the trick she and Dash used back in the day—grateful to say she spotted nothing but a doe grazing by a stand of trees.

Gemma found Buck and JoJo by following the music and trail of fans stopping by to say hi and grab a small bag of popcorn. The crowd was extra large tonight, most of them snapping pictures of the prince.

When John spotted her, she waved and tried to act casual. Like, *oh, you're here?* But when he offered his hand to hoist her into the truck bed, she felt self-conscious and wobbly.

His fragrance was clean and subtle and reminded her of the land after a cleansing rain.

"Seems we're the popcorn providers tonight." He handed her a small, red striped bag stuffed with popcorn. "The owner gave us these. People line up and we pass it over the side."

"Popcorn from the king of country music and crown prince of Lauchtenland." Gemma handed popcorn down to a dad and his two kids. "The movie will pale in comparison."

"No one outshines Bogie," John said, then added, "Jo didn't say you were coming."

"You sound disappointed."

"Not in the least."

The way he said, "Not in the least," as his fingers touched hers, passing along two more bags of popcorn, which she lowered into outstretched hands, made her shiver. There's no other way to say it. When she reached back for more popcorn, their eyes met and if this was a romcom, they'd be at the part of the almost-kiss.

But this wasn't a romcom, was it?

"Sir, is everything all right?" This from Gunner who'd posted himself directly below John to keep the curious and the royal hunters at bay.

"Of course," John said with a hitch in his voice. Then he smiled at Gemma in such a way she wanted to tap his arm and ask, *"What? What do you want to say?"*

"Hey, you two, stop with the oogly eyes, we're getting backed up." Haley stood by the popcorn machine with Cole, filling the kettle with kernels while Buck and JoJo loaded up the bags.

"What oogly eyes?" Gemma protested. "Please, just pass the popcorn up and we'll hand it out."

Meanwhile, Taylor and Jack worked the crowd and kept the line moving.

"Didn't I tell you, Gemma?" JoJo said. "We'd be serving popcorn all night."

"I'm shutting it down when the movie starts," Buck said. "Let everyone know."

Finally the lights flickered and the screen flashed with a '40s-era newsreel, updating them on the war in Europe. Taylor, Jack, and Gunner shooed away the remaining crowd, and Buck and JoJo hopped into the truck bed—which was fitted with two custom leather benches embossed with Buck's brand logo. The back bench was a touch higher than the front. Just like in a theater.

As the newsreel voice-over assured them of the Allies' coming victory, everyone found a seat. Since they were all couples but John and Gemma and Gunner, they cuddled close. Jack with Taylor and Haley with Cole.

The back bench had Buck and JoJo in one corner and John in the middle. Gemma took the other corner. Gunner chose to watch the film sitting on the roof of his rental car—which was next to Buck's truck. He collected four bags of popcorn and climbed aboard.

"Maybe I should sit with Gunner," Gemma said, thinking he looked a bit lonely, his long legs resting against the windshield, his popcorn lined up beside him.

John leaned to see around her. "I'm sure Gunner would appreciate—"

"I'm fine. Need my space."

Gemma laughed against her hand. "He heard us."

"The man has the hearing of a bat."

"Don't forget it either, sir."

"How are the lads and lasses?" John scooted a little closer to her. "Our pups? I almost stopped by after my meeting with Scottie."

"You should've. Of course, you'd have ended up working. How was your time with Scottie?"

"Good, I think. We're getting the hang of it, being siblings after thirty-plus years."

"Will she go to meet your mother?"

"Undecided. But we shall see. So our little charges are faring well? I find myself thinking about them when I'm not on shift. Wondering how they're getting on, laughing at some cute thing that happened while weighing or feeding. They've become friends, I suppose."

The prince looked at her a moment longer than necessary, waiting for her answer, but she was bottled up with a warm, gushy feeling.

"Um, yes, they're friends. Do...do you miss your friends?"

"A little," he said. "But not because I'm here. I've not seen them much since Holland died. We gathered a few times, but it was awkward. They acted as if she'd not died, treating me like before I was married. They didn't know if they should talk about her or not, or how to ask. Meanwhile, I was in a fog, not communicating clearly. My mate Lute finally said, 'We fear if we bring her up, we'll cause you pain. Yet if we don't ask, do we come across as if we don't care?' I had no answer, so we stopped trying."

"I wonder about Imani sometimes. Should I talk to her about her parents and grandparents?"

"Parents and grandparents?" He shook his head. "That's a lot of death for one young woman."

"Too much. She still has one grandmother. In Florida. We've started to touch on it lately. I hope she knows she can talk to me."

"You should ask her, Gemma. Looking back, I should've talked about losing Holland sooner but I just—"

"Couldn't. Believe me, I get it."

"Is that the reason for your shadows? Did you lose someone close?"

Her shadows? So, he saw what she tried to hide. Same as Haley and JoJo.

"Sort of, yes." If losing oneself counted.

"And sort of no?"

She glanced back at him, smiling. "And sort of no."

"Should I inquire further?"

"No, the movie is starting."

JoJo passed out more popcorn, the buttery kernels making Gemma's belly rumble, and passed around cold, dripping bottles of water from the ice chest.

Up front on the movie screen, the black-and-white images of the *Casablanca* trailer played.

"I'm looking forward to this. I've never seen it," John said.

"Makes two of us."

"Room for one more?" Scottie O'Shay emerged from a row of cars, wearing shorts and a blouse, her voice tentative but strong. Sure, she was an O'Shay. And a Blue.

"You came." John stood as Cole gave Scottie a hand up. "Lovely. You remember Gemma." He motioned for Scottie to climb over the first seat—which collapsed—and take a seat next to Gemma.

"This is some setup. Buck, I'll need to know who did the work. Dad would love this." Scottie sat next to Gemma, exactly where John directed her, and despite all internal warnings, Gemma was disappointed. She'd wanted to sit next to him but really, this was for the best.

Later, when she climbed into bed, she'd have a good talk with herself about crushing on a royal prince. The heir. The too-good-for-you guy from Lauchtenland.

146

Then she'd fall asleep and dream of his rolling accent.

"I hope you don't mind me squishing in," Scottie said with such sincerity Gemma liked her all the more. "Have you seen *Casablanca*? I haven't."

"Believe it or not, no. Sad for a former actress, isn't it?"

"Here we go." John handed Scottie a bag of popcorn and bottle of water, then motioned for Gemma to move over.

Move over? Which way? Toward Scottie or the side of the truck? She decided on the side of the truck, and to her surprise-slash-delight, John plopped down next to her.

Heaven help her but she felt a bit weak. She leaned forward to focus on the movie and to escape John's presence and fragrance.

"Gunner, you all right, mate?" John called.

"Fine, sir." He wadded up his popcorn bag and moved onto the next. Two down, two to go.

Then, at last, Bogie and Bergman were on-screen.

The front-bench couples cuddled, facing the movie. On the back bench, Buck and JoJo cuddled up. Scottie reclined with her long legs stretched toward the front bench, and while the space was tight, there was a good six inches between Gemma and John. Definitely no cuddling here.

Then Haley spotted Marjorie Wentworth, who'd been a good friend in high school, and invited her to join them. She crowded in next to Haley and Cole.

Then out of nowhere, Haley's brother Seth and his wife, Noelle, climbed aboard the tricked-out truck.

"Sorry we're late," he whispered, hunched over, trying not to block the screen. "The sitter couldn't find her car keys."

Holding Noelle's hand, Seth made his way to the back. "Hey, Gemma."

"Hey, y'all." Now which way did she scoot? Toward or away from John? What if he scooted closer to Scottie. What if this bench didn't hold seven people?

"Can we crowd in here?" Seth said, taking the popcorn bags Cole handed over.

"Absolutely." John slid toward Gemma, tucking in so tight their elbows touched. Now her crazy, runaway pulse was so loud she couldn't make out the dialog. Worse, she was absolutely crushing on the prince.

Shoot, she'd slept in the barn across from the prince for almost two weeks. This was no big deal. But oh, every time his arm touched hers, her entire body flamed. This. Was. A. Big. Deal.

But it shouldn't be. Couldn't be.

Cole stood up to fill his bag of popcorn from the machine.

"Down in front," Scottie called, and Gemma snorted a laugh. She covered her mouth with her fingers. Nice. Very elegant. Snorting a laugh.

Well, eventually she forgot about her seatmate and lost herself in the film, in the adventure in North Africa as Rick and Ilsa fought for freedom. Fought for love.

Finishing her water and popcorn, she cleaned her hands with a wipe from the container JoJo passed around then sat back, heart still engaged with Sam on the screen as he played it again.

She startled when a hand touched hers. John. Slowly, gently, he slid his palm against hers and entwined their fingers, igniting a five-alarm fire in her. What was he doing?

John reclined against the back of the seat, his shoulder touching hers. Oh, help but he was killing her. One tingle at a time.

Don't think. Don't analyze. Just be for once.

So little by little, millimeter by millimeter, she leaned against him.

Everything was fine until Ilsa pressed into Rick and declared with a weepy voice, "If you knew how much I love you. How much I still love you."

John sat up and yanked his hand from hers. Leaning forward on his arms, he watched the rest of the movie with a stiff, barriered posture and never once looked at Gemma again.

CHAPTER
FIFTEEN

JOHN

"**Y**ou should get some sleep," he said as he exited the puppy stall, his eye on Gemma, the memory of her hand in his haunting him.

He left the drive-in with her just before midnight—Gunner followed in his rental—and arrived at the barn for the midnight feeding.

Imani had prepped the bottles then texted Gemma.

Tina called. Needs me on the breakfast shift. Going to bed.

So Gunner volunteered to help. What a sight to see the squiggly, hungry puppies in the big man's hands.

At the moment, he slept in his motor, though John assured him he could sleep in the barn or go back to the pool house.

"You're my duty, sir. The motor's plenty comfy."

The cats meowed and rubbed against his ankles. They seemed to think the midnight feeding included them.

"What a long day." Gemma hung up her apron which covered her dress from the evening. Her hair fell about her shoulders, a bit wild and frayed from the humidity and he fought the urge to reach for her, hold her, tell her how much he loved holding her hand. Then again, he pulled away. "But the movie was good."

"Yes, very." Ilsa's confession to Rick echoed through him. The same one he'd made to Holland. *"If you knew how much I love you…"*

Wanting to hold Gemma made him feel untrue to Holland. Which was also unfair to Gemma. Even if he was completely ready to move on, he'd not assembled anything close to a whole, working heart.

All he had was a collection of broken pieces. A man still in love with his dead wife, chained by memories and what should've been.

The black-and-white feline with big ears and long tail curled around Gemma's legs. She scooped her up, set her on the workbench, and grabbed a handful of treats.

"I really should stop buying these things, they're too expensive."

"Which reminds me, I put some money on your account at the feed store yesterday."

She looked at him. "You didn't have to do that." She snapped the lid off the cat food container and filled the cats' bowls.

"I want to help out."

Gemma set the black-and-white, whom she called Tux, in front of the food. "What did you think of Rick ending up with the police chief instead of Ilsa? I suppose that's as it should be." She brushed past him, raising her hair from her neck, fanning away the heat. "She still loved Victor."

John reached for her without pausing to think or analyze. "Holding your hand sent me to the moon, Gemma. I'm not going to lie. I was all zingy and twittery, distracted. Who cared about Rick and Ilsa, I was with you."

"Zingy?" She grinned and zapped him with a current of romantic electricity. "Very poetic, Prince." She stepped out of his arms. "It must not have been a pleasant ride to the moon. You let go. When Ilsa told Rick she still loved him."

So she'd noticed. What did he expect? "I'm sorry. One moment I was with you, only you, thrilled to just be in the moment and not conflicted with life. Then Ilsa made that confession and I tumbled down a rabbit hole, back to misery, back to disappointment, back to all the memories. Holland and I had a similar confession. When we met, I felt like I'd come home to love. She was the one who would help me be king. You know, for all a man's bravado, he needs a woman in his life." He looked down and kicked his foot over the stone aisle. "So very much."

"For all a woman's bravado, I reckon she needs a man in hers. Wasn't it that way from the beginning?"

"There are days when I barely think of her and then something like tonight happens and she consumes me. I'm sick with missing her."

"Prince, you don't owe me an explanation. You held my hand, big deal. You'll go home in a couple of weeks and this will be a distant, if not forgotten, memory."

"Never distant, never forgotten." They leaned against the workbench, not moving, their glances passing. "Maybe it was just me," he said into the quiet. "But holding your hand felt like more than a 'no big deal.'"

"Not really." A shadow passed over her expression as she left the workbench for the puppy stall, and his curiosity piqued about what exactly lived beneath her veil. What was she working so hard to conceal?

"I like you, Gemma. A lot," he said, walking with her to the puppies. "In fact, had we met at another time—"

"If we'd met in another time, we'd not be having this conversation." She knelt by the puppies and pressed her hand on their cuddled, sleeping bodies. "I feel so protective of them. I'm not sure I can give any away."

"Surely you'll let me have Chandler." John dropped to his blankets and rested his arms on his raised knees.

"You want the runt of the litter?" Her smile was genuine and free from secrets. When she talked about her herd, the puppies, or Imani, she became determined and focused.

"I feel rather protective of him." *Of you.*

"He won't be ready when you leave."

"You could bring him over." He stretched out and scratched Chandler's ears. The little chap squeaked and squirmed.

Tweedy roamed between the two of them, sniffing, inspecting, making sure her surrogates were safe. Blue used the opportunity to stretch his legs and head outside.

"You know, it occurs to me you know more about me than I do you," he said after a moment.

"You're famous. I'm a nobody."

He raised his head. There was more than self-deprecation in her reply. "That's a rather harsh view, Gemma. How does a *nobody* take in an orphan daughter and rescue animals?"

"I did what anyone would do." Retrieving Phoebe and Monica, Gemma settled against the barn wall and cuddled the puppies in her lap. "Imani's parents were good friends. We went to high school together. They were the all-American type. Smart, good-looking, athletic. She was black and he was white. They dated all through high school and got married the summer after we graduated."

"There were no racial issues?"

"Some but not enough to stop those two. Plus both parents were successful, leaders in the community, and they helped to make it work. Althea and Ethan had scholarships to great colleges. Althea went to Howard, Ethan to George Washington, where he played basketball. Imani was a surprise honeymoon baby."

"Had to be rough on young students and one playing a sport."

"Their parents partnered to pay for a decent apartment and a nanny so they could get their work done. But really, if you knew Al and Eth, you'd know they'd have figured a way without help. They were driven and organized, knew what they wanted."

"You knew what you wanted too." Reading between the lines was a skill every lawyer *and* crown prince needed.

"You're trying to figure me out, aren't you?"

"Is that so wrong? We started this by saying you knew more about me than I knew of you."

Gemma didn't look up from the sleeping puppies, smile, or even smirk. "Althea and Ethan graduated with honors, and she had a job interview in Manhattan. That was her dream, to work and live in the city. She was on cloud nine. Since I first met her, like seventh grade, she said she was going to live in New York, have a high-powered career, then come home to HB and raise her family. While she and Ethan were apartment hunting, she dropped dead of an aneurysm. Ethan was devastated and really never recovered. Her folks were just as torn up. Al was a late-in-life child. Their only child. Ethan and Imani came home for support and he went to work for O'Shay's."

"Holland's death knocked everything out of me," John said.

"I can imagine." Gemma's look of compassion comforted him. "Althea's father died of a heart attack when Imani was like six or seven. Then Althea's mother died a few years later. About the same time, Ethan's father died of a stroke. So, here's Imani, barely ten years old, and her family is dying all around her. Ethan's mom connected with a high school classmate and eloped with him to Florida. For Ethan, his life was falling apart, and he lost all of his support. He started battling insomnia. They had a live-in nanny so Ethan would go for long drives in the middle of the night. Then two years ago, just as I was coming home, he died in a single-car crash."

John sat up and scooted against the wall behind him. He hated how cruel life could be. "I feel so powerless when I hear a story like this one."

"Imani asked me the other day if she was cursed. I assured her she wasn't. Not from where I sit anyway. She's so resilient. So whole, considering everything that's happened."

"Because she has you."

"Not sure that's in her favor." Gemma rose up and returned Phoebe and Monica to their siblings. "But I'll always be there for her. Always."

For someone so beautiful, who displayed strength and confidence, who loved others well, Gemma did not have a high opinion of herself?

"How'd she come to live with you? After her father died?"

"I'd been home about a month, just bought this place, when he crashed. A lawyer showed up and said I was in his will. If anything happened to him, Imani was to come to me. After Althea died, I vaguely remember him asking me something about being Imani's guardian. But I didn't think she'd ever come to me. I figured I was way down on the list after grandparents, family, married friends. Maybe he thought I'd be rich and famous, not, well, what I am." There it was again. The self-loathing. "Imani was supposed to be living in a gorgeous, big house with successful parents and siblings by now. Instead she lives with me in a broken-down '70s time capsule and shovels poop from rabbit cages."

"A little poop shoveling never hurt anyone." He loved her soft laugh. "Does it matter where she lives as long as you love her? And what's so wrong with you? You're a marvelous success. Everyone loves you, speaks well of you."

"Yeah, that's because they don't—" Gemma stretched over her hay bed, flat on her belly, and stared at the sleeping puppies. "Hey, cool, Scottie showed up tonight. At your invitation."

"I was surprised but glad she did. The relaxed atmosphere made it easier for us to interact. We made an appointment to meet at Java Jane's. Behold the power of a good film and buttery popcorn."

"She'll come around. Give her time. Being a queen's daughter is a lot to take in."

"But does she have time? The queen, my mum, has been in the hospital—" He stopped. Blast. The words spilled before he realized they were on his tongue. Gemma had that effect on him. Made him want to speak, share, let her in. Now she regarded him, waiting for more. "She's been, well, ill. Nothing serious but she spent a few days in the hospital. Mum is young and healthy, so this is just a hiccup, but still, if Scottie ever wants to know her mother... Gemma, do not speak of this to anyone, I beg of you. The Family has not gone public with this development. Not even to the prime minister. No need to alarm the land over nothing."

"Your secret is safe with me. But is she really going to be all right?"

"Yes." Spoken with conviction because he needed it to be true. But of course it was. Mum was a rock and a picture of health. "What time is it?" he said. "You should get some sleep. You have work in the morning." He shifted around so he could refresh his bed of hay. "Go inside, set your alarm for three."

"I think I'll bunk out here too. It's cooled off and—" She sat up and faced the window. "I think it might rain." The sounds of Hercules and Whinny could be heard in the barn. Little Silver clip-clopped around to peer at the puppies.

"Can I use your facilities? I brought my toothbrush and a change of clothes just in case."

"No, use the water trough." Her sober countenance broke. "Of course, you goofball. I'll go too and change."

John scratched Silver's muzzle as he exited. Seeing him, Whinny shied away, trotting back out to the darkness. "You'll see in the end, ole girl, I'm a good chap."

At the house, they changed and took turns in the loo. Then walked back to the barn in a comfortable silence, said good night, and just as they were about to douse the lights, thunder clapped and rain scattered over the tin roof.

Silver's tiny hooves crashed against the center aisle stones and into the puppy stall. She could be heard snorting from a back corner.

"It's all right, Silver. I'm here," Gemma said.

"It's almost as if she's run to mummy's room for comfort."

"But I should take her to her stall. I don't want her getting too riled and stomp on the cast of *Friends*. Come on, sweet girl. I'll give you a whole apple."

John watched Gemma's dark form move from the stall, a torchlight at her feet, Silver following with her head under Gemma's arm.

Comfort. It must be her superpower. Because whenever she was around, people, animals, maybe even the trees and grass entered into peace.

Rising up, he leaned against the stall opening, listening as she sang and talked to Silver. Another thunderclap and Silver snorted and stomped. Then he heard music. After a few moments, Gemma came down the aisle.

"I put on her favorite album."

"Which is?"

"Classical. Music says things to the heart and soul words can't touch."

"Our groom played music for Briley when he was in so much pain."

"Who's Briley?" Gemma walked past him toward the south opening. Should he join her or let her alone?

She stood in the middle of the opening as a shadow, arms folded, head back, hair cascading down her back. She seemed so comfortable in the dark. Like Whinny.

"He was Holland's horse," John said, making his way to where Gemma stood, haloed in light-filled raindrops. "She was riding him when she came off and hit her head on the rocks. He broke his leg. It's been a tough road of healing."

"If there's an easy road to healing, please direct me to it."

"I'll join you there."

Her laugh was sweet, low, and in an instant, he didn't want to stand six feet from her but hold her, touch her, kiss her. *Kiss her?* His blood ran warm and he retreated to the puppy nursery. He'd not do it. Betray Holland. He'd promised to always love her and no other.

Until death parts us.

But death came all too soon.

"I love the rain," she said.

John paused just inside the stall. The heat from the day, along with the heat lamps, clamped down any fresh air. The space felt suffocating. But the center aisle was a thoroughfare for the sweet, cool, dewy summer rain. A path back to Gemma.

"You looked so peaceful I thought you'd prefer to be alone."

"I'm always alone."

He made his way toward her. "I wish you'd tell me what bothers you."

Gemma stretched, palm upright, to catch the drops from the edge of the roof. "When I was a kid, Daddy and I would take walks in the summer rain. Did you ever do that? Play in the rain, walk in the rain?"

"As a boy. Sometimes with Mum and Dad. We had a governess who loved the out of doors. We'd go on picnics and hikes."

"Were your parents not hands-on?"

"They were. As much as time allowed. We certainly weren't raised like our grandparents, surrounded by nannies and governesses, shipped off to boarding school at six."

"What will you do when you go home?"

"Work, I suppose. As crown prince I'm part of the legal system and I also sit in on parliamentary proceedings. I have no vote, but I'm there to represent the people through the crown. I have my causes. The charities I patron. More than anything, I must find a path forward."

"And to raise a puppy."

He laughed. "Indeed. When should I expect delivery of little Chandler?"

"Mid to late August, I suppose. But I'm not sure how you'll get him."

"You won't bring him over?" Like Gemma, John offered his palm to the rain. The little chap Chandler would keep him connected to this curious woman, and the idea made him happy.

A streak of lightning announced the next roll of thunder and when it clapped, nothing came from Silver's stall. John looked back to see Hercules had come in the opposite door and was checking on the mini. Then he clip-clopped his way toward them.

His large frame dwarfed both of them, and John laughed as the big gelding rested his muzzle on Gemma's head. "Did you check on your lady, big guy?" She stroked his head and neck.

The three of them stayed that way for a long time. John had no desire to move but to just be. The rain seemed to do more than water the earth tonight. It seemed to water him.

Eventually Hercules returned to his barn apartment. Whinny remained outside in the downpour.

"Guess we should get some rest before the three o'clock," Gemma said, turning toward him. "It must be after one already."

She stepped. He stepped. They bumped into one another and without a thought, he took her in his arms, inhaling the scent of her hair, her skin, all the while desperate to quiet his pounding heart. She remained stiff and still beneath his embrace. After a moment, he released her but held on to her hand.

"I want to kiss you," he whispered.

"No you don't." She stepped away.

"But I do."

"Prince, please, there's no point in this. Trust me, you don't want to kiss me. There's nothing permanent here. And I won't be your midnight lover." She turned back to the rain. "Should I remind you how you pulled your hand from mine during a movie because you miss your wife?"

"I know, I know, but you're here and she is not. Good grief, I feel treasonous and resentful for even saying it but it's not like she's gone for the weekend or on a girls' holiday. She'll never be on this earth again. I am a widower. As much as I love her, there's a part of me that's banging against the box I'm in to get on with life. And life includes love."

"I get it, I do." He could tell by the clouds in her voice she understood. Maybe even returned some of his feelings. "But, Prince, I've kissed a lot of frogs in my time, I'm ashamed to say. Think twice about kissing me. Then think again."

"What are you saying? You have some kissing disease?"

Her laugh filled him with relief. "No, just that I've kissed a lot of men and I'm not proud of it."

"We all have a past, Gemma."

"How many frogs have you kissed?"

"Frogs? None, though Gus kissed a frog on a dare while at school. He was oh, nine or ten, and teased and mocked for being pudgy. He wanted to be one of the lads so they challenged him to kiss a frog. Instead of defending him, I stood there and watched." John shuddered. "I still feel horrible about it."

They stood side by side as another bolt of lightning lit the sky. He could just make out Whinny determinedly positioned under the pond tree.

"Do you want to kiss me?" he said.

"I don't think I've ever conversed this long about a stupid kiss. Yes, I want to kiss you but, Prince, the first woman you kiss after your wife should not be me."

"I demand an explanation." Time for his prince voice. He'd get to the bottom of this Gemma, self-deprecating, loathing mystery. It was probably something only she saw as catastrophic. "What are you not telling me?"

"Prince, go home. Find a Lauchten woman with a title and pedigree." She lifted her face to his and in the shallow glow from the barn lights, he saw the shadow loomed in her eyes. "I'm nothing special. Not worth kissing."

"Is this the boyfriend Matt's doing? Did he hurt you? What did he say to make you believe such lies? Forget him, Gemma. He's not worth another moment of your time, your thoughts. You *are* special." He took her hand and placed it over his heart. "Trust me, I'm a prince—I know these things." The heat of her hand radiated through his skin.

"You're making me almost believe, John. Matt's a rat fink to be sure, but if you must know, I'm the one who hurt me. I let myself down and I've no one else to blame."

"Then apologize and forgive yourself."

She tipped forward, pressing her forehead to his chest. "Easier said than done."

He raised her chin with a light touch. "I want to kiss that shadow out of your eyes."

Her eyes welled up and the shadow wavered. "I'm not sure anyone has that much power."

"Can I try?" Blast, but if he wasn't nervous.

A tiny tear tripped down the side of her face. "And if I swoon, will you catch me?"

"I caught you once, remember? But now that you mention swooning, I'm quite sure my simple kiss will prove disappointing. As you say, a kiss doesn't have that much power."

"I think we've talked about this for way too long."

He drew her close. "Then shall we get on with it?"

"Very romantic, Prince. Did you hear that, Hercules?" The big horse stuck his nose over the top of his stall and glanced down the thoroughfare.

Enough chatter, then. John slipped his arm about her waist and bent toward her. She hooked her hands over his shoulders as their lips met.

At first it was a bit underwhelming. Then, there was nothing but her warm, soft lips and the fragrance of rain, hay, horses, and puppies. The perfume of her life. And he escaped into it.

Way off in some distant valleys of his soul, the sound of a breaking box echoed.

When they broke apart, their eyes met, and without a word or even a sigh, they fell into another kiss, breathing to the rhythm of the rain. They were the only two people on the earth. John felt it.

He didn't register the sound of Hercules's big hooves clopping against the stones until his giant nose rammed him from behind, knocking him out of the barn and into a warm, muddy puddle. Hercules, apparently, was having none of it.

Laughing, John hopped up and reached for Gemma, dragging her into the rain with him. He hugged her against his hip, kissing her as the rain slaked their skin clear through to their weary souls.

"I thought we needed sleep," she said.

"We do." He took her hand and led her under cover for another kiss. From the puppy stall, he thought he heard his phone beckoning. No bother, he'd answer later. "Where were we?"

"I knew I loved the rain," Gemma said when their kisses began to fade. "We should, um, dry off." She lifted the lid of the blue tub and handed him a stained, tattered terry cloth that smelled of laundry soap.

He dried off as she flipped over to towel her hair, and when she rose up, the shadows in her eyes had retreated. At least as far as he could see.

He took hold of her and rested his cheek against her wet hair. "I'll remember this. Always." Blast! That was his phone ringing. Not the ordinary ring of friends and family but an urgent tone. "Excuse me, Gemma."

Answering his phone, he peered up to see Gunner standing in the barn, his phone in his hand, his expression somber. John tried but failed to stop the sinking sensation of bad news.

"Dad, hello," he said.

"Come home, Son." His voice crunched like gravel. "Mum's collapsed."

"I've been stalking IG accounts in America. I found this. It's dark but isn't that Prince John and the same woman he carried in his arms? Margot? Gina? @melissafarisreports. Can anyone confirm? I'll be so desperate if he's found love before I had a chance to go to the royal ball and sweep him off his feet. #Cinderellasyndrome"

— @ILOVETHEROYALS ON INSTAGRAM

"More and more I'm wondering the purpose of the Family. Why strap Prince John to a law of marriage in order to take his oath? The man is clearly mourning his wife. And really, Samm, I ask, isn't the age of royal houses over?"

— HAMISH FICKLE OF THE NIGHTLY SHOW WITH SAMM MAN

"Hamish Fickle, MP from Midlands, continues to challenge the monarchy. His young RECO party held a rally on Haxton University's Hax Square with thousands in attendance. 'I think he's the future,' said law student Lindsay Harrell."

— THE NEWS LEADER

"Well, Stone, we're not sure really. We've heard rumors the queen is in the Royal Louis Medical Center, but efforts to enter Her Majesty's wing have been thwarted. As information is released, we'll announce it here on the *Morning Show*. Also follow me on social media @melissafarisroyalreporter."

— *STONE BRUBAKER ON THE MORNING SHOW*

CHAPTER
SIXTEEN

GEMMA

How could a man she'd only known two weeks leave a hole in her heart? This was not supposed to happen. She blamed the puppies. They'd tenderized her, made her want to love, made her think of marriage and the whole silly white picket fence thing.

She'd hoped she'd get over those quirky, crushy feelings. But in the two weeks he'd been gone, she felt the same.

In the quiet moments of the day she returned to the magic of his passionate kisses and practically shoved herself into the impossible idea of loving him.

Standing at the kitchen sink, Gemma looked up as a clap of thunder rattled the windows. Since John had gone, it'd rained almost every afternoon. One inhale of the fragrant, dewy air and there she was, back in his arms, her head pressed against his sculpted chest.

She wasn't the only one missing him. Last night she found a newly mobile Chandler and ole Blue lying on the prince's bed, their noses pressed against the blanket.

"I know, sweet boys. I miss him too."

She'd returned Chandler to his siblings and sat with Blue for a while. Finally, she stopped procrastinating and made him get up so she could store John's bed in the loft.

"We all have to get over him."

The first few days he was home, he'd texted her throughout the day.

"Mum's feeling better. They're not sure what she's fighting. A virus or bacteria? It's all rather confusing."

"The puppies are moving about???? I'm missing it. Send more videos. Stat. (That's hospital speak for right now!)"

"Do you miss me? Of course you do."

"Buck says I took the truck keys with me. Ha! I must return to HB and give them back."

She responded with her own brand of jesting and sarcasm, sending videos of Justin snuggling Chandler.

But she'd learned better than to text when she was punchy and tired. She sent this to him around 1:00 a.m. after caring for a sick Miss Frances.

"Since you've gone, I can't breathe. Come home and be my oxygen."

"P.S. That was a line from a horrible play I was in my second, maybe third, year in LA. I keep trying to forget but bad lines resound as much as good ones."

She was mortified when she reread it the next morning. One, because she sent a line with so much subtext. Two, because she opened the door to talk about L.A.

But his reply eradicated her fears.

> "I'm thrilled you didn't come up with that ghastly line yourself. Your humanity is redeemed."

> "Sorry about that weird text. I was up with Miss Frances."

> "No worry."

> "Oh, I meant to tell you. Ran into Scottie in Java Jane's. She said she was sorry she didn't get to say goodbye. Maybe she's softening to her royal roots."

"Gemma?" Imani leaned against the kitchen counter. "Can I ask you something?"

"Anything."

"Are you in love with the prince?"

She looked up and out the sink window. "What? No. We're friends. Nothing more." Gemma rinsed the spaghetti pot and settled it in the drainer.

"If you were, like, would you move to Lauchtenland? What about me?"

Gemma dried her hands and motioned for Imani to sit at the table. Opening the fridge, she retrieved two ice cream bars she'd picked up from Pops Yer Uncle on her way home. On her way out she'd snarled at their First Place Three-Legged Race trophy.

"First, let's not invent a scenario to worry about. Second, you are my priority. Always. Any man who wants me has to love you." Gemma peeled away the wrapper and bit into the chocolate and caramel swirl. Pops was the best. Simply the best.

"B-but what if he doesn't? I'm not technically your daughter. I'd certainly not be his." Imani stared at her ice cream bar without interest.

"Do you think I could love a man who would not love you? Imani, look at me. It's not an option. We are a package deal."

Her eyes brimmed when she looked at Gemma. "My grand-mother didn't want me."

"Your grandmother is blinded by grief and pain and, if you ask me, selfishness."

"Seems like everyone around me dies. My parents, Mama's parents, Dad's father. If anything happens to you…" Imani tipped forward until her forehead rested on the Formica. "I'm scared." A soft sob accented her confession.

"Nothing's going to happen to me." Gemma set down her ice cream and knelt next to Imani. "If it was, it'd have happened a long time ago, trust me. I'm not going anywhere. You are my daughter. Say the word and I'll adopt you tomorrow."

In the span of a breath, the adoption word was on the table.

Imani sat up with a force, making her corkscrew curls bounce. "Y-you can do that?" She wiped her tears and conquered her sorrow with a smile.

"Yes, you're sixteen. All you have to do is ask. With your parents gone, you're legally free to do so."

"What about Gigi?" Was that a hint of hope in her voice?

"She has no rights, but if you want her to adopt you—"

"No, no, I don't." Imani unwrapped her ice cream. "Wow, this is cool. Can I think about it? I mean, I want to but I have to think." Gemma knew. Imani's MO was to think about things.

"Of course. I didn't ask you before now because I didn't want you to think I was trying to take your mom's place. But when you're ready, tell me and we'll get the ball rolling."

"Is it expensive? I could use my social security money."

"That is for college."

"But I'm getting a scholarship to play basketball."

"I like your thinking, but as your future legal mother, I insist on paying. Though I should check the refund policy—"

Imani flew at her, knocking them both to the scarred linoleum floor. "Thank you, thank you."

They lay there for a long, tearful, happy moment. Then Gemma said, "I think our ice cream is melting," and they pushed to their feet, laughing.

"Can I go over to Justin's?" Imani tossed her wrapper in the trash and bit into her melting treat.

"What? Now? After our huge mother-daughter moment?"

"I want to tell him, see what he thinks."

"Are his parents home?"

"Yes, his parents are home." Imani unhooked the truck keys from their spot by the door. "What do you think we're going to get up to at his house we couldn't get up to in the back of my truck? Or his?"

"That's it," Gemma said. "You're never leaving the house again."

"Gemma," Imani said, slowly, averting her gaze, twisting her foot to one side. "If *that's* going to happen, I promise to talk to you. Deal?"

The confession knocked the wind out of Gemma. More than the monstrous hug or the prospect of adoption. She'd have never talked to her mother about sex, about what she and Dash were up to on dark country roads when they were supposed to be at the movies.

"All right, deal."

Imani dashed out and Gemma finished her ice cream, then the last of the dishes and sorted through the mail and papers on her desk, but she'd been doing that job at the shop all day.

The last thing she wanted to do at home on a glorious Monday evening in August was figure out which papers to keep and which to throw away. She was about to give up and head to the barn to check on the puppies in the new pen Daddy built for them when an envelope with the return address of B. A. Carpenter caught her attention. This was her second one. And she'd received a call from the same number.

She considered opening it for a moment then dumped it along with the other "To the Resident" letters in the can by the desk.

As for the rest of the papers and bills, she'd leave them for now. A chore for another day.

She'd taken a water from the fridge when she spied Imani's order pad from Ella's Diner. She brought it home by mistake last night. An idea sparked. Pie. Gemma suddenly wanted pie. Tina Danner made the best cherry east of the Mississippi.

Gemma shot JoJo a text.

"Pie? Ella's? Thirty minutes?"

"Absolutely!"

Back in the day—'50s and '60s—everyone in town went to Ella's for pie and coffee after dinner. It was like a town ordinance or something—must eat pie once a week at Ella's.

If pie didn't suffice, they ordered an ice cream sundae or a root beer float.

She dashed to the bedroom, shed her hay-and-dust-infested clothes, then headed out. She'd just locked the back door when a dark sedan stirred up dust in the driveway. Gemma stepped off the porch, squinting to see who sat behind the wheel. No one she recognized.

The driver, a man in a buff-colored cowboy hat, pulled up to where she stood. "Gemma Stone?"

"Who's asking?" She glanced toward the road, calculating a path of escape, should the need arise. She used to be quite fast until the accident.

"Brick Aloysius Carpenter, Attorney at Law. You've not answered any of my letters, emails, or calls."

"B. A. Carpenter? You're real?"

He walked toward her with a large manila envelope. In his mid-60s, he looked a bit like the Columbo character Mama watched in reruns. Only a cowboy version. His gray hair was thick and unruly, sticking out from under his hat, which looked more and more tattered the closer he came.

His white shirt was cinched with a bolo tie, and his boot cut jeans flared over a pair of polished cockroach kickers. His brown eyes were sharp, steady, and intense.

"I'm in a hurry. So if you don't mind..." Gemma stepped around him toward her car. "If you're here on behalf of the hotel in Vegas, I'm not—"

"Ma'am, I represent the Kingston family. You're living on their land."

She stopped and turned, chilled by the August night air. "You mean it *was* their land. I bought it from the Samson Development Corp over two years ago. Paid cash. Don't try to tell me different. I have the deed."

She resented the tension she felt and the fact this man was ruining a beautiful evening and the reinstating of an old Hearts Bend tradition.

"Ms. Stone." B. A. Carpenter drew a little closer. "The Samson Development Corp is—was—fraudulent. They no longer exist. They never held the deed to this land. The older Kingstons left this place to their children." He offered her the envelope he gripped in his hands. "You'll see all the pertinent legal information is there."

"Excuse me, did you say Samson Development doesn't exist? How? I went to their office, met their lawyer."

"They rent out a building, hang around long enough to look

legit, all the while looking for their next victim. If not two or three victims. They're modern squatters. Find properties uninhabited with no loans or liens, create a quitclaim deed, which sadly no one researches or checks, and offer their desperate victim a deal too good to pass up. Did they tell you they liked you and were willing to let the property go at a loss?"

Gemma dropped like a rock but caught herself before she completely hit the ground. On her knees, she made her confession. "But I gave them all my money."

"Did they tell you they just wanted to give you a break in life?"

"Yes." She tried to stand but her legs refused to hold her.

From the start, she thought the offer was too good to be true. Twenty acres on this side of town for a hundred and fifty thousand. But everything seemed to check out. Even her friend at the county office said, "Go for it."

"Did they ask you how much cash you had?"

Gemma bent forward with a moan.

"And while they wanted three or four times that amount, they were willing to let it go to you for whatever you could pay?"

When she fell all the way forward, the sharp edges of tire-worn gravel bit into her hands and the back of her arms.

"Ms. Stone? Ms. Stone?" B. A. Carpenter leaned over her. "Can you hear me? Ms. Sto—"

"Now that he's back, can we expect to see some romance?"

– NEWS AT NOON WITH TAMMA TUCKER

"Prince John Deputized to Represent the Queen. What implications does this have on his investiture? Live update at five."

– LTV-1

"I mean it's ridiculous, don't you think? The queen is ill and we have to jet the crown prince home to swear a temporary oath as her deputy? What are the elected officials for if not to execute their duty to represent and protect the people? And we still have the issue of the marriage writ. If she dies, God forbid, and John is not married, has not taken his permanent oath, do we have a constitutional crisis? Does the government dissolve at once? We can't be formed in a dead queen's name, now can we?"

— VIDEO OF HAMISH FICKLE FROM THE PARLIAMENT FLOOR

"The Justice Ministry's investigation on the sale of the Midlands property to Reingard Industries after Eloise Ltd. filed a complaint against the textile giant last month is ongoing as well as the civil case between the two clothing manufacturers."

— CABLE NEWS PF

"Hamish Fickle is such a doll. Is it weird to have a crush on a political chap?"

— @IMYERGURL ON INSTAGRAM

CHAPTER
SEVENTEEN

JOHN

"**I**s everything ready?" John greeted the Steward of the Dining Hall, Latham, wearing a white tie, his skin and shoes buffed to a sheen.

"Indeed, Your Royal Highness." In his sixties, the man had been setting up for royal and state dinners for three decades. "The cocktail hour begins on the hour, as the guests arrive. You will dine at half past. The hall is ready, the table set, the menus and placards at every place setting. Chef George's staff has everything under command, so I expect no delays. A quartet will play in the foyer until the speeches. Do you have any specific questions?"

"What inquiries did the queen make before every dinner?" John shifted his shoulders against the stiff confines of his tuxedo. He missed the T-shirt and shorts he wore in the Tennessee barn full of rescues—including himself and a brunette beauty.

Their kiss in the rain still lived in his memory.

What might have transpired if he'd not been called home? He wondered if that early morning call hadn't rescued him from his own folly.

"She inspected the table, sir, then said, 'Very good, Lath. I see you have it under your usual control.'"

Without a reply, John walked the length of the dining hall, taking it all in, his nerves glancing toward the edge. He'd attended six or seven state dinners in his thirty-one years, but never as the leader, never sitting in the Head of State chair.

The hall glistened and glowed with wall sconces flickering against hand woven wall tapestries depicting Lauchtenland's history.

A row of Schonbek chandeliers showered light over a table set for a hundred and fifty with white bone china rimmed in gold. Polished gold and silver vessels awaited use on the buffet.

"Sir, is everything to your satisfaction?"

"Yes, as the queen said, I see you have it under your usual control."

Nevertheless, John shouldn't be here in place of the queen. She was the monarch, the leader of the land. The pundits took large swings at him when he took the temporary oath of office, to stand in for Her Majesty.

"What happened to the marriage writ? Are we just changing things as we go along, making up laws that suit us? If so I've got a few things I'd like changed."

"Should he marry just to be married? I don't get this writ. What is the point?"

"We've a temporary king? Does he have all rights and privileges of the office, of the throne?"

These comments and questions derived from the royal press rota. Then there was Hamish Fickle who challenged everything from the queen's health to the validity of John's new position to LTV-1's weather report.

"So we have a writ for the crown heir to be married before his investiture but now that the queen is under the weather, she's sanctioned Prince John to take her place? What are we doing? What is the purpose of the writ if he can just belly up to the throne?"

The man was an insensitive clod. But the Family as well as the Chamber Office remained silent.

John paused by his place at the head of the table. Tonight's dinner was for civic leaders in government, business, and charities.

He inspected the names of the guests on his right and left. Dad, thank goodness, was on his right. A mayor from the northern village of Wython, on his left.

John squinted at his name. This couldn't be correct.

Bor Short.

Surely Bor was short for Boris. The nickname combined with his last name created an unfortunate image. Nothing wrong with being short, but boring...

With a final glance about the room, he returned to his apartment. He'd planned to meet Gus and Daffy there, along with Dad, and come down together to greet their guests.

Gus waited for him in his living room, the remote aimed at the telly. "Did you see the news?"

"I see everything. I'm the temporary monarch. I've eyes in the back of my head, at my temples. Even on the soles of my feet. What news are you referencing? Hamish Fickle on the parliament floor? The Supreme Court cases? The Midlands property case?"

John headed to his dressing room, yielding to a strange urge to check his hair. Too much gel? If so, too late.

He'd just read the brief this morning about the Midlands suit. The Justice Ministry was still investigating—which he found odd. The land sale drew no red flags. Eloise Ltd., it seemed, was simply angry for the property being sold out from under them. Welcome to business. Reingard had offered restitution for the environmental surveys just this morning. Win-win as far as John was concerned.

Or was there more news about the writ and how John could not *legally* be the queen's deputy?

"They're saying a member of parliament is behind the Reingard land deal," Gus said.

John drew away from the mirror where he'd been inspecting his hair. Definitely too much gel.

"Lords or members?" Lords inherited their positions. The members were elected. Either chamber was capable of scandal, malfeasance, fraud, corruption. "Please tell me Hamish Fickle is caught up in it all."

Not nice, but a legal trial would get him off the talk show circuit.

"The little man with the big mouth? I don't think so. John, look here." Gus tapped John's shoulder. "Your tie is crooked. They don't know who's behind it. The typical 'Oops, there was a leak in the investigation' foul-up." Gus finished with the tie and patted his brother on the back. "Are you ready for tonight?"

"To eat and speak? How hard can it be? I've rehearsed my remarks so much I woke up this morning muttering, 'I'm delighted to welcome you to Perrigwynn Palace.'" A new revelation dawned. "You don't think they'll be disappointed to have me presiding instead of the queen?"

"Who cares? You're her deputy, the future king. Be confident. Forget Hamish Fickle and anyone who sides with him. The crown has survived a thousand years of ridicule and speculation, enemies and naysayers. Do you think one MP from a small county can topple us now?"

"Napoleon did a bit of damage."

"Hamish is no Napoleon." The brothers returned to the living room to await Dad and Daffy.

"You place the wreath on Holland's grave in a few weeks."

John stopped at the tea trolley for a quick, fortifying cup. "Your point being?"

"Your duty. Dating. Marriage."

"Good golly, has Mum drafted you to her side? Did she tell you I agreed to meet Scottie if she changed the writ?"

Gus made a face. "Did *she* agree?"

"Told me she had a meeting with Elias."

"She asked me to encourage you to date. Even suggested setting you up with some of Daffy's friends."

John dropped cream into his tea but didn't take a drink. "She has no intention of changing it, does she?"

"I wonder…" By his expression, John knew Gus was conflicted. "You know she's slow to change long-standing traditions and writs. She believes in them."

"Then you'll have to be the heir. You're married with a child on the way. It's perfect." John paced toward the window, the conversation unsettling, all the while bringing Gemma to mind.

"I know, let's hand the whole lot over to Scottie. She's strong. Determined."

"She's also never been to Lauchtenland or met Mum. I'm afraid that scheme won't fly."

"I refuse to marry without love. Marriage is too long and too intimate to go into it without affection, without common goals and dreams. I can't date with marriage as the endgame. It feels phony. Old Grandfather Louis would side with me were he alive. I know it. Besides, I've done my part. I married and was ready to take the oath. If Holland died even a month later, we'd not be having this conversation. Talk to God about why He took her from me."

The Port Fressa summer days were long and as John stood at the window, twilight barely colored the horizon over the bay.

"Mum would sooner change the writ than release her crown prince." Gus's voice was mellow and sincere. "But my daughter could still be your heir until you have children of your own."

"Daughter?" John turned around to see his brother's smile, so white and wide he'd guide the longshoremen home on a moonless night. "Congratulations."

"I wasn't sure if you wanted to know."

"Why wouldn't I? Of course I do." He offered to shake Gus's hand then drew him into a hug. "Let's pray she looks like Daffy."

"Every night." Gus's joy faded a little. "I can't help but think you'd have had your own son or daughter by now."

"Well, don't. It's enough to deal with Holland being gone. Besides, your blessing is my blessing."

Gus went to the door and looked down the hallway. Dad and Daffy should arrive any moment. "I think back to the day Coral Winthrop left me at the altar," he said. "When I thought my life was over. Now, I can hardly remember the pain. I'm married to a woman I love madly, and miracle of miracles, I'm good friends with the woman who dumped me as millions watched. God brought it all right. He did."

"For you, maybe."

"John, He will for you too. He can't abandon you. It's not in His nature."

Okay, fine. John let the conversation drop because in the past he'd tried to push back but he got a sermonette every time on the beauty of faith and believing in a God who gave His own life for him.

Him being a relative term. Crown Prince John Titus Edric Rein Blue? Or just mankind in general? There were moments when John believed the poor soul in the streets had more of God's attention than he did. Perhaps that was as it should be. The balance of things.

Still, little brother, also a prince, had had a supernatural encounter with a man he called Emmanuel. Even Mum claimed the occasional visit from this ethereal character. Yet John, the future king of Lauchtenland, had never met the heavenly man. Or been touched by God. Unless Holland's death was His finger. Then he had nothing to say to the Almighty.

Dad arrived with Daffy. John kissed her cheek, congratulating her on having a daughter, and together they started down the corridor to the center staircase leading to the grand foyer. That's when Dad pointed to John's empty hands.

"Where's the scepter?"

Of course. The royal scepter. The one the sovereign used to open every ceremony and dinner. Briggs reminded him only a short while ago the cedar-and-velvet box containing the wood, steel, and gold rod was in the queen's office.

"Go ahead," John said. "I'll get it and be along."

At the queen's office, John punched in her security code and entered. The space was eerie and quiet with Mum's continual absence, Mason not at his desk, phones not ringing.

He found the scepter box on her desk. Opening the lid, he hesitated. No one but the king or queen touched the scepter. At his investiture ceremony, he'd see the scepter, pay homage to what it represented, but even then, he would not hold it. Not until his coronation.

But as the queen's stand-in, he had no choice. Palms sweating, John started to reach for the ancient royal staff with the emerald-and-ruby-encrusted crown and polished brass stem, engraved with House of Blue cyphers.

Then he hesitated, an intuition warning him to consider his actions. Once he lay hold, he'd be changed. He'd be accepting his destiny, investiture aside. Was he ready?

Breathing deep, he overcame his slight trepidation and gripped the scepter, half expecting a flash of lightning and crack of thunder.

Instead, he felt at peace and little doubts faded away. He'd known his whole life he'd be king. But in this moment, he grasped the enormity of it all without fear.

Closing the box, he turned to go, but something caught his eye from the grounds below. Probably the dogs running free, their minders chasing after them. Glancing down, John expected the dogs, or members of the ground crew, but instead he spotted a man in a long anorak and wide-brimmed hat standing under the elm. Three stories down and a dozen meters apart, John felt as if they were face-to-face. The man's blue eyes radiated with a laser-like glow that cut through the glass and stone of the palace, through the bulwark John lived behind.

After a long, visual exchange, the man nodded, and for a second, the scepter glowed and burned in John's hand. Then the moment was gone. And so was the man.

"John, did you find it?" Dad stood just inside the office. "We must go down. The Family is never late."

"Yes, sorry. I'm just coming." He raised the scepter. "I have it here. In my hand."

And somehow in his heart, in his mind, and in his soul.

GEMMA

Three days after B. A. Carpenter arrived, announcing Gemma lived on stolen property, her house was full of Stones.

Mama, Daddy, Granny, Aunt Edwina and Uncle Bud, along with Hank and Betty, Al and Betty (yes, it got confusing), Bill and Nancy. Because even a crisis called for a good game of cards. And prayer. Cards and prayer.

Mama called everyone she knew to pray, announcing Gemma's shame and failure to the world. Even strangers on the street.

"My daughter got hoodwinked by land swindlers. She could use your prayers."

Even the guests at the Hearts Bend Inn got a full account as Mama made up their beds and emptied their trash. (She knew all this because Daddy gave Gemma a detailed account.)

Gemma Edwina Stone once again walked the journey of a thousand bad decisions. Now a thousand and one bad decisions.

Tonight Pastor Clyde came to pray after supper—which Gemma appreciated—though he was rather loquacious despite the heat of bodies gathered in the kitchen under a weak working ceiling fan. The old air conditioner huffed and puffed trying to keep the house cool, but its old motor wasn't enough against so many warm bodies and too many long-winded prayers.

Escaping outside after the prayer, Gemma sat on the back deck, grateful the August evening had cooled. Imani started school this week. She'd play a short volleyball season, then get straight into basketball.

Gemma anticipated a lot of nights at the Rock Mill High gym or traveling around the state for away games.

She welcomed the distraction. Because she still spent too much time thinking about the one thing she desperately wanted to forget. The prince.

She created a couple of social media accounts—with a fake name of course—and followed some of the royal blogs and the Perrigwynn Palace account. Prince John had a lot of fan accounts, as did his brother, Gus.

She tried not to look at her feeds often, but scrolling through various accounts had already become her nightly habit.

Worse, she dreamed of him. And also, she blamed the puppies. Everything about them screamed, "The prince, the prince."

They were growing up. By the end of summer, they should all have new homes. Except Chandler, because the prince wanted him. Gemma wondered if Scottie would go over any time soon. She could take Chandler with her.

By Thursday night, Gemma had enough. Especially after little Jimmy Peterman barged into the bathroom—the lock never worked—and announced to the world, "Miss Gemma's pooping on the potty. Mama, Mama—"

Embarrassment and limping A/C aside, she was suffocating. People were at the house when she went to work, when she came home, and when she went to bed.

They mopped, vacuumed, cleaned, did the laundry, and attempted to cook—all of which she appreciated—the good southern hospitality in a time of crisis.

Which led to a daily detailed account of every flaw in the house and every quirk of her broken-down appliances.

"The oven don't heat evenly. I think it's your coils."

"Did you know two of your burners are out?"

"What's with the washing machine tub spinning backwards?"

Yes, she knew all of it, but what did any of it matter? She'd lost the house and the land.

The worst part was when people wanted to help with the herd. Between telling them what to do and what not to do, and running interference for the rescues, the chores took twice as long.

Eventually every conversation ended with, *"Why don't you go on inside and see what Daddy and Mama are up to?"*

But enough was enough. Standing between the living room and kitchen, Gemma got everyone's attention. "Thank you all so much for your encouragement and help but—"

"That's my granddaughter, boys. Read 'em and weep." Daddy's voice cut through Gemma's.

At the kitchen table, Imani sat cocooned in the affection of the same folks who'd raised and helped raise Gemma. Daddy, Mama, and all the honorary aunts and uncles. Imani and Daddy just won a game of Hearts.

How could she tell everyone to leave when they loved on that girl so well? When they loved on her. When Nancy bustled about to cut Imani another brownie and scoop out vanilla ice cream.

The girl had no idea about B. A. Carpenter, the Samson Development Corp, and the great fraud, or that she now traveled with Gemma on her road of bad decisions. She had no idea her life was about to change. Again. Gemma envied her innocence. Envied that she believed the nightly crowd at the kitchen table just meant they'd suddenly become the party house.

About then Justin arrived. He melded into the glorious chaos, saying yes to a brownie and ice cream. Then Penny popped in.

Forget her announcement. Gemma needed to escape. Leaving the crowd behind, she headed for the barn.

Tomorrow, yes, tomorrow, she'd express her appreciation then ask everyone to pray for and support her from their own homes.

Never mind Betty's lasagna bubbling up in Gemma's rickety old oven, filling the house with aromas powerful enough to make a girl change her mind. But no. *No.* They had to go and she had to face a new future.

In the barn, the dogs napped on the stone aisle, cooling under the high ceiling fans, free from the inside chaos.

"Gemma." She turned as Imani called her name. "Do we have more soda out here?"

"Check the fridge." Gemma pointed to the old appliance in the far corner. The paint was chipped and faded, and the door had a dent the size of a horse hoof, but the sweet thing hummed with life.

"Did you see Memaw brought more groceries? There's food everywhere." The light of the fridge illuminated Imani's athletic form as she collected bottles of Orange Crush. "Isn't it fun to be the party house? Justin's parents always have people over. Can we do this more?"

"More? We have people here every night."

"True, we do." Imani grinned as she headed back to the house, her arms loaded with cold soda bottles. After a few steps she stopped and turned around. "Gemma, why is everyone here? Be honest."

Gemma shrugged, lacking the energy and heart to confess the truth. At least not yet. "I guess they thought it was time."

But Imani was a smart girl. Her mother's daughter. "Is everything okay?"

"Right as rain. Go on now before those sodas get warm."

On the other side of the barn, the goats stirred and bleated. "You've been fed. Miss Frances. You all right?" Gemma patted the mama goat's head. "Y'all go to sleep," she said.

At the puppy nursery, she stepped over the gate Daddy had recently installed and sat in the hay. The little rascals were milling about, playing, chewing on each other, and climbing on Blue and Tweedy.

"Clearly these puppies are more fun than we are." Gemma glanced up to see Daddy at the stall opening. Should've known he'd come after her.

Clearing the gate, he sat next to her with an *umph*. "How's little Chandler?" He searched for the runt of the litter who'd just collapsed after a wrestling match with Joey.

"Growing. I think I'm going to keep them all."

"Six puppies and five dogs? Quite a handful. I'm sure we can find good homes." Daddy cradled Ross against his neck, laughing when his tiny tongue kissed his skin.

"The truth is I have to find good homes for *all* of them. The dogs, the cats, the rabbits, the goats, Herc, Whinny, and Silver."

"If I could, I'd make this go away. Your mama got on me the other night for wasting so much of our money on schemes. Said we'd have had a nice nest egg by now. We could help you out."

"Not enough to redeem this place. Besides, I couldn't take your money. This is my mess." Gemma toppled sideways and wept softly against her father's broad shoulder.

"Life doesn't seem to be going your way, does it?" He kissed her forehead. "What about the prince? What does he say?"

"I've not told him, nor Imani, so don't tell her." She sat up and wiped her cheeks. "Daddy, don't get ideas about John and me. We were friends for a few weeks. Maybe what we both needed but he's off living his life, following his calling. Which is a very different life than mine."

But oh his kiss…

One day, when she was old and gray, with menopause whiskers on her chin, she'd sit in the back booth at Ella's Diner, smoke curling from her cigarette (even though Tina told her a hundred times to take "that thing" outside), ashes scattered over the table and into her coffee cup, and regale anyone who caught her eye with her story of the prince.

"You there, did you hear about the time I kissed the king of Lauchtenland? He was only the crown prince then but, honey, what a lover."

She'd exaggerate, of course, and over time forget the actual details because she'd embellished them for fifty years.

"Did I tell you about the time a crown prince and I slept in the barn on the hay. We had a passel of newborn pups, you see, and—"

"Imani's strong, Gemma. You should tell her. Best to find out now, and from you. With that lot in there, I'm surprised she doesn't already know."

"She probably does." Gemma sighed. "We talked about adoption. She's sixteen. All we have to do is fill out forms and see a judge."

She told how Imani wept on her shoulder, confessed her fears and insecurities, wondering if she was cursed.

"I want her to be as secure as possible, but how can I adopt her when I've no place to live? Her world's been pulled out from under her far too often, so when she finds out, I'd like to have some sort of plan figured out to lighten the blow."

"What about you? Your world's been pulled out from under you a couple of times."

Gemma picked at the hay beneath her legs. "I'm a victim of my own decisions. Including this recent blunder. Dash told me to get a lawyer."

"Your old boyfriend Dash? The fancy lawyer?"

"I ran into him when I was considering this place. He was in town visiting. But then I talked to Keith Niven, Hearts Bend realtor extraordinaire, and he said to do a title search, but the Samson lawyer said why waste the money? Told me they had other buyers chomping at the bit. I didn't want to lose this place so I signed on the dotted line. They had the deed. I had the cash. What could possibly go wrong?"

"Something is going to break your way, Gemstone. I know it."
Daddy patted his flat belly. "Feel it right here."

"Maybe. I don't know. But my life is here, so I'll start from
scratch and rebuild what we've lost. Imani leaves for college in
two years and I want them to be the best years of her life." Gemma
stood and looked out into the barn. "I love this place, Daddy. I've
healed here. So has Imani. Even the herd has healed."

Whinny trotted into the barn, down the aisle, and nibbled
Gemma's outstretched hand.

"Are you sure the Kingstons don't want to sell? Can't think
they care much about this place, leaving it empty for well over two
years."

"Someone in the family wants it. B. A. Carpenter was very
clear on the score. Besides, I couldn't afford it. This property is
worth one point two million."

Daddy let out a low whistle. "I wish I had the money…" His
confession faded. "How much time did they give you? Three
months?"

"Yes, but I want to go as soon as possible. The die is cast. Just
need to find a good home for these guys." She moved to Hercules,
who peered over the lower stall wall. "Now that I know, I feel like
a squatter."

"I'm afraid you inherited my gene for wild dreams and bad
decisions." Daddy returned the sleeping Ross to the puppy pile.
Tweedy and Blue had gone out for a late night stroll. Gemma was
pretty sure they were a *thing*. Maybe Blue would propose soon.

"Stop, Daddy, none of this is your fault. I love that you're a
dreamer."

"I'm getting a permanent job, Gemstone. No more driving a
truck. Cole Danner offered me a place on his crew. Paying me
more than I'm worth but I'll take it. My paycheck goes straight
into your mother's account too. She's going to give me an
allowance."

Gemma regarded him for a long moment. "So, you're going
cold turkey on your get-rich-quick ideas? No more 'This is the
one, Mauve'?"

"Nope. Cold turkey. Got me a Roth IRA, whatever that is. We finally saw the financial counselor your mother's been badgering me about. We're a bit late to the retirement game, but if we work another fifteen years or so, God willing, we'll be all right. Don't want our cares to land on you."

"I'm proud of you, Daddy," Gemma said. "Dreams come in all shapes and sizes. So does success. As far as I'm concerned, you and Mama are rich and successful. You love well and you're well loved."

"Let's hope the Good Lord sees it your way on my judgment day."

They chatted a bit more, filled the puppies' water container, and secured them for the night.

"I'll get rid of everyone in the house, Gemma. It's a bit much, I know." Daddy bent to pet the dogs sleeping in the center aisle and checked their water supply. "I'll make sure they're otherwise engaged the rest of the week."

Daddy always could read her like a book. She'd honed some of her acting skills lying to him about where she'd been and what she'd been up to. But the older she got the more she realized she'd not fooled him one bit.

"I met JoJo last week for pie," Gemma said. "Why don't we meet Mondays, get the old tradition going again? Tina's cherry pie will make all this land business go away."

"Like the old days? Why not?" Daddy wrapped his arm around her as they headed out of the barn. She limped a little too much. Still stiff from sitting cross-legged. "You ever going to tell me what happened out there in Vegas? Why you came home limping?"

"I told you. I was on set with Zac Efron, filming an action movie. We were supposed to make out, because we were in love, and jump out of an airplane at the same time. That's what hot undercover spies do. So there we were, kissing like passionate lovers, when the director cues us to jump. Out we go, lip-locked, and falling five thousand feet a second. Boy, was it windy up there. Finally, Zac pulled his rip cord but mine didn't work. I'm dropping like a boulder, thinking I'd better start talking to Jesus, when all of a sudden, Zac comes at me like a bullet—"

"Hold up, hold up," Daddy said. "Who is this Zac fella? When I asked about your hip before, you said you were filming a cowboy movie with Matthew McConaughey."

"Oh right. McConaughey. I did hurt my hip with him. The first injury. Zac was the second and the worst."

"What are the names of these movies again? I'd like to see them."

"Sadly, my part ended up on the cutting room floor."

"So exactly who is Zac kissing as he's falling five thousand feet a second?"

"The wind, Daddy. He was kissing the wind."

CHAPTER
EIGHTEEN

JOHN

August moved quickly toward Holland's memorial date. The bronze wreath was ready as were the guest list, musicians, and reception. He had a sense once that date passed, he'd turn a corner.

Briley's groom reported on the gelding's health. His leg was not improving but it wasn't worsening either. At one point he feared laminitis, but the digital pulse tests were negative.

John was grateful. The last thing he wanted on the anniversary of his wife's death was the loss of her horse.

Head down, focused on his work as well as the queen's, he read parliament briefings, staff briefings, and a summary from the Supreme Court cases since the monarch was the embodiment of the land's constitution.

The Midlands case had taken a dark turn with the Justice Ministry's Solicitor General citing a parliament member involvement.

John suspected MP Hamish Fickle. No wonder the man ran about the capital city trying to win a popularity contest, getting the people on his side. But no names were listed as of yet.

They're onto you, little Hamish Fickle with the big boasting.

He'd just moved from the queen's boxes to his own in-box when a new email dropped in from Taylor Gillingham. Right, the photographer from Hearts Bend.

"Your photos. I hope you like them. Click the link to download from my secure folder." Wasn't this a lovely treat?

The first image popped on his screen and transported John back to Hearts Bend, to the memories of Gemma, the herd, and how free he was from grief and life as a royal.

He'd not messaged Gemma in a while. He wanted to, but each time he typed her name into his phone, he quickly closed the app. What chance did their relationship have being so far apart? She clearly stated her home was in Hearts Bend. She planned to never leave. But he missed his friend.

He missed how she made him believe in love again. Just holding Gemma's hand sent his heart to the moon. Then, in one line, he came back to earth. *"I still love you..."*

As long as Holland's emotional confession echoed through him, how could he ever truly move on?

One by one, he opened and studied the photos. Taylor had a good eye and she'd captured him well. More than his image, but his heart. His favorite was one where he faced the lens, hands in his pockets, the wind bending the green branches around him, his expression like the days before death. He'd selected that one as a gift for his parents.

"Briggs, can you have this printed and framed? At least eight by ten. -PJ"

Gemma had been beside Taylor, smiling, observing, offering suggestions when the picture was taken. If he were honest, John was trying to look extra confident and dashing, hoping to impress her a little.

He moved on to the images of him with Gemma which knocked him back. Beyond her beauty, he saw the woman she must have been before her shadows. Easy-going, confident, and happy. A sense of connection electrified him.

He laughed at the images where Taylor photoshopped him into a tuxedo. Then he sobered. A thread of longing pulled through him. He wanted to be that man. The one standing beside Gemma, pledging his—

He rocketed from his chair. *No. Impossible. Stop this train of thinking.* He could not. Would not. Of course he liked her. Very much. She'd become a good friend. But love?

"You look rather serious." Gus walked into the office, bold as he pleased. "Hamish Fickle up to no good? Something in the queen's boxes?"

"Um, no, nothing." John stretched to minimize the pictures of him with Gemma, feeling a bit caught and exposed. Gus could read him better than anyone. "What brings you here?"

Gus sat, patting his belly. "Food. Daffy's at a luncheon. I wondered if you'd join me at Clemency Pub for a bite. We've not been in a while. I don't want them to think we're snubbing them."

"I'd love to but I can't. I've a mountain of work."

"Dinner then? Come to us. We've barely seen you since you arrived home." Gus reclined in the chair, stretching his long legs under the desk. "Have you had any response from the state dinner? You were a hit."

"They'd still prefer the queen." The sense of destiny infused in him from the scepter had waned during the week.

"The future king is a suitable substitute. Why do you knock yourself?"

"Is that what I'm doing?" John returned to his chair, his composure under control. "I'm merely stating fact. The queen is the preferred monarch."

"Doesn't change much," Gus said. "You're still the heir."

"But not officially. Not until the oath."

"Mum will change the writ. You won't have to be married. Public sympathy is growing for it."

"Public sympathy is growing for Hamish Fickle and his idea of no monarchy."

Gus laughed. "He's barely got a leg to stand on. He appeals to those who want change for change's sake. Most of them can't decide a uni track. The others are the old guard who'd oust the Blues in a thrice only to place the crown on their own heads."

"If Mum changes the writ, I'll take my oath."

Gus was silent for a moment. "Are you concerned for her health? I've never seen her like this. Weak, in pain, absent from her duties."

"The doctors will sort it out. She's Queen Catherine of Lauchtenland. The warrior blood of the House of Blue is in her veins. She'll come right in no time."

"I wonder if the blood is diluted after a millennium."

"Never!" John pounded the desk with his fist more in jest than anything, but the motion and sound rumbled through him and he almost heard the roar of King Titus I through the centuries.

Mum had to change the writ. Wife or no wife, he would be the next king. Titus didn't expect a king to have a bride. Neither did the Reins or any Louis's. Well, except the one King Louis who wanted his playboy crown prince to settle down.

Lost in his own world, John missed when Gus segued the conversation to Gemma.

"—the girl in the social media posts? You seemed comfortable with her."

"Gemma?" He remembered the photos. Should he share with Gus? "She's a friend. Nothing more."

"Good. Cause I'm not sure she'd be suitable for your queen."

"Why not? You don't even know her."

"Neither do you." Gus leaned forward, a look on his face John didn't recognize. "What do you know about her? Other than she's an American, which I don't trust."

"Please, Coral left you at the altar for a very good reason. You are both better off."

"Still, let's avoid foreign princesses, all right?"

"Yes, I know. What are you inferring?"

"Nothing. I'm inferring nothing." Gus stood.

"Gus, if you know something about Gemma, tell me."

"I don't. Honest."

The brothers engaged in a visual standoff until John said, "Who investigated her?"

"The same people who investigate all our friends and acquaintances."

"And?"

"And she was an actress. Not very successful. A few commercials. Sitcom spots. A small part in a movie."

"Does that make her unworthy of me because her career didn't land?"

"Certainly not. Just wanted you to be aware. There's a mysterious gap in her resume. She left L.A. for Las Vegas, then nothing until she returned to Hearts Bend."

"I think that's her own private affair."

"Very good. I'm going to lunch. Dinner then?" Gus backed toward the door. "Our place. Seven o'clock."

When little brother had gone, John fired off a message to the head of security.

"Send me all the data on Ms. Gemma Stone."

Dexter, the royal corridor footman, carried in a luncheon tray. Sandwiches and crisps along with bottled water.

John thanked him and retrieved a sandwich and bag of chips, as the Americans said.

Instead of sitting and reading as he'd been doing, he went to the window and scanned the palace grounds where the man in the anorak had appeared, gazing up from under the elm.

Who was he? What was he doing on the grounds? He should inquire of security.

Looking southwest, the late summer sun flooded Port Fressa like a golden river, warming the streets, the grounds, the structures, and every soul in preparation for Lauchtenland's long, grayish winter.

Farther west was the Heart of God—the six cathedrals built hundreds of years apart but which somehow formed a heart. When all their steeple lights were on, the heart could be seen from space.

The Heart of God...a man-made phenomenon. Or was it?

Up in the old hamlet of Dalholm, a grassy ledge had been carved out in the sheer rock cliffs above the North Sea channel. The sailors who hid there during a storm called it the Hand of God.

How they scaled the rock as the seas crashed around them remained a mystery. Or as the Northtons said, a miracle.

As a boy fascinated with a fairy tale, John had dreamed of his first kiss being beneath the Heart of God lights. But the moment had been stolen during a late-night summer party at the end of his first year in A-levels. Charlene Backus. He couldn't remember who kissed whom first, but at sixteen, the Heart of God was far from his mind.

Then with Holland, he decided to take her there on their first date. But she'd kissed him first, just as they'd finished dinner. She'd scooted to his side of the booth and dropped one leg over his and slipped her arms around his neck. By that time, all their engines were revving and it was impossible to stop and ask, "Care to trot over to the Heart of God first?"

"Sorry to disturb you, Your Royal Highness." Briggs stood just inside the office. "Two people are here from the Solicitor General's office. An Inspector Meade and Inspector Tolsma."

"Don't look so distressed, Briggs. Whatever you've done, I'll put in a good word for you."

He didn't smile. Not even a little. "They've asked to see you, sir."

John held his composure. He'd learned from the queen to never look rattled or surprised in front of the staff.

"Send them in. And thank you."

A man, Inspector Meade, and woman, Inspector Tolsma, dressed in business attire entered with solemn expressions. He bowed and she curtsied.

"Sorry to bother you, Your Royal Highness."

"Please, come in. How can I help?" John encouraged them to sit, but they remained standing.

"We are here on behalf of the Justice Ministry's Solicitor General's investigation into the Midlands case."

"Yes, I just read a briefing this morning. I've been following along. Is it true a member of parliament might be involved? Hamish Fickle is my guess. Corruption, malfeasance, and insider trading."

"Yes, sir." They glanced at one another. "Not MP Fickle, Your Royal Highness. But your father-in-law, Lord Cunningham."

"Cletus Cunningham involved in something illegal?" John walked toward the luncheon trolley for another sandwich half.

"He was the Solicitor General before he joined the House of Lords. He fights for justice under the law every chance he gets." He gestured to the tray. "Do you care for anything? Help yourselves."

"Yes, sir, we're aware of Lord Cunningham's resume. But he was named when the investigation began, and we've uncovered quite a lot of evidence."

"What sort of evidence? How can I help?"

"There was a gift given to his daughter," Inspector Meade said, slow, tentative.

But Tolsma went straight to it. "We believe Princess Holland was part of the conspiracy."

"The princess? Involved in a crime?" John scoffed. "I don't believe so. No."

"Did you ever see her wear a large diamond necklace, sir? About twenty carats? We've confirmed through multiple sources, even video evidence, that Luca Reingard—"

"The founder of Reingard Industries?"

"—gave the princess the necklace."

"Whatever for?" Reingard was one of those brash, bold, good-looking, thirty-something chaps with a steel jaw and a steely gaze. An entrepreneur with the Midas touch, he'd turned his father's small weaving business into an international textile company. *EuroFinancial* dubbed him "The Face of Tomorrow's Billionaire."

"According to testimony," Meade said, consulting notes on his phone, "she met Reingard in Brighton Kingdom at a marketing conference two years ago." Two years ago? They'd been dating. "He wanted to meet her father, who chaired parliament's Economic Development Committee. He stepped down six months after their initial meeting. Reingard wanted the Midlands land Eloise Ltd. was about to purchase. They planned to build a major plant and warehouse and expand Reingard Industries into Europe, Asia, even America, from our soil. They were also about to announce their IPO."

"And Holland knew all of this?"

"We're not sure what she knew." Tolsma stepped toward him. "Or you."

"Me? I knew nothing. She told me the necklace was a gift from her father."

"We've video evidence of the princess with Reingard." Tolsma offered her phone and John tapped the Play button.

Holland and Reingard stood in a large conference ballroom, chatting. The next frame showed them at dinner, the necklace resting below Holland's neck.

"We wondered if you had the diamond here."

"I know this diamond," John said, low, rattled, passing back Tolsma's phone. "But I don't know where it is. I only saw it once."

"Lord Cunningham claims he doesn't have it either," Meade said. "We've searched his home and office."

"What about his country estate?" John wanted to sit, to think, but he remained stalwart and on his feet.

"We're working on a warrant," Tolsma said. "Sir, do you mind if we look around your apartment?"

"You think it's here?" John said. "My in-laws came for Holland's things—clothes, shoes, bags, books, jewelry—two weeks after her funeral. I argued I wasn't ready but they insisted. Said it would help me heal and move on."

"Can we do our own inspection, sir?" Tolsma was all business. "It's desired evidence in a high crime and misdemeanor case."

"High crime and misdemeanor?" Which meant the Solicitor General aimed for impeachment of a sitting member of the House of Lords. What a weighty allegation and lofty goal.

The last Lauchtenland impeachment happened in the sixteenth century. "Is the crown being implicated in any way? Am I being implicated?"

"No, sir. Neither you nor the queen, but according to testimony, Princess Holland understood the diamond was a thank you for her part in the plan. She also bought shares under her maiden name in Reingard before the company went public."

She'd never said a word. Not. One. Word.

Once again, Tolsma asked to search his place. More specifically, where Holland dwelled. John escorted them from his office, down the hall to 2A in a swirl of heart-pounding confusion, striving to understand. Holland had always been open and honest. She wrote down her goals and values, and every few months reviewed them to see how she was doing. She asked John and other family members to give input.

But this bit of news she hid? It made no sense.

"This was her dressing room." John opened the double doors and stood aside. "Everything she wore was kept in here. Clothes, shoes, handbags, jewelry."

The inspectors combed through drawers and empty boxes, under things, over things, in the bathroom, and even through John's dressing room and bureau.

The only things Holland's parents left behind were her hairstyling wands, a set of trackie bottoms, and one pair of mud-stained trainers.

They were about to conclude their business when Tolsma retrieved a burgundy crushed-velvet box tossed to the back corner of a top shelf.

"Do you recognize this, sir? Did she keep the diamond in here?"

John rose slowly from the chair where he'd collapsed, shaking with anger, with loss, the sour taste in his throat sinking into his skin, his veins. "Like I said, I only saw her wear it once."

She wore it on a night he treasured. A memory of memories. They'd just returned from their honeymoon, blissfully in love. Tanned, happy, rested, hungry for each other. There were moments he thought his heart might burst for want of her. He missed her when she was out of sight. They called and texted all day if they were on separate missions.

But he first saw the diamond the night they attended LAFFA—Lauchtenland Actors and Film Foundation Awards.

Holland dressed behind closed doors, insisting she wanted to surprise him with her new gown. When she stepped from her dressing room, she stunned him in a midnight blue frock with a plunging neckline and a blinding jewel resting against her tanned skin.

"You'll be the most beautiful woman there." Then he touched the diamond pendant. *"Darling, where did you get this? Should I be jealous?"*

"Yes, it's from my other lover but I told him, 'This is the last one or John will be cross.'"

He laughed and wrapped her against his chest and kissed her lips down to her neck and shoulders, and to the spot where the diamond rested in the deep V between her breasts.

"John is something, but he's not cross."

"Darling." *She sighed with passion.* *"We have to go."* *Breaking away after a lingering kiss, she promised to meet him at this same spot after the gala.*

It'd been a passionate, frantic reunion and the necklace was the only thing she wore as they satisfied their desire for one another.

"So where—" *John held the diamond in his hand as she rested her head on his chest.*

"A gift from Father. I'm his only child and he wanted to send me off to wedded bliss with something special."

"Sir?" Meade touched his arm. "We're satisfied the diamond is not here." Meade then Tolsma handed John their cards. "Ring us, please, if you find out anything."

He never returned to his office. He poured a glass of port and sat in the living room until the only light in the room ricocheted from the palace grounds.

His wife, the woman who carried his child, the one he trusted with his life, his future, had harbored a lie. Worse, facilitated an illegal business venture.

As for her relationship with Luca Reingard, were they more than business acquaintances? Luca had a reputation as the billionaire playboy. Did she have an affair with him? If so, when? Surely not after they'd met and married?

His phone buzzed with messages but unless Port Fressa was being bombed, he didn't care. What couldn't wait until tomorrow?

If Mum was in trouble, Dad would knock on his door. He'd missed dinner with Gus but he'd text something had come up and ask for a raincheck.

The ancient clock on the mantel tick-tocked the hours. John dozed in his chair then awoke with a stiff neck, his glass on the floor.

His butler, Shaw, roused him for a late supper, but he wasn't hungry. Nevertheless, the man left a tray and turned on the telly to a favorite show.

The scent of grilled meat stirred his appetite after a moment, but he could only consume a few bites. He was too full of sorrow and confusion. If Holland were alive, what would she say? How would she make her case?

Reaching for his phone, John rang his father-in-law. The call went to voicemail.

"Cletus, it's John. Can you ring me when you've a moment? I'd like to talk to you about something. Thank you."

Gus texted around nine.

"Everything all right?"

"No. Chat tomorrow?"

"Chat now?"

"Tomorrow."

Finally he stripped for bed and stretched out on top of the cool sheets. But sleep evaded him. Rolling on his side, he pressed his face into his pillow, realizing he missed the scent of hay beneath his head and the lullaby sounds of squeaky puppies.

He missed Gemma.

At 4:00 a.m., when he'd rolled over for the thousandth time, he grabbed his phone.

"You awake?"

"What are you doing awake? It's only 10:00 p.m. here."

"Can't sleep."

"What's up?"

"I miss the barn."

"My palace for yours?"

"Deal."

"How's the queen?"

"Good. To be honest, struggling, but the doctors are hopeful. Please don't speak of it to anyone. I shouldn't have told you, put you under that pressure."

"Prince, trust me, I'm a vault. I'm sorry she's not doing well."

"Not sure exactly what's going on. Maybe autoimmune disorder."

"I'm so sorry."

"How's the herd? Are you looking after my Chandler? I'm coming for him, I promise."

"He's getting fat. Last night Ross challenged him in a wrestling match and Chandler almost won."

"That's my boy!!!!!"

"By the way, I think Blue and Tweedy are engaged."

"At last!"

"Want me to sing you a lullaby so you can go back to sleep? Do you have a full day tomorrow?"

"Meetings. But other things are going on."

"Wanna talk?"

"I wish you were here, Gemma, so I could tell you face to face."

"I wish I could talk to you face to face. Some stuff has happened here too."

"Like what? Shall I ring?"

"Easier to text. I might cry if I say it out loud. Basically, shew, here goes. I lost the property. Apparently if a deal is too good to be true, it is TOO GOOD TO BE TRUE. I was swindled, Prince. The property did not belong to the crooked people who sold it to me. I'm out $150k with no more money and no place to live."

"What? You're having me on... You're serious?"

"My stupidity has reached legendary status. I'm sick over it. I've not told Imani yet. I'm working on a plan so I can tell her the good news then the bad. Meanwhile folks have been coming to the house every night like some sort of wake, but they clean and cook. We've eaten well. But tonight we asked them to make it their last."

"Where will you go? What will you do?"

"Probably bunk in with Mac and Mauve, then try to find a place to rent. The herd will be moved to other homes and rescue farms. Blah, just typing it out makes me sad, furious, and humiliated. Dash, my high school bf who's now a lawyer, told me to do a title search, but the dev. company had the deed. What more did I need? Prince, this is par for the course. The last twelve years have been nothing but a series of bad Gemma Stone moves."

"Stop, you're being too hard on yourself. Anyone could've fallen for such a deal."

"Yeah, but they saw me coming, didn't they? Big L on my forehead."

"What sort of stupid things are we talking here, Gemma? Besides a land swindle?"

"You should get to sleep, Prince. How about that lullaby?"

He hesitated. Did he swap disaster stories with her?

"Two inspectors came by this afternoon. My father-in-law is under investigation."

"Goodness! Why?"

"Corruption, malfeasance, insider trading, and because of his position, high crimes and misdemeanors."

"High crimes? Sounds like a novel. What did he do? Did you suspect at all?"

"Insider trading stuff. Even worse, Holland was in on it. Bought stocks before the IPO and received a 20 carat diamond necklace as part of the 'deal.' Long story. See, I need face to face."

"Prince, way to bury the lead. Holland was involved?!"

Gemma sent a string of emojis which made him laugh despite himself.

"Thanks for listening."

"Are you okay?"

"No, but I will be. How can you give your heart and soul to someone to find out she's not what she seemed?"

"John, I know you're disappointed but she's not around to defend herself."

"She lied to me about the necklace. Said it was a gift from her father."

"Maybe it was."

"It wasn't."

"Fine but you cannot question her love for you."

"Can't I? Now I wonder if she only married me for my title and position."

"You don't believe that... I know you don't."

"Only because I don't want to, Gemma. I'm putting a permanent wreath on her gravesite this month. She will forever be a part of House of Blue history and now to think she used her position and her father's for financial gain?? She lied and cheated. Not just about how much money she spent shopping or on a pair of shoes. But about corruption. If she did it once, who's to say she'd not do it again? The worst part is the Cunninghams are wealthy. Why cheat and lie for more?"

"Because when money's involved there is no truth. Only money. Money equals power. You don't want to buy a bigger house or vacation chalet, you want to buy position, authority, favor. And I can't believe she's the first Blue to lie and cheat."

He laughed softly and sent an angry emoji.

"You know I didn't text you to make sense. You're supposed to commiserate with me."

"Then commiserate with me. How am I going to start over? I got nothing."

For the next hour they texted until she claimed she had to go to sleep or be a zombie at work all day.

"We miss you around here."

"Thanks for listening, Gemma. I mean it. I miss being there."

He fell asleep thinking of her as early morning light peeked around his window shades, his phone cradled against his chest. He'd just started to dream when someone rudely roused him awake.

"John, get up." Dad snapped on the end table lamp. "We're going to the hospital."

CHAPTER NINETEEN

GEMMA

Thursday morning The Wedding Shop storeroom was hot and airless. Gemma stepped from the long, narrow room into the circulating air of the mezzanine. The shipment from Elnora Brides nearly did her in—from wedding gowns to fascinators—but the shop was replenished with the latest in bridal fashion.

Since John's late-night texts last Friday night, their exchange lingered in her thoughts. She missed him. Felt for him over the mess with Holland. But why did he tell her? Why not talk to his friends and family?

She loved being chosen to hear his story. The whole thing continued the odd connection between them. But where could it lead? Nowhere.

Gemma brushed a bit of perspiration from her brow and paused by one of the gowns she'd just hung on the rack. Despite being wrapped in plastic, the milk-white gown was beautiful. It called to her. *Try me on.*

She resented the desire to dress in white and walk down a church aisle. Frankly, she blamed Taylor. She had no desire to marry until Taylor dressed her in a dozen wedding gowns, took a thousand pictures then sent them to her.

"The magazine loved them. They loved you too. I got props for choosing a great model. I owe you one."

You bet you do. Last night when Gemma opened the first set and saw herself as a bride, she welled up. Next came the pictures with John and she practically melted in her chair. She was wanting what she could not have.

Sure, despite all the internal pep talks about how her past didn't define her, shame still owned her. The more time passed, the more shame stretched out its long legs and possessed more not less. The emotion grew fat and happy, fed off her memories and mistakes. Time, the losing beast, was no friend. Didn't heal anything.

While she knew she'd never sink as low as she did in Vegas— oh, please no—she knew she'd have to confess her limps to some future husband. If she ever fell in love at all. Maybe she'd be fifty or sixty with arthritis and could blame her limp on old age.

Because if she ever told her man the truth, her shame would become his. He'd never see her the same. He'd never respect her.

"You did what *for money and fame?"*

Exactly what John said about Holland. Why did she facilitate corruption when her family already had money, power, and position? She misrepresented herself to John and now he was reeling from it. Any man who loved Gemma would face the same dilemma. Love her as he knew her before her story? Love her after?

If she didn't tell and he found out, his trust would be destroyed. Well, that's how she saw it anyway. Because she didn't trust herself.

Even worse than her time in Vegas? Her ability to make good decisions. She was batting zero here.

Matt Biglow? Rotten. The reality show? Abysmal. The farm? Swindled. A half dozen roommates she'd barely survived? Well, for that she was grateful.

Her mission in life was to find a new place for herself and Imani and great homes for the herd. Anything above and beyond was gravy.

At night she searched for rental property where she could transport the whole herd, but they were too expensive or too far away. One property looked promising, but the house was practically falling down and there was no barn.

So she gave in last night and told Daddy they were moving in. Yesterday he sent pictures of Mama's yoga/junk room being reclaimed as a bedroom.

"You'll be moved in and making dinner one night before Mama realizes it's gone. What's Imani's favorite color? I'm going to paint her room."

"Rock Mill High colors. Thanks, Daddy."

None of his get rich quick schemes ever panned out, but Daddy was the richest man she knew.

For now, she had to get out of the hot storeroom. Finishing with the Elnora shipment, Gemma collected shipping boxes, papers, and Bubble Wrap, kicking what she couldn't carry out to the mezzanine.

"Hello." A smallish woman with a piquant face stood by the stairs.

"Can I help you?" Gemma regarded her for a moment. She was pretty with a cloud of white, Brillo pad hair and fiery eyes. "Grandmother dresses are in the small salon." She carried the trash to the chute down to the outside dumpster. A Haley Danner invention. Wait. How'd this woman… The shop wasn't open yet. "Excuse me but how did you get in?"

Gemma peered down into the shop. The lights were off, window shades drawn, and the music wasn't playing.

"Did I leave the back door unlocked?" She reached for the woman, ready to usher her down the stairs and out the back door.

"I didn't come in the back door."

"Then how did you come in? Know what? Never mind. You need to go." Gemma reached for the elderly woman, but the spry thing seemed to walk through her hand.

"Don't be so hasty. I came to help you."

"Help me?" Gemma gave her the once over. Dressed entirely in white, she wore a simple, drop waist dress, stockings, and low-heeled slip-ons. She carried no handbag, phone, or set of keys. "I'm still curious how you got in here. Did Haley send you? As you can see, I've already dealt with our latest shipment."

Gemma bent for the packing papers and boxes she'd kicked

from the storeroom and shoved them down the chute. Why would Haley send her help? Especially a very tiny, frail-looking woman.

"I'm sorry I'm late, but I was busy on another assignment. Now, shall we get going with you?" With a smile on her bow lips, the old woman spryly walked to the storeroom. "It's in here, I think."

"Excuse me." Gemma pushed the door closed. "You can't go in there. This is private property. You need to leave." Her bold declaration was governed by a sense of foreboding. The show-runner for the Vegas reality show was a well-connected producer who looked and sounded like Aunt Bea from Mayberry. But she was a witch. Mean, controlling, and selfish.

"I see you're not going to make this easy. Now where is it? That sweet dress." While Gemma still leaned against the door, this little bit of a woman grabbed the knob and pulled it open.

How in the world—

"Look, Mrs. Whoever You Are, I don't mean to be rude but you must leave." In Vegas, Gemma had never learned to stand up to bullies with white fluffy hair, but today was a new day. She wasn't trapped in the dream Matt pitched about how this show "is going to rock your world. Make you a star."

Little did she know, rocking her world meant losing a piece of herself every week.

This teeny tiny buttinsky had to go.

"Where is *that* gown? Haley and JoJo's?" Hand tapping her chin, the woman scanned the dresses and all the labeled boxes.

Haley's intake of vintage gowns exceeded the space on the floor so she preserved the ones she didn't need immediately. The gown she and JoJo wore was very vintage, very special, and according to legend, almost a living, breathing thing.

"Please, don't make me call the sheriff's deputy." Gemma took the woman's arm to remove her from the room, but she didn't budge. Not so much as a wobble.

"Did I forget to introduce myself? That's been happening more and more." She offered her small, weathered hand. "I'm Adelaide."

Gemma glared down at her, arms folded. *And?*

"Yes, well." Adelaide withdrew her hand. "I'm here to help you."

"I don't need help."

"Well you see, that's the trick of it. You do. Ah, there it is." Adelaide pointed to a box on the top shelf. "Can you pull it down?"

"For what reason?" Gemma tried again to eject Adelaide from the storeroom, but she twisted free. "I'm still trying to figure out who you are and what you're doing here."

"They told me you'd be difficult but not this much."

"They?" She hated to admit it, but Adelaide's brand of crazy was entertaining. Also, very fragrant. A heady, spicy scent had begun to radiate from her. And for a moment, Gemma thought the old woman's skin sparkled. "Listen, I promise I won't hurt you, but have you escaped your family, or some hospital?"

"Goodness no. I'm completely sound." Adelaide fluffed her white, floating hair. "I guess I might as well say it, being how I'm late and don't have time to nuance things as I usually do. I can see you're a skeptic." Oh, Gemma was a skeptic all right. "Sweetheart, I'm your angel."

"My angel?" Gemma laughed. "Where were you two years ago when I needed you most?" She patted her hip. "When I got this? Is this—Oh wait, I know, Tommy sent you, didn't he?"

When she first moved to Tinseltown, she ran with a group of improv comedians. While she'd not seen any of them in years, this angel bit reeked of their inspiration. Especially Tommy.

He loved social media. Followed everyone from a six-year-old drummer phenom to royal families.

She'd been a bit of an ostrich about social media, but she knew about the viral post from the 4th of July, and the ones of her handing out popcorn with the prince. She'd been more concerned about Matt Biglow trying to seize an opportunity with her being on social media than Improv Tommy.

"What kind of angel are you?" Gemma said. "Guardian? Warrior? Watcher? Bumbling?"

"Bumbling? That's only in the movies." Adelaide pulled the stepladder around and took down the box she wanted. "I'm the angel of princesses."

"Okay, yeah, Tommy sent you, didn't he? This is *so* him. Angel of princesses. There's no such thing."

This whole scene was definitely a comedy bit. But still, how'd she get in? Did Tommy get Haley and JoJo in on it? Or hire an "angel" who also picked locks?

"Oh for heaven's sake, girl. The Lord sent me. He hinted I'd have to spell things out, but I believed you'd be a bit sharper."

"The lord? Is that what Tommy calls himself now? Lord?"

"Forget this Tommy chap. I'm talking the real Lord." Adelaide handed Gemma the wedding dress box—which consumed most of her tiny frame. "Some folks need revelation like a ton of bricks. Now, are you going to cooperate, or do I have to haunt you?"

"Haunt me? I thought only ghosts haunted people."

Adelaide looked toward the ceiling. "Can I request a new assignment? Princess duty is exhausting."

"Princess duty? That's all you got? Tommy is slacking." Gemma shoved the box back on its shelf. "Tell him it didn't work. I'm not falling for it. Sure, I met Prince John, and maybe we kissed—" Just saying the words made her shiver. "But we're friends. Nothing more. You tell Tommy—"

She was talking to herself. The storeroom was empty. "Adelaide?" Gemma exited the storeroom to the mezzanine. "Hello? What kind of angel deserts a girl when she's trying to understand?" Figures she'd have *that* kind of angel. "Adelaide?"

The mezzanine was flooded with a golden glow and the fragrance of a luscious, spicy oil. Gemma ran downstairs, checking the doors, even the windows. Locked. All of them. The shades were drawn and the Closed sign faced the street.

"Adelaide?"

Gemma didn't tell Haley and JoJo about her encounter with Adelaide, the so-called angel, if she was to be believed, who prepared princesses. Or the text with John.

"You've been quiet today, Gemstone." Haley set a cup of coffee on the office desk then sat in the nearest chair with a cup of her own. "Want to talk about it?"

Gemma finished what she was doing with the bank account then took a swallow of coffee. She didn't want to talk about Adelaide because the more she thought about it, the more she knew Tommy had pranked her. Even the swirling golden light could've been him. He moonlighted as a magician now and then. He had tricks. The fragrance was a bit of a mystery, but she'd not put it past him.

If it wasn't Tommy, then Adelaide was real. And Gemma was not ready to take that leap.

"Just this business with the farm. Can't sleep at night."

"Cole and I've been talking about it, wondering how we could help. He just finished a remodel on a house we bought to flip. We were going to offer it to you for rent or to buy at cost but Keith Niven had it to list and he sold it before it went officially on the market. You couldn't have brought the whole herd, but there was enough land for the dogs."

Gemma's tears came from gratitude. How humbling to have friends who discussed her life with a view of helping. Her experience in L.A. and Vegas with Matt hardened her. Told her everyone was out for themselves. *Get your own. No one will do it for you.*

"I appreciate you guys so much. You've been more than good to me. But Daddy's cleaning out two rooms for us. I'll figure something out." She forced a big smile and saluted Haley with her coffee.

"You'd tell us if you needed help. JoJo and Buck, Cole and I will do anything we can to—"

"I know and I appreciate it more than you know."

"What about the prince?"

"What about him?" Gemma turned back to the computer to check the shop email. "He's home. I'm home. Never the two shall meet."

"Really? You don't think—"

"No, I don't," Gemma said softly. "And if you're honest, you don't either."

Talking about him made her miss him. Since the strange mezzanine encounter with the real or fake angel—the princess preparer—she'd been thinking of John off and on all day.

Could she ever be a real princess? No. No! Certainly not.

The conversation flowed to the shop schedule. Haley asked for an early morning meeting with Gemma and JoJo to discuss fall marketing and Christmas season plans.

"Next Tuesday? I'll bring breakfast from Havens." Haley pulled out her phone to text JoJo.

"Haley, I know I'm not really a partner in the shop, so you don't have to include me."

"That's just it, Gemma. We think you'd be a great partner with us. I want more children. JoJo wants to get started on babies. Goodness knows she doesn't need shop money. We both want to help you."

A future. Haley spoke of something Gemma feared to envision. Her future.

Around four, Imani texted she *loved* school and was going with the gang to the Fry Hut, then to shoot hoops at the gym.

> "I love being a junior. Oh, and trig is actually fun. Ms. Parrish says I'm a natural with numbers. Maybe calc next year. Also, I'm running for student council. Yikes! I need to make a video tonight. Can you help me?"

> "Of course I can help you. BTW, your mom was brilliant at math too. Have fun with 'the gang.' Home by nine if you don't have homework. By eight if you do."

> "Done. Study hall."

Gemma set down her phone and stared toward the window. The shop office was her home away from home, her retreat when the world closed in.

"God, what do I do now?" The short prayer came from a deep place. She'd not talked much to God in the last decade, but maybe it was time to humble up and give Him a chance.

Gemma had yet to tell Imani they were moving. Though she was surprised Mama hadn't spilled the beans. Or one of Imani's friends, since Mama went around town asking folks to pray for Gemma. But so far, she seemed blissfully ignorant. Gemma envied her.

Meanwhile, she pressed forward with the adoption, gathering information, calculating the fees. She planned to tell her about the adoption when she told her about the move.

They'd go for pie at Ella's after dinner. When they were full of sweet cherries surrounded by a flaky crust, Gemma would drop the good news. Then the bad.

In the middle of the afternoon, Taylor texted she needed Gemma for another shoot. This time in Nashville.

"Big society wedding. Photographer dropped out. I got the call. This will be a big one. Care to help? December tenth."

"Okay, but if the bride doesn't show up, I'm not substituting."

"Spoil sport. Also, I'm doing some shots around town for an HB tourist campaign. Can you get free Saturday? It'll be a long day but the pay is good."

"Send the details. I'm in."

A few photos around Hearts Bend for the southeast wouldn't alert Matt any more than he was already. Or that shrew of a show-runner.

At home, Gemma fed the puppies, who ran and played in their expanded pen. Coming up on seven weeks old, the time had come to find them homes.

Haley was sending over a couple with their kids who were eager to get a puppy. Doc Goodwin phoned Gemma to say his granddaughter just bought a house and wanted a dog.

She agreed to those visits but she'd be inspecting the humans every bit as much as they inspected the pups. If she thought about the puppies leaving too long, she cringed and got all weepy inside.

After feeding the house dogs, she went to the barn. Hercules met her at the treat table and munched on his carrots as she brushed his coat. He rested his muzzle on her head as if to say thanks.

"How can I let you go, Herc?" A piece of her already broken heart cracked a little. "Do you think we can convince Mama you're a really big dog?"

He snorted, tossing his head. Silver came around for her treats and a good brushing. Last but not least Whinny, who seemed to understand the prince was no longer with them. She clip-clopped down the center aisle and searched for him in the stalls and across the yard.

"You should've made friends with him while you had the chance."

Whinny tossed her head in protest. *"You're not the boss of me."* Nevertheless, she came for her treats and brushing and, as always, dashed out to the field when Gemma finished, like she'd had a good day at the salon.

Hercules followed Whinny with a glance back at Gemma, grinning—yeah, he grinned—and trotted after the chestnut beauty. Silver checked on the puppies then tucked away in her stall for a nap.

How could this beautiful world that bloomed from the ashes of her old life be ending? How would the herd ever understand she didn't mean to betray them? Betrayal was a sensation she knew well, and it was bitter.

Gemma had just finished with the goats when a dark Range Rover eased down the driveway. The driver parked next to the BMW, and Scottie O'Shay stepped out.

Dressed in an O'Shay's shirt and dark slacks, her short hair styled in a way that accented the shape of her face, she looked like a young Queen Catherine.

When Gemma met her halfway, she spoke without preamble.

"The queen," Scottie said, her expression tight and drawn, "is not well. I don't know, John almost sounded as if…" Tears rose in her eyes. "I'm going to Lauchtenland and I wondered if you would go with me. I don't have any right to ask, we barely know one another, but I—I can't go alone. Not on this trip. Not to meet my mother. Dad has had a big meeting scheduled in Miami for six months. Besides, I think this whole reveal has thrown him for a loop as much as me. I thought we'd go back to the way we were before, but now I realize we can't. I can't. I know who my mother is and there's no forgetting." The commanding princess of O'Shay's Shirts quivered and her high, pale cheeks jutted over equally pale lips. Her eyes were full of frowns. "Gemma, if she dies and I didn't meet her because of pride or fear, or stubbornness or the possibility of pain, I'll never forgive myself."

"What about Shug? Or Fritz? Don't they want to go?"

"Are you kidding? Shug was mad as a hornet I found out. 'That was never the plan,' she said. She's still ruffled about it. Fritz would go in a shot if I asked, but I can't pit him against Shug. But even if I wanted him to come…" Scottie stepped closer, her hands locked and pleading. "It has to be you, Gemma. I've thought a lot about this. John knows you. He likes you. He brought you to Dad's for dinner as a sort of bridge. Now I'm asking you to be that bridge again. Please. I know you have Ethan and Althea Shumaker's daughter. If she needs anything while you're gone, I'll cover the cost. Car? Gas? Food? She can even travel with us if—"

"She started school. She has volleyball, her schoolwork, and a job. She's a starting outside hitter and an A student. Also a starting guard for Rock Mill High basketball."

"She sounds like her parents." Scottie graduated four years ahead of Althea and Ethan, and five ahead of Gemma, but everyone in town knew of the super couple who rocked the halls of Rock Mill High. "I'd love to meet her sometime." Scottie stepped closer. "But for now, I need you to go with me. I'm asking, begging. Please, Gemma. Like I said, I'll cover any care you need for Imani."

"She can stay with my parents."

"I'll cover your wages for the days you miss. In fact, I'll pay you to come with me. Like a companion."

"You don't need to pay me."

"Then a shopping spree. The Midlands is an excellent garment district. Dad's been wanting to look at a textile company there for a line of winter shirts. But my mission now is to see my mother."

No was not an option. Even if Gemma wanted.

"If you think I can help, of course. When?" She'd need time to make arrangements for the herd, the shop, and oh, she had a job with Taylor. Then there was Chandler. She *could* take him to John. But was she ready to let him go?

"Tomorrow."

"Tomorrow? Friday? Goodness."

"I know it's short notice, but a pilot friend of mine with a Gulfstream 650 is taking a couple of businessmen to London tomorrow evening. There's room for us. From London we head to Dover for the ferry to Port Fressa. I've got my assistant working on a hotel and transportation."

"Goodness." Gemma felt a bit wobbly. And oddly excited. "Let me make a few calls but if you really want me to go, then yes, I will."

Chapter
Twenty

John

In the low, golden lamplight of the hospital room, his mother slept. The only cards and flowers on the mahogany table were from the Family. No one else knew except the prime minister.

Not Mum's secretary or her personal assistant. Her hair stylist knew, however. Ingrid had been with Mum thirty years. She was a vault.

Lying there, Mum seemed at one with the white sheets, her complexion as pale, her frame buried under blankets. The blue lights of the monitor flashed and beeped.

Ingrid came round yesterday to wash and style her hair. She left it in long waves spread across Mum's pillow. The sheen and shine appeared out of place against Mum's frail, pale complexion, but John took it as a reminder of Mum's strength and health.

Since Dad roused him from bed in the wee hours of last Saturday, Mum declined rapidly. She had trouble breathing. She was weak and had trouble with her facial movements. The doctors, which were the best in the land, possibly northern Europe, were flummoxed, doing their best with her treatments. They concluded an autoimmune syndrome was attacking her nerves and muscles. Or a rare sort of virus. Or, or, or... They were guessing in the dark.

How dare some nasty foreign entity or body malfunction bring down such a giant? John wasn't sure the queen was even allowed to be sick let alone on the verge of...of...

He shot to his feet, not letting the thought sink in. *Death.*

"There you are." Mum's whisper whirled him around. "I was dreaming…of…you."

"Shh, save your strength." He pulled his chair to her bedside and reached for her hand. It was one extremity that didn't pulse with pain.

Her palm was soft and full of memories. He rested his forehead on the top of the siderail, unwilling to burden her with his tears.

"Will you promise me something?" she said, giving his hand a light squeeze.

He wiped his eyes with the back of his hand before looking up. "Anything. I promise." His grin was slow and wobbly. "Up to half my kingdom."

Mum responded with a weak smile and his heart sang a little. "Marry. Find love. Arrange the investiture. Be my legal and *lawful* heir. And be quick about it. I'm not doing very well."

"What about the writ?" He regretted the question as it left his lips. Who cared about the writ?

Just agree with her. Then defy her subtle hint of leaving this earth before holding her new granddaughter. This syndrome or virus was a temporary setback. Some sort of evil denying Mum her finest hours.

"You're going to get through this, Mum, I promise."

"You can't make such a promise, love. Now about your investiture." *Behold, sickness, she's queening it over you.* "It can happen the same day as your wedding."

"Mum, please, there's no one to marry. I'm not going to choose a woman unless I'm madly in love. Not for the crown, the Family, or Lauchtenland. I'm not. Sorry. Make Gus the heir."

"You want to abdicate then?"

The A-word. One the House of Blue despised. "No, but you're giving me no choice."

Mum tugged his hand, so he moved in closer. He could see she was in a bit of pain and tiring out already. He released his grip on her hand and regretted his outburst.

"Choose love, son. Choose."

"Yes, I understand and I will but—"

"Choose." She breathed deep, a smile on her lips, and closed her eyes.

He sat by her bed another hour while she slept. He'd never been much of a praying man but someone, something more powerful than disease and sickness must intervene.

John rested his hand on top of the blanket. "I've no right to ask, God, or even speak to You, but for Mum, the queen, say the word and she'll be healed." Did God hear a man with no faith? Well, not much. "Please."

With a glance at his watch, he stood. Dad texted he'd be along at six, or rather, someone would be along for the evening shift.

"Mum," he said, leaning close. "Will you do me a favor?" His eyes filled as he carried on her part of the conversation for her. "'Anything, up to half my kingdom.' Get up out of this bed. Live."

He exited into the Queen's Waiting Room, a large, plush space with a telly, food service, and couches that made out into beds. He expected to see Dad waiting with the protection officers, but the room was empty except for Gunner, Otis, and Hemstead.

The officers stood, and Gunner handed John a plate of puffs.

"When does the king consort arrive?" John said. Dr. Ritter limited Mum to one visitor at a time. Daffy and Gus were staying away until a firm diagnosis.

"We're not sure."

John stepped into the corridor just as a giant of a man with electric blue eyes came through the first set of doors. He wore a wide-brimmed hat and an anorak, the heels of his worn leather boots resounding against the marble with each determined, powerful stride.

It was him. The man from the lawn. The night of the state dinner when he'd gone back for the scepter.

"I'm here for the queen," he said.

Hemstead rose without a question and let him in Mum's room.

"Wait," John said. "Who are you?"

"Don't you know?" His words were sharp and commanding, and John felt both seen and rebuked all at once. "Emmanuel."

GEMMA

"The car is here." Gemma knocked on Imani's door, listening. It was a Friday night and she half expected her to have plans, but she'd been in her room since she came home from volleyball practice. At which time she declared, "I can't wait for basketball season."

"Imani?" Gemma knocked again.

A loud bump-bang was followed by a slam. "Hey," Imani said, leaning against the doorframe, one hand on her hip, her shirt twisted at her shoulders. Seeing behind her, Gemma noticed a rumpled comforter and the old window shade slightly off-center.

"What's going on?"

"Nothing." The teen added a nod and an awkward shift from one foot to the other. "Watching volleyball videos. Coach sent some plays we're going to run. Also, talking to Penny about basketball season. I don't think I'll play volleyball next year."

Gemma leaned to see farther into the room. Imani's phone lay facedown on her bed.

"I'm going to ask point-blank," Gemma said. "Was Justin in here?"

"What? No. Gemma, give me some credit." Her tone dripped with the defensiveness of a sixteen-year-old. A sound Gemma had perfected.

"Remember we have a deal."

"I know, I know. Deal."

They stared at each other for a moment, and as much as Gemma wanted to challenge her, she remembered how it felt not to be trusted. Of course, she'd deserved not to be trusted.

"I guess this isn't a warm goodbye." Gemma drew Imani into a hug. "Sorry for my suspicions. I've got to go. Scottie's here."

Imani's eyes welled up and spilled over. "H-have fun."

"Hey, what's wrong?" Gemma drew her into a hug. "Is it school? Justin?"

"Y-you."

"Me?" Gemma pulled back to see her charge, her ward, her pseudo-daughter. "What'd I do besides remind you we have a deal?"

"You're leaving. How do I know you're coming back?"

Gemma dried her cheeks. "Because I'm telling you."

Imani dropped down on her bed. "Mama and Daddy were supposed to come back. Granny and Gramps Cook, Grandpa Shumaker weren't supposed to die. Gigi Shumaker was just going to her high school reunion. Now she lives in Florida with a fat man named Rick." Add Rick to the list of nasty four-letter words. "Uncle Roy's left for Texas 'cause he met someone on the internet. You're flying to Lauchtenland on a private jet to meet a prince. How can I compete with a prince? And what if the plane crashes?"

Gemma laughed. Not intentionally, because Imani delivered a stellar argument. More because she heard herself in the girl's reasoning. How many trips down *What-If Avenue* had she taken? Especially since losing the property. But the funny part of the speech was how Imani believed she competed with a prince.

Even if Gemma had lost her mind and allowed herself to love him, she'd never confess it out loud. She would never allow him to hitch his wagon to hers. It'd ruin his life.

"First, I'm coming back. I've a job I love, a kid I love, animals I love."

"Okay, where are we going to live?"

"Where are we… Here of course."

"Cut it out, Memaw told me. She made me swear not to say anything to you. She says we might have to move in with them. We lost this place and we're broke."

"Good ole, Mauve. Wait until I see her. And we didn't lose this place, I lost this place. I'm sorry I didn't tell you. I had a plan to go to Ella's for pie, show you the adoption papers, and then drop the bomb. Do you still want to be adopted? I can't offer much but love."

Imani's tears glistened on her brown cheeks. "I want you to be my mom. Love is all I want and need. We can live with Memaw and Pops. I don't mind. And we have my money—

"Absolutely not. That's for your future." She'd work ten jobs to give them a home before dipping into Imani's account. "If you want a broke, failed actress who lost her last dream of owning her own place in a swindle, you can have me. I want you as my daughter. And I promise"—Gemma crossed her heart—"as soon as I get back, we're making you officially mine. Then you'll really be sorry."

Imani laughed but the truth was a boulder on Gemma's shoulders and back. A burden of her own doing.

"Bring me a souvenir."

"I will. And I'll call and text." Gemma started down the hall to the kitchen where her luggage waited by the back door. "Maybe I'll talk to Scottie on the way over. See about a job at O'Shay's Shirts." The idea of a nine-to-five about choked her. She'd have to start in the factory, running a machine or inspecting shirts, but if it provided benefits and a steady paycheck—

She'd hate to leave The Wedding Shop, but the time for dreaming, the time for having it her way was over.

"We have to give away the animals?" Imani said.

"We can bring the five dogs and maybe a puppy, but the others need more than Mama and Daddy's place can provide. Doc's already sending me names of good candidates."

"Justin and Penny want a puppy."

"Good. You'll see them all the time."

A horn blast was followed by a knock on the kitchen door. "Got to go, baby." Gemma hugged Imani one last time.

"Why can't things stay the same?" Imani said softly in Gemma's ear. "Why do they change? Why do people die?"

"That's life. But we can't sit still and do nothing. We have to live, overcome fear, and fight for the good sent our way." Nice sermon, Gemma. If only she believed it. "Granny Stone used to say fear will never steer you right."

When Gemma was in the hospital with a broken and bruised body, Granny's words whispered through her almost every night. The little lessons she preached while baking cookies together or going on country walks had not been in vain. Despite being the Yoda of Guilt, Granny was the Skywalker of Wise Sayings.

"W-what about the prince? I mean what if—"

"Hey, Miss Worrywart, get off *What-If Avenue*. It's a dead-end. Here's another Granny saying. '*What if* are the two most dangerous words in the human psyche.' She's right. Any decisions I make will involve you. Furthermore, there's not a snowball's chance Prince John of Lauchtenland and I will be an item. I'd not allow it."

"What do you mean you'd not allow it?"

A second knock rattled the back door, followed by a male voice in the kitchen. "Ms. Stone? We must get going." The driver reached for her luggage.

"I'll be back in a week." Gemma kissed Imani's cheek then hooked her travel backpack—a splurge from the new Mass General store—on her shoulder. "Mama and Daddy will be here this afternoon. I'm sure you'll be playing cards all weekend. You'll hardly miss me. Now, walk me out. Oh, remember to change the rabbit cages. We didn't do that last night."

"Why won't you allow the prince to fall in love with you? He already does, you know. Love you. Even Justin noticed."

Gemma's purposed laugh floated in the evening air. "You've been reading fairy tales." She passed her backpack to the driver who stowed it in the trunk. Then she hurried to the barn, slipped the sleeping Chandler into a crate, and walked back to the car.

Imani knelt before the cage door. "I'll miss you, Chandler. Remember I love you." Then she stood and hugged Gemma one last time.

"I love you, Imani. If I've not said it enough, I'm sorry."

"I love you too." Imani stepped back and wiped away the fresh tears. "Pops is organizing a guitar pull and barbecue for Saturday night. Justin's playing." She peered into the crate. "Tell the prince to send us pictures of him sometimes."

"I will. Now let me go." Gemma held off on a final warning about Justin, but Daddy was on the ball. Imani would be fine.

"Gemma, if he does love you—" Imani said just before Gemma climbed into the wide back seat of the limo.

"That means the world started spinning in the opposite direction. All this love talk doesn't matter. I don't love him. I'd never say yes to him."

Imani's hazel eyes popped wide. "Because of me?"

"No, because of me."

They were well down the road before Scottie spoke.

"I think Imani's right. John loves you."

"If that's true, stop the car, I'm getting out." Gemma checked on Chandler who was starting to fuss, then stared out the window as Hearts Bend faded away and Nashville drew near.

"Gemma," Scottie said as they neared the airport exit. "This journey will be one of discovery for both of us. I won't shy away if you won't."

Gemma glanced over at her. "I know who I am. I won't shy away from the truth. That's the best I can do."

"Whatever that means. At least promise me you'll have fun."

Gemma laughed. "Fun will be my middle name."

The flight over was luxurious. Gemma had never been on a private jet before and now she was spoiled for anything less. Flying commercial, even first class, would be like riding a cattle train.

When they arrived, the pilot balked at little Chandler being a passenger. But Scottie took up Chandler's defense, assuring her friend the puppy would not destroy the plane's cabin.

They had packed toys, food, and pee pads. One of those things would keep him occupied.

Turns out, Little Bing, which was Chandler's new nickname,

slept most of the way, waking up in time to charm a cabin of businessmen.

One man, a Music Row executive, texted his wife to go to the farm to choose one of the pups for their family.

"We lost our dog a few years ago and weren't ready for another one yet. We loved her so much, but this little guy has won me over." His wife kept asking for more videos of Little Bing.

They arrived in London mid Saturday morning and took a car from Heathrow down to Dover where they caught a ferry to Port Fressa. A driver met them in a dark sedan, chilled champagne in the back. Gemma pressed against the window as the car maneuvered the crowded, narrow, ancient streets.

The city was haunting, romantic, classic, timeless, modern, and old-world. Glass-and-steel structures scraped the late afternoon sky and cast long shadows toward the bay.

Memories of times gone by popped up on the edge of the road in the form of stone shops and thatched-roof homes. All buffered by a skinny walkway. The driver constantly muttered about pedestrians working around each other by stepping into the avenue.

They passed a red and gold brick building five stories tall stretching the length of a city block, flying the flag of Lauchtenland. Parliament, the driver said.

Then rising out of nowhere, a fortress of white stone and iron, spirals and turrets loomed ahead of them. Perrigwynn Palace. The royal standard flew from the top of each peaked rooftop and on every stone pedestal of the surrounding iron gate.

Gemma sank down in her seat. John lived there. In a palace. While sleeping across from him on a bed of hay in a horse stall, she never actually pictured his home residence.

Now she was really embarrassed she'd invited him into her 1970s kitchen with cracked linoleum floors and dark-paneled walls. But he called it cozy and reminisced over her Formica table.

On the flight over, she'd not allowed herself to think of him. But now, seeing his world, how vast and how different from hers, she felt small and insignificant.

What would she say to him when she saw him? If she saw him.

Scottie never really said Gemma had to go with her to meet with Prince John, or to meet the queen.

Scottie could deliver Chandler while Gemma could play the tourist. And what if—she'd never thought of this until now—the prince thought she was stalking him?

Gemma jerked forward when the driver slammed the brakes and gestured at a pedestrian. "Step out. Hit." His sentences were clipped and shortened, thick with his accent.

A few blocks more and he pulled into the Delafield Hotel entrance. A bellhop in a dark uniform trimmed with gold hurried to greet them and unloaded their cases. After a brief exchange with Scottie, he announced he'd deliver the cases straight to their rooms.

Then she concluded business with the driver, who slipped behind the wheel with a parting word. "Luck."

"Luck?" Gemma echoed.

"He speaks in shorthand, a dialect from Northton," Scottie said, walking toward the lobby. "My assistant told me about it when she was researching for our trip. They don't bother with unnecessary words."

"I think 'good' is a necessary word. How do we know he's not wishing us bad luck?"

"Let's believe it's for the good."

It was teatime by the time they settled into their suites. Scottie in Suite 401. Gemma in Suite 402, which came with a puppy play area. Very swank. Even Chandler thought so.

A porter from concierge named Arnez arrived with tea and cakes, then gave Gemma a tour of her quarters, showing her the hidden refrigerator, the dressing room, which was overkill, and how the shower, internet, and TV worked.

He pointed out the large binder with flyers from touring companies and restaurants and every possible thing a body could want to do or see in one of Europe's oldest cities.

When he was assured of Gemma's complete satisfaction, Arnez bid her a good afternoon then paused by the door.

"Begging your pardon, but have we met before?" he said. "I've seen you somewhere."

"I don't think so. This is my first time to Port Fressa. Ever been to Hearts Bend, Tennessee?"

"Never heard of it."

"There might have been a photo of me with Prince John. Online. But we're just friends, nothing more."

"Don't care squat about the royals. I'm a RECO man." In his early twenties, he seemed intelligent but edgy, an independent thinker, with a bit of hipster thrown in.

"RECO man?"

"Member of the Renaissance Coalition to remove the monarchy, peacefully of course, in favor of a full-on republic. Why should the House of Blue rule for a thousand years? What gives them the right?"

"The law?" Gemma took a shot.

Arnez laughed. "I like you. Spunky. Now, where have we met? I'm sure I've seen you somewhere."

"I was in a popular commercial a few years ago." Five, no six years. Already. Goodness. "During the American Super Bowl. I was the chip dip girl."

"I don't follow sports, especially American football."

"It was all over the internet."

"Yes, then that must be it. Only one commercial?"

"Several but that was the most popular. My hands, feet, and hair also appeared in several commercials."

"You're an actress? In Hollywood?" Arnez's interest seemed genuine. A bit of his swank hotel veneer faded. "I'd love to be in film and television."

"Former actress. I left California. If it's what you want, work hard and stay with it."

"Why didn't you stay with it?"

"I had other priorities."

"Ring if you need anything." But before disappearing, Arnez leaned around for a final study of her face, shook his head, and was gone.

His brief final inspection left her shaking. Moments like this were exactly why she'd never, ever be on a world stage. Ten years ago it was all she wanted. Now she'd live in constant fear that if she became known, she'd end up notorious. For all the wrong reasons.

In the meantime, she'd pour a cup of tea, eat one of the delicious cinnamon-looking treats, and let Chandler out of his crate. He was starting to stir.

Gemma stored her suitcase in the bedroom—she didn't bother to unpack—then let Chandler into his play area.

She'd slept and showered on the plane, so she was ready to go out, explore Port Fressa. It'd long been one of her bucket list cities.

Around five, Scottie knocked. "John is sending a car."

"Good. I've been thinking you could take Chandler to him."

"Instead of you? He knows you came with me because I begged you. Now get ready."

He knows? Why didn't he text. Why didn't she text? This was going to be awkward.

Next thing she knew, she was crossing the Delafield lobby with Chandler in his crate, his cute collie nose pressed against the metal door, sniffing the air.

"Are you nervous?" she said to Scottie as they climbed into the back of a tinted-windowed Range Rover. Because she was. What if it was weird between them? What if he acted all Prince John and treated her like Scottie's traveling companion? What if...

Get off What-If Avenue.

"I'm terrified," Scottie said. "You?"

"Perfectly calm."

"Do you always tremble when you're calm?" Scottie scratched Chandler behind the ears. "He's the only calm one in the car."

"The Chamber Office announced today Prince John will attend the North Sea Island Nations summit next month instead of the queen. This unprecedented move has raised questions regarding the queen's health. According to the *News Leader*, Queen Catherine has not been outside the palace since mid-July. With the crown prince not legally her heir, do we face a constitutional crisis if, God forbid, something happens to Her Majesty?"

— MELISSA FARIS, ROYAL REPORTER,
THE MORNING SHOW

"I don't know what to think, Hy. Prince John attending the North Sea Island Nations Summit instead of Queen Catherine… Rather last minute. It's in Port Fressa, correct? I find it all very odd. Do you think she's ill? And if so, doesn't the crown heir have to marry? I think the queen must change the writ. This is the twenty-first century. You can't force a man to marry for queen and country. He's still grieving his wife, for pity sake. It's loony."

— MADELINE ON THE MADELINE &
HYACINTH LIVE!

"The Justice Ministry announced arrests of four key players in what is now being called the Midlands Reingard Scandal. Sources indicate more arrests to come, perhaps reaching all the way to the House of Lords."

– PERRY COPPERFIELD, CABLE NEWS PF

CHAPTER
TWENTY-ONE

JOHN

The timing of Scottie's arrival coincided with the North Sea Island Nations Summit. But there was nothing to do about it.

The summit began Wednesday so he'd have to make the most of the few days before. Though he was fully aware Scottie didn't come to see him, did she? She came to meet her mother. Between Mum, Gus, and Daffy, she'd be well engaged.

Then there was the issue of Gemma. Scottie insisted she came at her request, but how could he spend a few hours with her? She'd become a good friend. Not to mention he was proud of his homeland and wanted to share it with her.

Maybe dinner Monday evening because Tuesday was a prep day and Wednesdsay morning he'd hit the ground running. The event concluded Saturday evening with a royal ball. What else?

He'd planned to attend alone, make himself available in the billiards room, and offer his dancing prowess to the women attendees.

But perhaps, *maybe*, could he entertain Gemma as his date? No, think again. Rumors would explode about a new love. While he battled his feelings for Holland over recent events, he wasn't sure he could commit to a new love.

For now, he waited in his apartment for Scottie and Gemma, a blend of anticipation and nerves.

He'd ordered finger food and drinks. Insisted only Dad, Gus, and Daffy be there to greet Scottie—he didn't want to overwhelm her. But Aunt Arabella insisted she be present since she was Mum's sister and had been with her through her most trying times.

John relented, but cousin Rachel might never speak to him again.

At the telly, Dad and Gus avidly cheered the Port Fressa Seamen, Lauchtenland's number one cricket team. By the sideboard, Aunt Arabella regaled Daffy with ghastly pregnancy and birthing stories. If she didn't stop soon, John would run interference. Daffy looked horrified.

Nothing but a typical, *average* family scene. It just so happened to take place in a palace. John inspected his place as if he were Gemma. While she'd made excuses for her run-down, out-of-date farmhouse, he found it charming and cozy.

What would she think of his dwelling? Pretentious? Ornate with coffered ceilings and gilded doors? Not very cozy? Not very charming?

"They're here, sir." Shaw stood at the door. "Miss Scottie O'Shay, Miss Gemma Stone, and young master Chandler Bing."

"Chandler? What's this?" John stepped in front of everyone to see Gemma carrying a wide-eyed, curious puppy peeking out from a black-and-white sling. "My little man. You brought him over for me?" He lifted the squirming puppy to his face. "Welcome home."

"Who's Chandler Bing?" Aunt Arabella's voice bellowed. "Isn't he a character on television? What show was it?"

"*Friends*," Dad said, stepping up beside John. "And I think this little chap is Chandler Bing."

"Chandler, meet your new family." John tucked the puppy close to his chest and shot Gemma a look of gratitude. Her smile took him back to their time together and he missed the man he'd been with her.

"Everyone, this is Scottie." He leaned to kiss her cheek. "And Gemma Stone." As his gaze lingered on her, he suddenly had a thousand things to tell her. "Welcome to Lauchtenland."

But he must focus on the guest of honor. Scottie. He introduced her to the Family using first names and omitting royal titles. Still,

Scottie and Gemma curtsied to Dad, Gus, Daffy, and Aunt Arabella anyway.

Chandler Bing on the other hand squirmed to be let down and immediately made his mark on the carpet.

"Shaw—"

"On it, sir."

There was a metaphor in there somewhere. John knew it.

While the star of the evening was Scottie, and maybe Chandler—even after his mess—the one that surprised him was Gemma. Nothing about the royal room, the Family, the atmosphere seemed to intimidate her. She was so at ease. So...so Gemma. He didn't get it. Why the hiddenness, the veils, the cloaked answers when they were together in Hearts Bend?

When will you tell me your story, Gemstone?

Seated on the far side of the living area, the girl who rescued things talked to Daffy and Dad, her hands animated with whatever story she told. She was a natural.

He sat with Scottie, Gus, and Aunt Arabella, trying to engage with their conversation but drawn to Gemma and the light coming off of her. Truly, when did she start letting her inner star shine?

He was about to say something to Scottie when Gemma's laugh interrupted his thought. Leaning toward Dad, she gestured and waved her hands about until Dad playfully batted them down and started his own gesturing to make his point.

Shaw circled the room, checking the food trays, clearing away empty glasses. John broke away from his circle to discuss Chandler's care and needs, requesting supplies to be purchased straightaway.

"I'll send someone now, sir," Shaw said. "I think he's a lovely addition to the household."

Scottie was on her feet when he turned back to the room. "While I've loved meeting you," she said, "especially little brother Gus and Daffy, I came to meet my mother."

She was a Blue all right. Taking command. Or perhaps that was an O'Shay quality she exhibited. Probably both.

Dad set down his tea. "I'll take you."

"I'm coming with." Aunt Arabella hopped up, reaching for her handbag.

"No, you're not." Dad wielded authority over his sister-in-law with expertise. "I'll give you a full report. But let's leave this to Kate's family."

"I am her family."

"Then her husband and children." Dad waited for Scottie to join him. "John, are you coming? Gus and Daffy?"

"Gemma will come with us." Scottie cast her friend a visual plea, which saved John the bother of finding an excuse for Gemma to come along.

"If she's going, I'm going." Arabella surged forward.

"She's here for Scottie," Dad said. "The room will be crowded enough. You'll see her tomorrow, Bella."

John looked to his brother, and as he hoped, Gus read his mind. "Dad, Daffy and I can't go but why don't you take Scottie, get to know her better. John you can drive Gemma, show her a bit of our beautiful city."

Smooth little brother. Everyone could see what he was doing.

As Dad and Scottie departed, Aunt Arabella followed, still arguing her point to be at this grand meeting. "I'm Kate's sister and Scottie's aunt."

Shaw excused himself and took Chandler to the kitchen for something to eat.

"Nothing too rich," Gemma said. "He's only seven weeks."

"Some broiled chicken, ma'am?" Shaw said. "No bones."

"That'd be fine." She gave John a shy smile. "Sorry, puppy mama syndrome." She spun around, taking in the room. "I've never been in a palace before. Very regal."

"If I didn't know, I'd think you frequented palaces often. You seemed so comfortable with Dad and Daffy."

"They were kind, talking to me first."

"I think you won them over. Hey, Gemma, can I ask why you and Scottie aren't staying at Perrigwynn? Why the Delafield?"

Gemma made her way to the window. "I think Scottie wanted the space, a chance to work things out without being watched."

She stirred the air as she moved, releasing the fragrance of the Tennessee grass after a summer rain. "I've always been curious about the Heart of God. Can you see the lights from here?"

"A few of them." He met Gemma at the large-paned glass and placed his arm about her—only to help her with the right vantage point—and directed her attention to the far, far corner of the city.

"I think I see it. There?"

"Yes, it's twilight but the lights are more vivid at night." His breath brushed her hair. "Isn't it odd how the most beautiful thing in the city is best seen at night?"

"Or how light is so powerful against the darkness."

When she lifted her face to his, he didn't think, just lowered his head for a kiss and the world faded away. He was lost in her, in the taste of her warm lips, in the memory of the summer where he'd lived without a care. If only for a few weeks.

When he raised up, her eyes sparkled, almost rendering the shadows powerless. But she pressed her hand against his chest and backed away.

"John, that night…in the barn. It was a moment but let's not start something we can't finish. You're not ready. I'm not available. Besides." She tapped her watch face. "We should go. Support Scottie."

"You're absolutely right. I was caught up in—" A fairy tale. Some part of him was still that ten-year-old kid who wanted the magic of *A Swan's Feather*.

GEMMA

She'd changed the feeling between them when she backed away. Naturally. But it came with a bit of regret, and she was trapped between the possible and impossible.

John retrieved a key fob as he spoke to Gunner via a smart device. "We're on our way down." Now he stood by the door, waiting. "We should go."

"I've upset you," she said.

"No man likes to be put off after he's kissed a woman, but you're right. We shouldn't get caught up in a fairy tale."

"Fairy tale? We're talking fairy tales now?"

He laughed to himself, jostling the key fob in his hand. "Mum used to read Gus and me an old family tale called *The Swan's Feather*. In fact my cousin Rachel has published the story as a children's book. It's about a prince who can't find his true love, then one day a feather appears in his life and leads him to his one and only."

"I don't have a swan's feather, John."

"I'm not looking for one, Gemma. Holland didn't come to me by way of a mystical, magical feather either." He opened the door. "Traffic should be light on a Sunday evening."

In the corridor, passing maids and footmen came to attention. Gemma saw, felt the reality of John's title and true stature. He was an honest-to-goodness Royal Highness. A prince. The entire world knew of him, watched him. He held a position of influence, a scepter he must wield with dignity and wisdom.

The ability to influence people for good had been one of her deepest desires when she'd struck out for Hollywood. For fame.

Until she ran headlong into a reality check. Even if she'd achieved her goal, she learned she'd have been one voice among the many. Her stage would've been nothing more than a clanging gong and crashing cymbal.

Now she had hope with Imani. Helping her launch into life filled her with hope. Being away from her the last twenty-four hours renewed her commitment and passion to give that girl every advantage. Life would steal no more from her.

Which was one more reason, among the many, why a serious relationship with a prince was out of the question. First and foremost, he wasn't asking.

"What are you thinking, Gemstone?" John used her nickname with warmth and affection.

"About Imani. What a privilege it is to raise her." She followed him through a paneled door down a back staircase.

"She's lucky to have you. Truly."

"Raising Imani is a great calling. I thought I had to be famous or rich to do good in the world. Your calling is grand and great, on a world stage. Mine is small and focused, on a small stage."

"Don't minimize your efforts while inflating mine. The best duty of any royal is to raise their children to have integrity and character. Especially because of their prominence."

"As they say," Gemma said, "the hand that rocks the cradle rules the world. Or in my case, the hand that raises a solid, healthy teen."

In the stairwell, lit with a row of recessed lighting, they were more alone than they'd ever been. The feelings between them popped and stirred.

"You changed me, you know," John began his confession. "I wasn't sure there was life after Holland and you showed me hope. You saved me, Gemma. Saved the king."

"You reminded me anything is possible. As long as we set our sights on reality." Gemma squeezed his hand. "I'll always treasure knowing you, Prince."

"Treasure knowing me? You make me sound like a chap you danced with at one of your proms."

"It's fitting. Because when it was all said and done, we left school to follow our own path."

"And never the two shall meet."

"Exactly."

"The trouble is, Gemma Stone, we did meet. And it may surprise you to know because it surprises me, I'm not sure I can easily forget."

Men in dark suits stood when they entered the Queen's Waiting Room, bowing to John and giving her the once-over.

The room was lavish with a thick, emerald carpet, tapestry on the wall, a portrait of a former monarch. In the far corner, two men watched a crime show rerun, while two others watched the door.

John introduced her as she chose the nearest chair. The men in black merely nodded.

"Let me check on things in the queen's room. Then you can come in."

"Me?" She shook her head. "I'll wait here." It was one thing to chat with John's father and sister-in-law in his apartment, but she'd not meet the queen when she was ill. And not in the emotional swirl of seeing her daughter for the first time since her birth.

"Are you sure?"

"This is Scottie's moment. Please tell her I'm here if she needs me but I won't interrupt."

When he'd slipped out, Gemma texted Imani.

"How's everything with Memaw and Pops?"

"Playing cards tonight. Learning canasta. Miss you."

"The herd?"

"Fat and happy. Herc misses you. Some folks are coming tonight to look at puppies."

"Inspect them well. Ask a lot of questions."

"Pops knows them. Says they're good stuff. How's the prince? Did you meet the queen? Penny says to get a selfie with her."

"Prince John is very well. And no, I will not get a selfie with the queen. This trip was for Scottie not me. Tell Mama and Daddy hi. Kiss them and all the herd for me. Even the mean Miss Frances."

"You can kiss her yourself when you come home. Memaw and Pops say they love you."

"I love you, Imani."

"Love you too."

She didn't know how long she waited for John, but she checked email, actually read more of the book she'd started on the plane, and was starting to nod off when John came in and motioned her forward.

"She wants to meet you."

"Who?"

"Mum. The queen."

She shook her head. "No, no, no. I couldn't possibly." Gemma looked down at her blouse and slacks. She'd made an effort to appear at the palace but not to meet the queen. "I don't think I'm dressed properly."

"You are perfectly acceptable. Besides, she doesn't care what you're wearing."

"But I do."

"I didn't care what I looked like when I met your parents."

She made a face and he laughed. "The king and queen of the card table? John, please, I love them but—"

"And I love my mum. She's a royal, yes, and very formal, but Gemma, she wants to meet you."

"You're just saying that to get me to agree."

He made a face, and she knew there was no getting out of it. The king consort suddenly appeared.

"What's taking so long? She's getting tired. Gemma, are you coming?"

"She's refusing, Dad."

"Come on, love," Edric said, a confidence on his aristocratic face. "She won't bite, I promise."

Okay, fine. Gemma stretched and squared her shoulders.

This is nothing more than an audition. Nothing more than a movie role. Let's see, what sort of character did she need to be?

A lady? A nobleman's daughter. Maybe a lady's maid if those still existed. Some sort of noblewoman? Oh, a businesswoman, an entrepreneur.

Stepping into character, she followed John and his father from the waiting room to the queen's room.

Gemma's illusions shattered when she saw a pale woman almost lost in a bed of white sheets and buried under white blankets. But her dark brown hair still had a lustrous sheen, an indication of life.

However, her attention was not on her latest visitor but on Scottie as she held her hand. Scottie's cheeks were streaked with black tear tracks, a ring of mascara under her eyes.

"Mum," John said, gently touching her shoulder. "This is Gemma, my friend from Hearts Bend. She traveled with Scottie."

The queen turned to her, focusing, adjusting her position. "Gemma, yes, John's spoken of you."

"It's a pleasure to meet you, Your Majesty." She bobbed down and up in an awkward curtsy.

"Thank you for bringing Scottie to me. I know it made her journey lighter."

"I did nothing, Your Majesty. She wanted to come."

"Ma'am," John whispered to Gemma.

"Ma'am," she said. Was she sweating? Yes, she was sweating.

"We've been having a good chat, Scottie and I." The queen shifted back to her daughter. "I can't believe she's here."

Scottie gripped her mother's hand tighter, her eyes full of tears, and pressed her forehead to the edge of the bed. Gemma walked around John and touched Scottie's shoulder.

"Is there anything I can do?"

She raised up and wiped her face, smiling amid the tears. "Just coming with me was enough. More than. Order whatever you want at the hotel, please, and charge it to the room."

"Hotel?" The queen's eyes sparked with life. "What's this? John, aren't they staying in the palace guest quarters?"

"Scottie preferred the Delafield."

"Absolutely not. Scottie will be moved into the Family wing immediately. Gemma may move with her if she likes or remain at the Delafield, but Scottie will transfer at once."

"Perhaps you should let Scottie weigh in on this one, Kate," Edric said.

"Why? She belongs at the palace. Scottie?"

"I thought, well, it would be easier for all if I stayed at a hotel."

"And what did easier ever do for you?" The queen laughed and raised Scottie's hand to her lips. "Please, for me. Move to the palace."

"Only if Gemma agrees." Scottie looked over, hopeful.

For a flash second Gemma resented this decision being thrust upon her. But her answer was clear.

"Yes, of course. We'll move to the palace."

"Good. Well done. I like you, Gemma."

With that royal approval, Scottie handed over her room key as Edric rang someone named Broderick to arrange for their things to be moved.

Outside, John led her to his car, Gunner heeling behind. "The queen is a force, even in her hospital bed."

"Very much. She didn't seem down for the long count. Is she improving?"

"This morning they diagnosed her with Guillain-Barré, a rare condition that causes extreme weakness, hinders breathing among other things. All the symptoms she's been battling. Now that they've caught the culprit, they can plan the proper treatment."

"Will she be all right?"

"Yes, with time. But recovery will be slow." At his car, John opened Gemma's door. "I shouldn't say it after our conversation, but it comforts me to have you here. Don't ask why or tell me I'm wrong, because it won't change how I feel."

She gave him a long, even look. "We all feel more confident in the company of friends."

"Well then, friend, are you hungry? I am. Let's eat."

North Sea Island Nations Summit Begins
Wednesday.

– THE NEWS LEADER

"Stone, it's just been confirmed the queen has a
rare condition called Guillain-Barré. I'm told by
experts this syndrome is a rare disorder which
attacks the body's immune system. Symptoms are
weakness and tingling in your extremities, shortness
of breath, prickly sensation in fingers and toes, and
double vision, among other symptoms. Recovery,
I'm told, is long, but the queen is in top physical
form and the medical staff and doctors predict a full
recovery."

– MELISSA FARIS, THE MORNING SHOW

A palace source leaked information on the queen's
mysterious daughter, Scottie O'Shay. Can we
believe she's come to meet her mother?

– @ROYALWATCHERONE

I'm gobsmacked! Out to dinner the other night with
my dad at Clemency Pub and look who I saw!
Prince John. Who's with him? Anyone know?

— @STEFWITHANF ON INSTAGRAM

CHAPTER
TWENTY-TWO

JOHN

The white feather on his bedroom mantel caught his eye as he readied for work Monday morning.

He reached for it and turned it in his hands. Why did Holland lie about the necklace? Did she know what was going on with Reingard? Did she send the feather the day of her funeral or was he believing in fairy tales again?

Peering up as if he might see or hear some celestial reply, John ran his fingers along the edge of the large plume. The feather was both firm and soft.

John returned the feather to its home on the mantel. In a week he'd place her bronze wreath on her tomb and say his final goodbye. But he had so many questions.

Leaving his apartment for his office, he rounded the corner and ran smack into Gemma.

"Good morning." He was pleased to see her. Very pleased. They'd had a lovely time at Clemency Pub the other night. The lads ended up joining them, all rather last minute, and Gemma was the queen, holding her own court with Larrabee, Lute, and Turner.

"You caught me. Snooping."

"You don't have to apologize. Have a look-see. I'd show you myself if I had time. Tell you what, I'll have Briggs ring the palace historian. He'll give you a much better tour than I."

"Really? Thank you. Scottie's gone to be with your mama. She left me money to go shopping. She's crazy. Like I'm going to take her money."

"She's grateful."

"I enjoyed last night with your friends."

"I think they enjoyed you." John glanced at his watch. "Blast, I must run. Though I'd rather chat with you, Gemstone. With this upcoming summit—"

"Go. Don't worry about me. I can get around on my own."

"And I will arrange a tour with the historian, I promise." They'd just bid one another goodbye when John called back to her. "I'm to attend a dreadful dinner tonight but will you be available around nine? I'll sneak away. I want to show you something."

"Can't you tell me what?"

"Surprise."

"See you at nine."

Gemma had just rounded the corridor when John turned back to his office. A glint of light caught his attention and he looked back to see a large white feather, identical to the one in his apartment, resting on the royal blue carpet where he'd talked to Gemma minutes ago.

Breaking News: The Justice Ministry arrested Lord Cletus Cunningham this morning at his home in Antaver Square. He is being charged with corruption, malfeasance, and insider trading in the Reingard-Midlands scandal. The House of Lords created a special council to establish High Crimes and Misdemeanors. Cunningham is the father-in-law of His Royal Highness Prince John."

– THE NEWS LEADER

"The Justice Ministry was clear. There are no links between Cunningham's crimes and the royal Family other than the now-deceased Princess Holland."

– PERRY COPPERFIELD, CABLE NEWS PF

CHAPTER TWENTY-THREE

JOHN

"**W**here are we going?" Gemma walked with him down Perrigwynn's foyer staircase and under the row of royal portraits.

"You'll see." This journey wasn't a big deal, but he was having fun, making the three-block trek down Clemency Avenue a mystery.

Gunner was off tonight so Otis stirred from his position at the bottom of the stairs and joined them as they headed around to the back exit toward the street.

The front was always heavy with tourists and the royally curious.

"Otis," Gemma said. "Where are we going?"

"Wherever His Royal Highness goes."

John laughed. "He's on my team."

"I'll bring my own security next time."

Next time? He slowed his steps as he peered over at her realizing he wanted a "next time." And another. And another. The sensation was rather odd yet exciting.

Otis stepped ahead of them as they made their way through the back gate. When he signaled all was well, John and Gemma entered the streets of Port Fressa. The air was scented with the sea and the sound of motors, horns, voices, and music that were a part of a major metropolis.

Crossing the avenue, he decided for small talk. "How was your day?"

"I toured the wharf. Ate at a place called Saldings on the Water."

"Saldings? Lovely choice. One of the best restaurants in the city."

They talked of food, and all the unique shops along the wharf, and then of John's preparations for the North Sea Island Nations Summit.

"It feels odd stepping into the queen's shoes when she's alive yet too weak to do her duty."

"It's good experience."

"Yes, but it still raises all the age-old questions. Do I have to be married to officially take my oath? I'm deputized now for an emergency but if she were to, well, pass on—"

"Know what I think?" Gemma said, sidestepping a band of professionals on their way home from the pubs. "Being a royal is complicated."

"No truer words were ever spoken." His hand brushed her as they jostled another clump of slightly inebriated chaps. His fingers itched to intertwine with hers.

Another block, the crowds thinned and the light from the Heart of God came into view. Gemma grabbed his arm.

"The Heart of God? This is where you're taking me?"

"Clever girl, you guessed." But how could she miss it?

Lights filled the Gothic towers and drained down through the arcade to the rose window. Then, as if propelled by some mystical force, the illumination spilled down the front of the structure and pooled in the roundabout, flowing toward the gurgling fountain in the center.

"Oh, John. I've seen pictures but—" She released him and moved straight into the radiant beams that seemed to dance around her. The light surrounded her head like an aurora and soaked into her long, wavy hair.

He was falling in love.

Overhead, the moon watched, and the stars bent low. Envious, John imagined, because he'd always sensed something different in the Heart of God, its converging blaze like no other.

"How did this come to be again?" Gemma slowly waved her

hands through the light as if through water. "I can actually feel it." She inhaled deeply. "What is that fragrance? Like a rich oil. Full of spices." She moved around the fountain as if trying to capture it all.

"I'm not sure." John inhaled, envious he could only catch a whiff of spices. "The cathedrals were built between the thirteenth and fifteenth centuries. Mystic monks wanted a place for the common man, the laborer, the slave and free, rich and poor, to commune with God."

"What about a crown prince?"

"If he believed."

"Do you believe?" Then she whirled toward him, tangled in light, stirring the fragrances. He barely caught a scent of cinnamon when Gemma stopped in front of him. "Wait, I know where I've smelled this before. At The Wedding Shop. An odd, cherubic-faced woman came in and she wanted me to try on JoJo's wedding gown."

"What? Why? That's a rather odd request."

"Tell me about it. I refused."

"Don't you want to try on a wedding dress, Gemma?" He reached for her hand which felt soft and silky in his.

"If I wanted to get married, yes. But no man—" She caught herself, ending her thought with a brilliant smile. "Anyway, the woman claimed to be an angel. But I thought it was a prank from my friend Tommy." Gemma raised her free hand as if to catch the light. "She had a fragrance about her I couldn't identify but now here it is in this heart."

John mimicked her move, trying to catch the same light, but all he caught was the ends of her hair floating in the salty summer breeze blowing off the bay.

"Do you believe her? Was she an angel?"

"Until this moment, I didn't know what to believe, but perhaps she was telling the truth. Also, when she'd gone," Gemma turned back toward the fountain, "there was a pool of light on the floor just like the one at the fountain."

"My mother and brother have encountered a man they call Emmanuel. He's perhaps an angel, some guiding force."

Gemma looked back at him. "God with us."

"Pardon?"

"Emmanuel means God with us. In third grade, I had a part in a Christmas play that talked about Emmanuel, God with us."

The second time she mentioned His name, the atmosphere popped and the Heart of God lights refracted with each syllable. God. With. Us.

A small laugh escaped Gemma and she walked deeper into the cathedral lights and John ached to follow, but his feet remained planted. All the while something akin to a low-grade fire ignited in his chest.

"Gemma—" He reached for her as she skip-danced past him. *Join her. In the mysterious light.*

He took a step then hesitated. He could fully sense the fragrance now. Even more, he couldn't take his eyes off Gemma.

He started to call her again, but the moment was sacred. Maybe even holy. Like the brief moment after Holland's funeral when he found the feather.

She was beautiful with the beams twisting into her hair, soaking into her skin, electrifying her clothes. Even her laugh expressed light.

Spinning, spinning, spinning, she stirred the atmosphere more and more until the light swirled into a cone and careened toward John, drawing the breath from his lungs. His strength left and he collapsed to one knee on the cobblestones. The oily fragrance saturated the air and covered him.

Then he heard the song of the stars. Incredible. Stunning. Divine. He reached for the light as Gemma had been doing and fell off balance. He laughed and tried to stand but the weight of the elements held him down.

Then, as quickly as it began, the experience ended. For one breath, two, three, John couldn't move. When he raised up from the stones, the Heart of God flickered and beamed with the average, everyday cathedral lights.

John glanced around for Gemma. He spotted her a few feet away, head down, shoulders shimmying, her soft sobs flowing beneath the babbling fountain. "Hey, love, it's all right, it's all right."

When he came to her, she fell against him, clinging, her sobs building, her tears soaking his shirt. Wrapping her up tighter, John rested his cheek on her head, then slowly began a gentle side-to-side sway.

Whatever they'd just experienced would take hours, maybe days, to unpack. Even then they might not understand.

As for her tears, they needed no explanation. They fell from her shadows, and if need be, he'd hold her until the light permanently shone in her eyes.

As she exhaled, releasing her tension, she reclined into him and John began to hum the melody he'd heard moments ago when he was kneeling down, listening to the stars.

Gemma

A soft rain cleansed Port Fressa by the time Gemma awoke the next morning. She'd slept deep and long, waking up in the same position as when she drifted to sleep.

The light from the Heart of God filled her and almost consumed her long after John delivered her to her guest suite.

She sat in the dark sitting area saying nothing, just being in a world where there was no Vegas, no broken hip, no shame, no fear. Without looking she knew the shadows in her eyes were rolled back if not gone.

Light always conquers darkness.

Kicking out of bed, she moved to the window and raised the sash, inhaling the glorious aroma of a summer rain. A pair of groundskeepers walked the lawn in raincoats and hats.

Then a footman or someone walked by with little Chandler, urging him to do his business, but the baby collie-mix didn't mind the rain. There were interesting smells in the grass.

Turning back to her room, she tried to think what she wanted to do today. John had meetings but in a hushed, emotional whisper, he asked her to attend the ball Thursday evening at the end of the summit.

She said yes almost before he finished asking. The feel of his chest beneath her cheek, the pump of his heartbeat in her ear, the warm embrace of his arms... She could deny him nothing.

In truth, she should pack her bags and run home. She was falling for him. But she could never let go, never tell him the truth. She was too ashamed.

Even after a night in the light, she never wanted John to know what she'd done on that Vegas stage. It would change how he looked at her and that she could not bear.

She heard a sound beyond her bedroom. A maid called out, saying she'd brought breakfast.

"Thank you." Gemma tied on the provided robe, complete with the queen's cypher, and made her way to the trolley.

She could tell John she couldn't go to the ball after all. Make up an excuse to go home. But oh, a royal ball with a royal prince. It was too much to pass up. But really, she shouldn't risk it. If her videos got out, she'd not only embarrass herself but her family, Prince John, and the House of Blue.

Where was the freedom she felt a mere ten hours ago? The sense she was no longer the woman who sold her soul for thirty pieces of silver. She was fresh and new.

Pouring a cup of tea then buttering a crumpet, Gemma sat at the dining table. "What do I do?" She swallowed. "God?"

One bite into her crumpet an idea hit and she stepped lively for her phone. After several rings, Matt Biglow's crumpled voice answered.

"Gemma?"

"Are you asleep?"

"Yeah, it's two in the morning."

Gemma glanced at the large, round clock on the wall of her suite. Ten o'clock in Port Fressa was two in the morning in L.A.

"Sorry. I'll call you later."

"I'm awake now. What do you want? I've tried to call and text you, but you never answer."

"I blocked you." She crossed the plush beige-and-gold carpet back to her breakfast.

"Six years together and that's how you treat me?" he said. "Blocked."

"Do you really want to talk about how we've treated each other?"

"Right, go ahead, what do you want?"

"I want an honest answer. Don't mess with me. I won't get mad or anything. Okay?"

"Depends. Will it incriminate me?"

"Where are the Vegas show files?"

After her accident, the producer dropped them like a hot potato, along with the cable channel, but Matt had uploaded an episode—the worst one as far as Gemma was concerned—on video sites, hoping the show would go viral and get network or streaming service attention.

"Destroyed," he said without pause. "A virus burned up my hard drive. I lost five years of work. I told you all of this in a text. But I guess it was blocked."

"You're telling me the shows, all of them, are gone?" She'd anticipated a battle with him but this was going splendidly. If the shows were gone, she was free. Safe. Her *what-ifs* perished.

"What's this about, Gemma?"

"I met someone. He's just a friend but he invited me to a rather public event."

"Are you talking about Prince John? He's the one who answered your phone, wasn't he?"

"It doesn't matter. Just promise me the videos are gone."

"I saw the viral post of him carrying someone across a finish line or something. The location said Tennessee and I knew it was you. Couldn't make out your face but I recognized your, um, shall we say, finer *assets*."

"Matt, the videos, please." Gemma sipped her tea but it had gone cold.

"Gone."

"Positively?"

"Very. Darn shame too. The shows were good. I was on to something."

"They were humiliating and degrading. What about the video or videos you uploaded?"

"Only one. Took it down. The uploads weren't good. I didn't want anyone thinking I produced shoddy work. Besides, Sandy threatened to sue me over them." Sandra Willet, the witch of a showrunner. "So are you and the prince a thing?"

"I told you, just friends."

"But you're going somewhere with him?"

"Will you give me your word? The videos are gone."

"Gemma, look, I know you're mad at me, *still,* especially if you blocked me, but I was trying to make something of myself and trying to create a breakout opportunity for you."

"You didn't tell me it would require selling my soul."

He laughed. "Sell your soul. Please. I don't remember you protesting very loudly."

Gemma shut out the memory of the show and her progressive slide into the stinking mud. "The show was one thing, Matt. You leaving me in a hospital for a month by myself is another."

"That was all your choice."

"Mine? You wanted me to leave the hospital and go back to L.A. with you when I couldn't even sit up. I was recovering from hip surgery and a concussion, Matt. You had no plan for my care."

"But I had a job. You know that thing we need to pay the bills, put a roof over our heads. *Hire* help."

"Go back to sleep, Matt. Sorry I woke you."

Gemma tossed her phone to the table, angry, thinking about the months she struggled on her own after surgery and the last of the lingering light from the Heart of God dissipated. She shouldn't have called him, but she wanted to know.

In hindsight, Matt's abandonment was the best thing that ever happened to her. It drove her home to Hearts Bend.

But all that was in the past. In the present she'd agreed to attend a ball with the prince. The press would be curious. They'd discover her name, her work, her hometown. They'd find old headshots and green screen auditions. Old roommates looking for the spotlight would appear out of nowhere. Even Sandy Willet would crawl out of the hole she lived in. Gemma lived too long in *that* world to believe any different.

Her Super Bowl commercial might get a second wind—which she could handle. What she couldn't handle was the video of her stripping across a Vegas stage.

Still, in the midst of her dilemma, was the echo of John's heartbeat and the tender, soft, and peaceful song he hummed as he held her close.

"The probe into the Reingard Industries scandal continues. At his grand jury hearing, Lord Cunningham professed his innocence and indicated his political rivals set him up. Also on LTV-1 *News at Six*, updates on the North Sea Island Nations Summit, the upcoming royal ball, weather, and sports."

— LTV-1

"The NSINS closing ceremonies were held today at Perrigwynn Palace. Prince John's ending remarks called for joint economic and human rights efforts while championing the purpose of the royal houses of Lauchtenland, Brighton Kingdom, and the Grand Duchy of Hessenberg. His Royal Highness's comments were countered by Hamish Fickle, MP and leader of the RECO party, saying it's time for a new day, a new government across the North Sea nations."

— CNC, YOUR CABLE NEWS CHANNEL

"We are so excited to welcome our guest, Princess Rachel, to talk about her new book, *The Swan's Feather*. Give her a warm Tuppence Corbyn welcome."

— TUPPENCE CORBYN & FRIENDS SHOW

Ahh!! I have an advance copy of Princess Rachel's book. Signed!!! I can't wait to read it.

— *@STEFWITHANF ON INSTAGRAM*

"We'll be on the red carpet for the royal ball posting live starting at six o'clock. We can't wait to show you the best styles on parade."

— *THE LAUGHTEN LOUD!*

Can't wait for the ball! Who do you think the prince will take? He can't go stag, can he? Also, does he really have to marry to be our king? Seems ridiculous. And Hamish Fickle is so cute! Anyone?

— *@JUSTHEREFORTHEPARTY ON INSTAGRAM*

We've just seen King Nathaniel and Princess Susanna arrive. She's stunning in a rich purple ball gown with a crystal belt. Waiting now for Prince John. Insiders tell us he will be arriving alone.

— *@ROYALWATCHERONE*

CHAPTER
TWENTY-FOUR

GEMMA

Going to a royal ball required a gown, hair, and makeup. And not just any gown or any kind of hair and makeup, but the royal kind.

An enthusiastic Scottie insisted on taking Gemma shopping with her while the queen was attended by her physicians. But their ventures to the Port Fressa fashion district were fruitless.

Then the queen was released from the hospital on Wednesday morning, so Scottie spent all of her time now in Apartment 1A.

"We're going to watch movies. Her favorite and mine. We have so much in common, Gemma. It's freaky."

Scottie had changed before Gemma's eyes. She was softer, brighter, speaking in low, slow tones as if some part of her had finally come to a place of peace.

Meanwhile, Gemma still had no gown. She was headed out to shop again, ready to load up her already-burdened credit card when Princess Daffy knocked on her door.

"Can you come to my place? I want to show you something."

"Let me change and—"

"You're fine. Gus is at a summit dinner tonight so it's just us girls."

Down the hall and around the corner, Gemma walked toward 3C with the princess.

"How do you find Port Fressa?"

"Lovely. So much to see. I had a tour of the palace with the royal historian yesterday."

"I worked for the Royal Trust before I married Gus. I love Lauchtenland history. Here we are."

Daffy and Gus's apartment was large with a simpler color palette, modern décor, and hardwoods instead of the standard carpet. But the thing that caught Gemma's eye was the gown hanging from the dining area chandelier. She'd never seen anything like it.

"Well?" Daffy said. "What do you think?"

"I think... Wow." Gemma's attention drifted to Princess Daffy's very round middle. "Is it your ball gown?"

"Gus and I are sitting this one out. I thought you'd like to wear it. Have it, really. I've never even worn it."

"Mine?" Gemma circled the dress, inspecting the material. It was a rich silver crepe de chine with a deep V-neck and a fitted bodice that anchored a flared, floor-length skirt intertwined with heavy cotton flowers and leaves. The most incredible part was the feathers. So many beautiful feathers. Layers of icy-white synthetic feathers—swan feathers—anchored the hem.

"What do you think?" Princess Daffy said.

"You can't give it to me. You'll want to wear it someday. How about if I borrow it?" Gemma inspected the waistline. It'd be tight. But maybe...

"Come on, try it on. And I have a special pair of shoes you can wear. What size are you?"

"Eight and a half." No one had size eight and a half.

"I knew it. I knew it," Princess Daffy said. "Come on, let's get you in this gown."

In the dressing room, Gemma slipped from her jeans and T-shirt and returned in bra and undies, feeling a bit unprepared for this.

The princess stood on a chair and directed Gemma to slip under the gown's hem and massive the skirt—arms up mind you—then she would help fit bodice.

"Brace yourself," Princess Daffy said. "This gown weighs a ton."

On first try the layered, textured bodice landed on Gemma's face. That inspired a good laugh. Then Daffy adjusted her aim and at last, the straps rested on Gemma's shoulders. Daffy stepped off the chair, maneuvering easily despite her round belly, and fastened the long row of buttons.

"Oh, Gemma." The princess flared the enormous skirt with the short train, adjusting the layers of silk, organza, and feathers. "The feathers seem to come alive, as if they belong to you. Do you feel like you can fly?"

Gemma moved to the mirror. "Goodness." It was too much. All too much. A week in a palace, being friends with a prince, soaking in the light from the Heart of God, and now wearing this amazing, *amazing* gown that was intended for a princess.

"Are you all right?" Daffy's form appeared in the mirror beside Gemma.

"Yes...no." Gemma reached for the nearest chair, stumbling under the gown's weight. She'd have to get used to it. "I'm a bit overwhelmed. I don't deserve your kindness and I should be honest about who I really am and what I've done but—"

A door chime interrupted her almost-confession.

"Hold that thought." Princess Daffy hurried off and Gemma decided to not hold *that* thought but to toss it far, far away. *Just be in the moment.* Why did she have to drag her past with her everywhere like some sick badge of honor?

What was the experience in the Heart of God for if it didn't move her forward?

Princess Daffy returned. "My stylist will do your hair and makeup tomorrow night."

"Why are you being this kind to me when you don't even know me?"

"We like you, Gemma. We see how John's changed since he met you. Holland's death really shook him."

"I don't really feel worthy, to be honest."

"When I fell in love with Gus, I knew I wasn't good enough for him," Daffy said. "Plus, the queen would never let me in the Family. I knew the great secret. Scottie."

Gemma let herself relax, finally letting go enough to enjoy the moment.

"My mum was Her Majesty's secretary before she went to work at the Royal Trust. I used to run around the palace with the princes and during a hide-n-seek game, I hid in the queen's closet. I overheard her on the phone with Scottie's father. I was young and didn't understand the nuances but I knew I'd just heard a great secret. I told my mother, though, who told me to write it down in a book and forget it. Fast forward twenty years and the blame thing fell into the hands of my friend and TV presenter Leslie Ann. And here we are."

"Princess Daffy, I'm not looking to marry John or anything. We're friends. That's all."

"If the look in his eye as well as yours is just friends, what must Gus and I look like to everyone? What's wrong with being in love with him? If he's the right one, things will work out. I was engaged to someone else when I realized I loved Gus. Of course, I refused to believe it until I met this very odd woman. Very mysterious. Adelaide."

"Adelaide?" Gemma shifted in her chair, adjusting the heavy skirt away from her legs. "Piquant face and Brillo pad hair?"

The princess gripped Gemma's arm. "Have you seen her?"

"I have. She came into The Wedding Shop where I work," Gemma said. "She claimed to be an angel, but I was pretty sure she was sent by a friend as a joke. He likes to punk people."

"Did he send her to punk me too?"

"Well no. But he could've heard your story?"

"I've never told my story about Adelaide to anyone but Princess Corina from Brighton Kingdom. She was the first to meet her. Then she visited me and now you. Gemma, she's no ordinary angel. She prepares future princesses."

The chill of recognition spread through her. "That's what she told me but I thought she was making it up."

"Daffy." Gemma reached for her arm. "Adelaide is for real?"

"She's for real. I don't understand it all, but when heaven decides to invade earth, who are we to argue? Oh, shoes." Daffy pushed up from her chair. "Pregnancy brain. I'll be back."

When she returned, Daffy placed a pair of crystal-studded shoes with red soles at Gemma's feet.

"These are very special shoes. Princess Susanna of Brighton Kingdom wore them to the ball where she and King Nathaniel fell in love. She had a different sort of angel, a woman named Aurora, who gave these to her. Then Susanna gave them to me when I attended John and Holland's wedding ball. Gus didn't know I was going to be there. His face when I came running toward him, across the field to where he stood... Well, my heart nearly burst. I'll never forget it." Daffy's eyes glowed as she handed the shoes to Gemma. "Now I'm giving them to you."

"Give? Lend. I'm not taking your angel shoes."

"You will if I say so. And keep an eye out for Adelaide in case she visits you again." Daffy stood back with a glow of admiration. "You are going to steal the show tomorrow night, Gemma."

"I don't know about that but I'll try my best to have a good time."

She'd dance with John in this one-of-a-kind gown, wearing a pair of Cinderella shoes in front of five hundred pairs of eyes and past a slew of hot, gossipy whisperers.

Maybe the point of her prince journey was to realize how foolish she'd been the last two years. Terrified, almost paralyzed with fear over people finding out she'd surrendered everything she believed in, every core value for fame and fortune.

Maybe that's what Adelaide the Angel was really trying to tell her. To merely think of herself as a princess.

Gemma had wrapped herself in guilt and shame, almost proudly, and refused to see herself any other way. She could fake it with friends and family, even John, but inside, she knew the whole truth. Saw the real woman beneath her talent, her beauty, and even her kindness.

But the Vegas files had been destroyed. God, or fate—hey, maybe Adelaide—had been looking out for her.

Got to say, it was nice to have a touch of supernatural on her side.

GEMMA

She finally knew what it felt like to walk on clouds. Even under the weight of the gown and wearing a new pair of heels, she floated through every dance.

She and the prince only left the dance floor when the orchestra took a break. Then John shuffled her off to a private room for hors d'oeuvres where she met King Nathaniel and Princess Susanna, Prince Stephen and Princess Corina from Brighton Kingdom, and Grand Duchess, Princess Regina from Hessenberg and her husband, Tanner.

All the princesses were southern American girls, and the moment they met it was like old home week.

After hours of dancing and twirling to stringed waltzes and stumbling through quadrilles, she was warm and energized, drinking in the magic of it all. The splendor.

When John suggested, "Let's get out of here," he took her hand as she gathered the heavy skirt, leaving the bright and vibrant ballroom with its gilded walls, glistening floor, and crystal chandeliers for the glorious darkness of a half-moon night.

Laughing, feeling as if they were getting away with something, they ran down the Queen's Avenue with abandon toward Clemency. Toward the Heart of God. And the crystal shoes bore with her.

"Gunner will be miffed we left him behind," John said.

"Should we tell him?" Gemma stumbled on a crack in the concrete and fell into him. He caught her about the waist and pressed his forehead to hers.

"We've got to stop meeting like this."

"I think you stumbled first. Just like on the Fourth of July."

"No, it was you. I think you wanted me to carry you."

"In your dreams. And like you could carry me in this dress." She turned away from him, but before she could take a step, she was in his arms, her face inches from his, the dress's skirt cascading down.

"Where should we go?" he said.

She was about to say "put me down" but instead she wrapped her arms about his neck. "The Heart of God, of course."

When they arrived, the cathedral lights seemed to blink and wave in greeting. John set Gemma on her feet but they fell against each other. Gemma stretched her hand to the fountain's cool, flowing water.

When she looked up at John, he held her close and kissed her.

"You made me proud tonight," he said, his lips against her ear. "Everyone loved you. The Hessenberg ambassador wanted to know where I'd been hiding you and from what aristocratic family you hailed. I said, 'She's from Tennessee.' He said, 'An American? Not another one,' but he was smiling." John kissed down her cheek to her lips. "Truly, love, he admired you."

"He barely knows me."

"Your dress reminds me of the fairy tale, *The Swan's Feather*."

"The one your mother told you?" Gemma stepped back. His kiss was awakening things in her she'd rather leave asleep. "Prince, this is not a fairy tale."

"When Holland died, I found a swan's feather on the abbey floor. But there were no swans in the nave. Then the other night, after we talked in the corridor, I found another feather."

Gemma made a face. "What are you saying? This dress with feathers is a sign? John, we're not living in a bedtime story where everything works out. Where feathers appear out of nowhere to guide us to our destiny and happily ever after."

He reached for her and she didn't resist. Resting her head against his chest, she let herself just be in the moment—standing with this amazing man in the Heart of God, listening to the music of the fountain...

Let this be her happily ever after. Even if it only lasted a night.

"I know we don't live in a fairy tale, Gemma. But I also know I don't want you to go home Sunday." The prince began to move in a melodic sway, humming the same tune from Monday evening, and Gemma flowed with him in body, mind, and soul.

"Gemma, don't you think—"

"Shh, Prince, let's just enjoy the lights, the fountain, you and me, this dress of feathers—"

"Which could be a sign." He leaned to see her face. "I find two random feathers and then you walk out of your suite bedroom wearing a million of them."

"Remember this feathered frock belongs to your sister-in-law."

"But now it belongs to you."

"Tomorrow it will be Princess Daffy's again." Gemma pulled free of him. He was dreaming too much. Talking crazy. "Prince, we've had a marvelous time together. I admire you, and am so grateful to have met you, but this is the end of the line for us save a Christmas card here and there."

"It doesn't have to be the end, Gemma." His low tone made her shiver. Where was he going with this? "I've been thinking—"

"No thinking tonight. Just pretend *this* is forever. And when the clock strikes mid—"

"Marry me."

His question startled her, and suddenly she felt the entire weight of the gown. "What?"

"Marry me. I realized this week you're my best friend. I want to talk to you first thing in the morning and in the evening before lights out. When something interesting, or not so interesting, happens I think, 'Wait until Gemma hears this.' So why not marry? As you know, I need a wife—"

"John, the clock has struck midnight. The spell is broken. We go back to our real selves You cannot marry me. I live in Hearts Bend. I have Imani. She wants to graduate from Rock Mill High. And you, *you*, simply cannot marry me." The very idea of what the press would unearth if she married this man made her weak where she stood. Despite Matt's assurance the videos no longer existed, she'd taken a huge chance stepping out with a crown prince tonight. "John, I'm not royal material, trust me. I'm starting to think they put something strange in the punch at the ball tonight that's making you actually believe in fairy tales."

"My darling, you are perfect royal material. Smart, loving, kind. Beautiful. We can work out the details with Imani." The light of the cathedrals illuminated the seriousness in his blue eyes. "Having my best friend with me on this journey makes my heart light."

"John, listen to yourself. Please." If she said yes, she'd have to tell him about Vegas and that she could not do. Ever. She turned toward the street. "We should go."

Upon her words, the cathedral clocks pealed the hour, striking the twelve chimes of midnight. When the last bell rang out, the night was over and as far as Gemma was concerned, the magic, the spell, was broken.

"That's it?" Prince John said. "'We should go?' You're not going to even consider my proposal?"

She turned to face him. "All right, I've considered it and no, I won't marry you."

"Why not?"

"Do you even love me?" Gemma dragged herself and the heavy dress back to him.

"Do you love me?"

Yes, she did. The truth beat in her chest. "John, this summer has been *unusual* to say the least. But let's not mix up our friendship with real love."

"Being best friends is the perfect start for us. I'm not sure I could even say that about Holland. I want to be with you, Gemma. If our kiss that night in the rain is any indication of our, shall we say, *chemistry*, I know I can love you like a man should love the woman he married. We're good together and tonight I saw how well you fit into my world."

"You're caught up in a moment, Prince. The lights in the Heart of God, the chimes, the air, the music, and the whatever happened here Monday night. But you're not ready to get married again. You said so yourself."

"Because I was grieving and scared. What are you afraid of, Gemma?"

"How much time you got?" She smiled which relieved a bit of the tension. "Look, by this time next year, you'll have married a gorgeous Lauchten woman with raven hair and ruby lips, who's a brilliant entrepreneur of some kind and represents the future of your people." She grabbed a handful of the gown's skirt—which felt heavier than ever—and stepped toward the curb. "Trust me, I'm not that girl."

Gone, gone, was the mystery of the Heart of God, the swirl of the light, the fragrance, and the freedom. She was back in the dark pit of her past.

"Gemma." His voice was stern. "What are you not telling me?"

"Nothing." From the corner of her eye, she caught a glimpse of Gunner who stood off to the side, watching and waiting.

"I know there's something. Tell me. Is it losing your property? Someone swindled you. It could happen to anyone. But I can help with that, I can. What if we keep a residence in Hearts Bend?"

She held her reply as she walked into the night. Another word and she'd burst into tears.

"Gemma, wait. Gemma."

CHAPTER
TWENTY-FIVE

JOHN

She had a secret. He knew it. But she refused to tell. Brushing his teeth to the solitary chime of one a.m., John tried to imagine what she held close.

If she couldn't tell him, maybe he'd overestimated their connection. Their friendship. The passion he felt when he kissed her.

As he rinsed his toothbrush, an idea flashed. Her Majesty's Security Detail had sent over a dossier on Ms. Stone a few weeks ago but he'd been on his way to a walkabout at the time. He tucked it in a drawer for later inspection.

Then, in the course of things, he decided not to look inside. If there was some dark secret she harbored, who was he to ramrod his way through? Wasn't the news hers to tell when she was ready?

But now, he had to know. Leaving his apartment, he made his way to his office, the footman on duty eyeing him from the other side of the second-floor gallery. Hadn't he ever seen a man in his pajama bottoms before?

Clicking on the desk lamp, John pulled out the dossier. If there was something, Her Majesty's Security would find it.

Born in Hearts Bend, Tennessee. Date of birth. Parents' and grandparents' names. Salaries. No family criminal record. None. So that wasn't it. Gemma graduated salutatorian. She never said. Was a cheerleader during football season. Played basketball.

Moved to L.A. fourteen years ago. Spent a year in Las Vegas before coming home. Was in the hospital. For a month. Ah, so that was the source of her limp. But what was so bad she couldn't tell him?

Returned to Hearts Bend upon release from the hospital. Bought the property, the farm, for a hundred and fifty thousand dollars.

Boyfriend: Matt Biglow.

Then came driver's license pictures. Just before turning to the final page, he closed the dossier.

He'd seen enough. If there was more, he didn't want to know. He'd had enough with the women he admired harboring secrets. If there was something in Gemma's past she didn't want him to know, who was he to unearth it?

Perhaps she was right. He was reading too much into their unusual summer. She'd turned him down. Let that be the end of it.

Move on, mate. From now on Gemma would simply be the woman who helped bring him out of his grief.

John tossed the dossier in the rubbish and headed back to apartment A2.

He awoke to the sound of rain and an urgent-sounding door chime. He rolled over and buried his head under his pillow but he could still hear Shaw.

"He's still asleep, Your Royal Highness."

"I'll wake him." Gus. What did he want?

"Good, you're awake." Gus pulled John's pillow from his head. He wore short trousers, boat shoes, a sweatshirt, and a slicker.

"Aren't you supposed to be sailing?" John said, getting out of bed, tugging on a T-shirt before heading to the tea trolley.

"We've delayed an hour. Mum had a rough night and Dad wanted to make sure she was sorted before shoving off. And it's raining. But the weather presenter says the clouds will roll away by midmorning."

"Is Mum all right?" John popped a puff in his mouth. "Should I go see her?"

"The nurse is with her. Check on her this afternoon." Gus sat at the dining table looking solemnly at John. "Have you seen it?"

"Seen what?" John fixed a cup of tea and dropped a few puffs on his plate.

"The video of Gemma?"

"What video?"

Gus opened his phone then slid it across the table toward him. "It's all over the internet."

John tapped the screen with a sense of dread. The play button waited on the video Gus queued up. Would he see what possibly was on the final page of her dossier?

John set the phone down. "Do I want to know?"

"Probably not but you should."

With a deep inhale, John grabbed the phone and tapped play. Then *swoosh*, a spotlight hit a long runway and Gemma paraded toward the camera, wearing nothing more than strategically placed leather straps. Her short hair was slicked back. Her features accented and highlighted with makeup but there was no life in her eyes. Vacant. She looked vacant. When she began her routine, John tossed the phone to the table.

"Is this a show in Vegas?"

"It was supposed to be but it never saw the light of day. However, one film buff saw it when it was online and downloaded it. He's a porter at the Delafield. He recognized Gemma. He uploaded it early this morning."

"I asked her to marry me last night." Now he knew why she refused to tell him. Why she refused his proposal.

"You what?" Gus said.

"She turned me down. Joked about the spell being broken when the cathedral clocks struck midnight."

"John, our life is not your *Swan's Feather* fairy tale."

"It's Rachel's fairy tale now."

"You know what I mean. Whoever you marry impacts us all. Impacts Lauchtenland. Never mind the gossip and scrutiny Gemma would be subjected to. When she goes home, all of this will mercifully go away." Gus sighed. "Eventually. The Chamber Office line is jammed with calls. Hamish Fickle is out there asking why you brought a woman of the night to a formal, state function."

"She's not a woman of the—" He shoved away from the table. "I need to talk to her."

"And tell her what?"

"That she's still my best friend and I think, no, I'm sure. I love her."

GEMMA

He'd proposed. Of all the things she imagined between them, a true and honest proposal was not one of them. She'd not allowed herself to even pretend it was possible.

Then there he was, asking. While standing in the Heart of God. It was romantic and serendipitous. And not real. They were both caught up in the beauty and sensations of the Heart.

God would not want her to marry Prince John. He knew what she did and yes, though she actually felt forgiven after Monday evening, that didn't make her fit for a queen.

In the meantime, she lay awake long after she'd crawled into bed and stored her memories. The colors, sights, and sounds of ancient Port Fressa. The music of the ball. The timbre of John's voice.

Over time, everything would fade—like all summer memories—but she'd treasure them for now.

On the end table, her phone chimed. Scottie texted asking to meet for breakfast.

"I want to hear about last night and also I'm extending my stay."

"Give me twenty minutes."

Across the room, the swan gown hung from the top of the closet, the skirt just barely touching the floor.

Gemma kicked out of bed to walk over, and traced her hand across the embellishments, down to the feathers. "Thank you."

In the bathroom she started the shower. Princess Daffy's stylist had lacquered Gemma's hair something fierce. Finding the palace's laminated apartment intercom guide, she punched in the numbers for 3C, the spare heir's apartment. There was no answer so she left a message regarding the gown.

"Shall I bring it to you?"

With a final glance at the dress, she reached for her phone. She'd not taken a picture of it. Haley and JoJo would go bonkers.

She took a couple of shots then, on a whim, checked social media. Why not? She'd find a picture of her in the dress—there were so many cameras aimed at John last night—and send it to Hal and Jo, Mama, Daddy, and Imani. Though Imani followed the House of Blue accounts and would probably know more than Gemma.

Finding one of the royal fan sites she checked after the prince had left Hearts Bend, she dropped to the bed when the first image on her screen was of her and Prince John walking into the ballroom. He looked stunning in his tuxedo with his rakish smile and rich, dark hair.

You love him. So, what does it matter? I'm going home.

There were a lot of comments about how beautiful she looked—thank you—but more on how stunning the dress was.

Checking another site, she squinted at the first image. It was very dark. The text below read, "Gemma Stone a stripper?"

What? Gemma slipped from the bed to the floor. "Matt Biglow…no, no, no. You promised me."

Wait, maybe someone from her past hopped on one of these sites and *said* Gemma was a stripper but without any evidence. Besides, *she* wasn't a stripper. She merely played one on a fake reality show.

Drawing a deep breath, she tapped one of the hashtags to find hundreds of clips of her single performance. The one she'd spent twelve hours shooting, devoid of her soul, grateful for the merciful fall from the stage that broke her hip and miraculously ended the show's chance of ever being seen.

News outlets, blogs, royal watchers, and fans, everyone was posting some version of the video. Thank goodness she fell before the final, *um*, reveal.

She'd never forgive herself for letting Matt and Sandy talk her into that *stupid* show.

Gemma looked up as a splatter of rain hit her window. Go! She had to...go. Now. Get out of here. She ran to the door before realizing she was not dressed. Nor did she have any of her things. She snatched her suitcase from the dressing room, tossed in her pajamas, and the rest of her clothes, then swooped up everything from the bathroom. Meanwhile, the shower continued to run.

Wrapping her hair in a topknot—she'd have to live with the lacquer—she stepped into the large tile-and-porcelain stall, did a five-second wash, dried, dressed, and loaded up her travel backpack.

The suite doorbell chimed when she paused for one final sweep of the room. *Quiet. Don't move. Whoever you are, don't come in, please don't come in.*

A muffled voice called her name. Gemma held her breath, waiting.

Just let me go without being seen. Please.

No doubt the Family, the footmen, and the butlers had watched the video by now. John had seen the video. This was worse than just telling him. Now he was seeing. Even more hideous, if that's possible, by the time she landed in Nashville, everyone in Hearts Bend would know her shame.

She was going to be sick. But there was no time.

Waiting, listening, perspiration stinging down her back, the bell ringer must've gone. Gemma exited the bedroom just as the suite door clicked. She was caught. Found out. The intruder was a pretty, dark-haired maid.

"Begging your pardon, miss, I thought you'd gone."

"On my way." She hitched her travel pack over her shoulder and dragged her suitcase over the carpet. "Is the hall clear?"

She nodded and Gemma scooted past her without a word, gathering all her steel and courage.

Instead of going down the main stairs and past the footman, she headed toward the south corner of the palace—she'd discovered the hidden stairs while on tour with the palace historian—then toward the gate she'd exited with the prince and Otis.

She cleared the door without seeing anyone else and ran, dodging raindrops as she hurried down the walkway, barely able to control her legs.

But the gate was locked with a keypad. *Of course*, it was locked. Gemma jerked on the wrought iron with a rush of tears. "Please, let me out!"

A buzz sounded and the lock released. Gemma pushed free with a glance over her shoulder to see a footman watching her go.

Making her way to the taxi stand, the rain picking up a bit, she dialed Matt. She didn't care what time it was in L.A.

"You liar," she said when he picked up. "I asked for one truthful thing, but no. One night was all I wanted. One beautiful night. Why did you do it? Release a video."

"Let me guess, is this Gemma?"

"Like you didn't expect this call. You told me you didn't have the videos. Promised me."

"I don't. What is going on?"

"One of the Vegas show is online. I think it's the one where I fell from the stage."

"What do you mean, online?"

She gave him the hashtags to search, and after a moment he let out a long, weighty sigh.

"Gemma, I'm sorry, but I didn't do this. Hold on."

She arrived at the taxi stand, thankful to find a car waiting. "Airport, please."

The driver helped her with her luggage, looking closely at her. Had he seen it too? When she crawled into the backseat, she sank down to hide her face.

Then she lost her battle with her tears. This was par for the course. Her life. Journey of a thousand bad decisions.

"You there?" Matt said.

"Yeah." Gemma kept her voice low, close to the phone.

"The videos were uploaded by a kid named Clowney. His bio says he's a movie buff, wannabe producer-director, works in the hotel industry. Am I still blocked? Can I send you a pic?"

"Send it." When Matt's text pinged in, she recognized the man at once. "Arnez."

"You know him?"

"He was a porter at the Delafield Hotel. He said he'd seen me somewhere before, but I thought he was making it up. Flirting or something."

"He must have found my site when I put the video online after the network lost interest."

She wanted to hate Matt but at the moment, he was the only one who really understood. To her chagrin, he also sounded sorry and sympathetic.

"Why did I let you talk me into that stupid show? Why?" She fell over onto the seat. "I knew this day would come. Gemma Stone, this is your life."

"If it's any comfort, I didn't want that show in the light of day either. I'm working with Jeremiah Gonda on a project and he is very selective. He'd never have hired me if he knew I was a part of something like that."

"Showgirls, you said. We were supposed to be about showgirls."

"I know but Sandy took it in a different direction and we went along."

She hated the pronoun we. But he was right. She and the other nine girls in the show agreed to the modified premise.

"I knew this would haunt me sooner or later."

"Again, I'm sorry. But I was trying to make something happen for us. What do you want from me? I can't undo it."

Her tears pooled on the worn leather seat. "I want my dignity, Matt. Give me back my dignity."

"Yeah, that'd be great if I took it. Truth is, Gemma, you gave it away. We all gave away our dignity. If you want it back, go get it."

"Too late for that, isn't it?"

"As a matter of fact, no. Let this be my final advice to you. Don't let this get you down. Beat it, Gemma. Don't let it beat you."

She sat up and dried her eyes. "Thanks, Matt. I mean it."

At the airport, she sat in a corner and searched for a flight back to Nashville. When nothing popped up, she got in the long line up to the ticket counter. From her travel pack, her phone pinged and dinged, but she refused to answer.

The ticket agent informed her she could not exchange her Sunday morning first-class ticket for another flight. Even more joyous, there were no seats on a Nashville flight until tomorrow. But if she wanted, she could purchase the only remaining seat on a flight to New York.

Last row. Middle seat.

Gemma slapped down her credit card. "I also need the first flight to Nashville." The ticket agent typed and frowned, sighed, then typed and frowned again.

Maybe she was paranoid, but she kept feeling the heat of second glances. Heard the mumbling of "on the internet."

After an *eternity*, the agent announced Gemma was booked through to Nashville. For two-thousand-fifty-one dollars and sixty-three cents.

Gemma breathed a sigh of relief. Best two grand she'd ever spend.

She arrived at her gate hungry and on the verge of tears. No, not tears. Meltdown. The reality of it all began to anchor in. A familiar panic stirred but she was too weary, too angry, too sad to give in to it.

Grabbing a sandwich and chips, she returned to her gate and waited to board. Once she was in the air, she'd have eight hours to work on her explanation, find some sense of the girl she was yesterday, before the video shocked the world. And tell herself over and over she was not the girl in that dark video anymore.

She was the girl from the Heart of God. The girl full of light.

CHAPTER
TWENTY-SIX

JOHN

A ugust twenty-first. How things had changed since he buried his wife a year ago. John stood alone on the lush, green plot of ground of the Royal Memorial Garden where his wife would be remembered forever.

The granite headstone had been polished to a sheen, and when a slice of evening sun broke through the summer clouds, John walked on a lighted path.

Placing the final bronze wreath on the hook of an iron pole, he said a few words in private. The roto surrounded him, their cameras whirring and flashing. Boom handlers stretched their microphones to catch one word, any word, of his memorial sentiments.

His parents waited behind him in dark attire and solemn expressions. Holland's parents, Lord and Lady Cunningham, were *unavailable*.

Cletus was out on bail, now campaigning he'd been framed. John anticipated he'd implicated Holland, his own daughter, to maintain his innocence.

A quartet of trumpeters began playing Lauchtenland's national anthem, and John knelt down to place his hand over her name.

Her Royal Highness, Princess Holland Caroline, House of Blue

"I wish you were here to tell me what happened. Why did you lie to me about the diamond? I wish you were here because that was our plan."

The trumpeters moved from the anthem to an old Lauchtenland hymn. John stood. Time to begin again.

Holland was gone. Gemma also. At least now he understood why she refused to talk about her Hollywood career. Why she said they would never be more than friends.

Still the images of her swaying through the orbs and beams in the Heart of God would forever live in his mind. The light loved her. He loved her.

He retreated and bowed to his parents, who moved forward to pay their respects, Mum leaning on Dad.

John stood with Gus and Daffy. Since the day his brother had shown him the video, they'd not spoken of it.

Gemma slipped away five days ago without a word. A footman confirmed she left out the southern gate. Were all the women in his life to harbor some dark secret? Holland. Gemma. Even Mum, who concealed Scottie for thirty-five years.

He'd been tempted to text Gemma. But what could he say?

"Is this what you didn't want to tell me?"

Maybe their friendship wasn't as deep as he believed. Perhaps his feelings were all one-sided.

John smiled as Mum approached, leaning more on her cane than Dad. She faced a long recovery, even with treatment. Still Guillain-Barré had never gone to war with Queen Catherine before.

Dad proclaimed Scottie's visit as Mum's number one tonic. She'd returned home yesterday but she and Mum seemed to have a constant text running.

When the last song was played, John returned to his car and waved to the roto—which was made up of familiar faces. Men and women he knew well. They'd be kind today, speaking of Holland's accomplishments and avoiding the latest news.

He paused for a few questions, Gunner and another protection officer by his side. The questions were soft and friendly. Until John said he must move on.

"Was Holland involved with the Reingard scandal? Did she ever say anything to you?" Once Perry Copperfield breached the barrier, everyone started talking, firing off questions about Lord

Cunningham, Holland's involvement, the reality of conviction.

"Let's wait to see what the lawyers have to say, shall we?"

"What about the woman in the videos? Gemma Stone. Are you romantically involved? Is she a fit future queen?"

"Prince John, did you know about her Vegas career?"

He answered with a wave and ducked into the car with the flapping royal standards. As they cleared the garden gate and moved into Port Fressa traffic, Gunner tapped something into his phone, then tucked it away. John gazed over at him.

"Do you have something to say?"

"It wouldn't be proper."

"Say it if it's worthy."

Gunner fixed his attention beyond the window to the passing buildings and shops on the western side, the oldest side, of the city.

"Don't give up on her." He gave John a look. "I watched her in Hearts Bend and again when she was here. She's the real deal, sir. I know you see it because I observed you with her. I know the recent *findings* put her in a bad light, but whatever made her *perform* in that video is not who she is now. We all make mistakes."

"I'm not judging her for it, Gunner. By the vacant look in her eyes, she didn't want to be there. But will the Family, the country, accept her? Does she want this little bit of information following her the rest of her life? We're talking the House of Blue and the monarchy. We may live in a world where morals are wide and varied, but there are some lines that cannot be crossed."

"If Princess Holland were alive and you learned the truth about her misconduct, would you toss her aside?" Gunner was finding many worthy things to say. "She'd have broken some moral code. Corruption, insider trading, malfeasance."

"If we were already married, no. Besides, Gunner, Gemma has made the decision for me. She doesn't want to marry me. Now I know why."

"She left to protect you," Gunner said. "That makes her a hero in my book."

277

"No one is asking for your book."

"If she's your friend, if you care about her at all, you must reach out. She'll think the videos have disgraced her in your eyes. Or that you're turning your back on her. Show her you love her and forgive her."

"You sound like the reverend at the Christmas Eve service. And what's for me to forgive? What she did in her life before me is not my concern. She didn't cheat on me or lie to me." No, lying was all Holland.

"Do you love her?" Gunner fearlessly crossed the boundaries between royal and staff.

"You know as well as I do if we married the video will haunt her the rest of her life. Do you want to subject her to scrutiny and ridicule for the next fifty years? Even beyond her natural life, in the history books." John held up his palm as if reading from some book. "'Before becoming a princess and queen of Lauchtenland, Gemma Stone was an ambitious actress. She eventually took a role as a stripper, which came to light when King John invited her to attend the stupid NSINS Ball with him.'"

"Henry the VIII was a lusty man," Gunner said. "Murdered his wives in order to move on to his next conquest. Our Prince Louis V only settled down after his father forced him. But everyone knew he was on a first-name basis with the women at Madam Le Crux's."

The motor turned in to the palace and round to the main entrance. A footman hurried to open John's door. "Good night, Gunner."

"One more thing, sir. If I may?"

"Why stop now? What is it?"

"I spend a lot of time observing people. I can read faces. Gemma loved you from the moment she clapped eyes on you. If I were you, and I'm not, I'd not let someone like Gemma go without hearing the whole story. Love is a precious gift, sir. Don't waste hers for you on technicalities like what the press will say or history will write. In fifty years, no one will remember anything but your good works, the strength of your reign, and your love for your wife."

CATHERINE

Edric entered as she turned off the news.

"Dinner's almost ready," he said. "I feel like a rebel eating in the living room on telly trays. Mum never allowed it growing up. I only experienced it at friends' houses."

He lowered to the chair next to the couch where Catherine reclined under a blanket, her e-reader on the coffee table, her phone cradled in her lap.

"I know that look," he said. "What are you thinking?"

"I was reading the briefs on the Reingard case. It's clear Cletus Cunningham was involved."

"And Holland?"

"Yes, but I'm not sure how much."

"Anything pointing back to John?"

"No, thank goodness."

"Then there's the Gemma Stone video." Edric helped Catherine sit up as the footmen carried in their dinner.

"Mason tells me it's all over social media." Catherine stared at her plate. She was too sedentary to have much of an appetite.

"Have you spoken to him?"

"I'm giving us space. I'm not ready for a tense row with my son. Just thinking about it wears me out."

"Why does it have to be a row? He's as shocked as we are."

"But you know what I have to say and he'll push back." Catherine's phone pinged. Scottie. Her daughter. "Scottie is sending me pictures of her home. Her design taste is excellent."

Edric leaned over to see the photo. "Don't you feel silly you sent John to meet her instead of going yourself?"

"Hush. Don't question your queen."

"I suppose it worked out. You'd have been ill in America, and John created a nice bridge between Scottie and us."

"That's what Scottie said about Gemma. She was the bridge

between her and John. That's why she invited her to come as a companion."

"Do you think John loves her?" Edric said.

"I don't know. We'll have to ask him. He's only known her a couple of months. What about Scottie? Do you like her? Tell me honestly."

"I like her very much." He cut a bit of chicken. "She's very keen and sharp. I'll do my bit as the doting stepfather."

Catherine smiled and cut a piece of chicken. "We talked of a family gathering at Christmas."

"Really? Just us or the O'Shays as well."

"Just us. Then later the O'Shays perhaps."

"What if he loves her?"

"Who?" Once she started eating the chicken, she found she was hungry.

"Gemma, who else? I think John's very keen on her."

"Edric, you know what would await her if she joined the Family. Gossip, ridicule, scrutiny. The video will never die. Do you really think John loves her? He's disappointed in Holland, I know, but I think he's still in love with her."

"He's told you this?"

"Are you going to challenge everything I say? Pour me some water, please."

"Not to change the subject." Edric filled Catherine's glass, then his own. "I've been thinking about Hamish Fickle's little anti-monarchy campaign. Why not invite him for an audience with you? Get him on our side."

"Go on," Catherine said.

"If you ask me, he just wants attention. Validation. Like the boys used to do when they were young. We'd spend an evening with them and they'd be fine."

"If he's looking for approval, he chose a poor path by going into the parliament."

"Let's invite him here. You listen to his complaints about the monarchy, his plans to improve things, affirm him, and voila, he's on our side."

"I wonder at your recollection. There are a good many politicians who have never wanted to be on *our* side."

"We have to win one over sometime," Edric said.

"From what I can see, Hamish Fickle's plan for government improvements is to do the same thing a different way. Only with him in charge."

"Of course, he's young, isn't he? For him, history began the day he was born."

"All right, I'll invite him to the palace," Catherine said. "But I get to say I told you so."

"As do I, my darling. As do I. Now what's on the telly?"

Catherine reached over to squeeze her husband's hand. He was a gift. A compliment to her. John must find the same sort of love to walk with him through his reign.

And Catherine, the mother, and Queen Catherine, the monarch, knew Gemma Stone was not the one.

Then again, Emmanuel, whom she'd not seen since his visit to her hospital room, might have a thing or two to say about John's future bride.

If he had plans to speak to her son, then he'd best get on with it.

"Can our crown prince and future king marry a woman with a sordid background? If he did, he wouldn't be the first. On the blog today, the scandalous love affairs of Europe's royal families."

— *LOYAL ROYALS BLOG*

If you ask me, the prince should run from this girl. Why? Those videos will follow her the rest of her life. Who'd want that? Give her some privacy.

— *@STEFWITHANF ON INSTAGRAM*

"Prince John lays the final memorial wreath on Princess Holland's grave amid questions of her involvement with her father in the Reingard scandal."

— *THE NEWS LEADER*

"My heart breaks for Prince John. Maddie, look at this image of him alone at her grave. Solemn and dignified. I'm weeping, truly."

— *HYACINTH ON THE MADELINE &*
HYACINTH LIVE!

CHAPTER
TWENTY-SEVEN

GEMMA

She arrived home on a Sunday afternoon. Forty-four hours after she left Port Fressa.

A delay at LaGuardia was followed by a flight cancellation which stranded Gemma until Sunday morning.

They'd just started boarding the eight o'clock flight to Nashville when the gate agent announced the toilets were broken so they were going nowhere soon.

Couldn't they all just hold it for the two-hour-and-forty-minute flight? Anyone ever stood in a line to ride Space Mountain during the height of Disney tourism?

At least, praise God, she made a twelve-thirty flight—back row, middle seat—and when she rolled her luggage through Nashville's airport to catch an Uber ride home, she paused to kiss the ground. Literally.

Good news though. During her layover at LaGuardia, she'd rented a shower and washed the lacquer from her hair. Two hours, five bottles of travel shampoo, and a thousand gallons of hot water did the trick.

When she returned to her gate, her skin beamed like she'd spent a week on the beach without sunscreen.

At an overpriced women's store, she purchased a change of clothes. Then she paused at the bookshop when an interesting-looking novel caught her eye. Back at the gate, she curled up with a sandwich, chips, and water ready to get distracted from her life with a good story.

But after an hour of reading the first paragraph over and over she gave up. Tired, unnerved, restless, and shamed, she just wanted to go home and hide. Home and hiding worked for her. Even if she only had her home for a few more weeks.

During the long flight over the Atlantic, she ate about ten mini bags of nuts and pretzels and slept fitfully. Yet twice she fell into a deep sleep where she dreamed of dancing through the lights in the Heart of God while wearing a gown of swan's feathers, a handsome, glorious prince watching in the distance. Just as he reached for her, a bump of turbulence jolted her awake.

While awake, the whole mess was a nightmare. She couldn't stop thinking about it. Couldn't stop imagining the prince's reaction. She grabbed for another bag of snacks every time.

What must he think? Did he watch it? The whole thing? Was there any room for her to explain? To tell the rest of the story? How she fell from the stage because of swaths of bright lights and shadowy darkness. How she hated what she was doing so much she'd mentally checked out.

On the flight to Nashville, she began to prep for the family. For her friends. What would, *could* she say to them?

"Oh yeah, I filmed a risqué show in Vegas. Anyone up for pie at Ella's?"

When the Uber driver, Burt, turned onto the farm's driveway, Gemma felt as if time had stood still. As if the hour was the minute before she left with Scottie. As if the past week hadn't happened. As if there was no video. As if there was no shock and shame.

Mama and Daddy greeted her with enthusiastic, in fact, overly enthusiastic hugs, and escorted her inside where the old stove had managed to bake a lasagna.

Over salad Daddy announced he'd fixed the leak in the bathroom sink.

"The Kingstons will probably gut the place but at least they'll know it was in good hands with you."

Over lasagna, Mama regaled them with housekeeping tales from the Hearts Bend Inn.

"The man left a pile of sunflower shells six inches high beside his bed. Just left it there! Can you imagine?"

Over dessert—cherry pie from Ella's—Imani talked about school, volleyball, the upcoming basketball season, Justin and Penny, and her bid for Junior Class President.

"I'm running against Blake Gooch and everyone says he's the best-looking guy in our class. But I'll crush him during our debate."

That's when she dashed to her room and returned with a set of debate-crushing three-by-five cards.

Afterwards, Mama cleaned up while Daddy and Imani insisted on taking care of the herd.

"You just rest. Long trip home," Daddy said.

Not once did any of them ask about Port Fressa, Prince John, living in a palace, or the magic of attending a royal ball. Though Gemma could see a thousand questions looming large in Imani's hazel eyes.

But any story of Lauchtenland led to questions about the video. Not to mention the secret even social media couldn't dig up.

Prince John had proposed. And there she found a bit of a silver lining. The one good decision on her journey of a thousand bad ones. She'd turned him down. It made her breathing easier. Her anxiety lighter. Prince John from the House of Blue would not be saddled with her story for the rest of his life.

She was proud of herself. Truly. Then it took the rest of her effort to not admit she was in love with him. But she had the rest of her life to get over it.

Sunday night she slept hard. Monday she grounded herself in her day-to-day, unpacking, doing laundry, spending time with the herd, loving on the puppies, sitting under the trees by the pond, and burning the midnight oil to pack up the house.

Tuesday, she returned to work where Haley and JoJo—who were never shy about prying into Gemma's personal life—said not word one about any of it.

They talked about the shop, their plans for the weekend, Buck's new song, Cole's new construction project, and how Haley's daughter Emily, two, had picked out a song on the piano.

"She's a prodigy, I just know it."

Breath-by-breath, morning-by-morning, day-by-day, Gemma put the past behind her and pressed toward her future. It was the only way to survive.

August turned into September. The first Saturday turned into moving day.

The Music Row exec from the private flight over to London came over with his family to pick out two of the puppies. They left with Ross and Rachel, and two very happy children.

Penny adopted Joey and Justin's mama took Phoebe home in a monogramed wool-lined bed.

The rabbits went to a petting zoo in Cincinnati. The goats were adopted by a farm in Ashland City. The folks there loved Miss Frances. Hooley called and said he'd take the barn cats.

"Doc says they're fixed so I won't have to worry about kittens but I just love a barn full of cats."

Suddenly the barnyard was lonely, and Gemma began to feel lost, unanchored. At this stage in her life, she intended to feel like she had a handle on things. At least what the next five to ten years might look like. Instead, she was broke and moving home with her parents.

At least she had Imani. She was Gemma's bright future. She'd give her all to her.

In all of this, one little thing nagged her from the back of her mind. Her so-called best friend, Prince John, had gone silent. She'd not even had so much as a text from him. Admittedly her phone was shut off for the first two days, but now, after some of the brouhaha had died down, didn't he want to talk?

Was the ball in his court or hers? If she called, she felt like she'd just be making an excuse. If he rang, she felt she'd be giving more of an explanation. The outcome would be the same—a goodbye—but she'd feel better with option two.

Then there was the night she couldn't sleep, and perhaps had temporarily lost her mind. Gemma scanned the comments on a picture of her with the prince. They were brutal and mocking, as if those two-dimensional people didn't possess real, beating hearts.

Some dude named Hamish Fickle made a career of bashing the royal family and challenging Prince John's character. The House of Blue maintained their dignity and never responded.

Silence often required more courage than speaking out.

A few days later while at work she saw a news story of Prince John laying the final wreath on Holland's grave.

Dressed in a black suit with a white shirt, his hair shiny and styled, he looked every bit like a regal, royal prince doing his duty. But when he turned to the cameras, he looked like a man who'd buried his new wife and newly conceived child. Sad and sober, he moved slowly as he balanced the weight of his world.

Not only did he lose his wife, but thanks to the Reingard scandal, he lost the woman he thought he knew.

She almost texted him that day. Almost. But decided to let him move on and in doing so, realized she took the first step in reclaiming her dignity.

By the time moving day rolled around, she almost felt like her before-Lauchtenland self and inched toward her before-Prince John self.

Daddy arrived early with one of Cole Danner's work trucks and a couple of the younger guys to load up Gemma and Imani's bedroom furniture. That was about all they came with so that was all they were taking.

She wanted the Formica kitchen table, but B. A. Carpenter made it clear it was not to leave the premises.

By noon they'd loaded up Justin and Imani's truck with boxes and suitcases, dog beds and two fifty-pound bags of dog food.

All in all, she felt strong, like she was commanding life. Making lemonade, you know? The day dawned with a bright sun in a blue, cloudless sky and just a touch of fall fragrances in the summer breeze.

Then as she cleaned the last of the papers from the desk tucked into the kitchen corner and powered down her computer, the screen door slammed behind her as Daddy stepped inside.

"He's here."

Everything changed. Her faux sense of confidence. Her propped-up hope. Jeb Kornowsky had come for the horses.

She kept her back to Daddy, shuffling through a stack of junk mail like she might find she'd won a million dollars, a sadness pouring through her.

"Gemma," Daddy said. "I know this ain't easy but—"

His gentle confession popped her building bubble of emotion. "Easy? Do I act like any of this is easy? Do you think losing my precious farm, my herd, my furry family is not ripping out my heart? This isn't one of those, 'You'll get them next time, Gemstone,' moments, Daddy. This is, 'You screwed up. You make bad decisions.'"

"Don't put words in my mouth. We've done talked about this and—"

"You're too kind to me. You give me too much credit. Daddy, you've not said one word about the video. I know you know. You may not have seen it. Oh I pray to the good Lord you've not seen it—"

"I haven't. Your mama's seen a few seconds. All the boys at work have seen it." Was there a slight blush on her father's whiskered cheeks? "Some of them many times."

"Then say something. Your silence is killing me. I didn't even realize it until now. Tell me how I lost my way, gave up my values and virtue, surrendered my reputation and dignity, all for a shot at fame. Tell me how I let myself, you and Mama, the family, the town, down. I was the golden girl, Daddy. The one who was going to change the world, do good, help people, set an example. I was smart, beautiful, and talented. Now look. I walk with a limp and my former golden glow is draped with a black curtain of shame. Scottie O'Shay didn't lower herself for a shot at something better. She worked for it."

"Scottie O'Shay had advantages that you didn't. I'll take the blame for that."

"No, Daddy, I'll take the blame. You and Mama raised me right. I chose my own path of destruction. I guess I can tell you now Prince John proposed to me. Yeah, he did. The night of the ball. But I turned him down because I knew what type of person I'd been in Vegas. I was afraid if I stepped any further onto his stage, one of those shows, especially the one your coworkers have lingered over, would make it to the surface. Matt assured me they'd been destroyed with his hard drive. But ah, we were foiled by a nerdy porter at the Delafield Hotel who'd discovered it when Matt uploaded it a couple years back. He took it down but it was too late. When I saw it blew up the internet, I knew, *I knew*, I had to run. So don't tell me 'this ain't easy,' Daddy. Tell me how much I've disappointed you. How I've let myself and everyone down. How I don't deserve a man like Prince John. Shoot, even Hooley can do better than me and he's missing half his teeth."

"Don't seem like I need to say anything. You're doing a mighty fine job of beating yourself up. Seems you have it all decided."

"Am I wrong? Have I missed something?"

"You have it all wrong, Gemma. But we ain't got time for this. Jeb is here." Daddy pushed open the screen door. "We didn't ask you about it because you didn't seem to want to talk about it. But if you want to know what your mama and I think, ask. Don't assume. Don't think and speak for us. In that, I know we raised you right. Now come on."

Gemma bowed her chin to her chest, sniffing back the tears, Dad's rebuke tender and kind. Tearing a corner of the roll of paper towels on the kitchen table, she dabbed the tears from her eyes and headed out.

A glint of light bounced off the cracked mirror tacked to the doorpost. She leaned for a close look. Her hair was knotted on her head and her T-shirt said *Port Fressa Wharf.*

To her surprise, there was a bit of a glow about her. Maybe her speech to Daddy freed her up a bit. But this sort of light seemed to sparkle. It reminded her of the Heart of God.

The bags under her eyes were faded and her formerly pale lips boasted a rosy hue. She was going to have to speak her mind more often.

Taking a step back, Gemma rose up on her tiptoes to examine her breasts and waist. She wasn't the bag of bones she'd been before the accident. She actually liked her curves. They'd filled out the feather dress rather nicely.

She leaned just a bit closer and smiled. The light in her eyes seemed to sway and swirl, and goodness but if she didn't bring home some of the Heart of God light.

Gemma unhooked the mirror from its nail and settled it in one remaining box. Sorry Kingstons, but she was taking this with her.

Outside, she met Jeb Kornowsky in the yard as he stood by the open trailer gate. "Gemma."

"Jeb."

On the other side, Justin and Imani sat on her lowered truck gate. Twenty yards away, Gemma could see the tears in her eyes.

The herd was leaving. After she'd promised them a forever home. But Jeb was a good man.

"I'll take good care of them, Gemma. I promise."

"I know, Jeb. Doc said we couldn't find a better place."

Gemma turned as Daddy led Whinny out. That's when it hit her. A deep sensation of loss. Hold onto the girl in the cracked mirror. Hold onto the girl that understands life moves on.

Hold on...hold on. But the tears were rising hot.

Daddy handed Whinny's reins to Jeb.

"Up you go, girl." Jeb owned a large spread northeast of the new highway. His daughter and son-in-law just moved back to HB with the grandkids, so the horses would get plenty of attention and love. And carrots.

Settled in her stall, Whinny stuck her head through the drop window with a snort. Gemma gritted her teeth and breathed against the sting of emotion.

"She doesn't want to go," Imani said with a sob.

"She's fine, Imani-girl." Daddy handed over Silver to Jeb. "She's just saying goodbye."

Silver pranced toward the trailer like she was queen of the parade and trotted up the ramp, smiling at her view of the world from her low window.

"What adventure are we going on now?"

Oh Silver you do make me laugh. I wish I was more like you.

Steady. Steady. No tears, no tears. Jeb's place was a good place. His grandkids would spoil the herd rotten.

But she wasn't prepared to see Hercules. The big boy walked so steady, so graceful toward his new ride. His giant hooves crushed the gravel, then banged up the ramp. When he appeared in his window and gazed toward Gemma, she buckled to one knee.

How could a Clydesdale make her feel so loved? So forgiven? His expression was kind and gentle, as if he understood. As if he wanted to say, "Thank you."

The yard reverberated with the clank of Jeb closing the gate and dropping the pin.

"You've done a mighty fine job with them, Gemma," he said. "Especially Whinny. She's not afraid of men anymore."

"It—it was the prince," she answered while staring at her teardrops in the gravel and dust.

"You girls best say goodbye." Daddy's large, kind hand touched her shoulder. "Gemma? Imani?"

When Imani moved, the old truck gate creaked. Gemma tried to stand but Blue was leaning against her. For her strength or his, she couldn't tell. Maybe both. Then another dog, probably Tweedy, sniffed her hair. Marcus, Barksy, and Hal were last seen under Imani's dangling feet.

"You and Imani are welcome anytime," Jeb said. "Even if Winona and I ain't there."

Gemma nodded her thank-you and accepted the hanky Daddy shoved into her hand. When she stood, Imani was loving on Silver, then Whinny.

"Y'all be good," she said. "I'll see you in a few days at Mr. Jeb's. Now look, Whinny, be nice to Silver, and don't give Herc a hard time, he's in love with you. I'll miss you something fierce."

Justin followed, saying his piece. Then Daddy got in line. Even Blue trotted over and raised his paws to the side of the trailer.

At last it was her turn. But she couldn't—

"Gemma," Daddy said. "Jeb's a busy man."

"Right." She wrung her hands together as she stepped forward with the goal to be as upbeat as Imani, but her voice betrayed her.

"You heard Imani, y'all. Jeb's a good man and we'll visit. You'll be well loved at his place."

Whinny tossed her head with a neigh and snort. *"I'll be the judge of that."*

"Silver," Gemma knelt beside the mini. "Look after everyone. You know you're the boss, right?" Silver mopped up Gemma's tears with her thick lips.

"Oh, Races to Win...you're a beauty. But remember how you've learned to trust. And Imani's right, Hercules is in love with you."

The thoroughbred gently brushed her nose against Gemma's cheek.

Last but not least, Hercules. Gemma rested her forehead against his majestic muzzle and her reserved tears overflowed. "I'm going to miss you the most. You saved me as much as I saved you." She looked into his eyes and stroked his head. "You will always have a part of my heart."

Hercules stretched down until his chin rested on her shoulder— his version of a hug—then he sweetly tasted her hair. His version of a kiss.

She stayed with Hercules for a long time, crying softly, shoving aside memories of when he first arrived, to the first night in the barn with the puppies and the prince, to when Herc smiled and ran after Whinny. To the night the prince kissed her, and Hercules knocked him into the rain.

Eventually Daddy cleared his throat and she couldn't delay any longer. Gemma stepped back for a final speech.

"Listen, y'all are going to have so much fun with Jeb and Winona. They have a passel of grandkids and you'll get so many carrots and apples you'll be sick of them. When I visit, I expect to see you grazing and happy, maybe hauling some kid around on your back."

Whinny gave another snort. *"A child? So beneath me."* Such a diva.

Silver smiled and looked as if she were in awe that little people would be around. *"Someone my size."*

Hercules raised his nose as if he were the guardian of the galaxy. *"You can count on me."*

"I love you guys." Wiping her face with the back of her hand, Gemma turned to Jeb. "Best go before I change my mind."

"I mean what I said, Gemma. Come by any time." He climbed into his truck, fired up the old diesel engine, and eased down the long drive toward River Road. Blue once again leaned against her leg.

"Don't worry, boy, you're staying with me."

Daddy gave Gemma a strong side hug. "I hate this for you, Gemstone. I really do. You'll land on your feet, I promise."

"You're an eternal optimist, Daddy." She kissed his cheek. "And about our exchange in the kitchen—"

"Don't give it another thought. We'll talk when you're ready. But just so you know, your mama and I couldn't be any prouder of you. Yeah, we wish you'd not made some of the choices you made but you navigated them with class. You came out ahead. That takes courage, Gemma."

"Thank you," she whispered.

Daddy grunted and cleared his throat. "I best be going. Promised Deacon Eldredge I'd help with repairs at church."

"And we're going to finish moving. Imani, do you want to do one last check in the house?"

"I did this morning." She wrapped her arms around Gemma and set her head on her shoulder. "We'll be all right, won't we?"

"More than all right. We're going to get the adoption done and face the world together as a real mother and daughter."

Imani wiped her eyes with the edge of her T-shirt. "Can we have a movie night? So I don't think about today very much."

"Absolutely. Something funny. Cheer us up."

She ran to tell Justin who smiled and wrapped her in his arms. *Treat her right, boy. Treat her right.*

With the truck and the BMW loaded, Gemma was ready to lock up the house one last time. Imani and Justin headed on over to Mama and Daddy's and Gemma faced the house.

"You rescued me. I'm grateful. I had big plans for you but now someone else will redo your plumbing and walls, floors and doors."

She inserted the key in the lock then stored the key under the blue-glazed ceramic pot she bought at the hardware store.

Starting toward her car, she was suddenly lassoed by the breeze and turned toward the back of the twenty acres. The tree branches swayed as if waving goodbye and the ripples running across the top of the pond water restarted her tears.

"We were supposed to grow old together. But these have been the best two years of my adult life."

Leaving Hollywood and Vegas was not a loss. Leaving Matt, not a loss. But leaving this place, with the green field of wildflowers and the place where she learned to laugh again, was a huge loss.

Yet, the farm was also a reminder, if she could hold onto it, that redemption had a place in everyone's life. That beauty could come from the ashes.

Even for someone like Gemma Stone.

"MP Hamish Fickle is with us today. Mr. Fickle, you said something just before the break that made my mouth drop. The queen asked you to 'join her team'?"

"That's right, Tamma. And thank you for having me. She wanted me to help smooth the way for Prince John and change my stance on the monarchy. But she doesn't get it. As leader of the RECO party, and we are growing, I'm about every Lauchten being their own king and queen. This aristocratic class has to go. Time to end the old order and usher in the new. Besides, Prince John, we've learned through recent events, is no leader. My goodness, he brought a Vegas stripper to an international summit ball. Don't get me started on his wife, *Holland*. She'd be on trial for corruption and insider trading if she were alive. Our future king has absolutely no discernment. The Reingard case is ongoing so we don't know the outcome, but our own crown prince could be implicated. What did he know? If anything. The thick walls of Perrigwynn Palace hide many secrets. But Hamish Fickle is on the scene. You can run but you can't hide."

– NEWS AT NOON WITH TAMMA TUCKER

Our royal family is falling apart. I'm thinking of joining the RECO party. Hamish Fickle makes sense and he's so sexy. Anyone else?

— *@STEFWITHANF ON INSTAGRAM*

"Justice Ministry Indicts Three Environmental Agency Officials in Reingard Case"

— *THE NEWS LEADER HEADLINE*

"Is it possible the queen is losing her touch? Has this Guillain-Barré disease confused her? Muddled her thinking? If Queen Catherine, the queen of diplomacy, couldn't convince MP Fickle to join her team, and the prince has not yet officially taken his oath to be our next legal sovereign, we may be seeing a historic shift in Lauchtenland's society."

— *STONE BRUBAKER ON THE MORNING SHOW*

CHAPTER TWENTY-EIGHT

JOHN

Mid-September arrived with brisk breezes, and John embraced the anesthesia of the cold, North Sea air.

He also buried himself in work. Besides his patronages and handling the queen's business, covering her schedule, he also joined the High Court on a case involving privacy rights.

Last night he reviewed the case in preparation for opening arguments.

But this morning as he read memos and correspondence, sorting out a few issues to be taken to Her Majesty, he battled weariness. Was any of this worth it? Had the time come for the House of Blue to fade into history? Maybe MP Fickle and his ilk were right. What need did modern society have for aristocracy and royals?

He also battled loneliness. It wasn't a new sensation for him. He felt it often when he was in school and at uni, always so keenly aware he wasn't just "one of the boys."

But he never felt lonely in Hearts Bend. Around Gemma.

He missed the life he should have by now—one with a wife and a family. Of course, they'd be embroiled in scandal.

Days would pass without even wondering about his son or daughter. Then he'd see Daffy and wonder. He desperately wanted to be a father.

John shifted his shoulders, shrugging off his contemplations. They were making him anxious.

"Count your blessings instead, mate."

He had good friends and a loving family. Shelter, food, clothing.

Though Hamish Fickle was becoming more of a nuisance. He took every opportunity to remind the people of John's weaknesses. He challenged John's character and judgment. This week he mocked the queen and her magnanimous effort to understand him, join forces.

Mum said it best. Fickle was a little man with a big mouth. If he really wanted political change, then he'd get off the talk shows and into the political ring. He'd engage in debates and share ideas with his colleagues. Maybe he'd even listen more than he'd talk.

His father-in-law was also becoming a nuisance. After his arrest, Lord Cletus Cunningham was released on his own recognizance. But instead of going away quietly, he'd implicated his own deceased daughter in the case.

"I was a fool to follow her blindly. But I trusted her. I was under the impression I was fighting for the people of the Midlands. I was also told Eloise Ltd. had backed out of the land deal."

Lord Cunningham was undeserving of his title and his position.

However, there was good news in his world. Mum was on a slow mend, and Dad took extra care to ensure her rest. She worked a few hours four days a week and insisted they maintain their Sunday evening family dinner table.

On Friday nights, John met his mates at Clemency Pub for a pint and a lot of "What's up with you?" conversation. They never asked about Holland or Gemma. He was grateful.

A few nights ago, he'd dined with Sydney Templeton. Larrabee had mentioned she'd asked about him and during a quiet, lonely evening he rang her without debating the idea for hours.

She was lovely and charming, educated, very beautiful, hailing from the right pedigree for a man ascending the throne. She'd make a stellar future queen.

They dined at Rico's on Queen's Avenue. Their conversation was intelligent and lively. But when all was said and done, she did not fascinate him.

She was not the woman he'd cut open his chest for and hand her his heart. She was not Gemma.

Which created a whole other conundrum. He was truly in love with Gemma Stone.

"I'm sorry to disturb you, sir." Briggs stood at the office door. "But Wilford is on line one."

"Wilford?" He was Briley's groom. John closed the purple "box" he'd been staring at for the last ten minutes and reached for the landline. "Is everything all right?"

"I'm sorry, sir. I should've called sooner but I wanted to be sure. He's—"

"Wilford, say no more. I'm on my way. Don't do a thing until I arrive." Wilford tried to respond but John had already replaced the receiver. "Cancel my appointments," he said to Briggs on his way out. "I'm going to Hadsby."

Briley. John's last connection to Holland other than her parents. Now it seemed he was about to meet his demise as well. His broken leg just wouldn't mend.

John headed straight for the garage. Maneuvering Port Fressa traffic, he finally hit North One at top speed. He'd arrive at Hadsby Castle in the Old Hamlet section of Dalholm in less than three hours.

Hang on, Briley. Hang on.

After Holland died, he'd stabled Briley at the castle mews and hired Wilford to mend his broken leg. But the struggle had been long.

"God, if You hear a fool's prayer, please save him."

The afternoon sun spilled down the face of the Highcrest Mountains and the sight gave him some hope. Driving straight to the mews, he hopped out almost before the motor stopped.

"Wilford?" John walked down the wide brick center aisle toward Briley's stall. "Where is he? I must see him."

But Briley's place was vacant. John expected to see a weary groom beside a weak and sad gelding, and a sober veterinarian ready to pronounce death.

"Wilford, are you here, man?"

Emerging from the other side of the stable, he found the groom atop a spry Briley, who trotted with ease, tossing his head, happy to be free.

"Can you believe, Your Royal Highness? Healed. Raring to go." In his excitement, Wilford's Dalholm speech was even more pronounced.

"I can see. Wilford, what happened?" John pumped the air with his fist and whispered, "Thank You."

"One day. Poof. Fine." Wilford kicked Briley into a canter. "Not afraid." Briley raised up and pawed the air and when he came back down, he galloped toward John, tossing his head.

John grabbed the bridle and patted the gelding's muzzle. "You're back, ole boy, you're back."

"Miracle, sir. Miracle." Wilford's weathered smile said there was more to the story. "A few days past, a new vet, eyes so blue—"

"Tell me in the Queen's language not in Dalholm shorthand." The unique cadence of the Dalholmians was fun in the pub or at a dinner party but not when trying to understand a miracle.

"Sorry, sir. A few days ago a new vet came round. Strange chap with the bluest eyes I'd ever seen. They were like lasers. Dressed odd too. He wore—"

"A wool anorak and a wide-brimmed hat."

"You've seen him too? Ernst down at the Belly of the Beast calls him Emmanuel. But I've never clapped eyes on the chap before. Anyway. He strolled into the stable and asked to see Briley. Didn't see any reason not to let him. Not sure how he got on the grounds except maybe our regular vet sent him. Or you. Anyway, he spent about an hour with Briley and left. Didn't say a word the entire time. The next day one of the groomers had Briley walking the aisle. Said he wanted out. Then today, well, you see for yourself. But I say keep an eye on him. Don't let him do too much. He may look healed, act healed, but—"

"Let him run, Wilford. Let him run. Let him do what he was born to do."

When Wilford gave him the word, Briley sprinted away, racing free over the meadow, the tall grass almost parting, making a way.

John ran after them as horse and rider disappeared down a slope and onto the flat plain above the sea.

"*Yeahhhh!*" He jumped, waving his hands, shouting, "Run, Briley, run!"

In a season of surprises, scandals, goodbyes, and endings, Briley was mind-blowing surprise. An example of silver linings. A symbol of life after death.

If an encounter with Emmanuel—God with us—restored a horse, think what it could do for a future king.

GEMMA

She'd been settled into her new, old room about a week when she reached for her last suitcase.

Her closet and dresser were filled to the gills but she wanted everything unpacked and as organized as possible. It helped her adjust to this new way of living.

Opening the case, she almost passed out. Truly. The amazing, crystal-studded shoes Princess Daffodil lent her for the ball had come home with her.

Impossible. She was sure she left them in her suite by the feathered gown. And she'd not taken this little case with her to Lauchtenland. How did the shoes end up inside?

With a cold dread, she'd messaged The Chamber Office at once, asking for instructions on how to return them. But so far, almost two weeks later, she'd not heard from them.

Should she just mail them to the palace? Let them sort it out? What if they got lost?

In the ensuing weeks, Gemma spent a lot of evenings at Ella's Diner. Imani was off with schoolwork and clubs. She'd been elected Junior Class President. She had volleyball practice and soon, basketball. If she wasn't tied up with practice or projects, she was with Justin and Penny.

Gemma missed her but she remembered what it was like to be sixteen.

She ate dinner with her parents then excused herself before the card playing friends arrived. At twenty-nine, she wasn't ready to be drawn into their life of hearts and pinochle.

Every evening she returned from Ella's with napkin notes stuffed in her bag. Then she stored them in a box in her room.

One sip of her coffee or tea, or hot chocolate, and she had an urge to write. Tell what happened in L.A., in Vegas, this past summer. Just pour it out. Get rid of the acid and the bitterness.

During one such frantic writing session, Tina came by with a large stack of napkins and set them on the table, then kept going. Later when Gemma cashed out she said, "You know about this new invention called ruled paper? Also, these handy devices you hold in your hand and type. Tablets. Phones. Even a laptop."

"It's cathartic to write with pen and paper. Or in my case, napkin."

She wrote about the lights and fragrances of the Heart of God and how she felt different, cleansed, after being filled with the heart's glow.

She described the ball and dancing with a prince. She wrote about the puppies and the herd.

Then there was the weird Brillo-haired lady that Daffy also knew. The more she thought about it, the more it seemed less of a coincidence and more of a divine plan.

But Gemma was no princess. What did she and Princess Daffy have in common?

She scribbled about her land-purchase folly. That was an entire napkin pack according to Tina.

Last but not least, she wrote about the Vegas video going viral. Surely everyone in town knew about the land deal and the video by now. Even stern-lipped church ladies wanted to see how Gemma Stone took off her clothes on a Las Vegas stage so they could be appropriately appalled.

She wrote about her kitchen conversation with Daddy. About his love and affirmation. She wrote about the cracked mirror and the slightly new look in her eye.

She wrote that she loved the prince.

But these were notes for her eyes only. No one would ever see. Well, not until she was eighty-five and decided to write her memoirs.

On her days off she visited Hercules, Whinny, and Silver. They were so well loved she was almost jealous.

The family in Nashville sent pictures of Ross and Rachel sleeping in the children's beds. Penny and Justin kept Gemma informed on Joey and Phoebe. And Mr. Paul, who finally came for Monica right before the move, said he never had a better creature living in his house.

"Including my wife." There was certainly more to that story.

Writing about her past was one thing. The words flowed. But where she fumbled was her future. Last night she grabbed a napkin and wrote GOALS on the top.

Nothing. Blank.

This afternoon, she set an appointment with a social worker to get Imani's adoption into motion.

"Anyone home?" Gemma stepped into the kitchen and settled her Prada on a hook by the door. "Mama? Daddy? Imani? Anyone home?"

Except for a light over the stove, the place was dark. Gemma switched on the kitchen wall lamps.

"Imani?"

Her truck was out front as well as Mama's car. Gemma walked through to the living room where she found Justin sitting in the shadows, the only light coming from a light on in the bedroom hallway. He jumped to his feet, a nervous twitch.

"Miss Gemma."

"Justin." She gave him a stern look. "What are you doing here?"

Beyond the walls, the dogs barked to be let in. Gemma reached for the back door. All five scrambled inside over the high wrought iron steps.

"Waiting for Imani. We're meeting my folks at Ella's for a burger. She said she was going to text you."

"She didn't." Burgers at Ella's? Something didn't add up. This whole scene was suspicious. Very suspicious. "Where's Mama?"

"Don't know." With a shrug, he averted his gaze to his feet. He couldn't look her in the eye and there was only one of two reasons for that as far as she was concerned.

Gemma invited him to sit then made her way down the short hall to Imani's room.

"Imani." She tapped on the girl's door.

"Gemma?" Her surprised voice was followed by a bump and bang, then the door swung open, a breathless Imani shoving back her hair and yanking her jeans at the waist. "Hey, what are you doing here?" She looked away, pretending to search for something on her dresser.

"I live here. What's going on?"

"Nothing." Imani looked at Gemma, her gaze barely holding on.

"Justin's here."

"Is he? Really? I didn't hear him come in." Imani started past Gemma but she caught her by the arm.

"Why are you in your room, door closed? Why did you open the door breathless and adjusting your clothes?"

"Because I was changing. Geez Gemma. Stop accusing me. We're going to dinner with Justin's parents. I texted you."

"I didn't get it."

"Well, I know I texted you."

"You didn't know Justin was here? How come his truck is not out front."

"His truck is in the shop. His friend Cap dropped him off after band practice."

"Oh not at his own house where he could ride to dinner with his parents?"

"We wanted to ride together. Gemma, what's with the third degree? Besides, JoJo asked me to help with the Christmas play this year at the Kids Theater," Imani said. "Justin volunteered too. We're meeting her at the Kids Theater before we eat. Afterwards we're helping with the town's fall decorations. We'll be at the

Gardenia gazebo. Then I'm taking him home." She made a face. "Do you approve of our plan?"

Gemma folded her arms. "I will when you tell me what you do in your room, making a racket, door locked. Changing your clothes."

"Am I not allowed to change my clothes?"

Gemma stepped into the room and shut the door behind her. "What's going on?"

"Nothing."

"Imani."

"Gemma, I'm telling you, nothing is going on."

Gemma glanced back to the mirrored closet doors and caught the corner end of a large box. "What's this?"

Imani jumped in front of her. "Nothing. It's private."

"What kind of private?" Gemma pushed aside the doors. "What's in the box?"

Imani's eyes filled. "Something."

"Why can't you tell me?"

"Gemma, you don't own me. Even if you are about to be my mom. I'm sixteen. Not a child. It's my private stuff. Don't you have private stuff you store in a closet?"

"You want to talk about the video? Then let's talk."

"No, I don't want to talk about the video. Only that I defend you every day at school. Justin punches guys who are watching it in the locker room. I know you had your reasons, but you have a lot of nerve coming in here and acting like I'm up to something with Justin when I'm not."

Gemma dropped down to Imani's bed. "I'm sorry, Imani. How embarrassing for you. And you're one hundred percent right. I have no business treating you like how I was at your age." She pointed to the window. "Dash used to sneak into that window. Or I'd sneak out. We told my folks we were going to the movies, then go park in the woods off Ox Bottom." Gemma flopped back on the bed. "Don't even get me started on the road I traveled to win fame and fortune. Sold my soul and sacrificed my body."

Imani sat next to her. "Is that how you broke your hip?"

"Yes. I fell." She forced herself to look Imani in the face. "If you don't want me as your mama anymore, I'll understand. I keep waiting for your grandmother to write to me, tell me she saw the video on Facebook and how unfit I am."

"I want you to be my mom. I mean, no other girls' mama has a rocking body like you."

Gemma's burst of laughter was followed by sobriety. "Don't joke about it. I was nothing but skin and bones. Please do not admire me. Imani, you cannot know the shame. Taking off one's clothes for entertainment is not freeing, it's humiliating. I had to lie to myself every day we filmed to get through. It was blessed relief when I fell."

"Gemma," Imani began, her voice low. "It's not that I don't have feelings for Justin. You know, like *that*, but I'm not ready. Granny Cook used to preach to me even as a kid how a girl had to wait. Boys too. I didn't really know what she was talking about, but I know my parents waited for marriage. I kind of had it in my head I would too."

"Why didn't you tell me?"

"I don't know. It's kind of awkward."

"Tell me about it. I never talked to my mama."

"Gemma, Justin's a good guy. We've talked about sex because his dad told him to. He knows I don't want anything physical. Well, except I do like to kiss him." She blushed. "It's gotten out of hand a few times."

"You know, when I moved to L.A., I was going to be the girl who did it right. I knew of actresses who refused to bare all for a part. Who understood dignity. I planned to work hard, study the craft, network, audition, audition, audition, and earn each role for my talent, not my exposed body. But after a few years, when things didn't break open for me like I thought, I got desperate. Running with the crowd I did, my values and morals slipped. Then Matt came up with the Vegas idea and…" Gemma held Imani by the chin. "Never, ever let some man make you do something you know in your heart is wrong and shameful. Hear me? For that matter, don't let any woman either. I'll tell you, the other actresses on the show and the female producer were no picnic."

Imani stood to retrieve the box, bumping and banging it against the closet walls. "I found this after Granny died and Uncle Roy was cleaning out the house. He was going to throw it away." She raised the box lid to reveal a mountain of white silk, lace, and tulle, along with a photo album. "It's Mama's wedding dress and their wedding album. When I miss them, I put on the dress and look through the album."

"Oh Imani." Gemma reached for the book, her tears already spilling over. "You didn't have to hide this from me."

"I didn't want you to feel bad, and...I don't know." She shrugged. "It felt personal. As if I was spending time alone with them."

Gemma squeezed Imani's arm. "And here I was badgering you. Please forgive me. But anytime you want to talk about them, come to me. I can tell you all about their relationship, how much they loved each other, and their wedding day. How proud your grandparents were on both sides when they graduated from college with honors and went looking at Manhattan apartments. Though don't get me wrong, neither side wanted Yankees in the family."

"Was it hard for them? Being an interracial couple?"

"Some. Hearts Bend had been through racial strife in the past, but your parents knew what they were about. If they encountered anything negative, they just went on with their business, their life, their goals. They had the support of their families and friends."

"Justin's parents don't care I'm interracial."

"Why should they? I don't care that Justin is white."

Imani laughed. "I'll tell him. He'll be relieved."

Gemma tapped the teen's heart. "It's what's in here that counts. Don't let anyone tell you differently. Don't let anyone define you but—"

But who? Herself? She was only as strong as her weakest link. Gemma wasn't doing well defining herself.

"God?" Imani said. "Granny Cook talked to me about God. A lot. I didn't understand half of it but I had a dream about her the other night. She'd written everything down in a book and I was reading it."

"Now that's a cool way to hear from your Granny. Did she have any wisdom in her book for me?"

"Forgive yourself."

Gemma's eyes spilled over. "Easier said than done. Please keep that in mind as you go through life and make decisions."

"I will. I promise. And I'll talk to you, no matter how awkward, if I change my mind about, you know, things."

"Good." She kissed Imani's temple. "But don't. Your mama would be proud of you."

Imani took the photo album. "You're in almost every picture. One day can we go through the photo album and talk about them?"

"Of course. And I'm not proud of being in every picture. What was I thinking?"

"You're so funny. I know you have all the stories."

"Name the day and we'll trip down memory lane over a bowl of buttery popcorn. Even better, I'll get your parents' friends to come over. Haley and Cole, Buck and JoJo, Taylor and Jack Gillingham. We all have stories."

"There are days when I never think of them. It's as if they never existed. I feel guilty about it." Althea's dress was still folded in Imani's lap. "Every person whose blood is in my veins is either dead or moved away."

"Your gigi will come around. There's nothing saying you can't call her."

Imani shrugged. "What if she doesn't want to hear from me? Besides, you, Pops and Memaw are my family now."

"We are but we can still include your Shumaker and Cook relatives. Hey, I think you have second cousins in Arkansas and Texas. We can reach out, see if they want to get together. And when I adopt you, if you still want me to, we'll slice our hands and mingle our blood like old-world societies used to do when they formed a covenant."

Her eyes widened. "You'd do that for me?"

"Really? I was joking, but yeah, if you want. Yes. Of course." *Absolutely*.

Imani folded the dress back in the box. "I get scared sometimes. Like everyone will leave me. I don't want to say anything because I don't want you to think, like, you're not doing a good job. You are, Gemma. I promise."

"I won't leave you."

"But what about the prince?"

"What about him? He lives four thousand miles away. I haven't even heard from him since I came home. Consider it a summer love."

"Was it? Love?"

"Okay, consider it a summer friend-fling."

"Imani?" Justin's voice pushed through the door. "We should go. We told JoJo we'd meet her at five-thirty."

"Go," Gemma said. "I'll put the dress away."

"No, I want to. It was my mama's." Imani carefully folded up the gown then slipped the photo album underneath. She slid the box back into the closet then checked her appearance in the mirror. She started for the door then looked back.

"Gemma, I know the video is embarrassing. But if the prince rejects you for that, especially without an explanation, he's not the prince I knew in the summer."

"Oh, Imani, he's in a difficult position. He's a leader. A ruler. The woman he marries must be above reproach. Set an example. Let this be another lesson to you. Don't do, say, post, or share anything on social media you'd not want anyone to see. That you wouldn't want someone to uncover ten, twenty years from now. It could hinder you from getting a job or some grand opportunity. Character and values matter, Imani."

"Our teachers tell us not to think no one reads our posts."

"Imani, we have to go," Justin said.

She opened the door and a blushed-cheeked teen boy waited on the other side. He was a doll. "One sec, Justin."

"I'll be outside." Justin backed away from the door. "Night Miss Gemma."

"Give my love to your parents."

Imani turned to her. "One question. Do you love the prince?"

"He was my friend. He said I was his best friend."

"But do you love him?"

"Imani, I—"

"Gemma, yes or no. Do you love him?"

She was about to answer honestly when a door slammed and Mama called out she was home. Then Daddy. Next the dog barking frenzy began, their yips and snarls filling the double-wide. Last but not least, Mama announced fried chicken for dinner.

"We should get out there before Daddy feeds all the dark meat to Barksy," Gemma said.

"Tell me." Imani gripped Gemma's arm. "Please."

"What was the question again?"

"Do you love Prince John?"

Imani's question was so sweet, so sincere, Gemma could not stop the tears. "Yes, I believe I do."

CHAPTER
TWENTY-NINE

JOHN

H e traveled to Dalholm every weekend in September. Briley grew stronger and braver each week.

Wilford was a splendid groom but he took no credit for Briley's health other than to say he'd attended the beast.

"It was that man, Emmanuel."

Yet John was beginning to doubt Emmanuel. Why the mystery? Why come and go without a word? What was his scheme?

On this Saturday night, he joined Wilford—with faithful Gunner at a table by the door—at the Belly of the Beast for fish and chips, and a pint or two.

His Mondays through Fridays were stressful between the court case he sat on, filling the queen's duties as well as his own, and dodging the continued fallout of the Reingard case.

The Solicitor General's office of the Justice Ministry found there was enough evidence to indict Lord Cunningham. He would stand for trial.

His reaction was vicious, pledging to take down everyone with him, including the House of Blue. He found an immediate ally in MP Hamish Fickle.

The social media threads were explosive as well. No member of the House of Lords had been indicted since the eighteenth century.

If John was called to testify, he had one simple, truthful answer. *"I knew nothing about it."*

Tonight, the Belly was lively. Every table full and popping with the native shorthand. It was the rhythm and music of the pub.

"On me." Ernst, the proprietor of the oldest pub in Dalholm, maybe even Lauchtenland, set down a plate of battered, deep-fried fish. "Horse? Good?"

"Yes, Ernst, Briley is still good. He's fantastic." There was a concern Briley might develop laminitis, but Wilford cleared him last week.

"Marvel, yer maj." Yer maj was Ernst's accepted nickname for the princes.

The large man moved to stir the fire then welcomed a man at the door. "In. Sit. Pint?"

After his fair share of fish and chips, Wilford downed his second pint and pushed away from the table. "Home. Wife. Good day, sir."

John laughed. "Give your wife my regards."

"She'll be thrilled."

John shook the groom's hand. He was the man who'd brought a piece of his heart back to life through a chestnut gelding. "Next week?"

"Your Royal Highness, I know you're a busy man. You don't have to come up every weekend—"

"But I want to, Wilford. I need to. This place puts me at ease. Hadsby, the mountains, the old hamlet, the Belly of the Beast."

"See you then." Wilford backed away and offered a curt bow. He waved to Ernst on his way out. "Good one."

John returned to his chair, picked at the remaining filet, then shoved the plate aside. Staring into the fire, he reclined against the murmur of voices, the spikes of laughter, the hammer of a pint hitting the table.

"Prince. Tell. What's up?" Not only was Ernst the proprietor, but he was a longtime friend of the House of Blue, especially of John and Gus.

Kicking out the chair across from John, the big man with the braided beard sat, the scuffed and scarred wooden legs creaking under his aproned girth.

"What do you mean, what's up? All is well. Briley is his old self if not better." John raised his pint with a glance toward the faint light of Wells Line beaming against the paned glass windows. "I needed a miracle, Ernst."

"Yes, amen." Ernst slapped his large palm on the table then pointed at John. "You, girl." He furrowed his forehead until his thick eyebrows became one. "Insider trading? Video?"

"Ah, I see you're up-to-date. Tell me, friend, do you think I'm cursed?" The question came out of nowhere, but John guessed he'd been pondering the possibility for a while.

"Cursed? Nonsense."

"Then what? My wife died four months into our marriage. Now I learn she had dealings with Reingard. Then I met a lovely American woman that maybe, I'm not sure, maybe I could've loved, only to discover her secret career as a reality show stripper. While I can see my way clear to overlook her past, my family, my country may not be as generous. I'd never subject her, as my wife and best friend, to fifty years of 'The queen, a former Las Vegas stripper,' which you know will become a part of her story. Forget that she was a completely legitimate actress ninety-five percent of her career. Commercials, plays, even movies. Putting together what pieces I know, the reality show was just another acting job."

"You? Your heart?" Ernst tapped his own chest. "Want?"

"A do-over. A rewind. Go back to the day Holland went for a ride. No, the day I met her. I'd love to ask more questions." He sobered and stared into his empty pint. "I'd love to hold my child."

"Ah, Prince." Ernst slapped his hand over his heart. "Peace."

"We were just about to go public with the news."

"Better days ahead."

"If not, I don't want to see worse."

"But you?" Ernst said again. "What want?"

John sat back with a deep inhale. What did he want? His brain felt muddled at times, like he was lost in a fog with no end.

"I want to know if she really took a bribe from Luca Reingard. Did she participate in some scheme to cheat Eloise Ltd. out of their land deal? Did she know Reingard was expanding and buy stocks? Was she involved with insider trading? But why? Ernst, that's not the woman I married. All this news makes me feel like I lost my wife all over again. Did I know her at all?"

"And the American?"

"Gemma Stone?" Saying her name brought a ping of joy. "Crazy to say, Ernst, but she's my best friend. I've not talked to her in a month, but I think of her every day. I want to talk to her. But where do I take it? She lives in America. I live here. She's given no indication she'd embrace a royal life. She turned down my marriage proposal. She left without a word. Though now I know why."

"What hold up?"

John made a face. "Everything I just said."

"Excuses."

"Or valid reasons," John said. "Even wisdom."

"Scared?"

"Of love? Not anymore. I'm a bit unsure, but I'm not scared."

Ernst angled over the table. "Love. Rare. Don't miss."

They faced off for a few seconds. "Ernst, I *did* propose," John said. "She turned me down. Said the Heart of God clocks had struck midnight and our spell was broken. She's was probably right. I was caught up in the moment and the fact she wore a gown covered in feathers."

"She scared."

"Maybe for good reason."

"*Pfffbt.* You make too much. Love. Rare. Don't miss."

Did he love her? Enough to endure the public scrutiny? The bigger question was if she loved *him*. Enough to endure the tabloids, the gossip, the invasion of her privacy. It was a very tall demand.

"Mind if I join you chaps?" The man in the long anorak and wide-brimmed hat from the palace grounds and the hospital, from Wilford's story, pulled up a chair.

"Emmanuel. Down mountain? Goodness. World ending?" Ernst snapped for Betsy to bring the man a pint.

"The world is not ending just yet, my friend. But you're ready when it does. Stay alert." Emmanuel laughed with Ernst. A sound

John felt in his belly. "A pint and some of Stella's good battered and fried fish sound good."

Ernst's eyes glistened as he patted the mountain man on the shoulder. "Prince?" he said with a sniffle. "Emmanuel? Know?"

"We've seen one another."

The big man with the bonfire eyes offered his hand. "Emmanuel, and it's my pleasure, Your Royal Highness."

"Likewise." Emmanuel's grip was strong, warm, and electric. Moments after John drew away, his fingers still sparked.

They engaged in a simple chat to the ebbing and flowing noise of the pub. A man from the kitchen tossed another big log on the fire, and the flames shot up. Emmanuel watched, a calm on his face John didn't recognize. It was regal, sublime, and timeless.

"Who are you?" John said more to himself than Emmanuel.

"A friend. Comforter. Counselor."

"Healer?" John leaned toward him. "What did you do when you visited Briley? Why did you visit Briley?"

"I watched him running over the plain the first day Wilford let him run. So powerful, so assured, doing what he was made to do."

A sense of yearning gripped John. He wanted to run, do what he was born to do. This man was a spiritualist.

"I've seen you in the palace gardens. I saw you visit the queen at the hospital. Who are you and what do you want from me?"

Ernst appeared with the affable Stella, his wife, and set down a pint and plate of fish for Emmanuel.

He took a long drink then sampled his fish. "Ernst's food is the best around."

"Yes, it is." But he didn't want to talk about Ernst or Stella's cooking.

"You loved Briley, Prince John, even when he was struggling. You hired the best groomsman and doctor to give him care. You didn't give up on him when others told you to put him down. Now look, a year later, he's come right."

"I always believed in him, in Wilford and the team. But you were the one who made all the difference."

"What about Gemma? Gemstone, as her father calls her. Are you going to put her down?"

Gemstone? "See here, I demand an explanation of your intimate knowledge of my life. My friends."

Emmanuel sighed as he swallowed another bite of fish and reached for his napkin. "I was thinking when you love someone, truly love, you stand by them when the chips are down. You don't give up. If you can give Briley all the chances in the world, why not Gemma? You've certainly been given chances to be who you were made to be."

"Briley is a horse. Gemma did something she's not proud of. Do you want me to subject her to ridicule the rest of her life?"

"Shouldn't she decide? Are you choosing for her or yourself?" Emmanuel waved to a sorrowful-looking woman sitting alone two tables away. She immediately perked up and smiled. "You are disappointed in Holland, but that does not negate your love for her or hers for you. Gemma, your best friend, as you say, has a dark past she's not proud of, but a friend, I've found, sticks closer than a brother. Of this I am very familiar."

"How do you know all of this? Are you an, an—" John couldn't say it. He was a man of science. Of letters. "An angel? A spiritualist? What?"

"Many years ago, when I was going through a particularly trying season, I wanted nothing more than my friends to be with me."

John hated the non-answer answer. "And were they?"

"Almost to the bitter end. Then I was alone, but my father saw me through."

"Are you saying I've turned my back on Gemma?" He confessed what he knew was true. "I'd still like to know who you are and how you know anything of my relationships."

"Have you reached out? Telephoned? Texted?" Emmanuel dipped his fish into the creamy sauce, then worked on a chip or two.

"She left without a word. I decided she wanted it that way. What else was I to do? I have enough with Mum's illness, the memorial ceremony, and the wretched investiture, and the accusations against Holland. Not to mention the antics of Hamish Fickle."

Any more excuses in the box?

"One blessed thing about Gemma Stone," Emmanuel said. "You know all of her secrets going in. She may not have told you her secret, but she never lied about it. She wanted your respect, John. With Holland, you knew none of her secrets, but you must forgive her. Forgiveness is free. To ask for, give and receive. It's eternal and the most liberating thing a man can do. On top of that, it costs you nothing, yet gives you everything."

John gave his attention to the fire to avoid the embarrassment of tears.

"He who's forgiven much loves much."

"Are you saying I need to be forgiven? That I'm a sinner?"

"There's only one man in all of humanity who never sinned, and I don't believe you are him."

John laughed. "Well, you have me there, Emmanuel."

"My dear friend, you will never know the truth about Holland. She's left this life for another. Forgive her and move on. Now Gemma, oh sweet Gemma, is called to greater things but she believes she's disqualified herself. If you ask her the truth, she will tell you, John. She needs her best friend."

"She has a funny way of showing it. She's not reached out once."

"Nor have you so the field is even."

"You have me there."

"I have one question for you."

John waited, slightly irritated but he had to listen.

"What are you doing sitting here?"

"Can I propose my own question?"

"Please." Emmanuel waited.

"What do you want with me? Why are you...chasing me?"

"Don't you know? I came to set you free."

John felt as if the logs on the fire had fallen on him. Perspiration began to soak his skin and he could feel it dampen his shirt. His heart became a drum against his ribs, and for the life of him, he felt a wind against his face and hair. Tears pooled in his eyes until Emmanuel became wavy lines.

"I've not always been a good man, a good son or brother."

"Shame weighs every soul down. But you don't have to stay down."

Another wave of heat and John felt as if he'd tumble from his chair. Emmanuel stood, left payment on the table, then touched John's shoulder.

"I'll see you again soon."

Something akin to a shock zapped him and for an intense second, he shook. Then he collapsed, sliding down in his seat.

"Ernst, night. Stella." Emmanuel bid farewell to the proprietor and his wife. "Your Royal Highness," he said to John, "remember, a cord of three strands is not easily broken."

Unable to speak all he could do was nod.

"You've two feathers, correct?"

John gathered himself and sat up. "Yes, sir, swan feathers. But how do you know— Never mind. You just know, don't you?"

"There's a third somewhere. Find it. You'll be pleased."

"A third? Where? What does it mean?"

"Goodnight, Prince John. And remember, God is with you."

CHAPTER THIRTY

GEMMA

Her morning routine was off. Even though she had no animals to feed, she still woke up at 5:00 a.m., showered and dressed, quietly scrambled a couple of eggs, and ate them on the front porch steps as the first rays of light broke the night sky.

By seven-thirty she bid Imani, "Have a good day," then headed off to the shop for a day of cleaning, sorting, rearranging, filing, paying bills, answering email, and scouting out new vendors. In her spare time, she researched ways to stage a photo shoot for the next time Taylor Gillingham called for assistance.

At nine, she retrieved the morning pastries from Haven's and ate her first one while it was warm and fragrant, pairing it with a fresh cup of coffee and cream.

A couple of newspapers reached out for an interview, including Lauchtenland's *News Leader*. She deleted every email. She wasn't even sure how they'd found her.

But on this particular morning, October having just arrived with a crisp breeze and scent of fall, she was deep in the inventory closet once again, reorganizing from a frenzied weekend with a large bridal party, when she heard a sweet "Hello?" float across the mezzanine.

Adelaide.

At the same time, her phone pinged with a text. She rolled her eyes at the name on the screen. What did he want? Mr. B. A. "Take Away My Land" Carpenter.

"Gemma, could you meet at the Kingston place this afternoon at 5:00?"

The Kingston place? Now she realized why she'd not named the farm during her short tenure. It was never really hers.

"Need to sign some papers. Legal mumbo jumbo releasing you of all claim. Also, an affidavit assuring you knew nothing of the fraud. They won't press charges."

She resented the very idea of pressing charges, but she was grateful they believed her story.

"I'll be there."

"There you are." Gemma tucked her phone in her pocket and turned to greet Adelaide, her cloud of hair fluffed with the lingering summer humidity. "I've something to show you."

"What are you doing here?" Gemma stepped back as the tiny woman barged into the storeroom and made her way to the vintage boxes. "Princess Daffodil told me about you. Is it true? You haunted her too?"

"I never haunt. And yes, I visited her. 'Twas me job, love. I have something special for you to try on." She jumped up, yes, jumped, reached the box on the top shelf and pulled it down.

Okay, maybe she was a bit of an otherworldly creature.

"That's JoJo and Haley's wedding dress." Gemma pointed to the box.

"Indeed. But it's more than something you wear once and put on a shelf." Adelaide carried the box, which was half as tall as she, out to the mezzanine and removed the lid. "I don't know why the brides always try to box it away. Lights are supposed to shine, you know."

"What else do you do with a bridal gown after you've worn it?"

"This particular gown represents so much more than a wedding day. It represents healing and hope, redemption. That's why it fits every bride who tries it on. Now, let's see…" Adelaide stepped back into the storeroom, searching for something. "Know what, we won't bother with shoes. This is a barefoot moment. Besides, the heels with the crystal studs will serve on your day. Isn't this fun? We'll be shipshape soon."

"Crystal studs? How do you know about them? And what day are you talking about?"

"Shall we get started?" Adelaide pulled a Mary Poppins and all but disappeared into the box as she removed *the* wedding dress, the ivory satin spilling from her hands. "Go put this on."

"Adelaide, I've already put on several wedding gowns this year for a photo shoot. I'm not doing it again until it's for real. If I ever get married at all." Pure bravado. Every word. She was shaking like a leaf. Adelaide's presence was breaking down all her resistance.

"Now get going." Adelaide held on to the dress and pointed to the changing area.

But Gemma couldn't move. She recognized the V-neck, the swag front, and the three-quarter sleeves from the photos on the wall behind the desk. She knew the stories of the mystical gown that fit every woman who tried it on. How the dress found the next bride and transformed them. Poppycock and fairy tales as far as she was concerned. "Haley and JoJo would not thank us to mess with their wedding dress. Even if you are an angel, Adelaide."

"It's not their decision, is it. Get going." Adelaide's big white smile ignited a heat around Gemma's heart. The familiar fragrance from the last time Adelaide visited the mezzanine, and from the Heart of God, swirled around her.

"Hurry now, out of your things. Go behind the screen." Adelaide worked the gown's long row of buttons, the tip of her pink tongue resting on the corner of her mouth.

"I can't." Gemma snatched the dress from Adelaide with every intention of folding it back into the box and confessing the whole ordeal to her bosses and friends.

But the moment her hands touched the satin and silk, the heat intensified as did the fragrance. She began to tremble, feel as if she were coming undone.

"Go on now." Adelaide shoved her toward the dressing screen. "I don't have all day."

"Why, you have another princess to spook?"

"Actually, I have other duties. Princess duty is just one. Now go."

Fine. She'd get this over with, write it down in a diary—note to self, buy a diary—and get on with her life.

"You know, I need a place to live more than I need to try on this wedding dress. And oh yes, I'm not getting married. I don't even have a boyfriend."

"One thing will take care of the other."

"What does that mean? I'm going to meet a man who'll sweep me off my feet and rescue me? Last time I was swept off my feet, I got a broken hip and a world of pain. Besides, I can take care of myself, thank you very much."

"Goodness, such a lecture. Now put on the dress," Adelaide said. "You're the chattiest princess I've ever served. Careful now. It is well over a hundred years old."

"Princess." The term iced her semi-enthusiastic protest to these proceedings. "What are you talking about?"

"I'm talking about this wedding dress going *royal*. Taking it to the palace."

"What? You can't be—"

Adelaide raised her soft, pearly hand. "Go."

Oddly enough, Gemma obeyed, disappearing behind the changing screen. She removed her clothes and stepped into the skirt of *the* dress, the one of legend, the one that former brides claimed represented the Gospel of Jesus.

Raising the bodice over her hips and up her waist to her shoulders, she half expected a lightning bolt to crash through the roof and prevent her from soiling this beautiful, historical, if not divine, gown.

"How's it feel?" Adelaide said.

"Weird. Really weird." But good weird. She was beginning to get caught up in the mystery. Might as well see where this particular journey ended. Goodness knows, she'd taken enough bad roads on her own. Maybe Adelaide would give her a different ending.

Either way, this was a whopper of a chapter to add to her embellished prince story fifty years from now when she held permanent court in a back booth at Ella's.

"After the ball and everyone in the world knew some no-name chick from Tennessee took it all off for a reality show that never saw the light of day, an angel haunted me. Honest to goodness. I'm dying if I'm lying."

Adjusting the gown to fit her shoulders and torso, the dress began to wrap around her, embrace her. Squinting against a rush of tears, Gemma *knew* something was shifting in her.

But she wasn't ready. She was used to the girl with the limping hip and wounded heart. If she changed, became someone else, how would she manage her world? All of her tiddly winks were carefully laid out.

Even worse, what if an encounter with an angel and this timeless wedding dress produced no change in her at all? What if she'd be just as guilty, just as shame-filled as before?

Gemma pressed her hand to her queasy belly, her palm brushing a row of silky, incandescent pearls.

"Come round when you need buttoning," Adelaide said.

"O-okay." Clearing her throat and breathing deep, she adjusted her arms in the bell sleeves and when she moved around the room divider, she couldn't stop the tears.

Also, she could've sworn she heard the sound of a chain unlocking.

"Well, love, aren't you just, just, *ummm*." Adelaide smiled, her sapphire blue eyes shining as she inspected Gemma. "Just as I pictured. Beautiful." Adelaide began to work the buttons. "Nothing like the gown you wore to the ball. That was something, wasn't it? But it had no power to change you. It was a man-made gown intended to be more art than dress. But this gown was sewn with love. Meant to unite, meant to heal and bring peace. This gown God had in mind from the very beginning."

"You mean to tell me God Himself wants me to wear this dress?" Gemma looked over her shoulder and down at Adelaide. "And the others? He wanted them to wear it too? You're not going to be able to button it up. It's too small. I'm taller and thicker than Hal and Jo."

"There. Done." With a soft pat on her shoulder, Adelaide guided Gemma toward the floor-length mirror where a blend of warm and bright lights seeped into the antique threads, then through Gemma, chasing away her shadows. "How lovely and fine you are."

Gemma refused to look at first. Not full on anyway.

"Look up, love," Adelaide said.

Gemma complied with a quick glance, only to be captured by her own image.

A sob burst through as she pressed her fingers to her lips. Until this moment, every time she caught her reflection in the mirror—not the cracked one by the door at the house—she saw the girl she despised.

She'd relied on her acting skills to front happiness and confidence. Fake it until you make it, right? But every time she was alone and passed by any mirror, she loathed herself.

"What do you see?" Adelaide said.

Gemma shook her head. "I can't…"

"Would it help if I told you I've helped princesses before who felt lost and broken, and even more unworthy than you?" Adelaide very casually fluffed the skirt again which seemed to grow fuller and wider each time. "There, I think you dreamed of a large, sweeping skirt, didn't you?"

"I wish you'd stop calling me a princess."

"But it's who you are. Your identity is a disgraced actress, but your essence, if you choose to believe, is a princess. It's there for the taking with access to the highest of all royal thrones."

Gemma looked into Adelaide's face and suddenly they were the only two on earth. She wasn't the Gemma of yesterday or even sixty seconds ago, she was new and clean, redeemed. A fresh light washed the mezzanine, rising like a river and soaked every part of Gemma.

Her darkness could no longer hide. Another sob rolled through her and echoed in the room. A wail of sorrow and regret. The light continued, moving and shifting, accenting the gold threads of the gown and weaving through Gemma's hair.

She tried to find Adelaide but she was obscured by the glow. All she could see, and feel, was light. Good, clean, redeeming light.

"Oh, why? Why did I do it?" Gemma slowly sank to the mezzanine floor. "I'm sorry, so sorry. For everything. For everything. I don't want to ever do it again. Ever." Her forehead touched the wide, polished planks. Her tears filled the scuffs and scars. "Lord, here I am. If you want me… I'll be your princess."

The fragrance of spices grew stronger then faded, and peace began to press into her from the gown. A laugh bubbled up instead of a sob. Then another. And another. With each one, the echo of breaking chains followed.

She was free. Free! Jumping up, Gemma spun to celebrate with Adelaide, but when she glanced about, she was alone and under the normal lights, normal scents of the mezzanine.

"Adelaide?" She ducked into the storeroom. No angel of princesses was to be found. "Adelaide?" Gemma stood in the middle of the room and looked up. "I think you can hear me so thank you. I believe."

Gemma took one last look in the mirror, expecting to see her sad eyes propped above dark circles and pale lips. But what she saw changed her even more. A spark of life. Hope. Even more than what she saw in the cracked mirror. And there was a touch of pink on her lips and cheeks.

With a final glance at the dress, she wondered what happened now. But even more important, how was she to get out of the dress with a bazillion buttons?

"Adelaide, you must come back and help me." She didn't want JoJo and Haley to catch her in their dress. Not until she had a chance to explain.

But she wiggled and tugged, working the buttons, and at last she slipped free from the wedding dress. As she carried it back to its box, Gemma stopped short.

There on the floor was a large white swan's feather.

QUEEN CATHERINE

She hated the weakness, but recovery from this particular affliction took time. Apparently, she was blessed to be alive and kicking about, such as it were.

Edric fussed over her, as did her new maid, Ebba, an older woman with more nursing than fashion training, and her dear sweet Mason.

John was doing a splendid job with her duties. He read her daily boxes, kept her diary commitments and the Family business moving forward.

To her surprise, she found the forced, semi-retirement refreshing. She hid away from the world, from the business of the crown, and became Catherine, a wife, mother, sister, friend.

She missed Scottie. When she'd first gone back to Tennessee, the two of them texted or called at least once a day. But by the time October presented itself on the calendar, the messages were down to once a week.

They didn't know each other well enough to keep the conversation going. Their shared memories consisted of less than two weeks. What was that against a lifetime?

They'd talked of Christmas but really, would Scottie travel over again? She had her own traditions, friends and family. As did Catherine.

Fighting for her health made her all too aware of how quickly things could change, how short and fleeting life was.

"He's here, ma'am." Mason stood in the doorway. "Are you feeling all right? I can turn him away."

"Certainly not. We made an appointment." Catherine pushed to her feet, drawing strength from thirty years of political and social meetings.

"Your Majesty." John entered, faced her with a bow and took her offered hand.

"Thank you for coming." She sat and motioned for him to sit across from her.

"Is all of this necessary?" John said.

"This is a formal meeting, so yes. You know we tried to get Hamish Fickle on our team."

"How could I not? He mocks us every time he opens his mouth."

"Best to ignore him at this point. People will tire of him," Catherine said. "But you, my dear boy, need to start making your mark. Get on the talk shows."

"You're joking, right? I'm not going to become a talk show puppet."

"No one is talking puppet. We can partner with the right shows and presenters. But we must move you away from the topic of the, um, the—"

"Vegas stripper?" His voice carried a bit of defiance.

"I wasn't going to say that, but yes."

"As you pointed out about MP Fickle, we'd do best to ignore it. Let it die. You know if I go on talk shows, all they'll want to talk about is Gemma."

"Are you still in touch with her?" Catherine said.

"No." The sadness in his reply made her flinch. "She probably thinks I hate her, but I don't. I'm giving her space."

"What about Sydney Templeton? Have you seen her lately?"

"I see your spies are hard at work."

"She's perfect, if I can use that word."

"Sydney is pretty special."

Catherine leaned toward her son. "Then get on with it."

"With what?"

"Marriage. Just make sure she doesn't have any Holland-sized secrets. Her father's not in the House of Lords since he's sadly deceased. So there'd be no tomfoolery there."

"You want me to marry her?" John was on his feet, pacing.

"With MP Fickle on the loose, we need your position as our next king tied with a neat, pretty bow."

"I have other plans. Beginning with you changing the writ. You promised me you would if I went to meet Scottie."

"As I recall, I said I'd look into it. I did take a meeting with Elias and we believe, considering your current widower status and the trouble Fickle is stirring, the writ must remain intact."

"No, the writ must change. Then I will take my oath and the crown will be secure."

"But if you don't marry—"

"Gus's child will be my heir. Mum, what's going on?"

She sighed, her expression sober. "I fear if I change the writ you will not marry. That a change now from the crown while people are being stirred to think it's time for something new, something different, will make it appear as if we are weakening. Fickle will take a well-aimed shot at our bow." She shoved to her feet with a remarkable strength. "The damage could be irreparable."

"Has your illness gone to your head, Mum?" He dropped all the formality of a royal audience. "Irreparable? Because you changed a writ to allow the crown heir to swear his or her oath of allegiance without a spouse. You cannot believe people will balk at such a modern move. In fact, I believe they'll see it as the House of Blue becoming more relevant. How many Lauchtens are really for the monarch to go away? A few rabble rousers at Fickle's campus gatherings? And you know he'd not be the first MP or lord or political opponent to take a shot at our bow. We're still here. Stronger than ever."

"Beautiful speech, son. But the writ stands." Catherine practiced that line for the past week.

He moved with frustration around the audience room. "What if I promise to marry within the next two years?"

"Six months."

"Six months? You cannot be serious." Then he swung around to her. "Whoever I want?"

She narrowed her eyes at him. "What do you mean? I should tell you I've reached out to Sydney's parents. We might have a dinner. Here."

"Go ahead but I won't be there." By his tone she understood he battled the call of duty over the call of his heart.

Welcome to the crown, my son. She knew the feeling all too well.

"My father gave me an ultimatum when I returned home from America. After leaving Scottie with Trent. I met your father within the month, and we've been happy and in love for thirty-six years."

"I'm not you. I'll marry who I want, when I want."

"Within the next six months."

"Why six months? What's the rush? Are you going somewhere?"

"No, but this bout with Guillain-Barré has made me realize we cannot delay the investiture. I'll sleep easy at night knowing you are my full and rightful heir."

Hands in his pockets, John stared at the window for a long while. At last he said, "I met an interesting man in Dalholm. Emmanuel."

"You saw Emmanuel?" The holy man now appeared to her firstborn.

"We chatted at the Belly of the Beast. I think he healed Briley. Know what he told me?"

"What?" Catherine wasn't sure she wanted to hear the answer.

"That my best friend needed me."

"Your best friend? Really? That's rather curious. Did he mean Larabee? Or perhaps Lute?"

"He meant Gemma Stone. And guess what, Mum, I proposed to her. After the ball."

"You what?" Catherine rose from her chair. "I hope she had the good sense to turn you down."

While she did not want to be judgmental or small-minded—people made mistakes, she certainly had—she hardly thought this American *showgirl* was right for the crown.

"She did but I never accepted her answer."

"Thank goodness." Catherine pressed her hand over her thumping heart. "And you don't have to accept her answer. She said no."

"Emmanuel told me to go to her."

"Emmanuel told you to go to her?"

"I've been putting it off for fear of... I don't know. Fear of you. Fear of fully letting go of Holland and the past. Fear of falling in love and losing Gemma like I lost Holland. Fear she'll turn me down again. Fear of what the people will do to her if she agrees to our global fishbowl."

"Emmanuel told you to go to Gemma Stone? Are you having me on?"

"He told me to go to my best friend." A flicker of determination crossed his fine, chiseled features—so much like her father's—and she knew he'd settled something in his mind. "Gemma is my best friend. I told her so when I proposed. Then Emmanuel came into the Belly of the Beast and changed me. Mum, you don't know Gemma but I promise you, she is much more than one tawdry story."

"And you really love her?"

"I'm on my way, yes. She was my friend first. Now, I fall more in love with every thought of her. It's different than with Holland who seemed to fit some predetermined mold. She was everything I wanted as a future queen. And I did love her. But with Gemma I'm nothing more than an ordinary chap falling for an ordinary girl. She makes me want to be a better man, Mum, and that will make me a better king."

"You are sure?"

"Emmanuel seems to be sure."

"Well then, if Emmanuel is sure, you have my blessings. Do what you must." She was proud of him. He'd chosen Emmanuel over her. Over the people.

Oh, her precious son. He was going to make a fine king.

CHAPTER
THIRTY-ONE

GEMMA

There comes a time in every girl's life when she must honestly answer the question, "How'd you end up here?"

By getting up from the dirty floor on which she'd landed and choosing to walk toward wholeness. One step, one limp, at a time.

A week and a half after a tiny little angel and an old wedding gown set her free, Gemma was becoming the woman she always wanted to be. A friend, a daughter, a mother. A change agent for good.

It wasn't some big charity or national cause. Imani Shumaker was just as important and Gemma was proud to be her mama.

After the wedding dress day—which she confessed to Haley and JoJo and they all cried—Imani's adoption hit the fast track.

Before she knew it, they were before the judge to be officially united as mother and daughter. Gemma Stone and Imani Shumaker Stone.

Last night Justin's parents hosted a grand barbecue in celebration with smoked ribs, coleslaw, baked beans, corn on the cob, homemade ice cream, and a rousing cornhole tournament. Daddy got his buddies together for a guitar circle and the party roared on until one in the morning. No one cared it was a week night.

Imani hugged and kissed Gemma a thousand times, each touch, each move toward her solidifying their bond. Take that mistakes. Take that death.

Tonight when she ran onto the volleyball court for her final home game, Gemma would cheer as her real mother.

Anyway, back to the wedding dress. Haley and JoJo listened intently as Gemma told the story of Adelaide-the-angel and how putting on the gown had changed her. And never once did they state the obvious.

"You don't even have a boyfriend let alone a fiancé."

When Gemma finished her tale, the three of them sat in the office for a long time not saying a word.

Finally, Haley said, "Don't know how but that dress is more than a wedding gown."

"It's represents the Gospel," JoJo said.

Then this afternoon, B. A. Carpenter rang again.

"Can I ask you to meet me at the Kingston place again?"

And *that's* how she ended up here, flying down River Road with the top dropped on the BMW, the temperature in Hearts Bend finally more like fall than summer.

She had no idea what Carpenter wanted but frankly she didn't care. She found joy. Peace. Gratitude.

Keith Niven sent a link to a really cute little cottage out by the old, abandoned railway caboose that was for sale. She was going to check it out Saturday morning.

As much as she loved the farm, saying goodbye actually broke her last ties to Vegas. In her short hindsight, Gemma concluded it was a good thing.

Then again, if it wasn't for the farm and the newborn puppies, she'd have never become friends with the prince. She'd have never danced at a royal ball or been filled with the light of the Heart of God.

Maybe she'd have never met Adelaide, the princess angel. No use denying it. God was up to something. All she had to do was say yes.

Arriving at the farm, Gemma slowed and turned down the driveway. B. A. Carpenter was already there, walking the grounds with his hat pushed back on his head. When he saw her, he came her way with a nod and sheepish expression.

"Howdy, Miss Gemma. Sorry to have you come out here again so soon but—"

"What do you need? Is something wrong?" She glanced around. "Everything looks like I left it."

"Well, there's something in the barn that isn't quite right, and I wondered if you could help me explain to the Kingstons…"

"Sure, if I can. There was a lot not right with the barn when I bought the place—" Gemma hesitated at the barn door. Did she smell pizza?

She looked back at B. A. Carpenter. "Is someone else here?"

"The new owner. He wants to meet you."

"The new owner…a Kingston?" Gemma made a face. "Why?"

"Sometimes why is not the right question to ask, Miss Gemma."

JOHN

Once upon a time Prince John believed in fairy tales. And after this summer, he still did. He'd also discovered the author of his love story had a divine sense of the happily ever after. He was finally launched out of a horrible Act One and into a promising Act Two.

Crown Prince John was no longer bound by grief. He was free to love.

And, after three weeks of intense communication, working late into the night, he was about to execute his romantic plan. At least he hoped it was romantic. In hindsight, it might have been wise to communicate with his intended a time or two before springing the whole palaver on her.

Best of luck to you, mate.

He jerked to attention when he heard footsteps and reached for the light switch. He'd been so focused on details he'd not prepared for nerves. He was sweating now that he stood in the barn, the puppy stall wrapped in a thousand twinkle lights, soft music queued to play from a portable speaker, the round table in the corner draped in blue linen cloth, holding a bucket of champagne and a hot pizza from Angelo's. Would Gemma remember their first meal together was pizza?

He should've called her. Texted. Kept up the appearance of being friends. But once he decided, he put all his efforts into making his second proposal one she could not refuse.

Also, he feared if he talked to her, even texted her, his mounting love would just spill out. And he needed to tell her in person. Let her see in his eyes, hear in his voice, her past did not matter to him.

Mac and Mauve, their haul of friends, Imani, Justin, and Penny, were his boots on the ground. To his surprise, they kept his secret well. Then five days ago, he'd arrived at Buck and JoJo's to hide out until he could conclude business with the Kingstons through B. A. Carpenter.

Which brought him to this moment. Gemma arriving at the barn. He'd flip on the lights—which he hoped reflected those from the Heart of God.

In the meantime, he'd started a face-to-face relationship with Imani. She must know she was as much a part of his plan as her mother.

Last night they'd dined in secret on Buck's back deck.

"If I'm marrying Gemma, I'm making a commitment to you as well. You will join my family and if you want, I will be your father."

There were lots of tears, laughter, and goodness, the girl could rattle off the deepest, most thoughtful questions.

"Can I finish high school here?"

"Can I keep my parents' name if you adopt me too? Do you like me this much?"

"Can I think about all of this?"

"What exactly is royal life?"

"Would I get an allowance?"

John answered yes, yes, yes, yes and yes, and a lot of *We'll talk* replies. But mostly assured her he liked her a lot. Even loved her.

There were things to work through but in the end, he had Imani's blessing to propose to her mother.

He'd never forget her expression, her soft tears, and the way she flew into his arms. "Yes, please, make her happy."

He'd cleared the parent hurdle, the daughter hurdle, and now for the fiancée hurdle. Words like *insurmountable* and *fortress* came to mind.

GEMMA

Standing in the dark center aisle, she glanced back at B. A. Carpenter who was hustling to his car.

"What am I doing again?"

"Go on, you'll see."

Gemma turned back to the barn and the stalls. "Hello? Mr. Kingston?"

Lights flashed on, flooding the aisle and spilling out from the old puppy nursery. Music sounded, drawing her farther in.

"Mr. Kingston? It's me, Gemma." She'd never met the man before so she didn't know what to expect—or what this was all about—but she was quite sure she didn't anticipate Prince John stepping out in front of her.

"I'm not Mr. Kingston but a future king. Will I do?"

With a low gasp, she stepped back, wrapping her arms about her waist. "Prince, what are you doing here?" She loved how his blue eyes glistened. Hated how her soft voice quivered.

"Well, it occurred to me my mother was never going to change the marriage writ and I had to get on with finding a wife. Then I said, 'Prince, you actually proposed to a lass who turned you down but I think she needs a second chance.'"

Gemma shook her head. "No, John, no, I can't let you do this."

"But oh, I beg to differ, darling." He walked toward her, reaching for her hands. "You see, not only are you my best friend, but I love you. I fall more in love with you every time I see your face in my mind's eye."

"But you know the truth. Which is all well and good if we lived in a barn, but we won't live in a barn, Prince John."

He kissed her forehead. "Call me love or darling, babe or honey, but not Prince John. And no, we won't live in a barn but in a very giant fishbowl, but I think we can be the sharks those pariah need."

A tear dropped onto the back of his hand. "So much has happened since I came home. I've changed. Healed. But John, darling, love, honey, and babe, I cannot let my mistake plague you and your family."

He touched her chin and raised her gaze to his. "Do you love me?"

"More than I care to admit."

"Then marry me. We'll face whatever scandal comes, together."

"But you already know how it will be. Honestly, how's it been for you since the video went viral? That MP Fickle loves to bring it up every week."

"Who cares about him? Let him fight his own battles. We will focus on our love, our lives, and making a difference through the House of Blue, strengthening a thousand-year reign. Even Jesus's lineage had a prostitute."

"If you're trying to cheer me up—"

"I'm trying to get you to marry me." He tugged her toward the stall. "I'm hungry. Let's eat."

"John, darling, love, honey, babe, this is amazing." Twinkle lights dangled from ceiling to floor. Stringed music spilled from two little speakers. The hay had been swept away and the floor covered with a deep purple rug embroidered with the queen's cypher. C R I.

"Champagne and Angelo's pizza." He held out her chair.

"Like on our first date. Except without the champagne."

But before she could be seated, he hooked her to himself and kissed her. "I think I knew the moment JoJo paired us together in the 4th of July race I wanted you in my life. I knew you were special, Gemstone. But I really knew the afternoon of the wedding dress shoot. Marry me?"

"But darling, love, honey, babe, there's so much to work out. Imani's doing well in school and—"

"I guess I have to lay out my entire plan. You're a tough one to get a yes from, Gemma Stone. I bought this place."

"What?"

"Your dad helped me track down Mr. Carpenter and I made an offer to the Kingstons. They accepted. This is our place now. I've set aside a remodel budget. Your parents have agreed to move their trailer here until we can get the house plans set. Cole Danner will be our contractor. We'll live here, if you don't mind, as much as possible while Imani's in school. I can travel back and forth as needed. You can come with me and Imani will stay with your parents. And yes, she loves this plan. I already asked her permission to marry you."

"And she said yes?"

"After several dozen questions, yes."

Gemma laughed. "Sounds like her."

"I won't lie to you, Gemma. Life with me won't be easy. It won't be fair. But I promise you a loving husband, a loving home, and if you want, a loving father. I mean, I hope we have children. The queen is counting on an heir and—"

She couldn't resist another moment. Raising up, she kissed him, her hands wound into the oxford threads of his princely O'Shay shirt, the scent of his skin like the field after a rain.

When she pulled away, he was breathless. "Can I take that as a yes?"

"I might be crazy after what I've been through the past few years, but I love you, Prince John, darling, love, babe, honey."

"Is that how it's going to be? All my pet names because you love me so much?"

Gemma pressed her forehead to his chest. "I love you more than I knew. More than I thought I had a right."

If Hollywood, Matt, Vegas, and a viral video maximizing her shame led her to this, she'd take the journey of a thousand bad decisions all over again. Okay, maybe not every bad detour but it was her life, her journey, in which all things worked together for good.

Even better, she had her very own princess angel. Finally, Adelaide made sense.

"What about your parents? The Family? The government of Lauchtenland?"

"The queen understands. She's happy if I'm happy. Look, there is a lot to tell you. A lot to unpack, but it changes nothing about how I feel. About what I know is right. Are you willing to step out in courage with me?"

"You haven't even asked me about the video. The show. What I was doing on that stage."

"I'm curious, certainly, but in the end, whatever reasons you give me won't change my feelings or my mind. I want you to marry me."

"Then please, let me tell you. I can't marry you otherwise."

The prince nodded and gave her arms a squeeze. "Go on then."

Suddenly all the important details and reasons she'd collected to be her explanation vanished. Her newfound boldness waned. Was she really the woman being washed by light in the Heart of God? While wearing a mystical wedding gown?

"Gemma?" John said.

"Sorry, now that I'm free to speak about it, I can't. I almost don't want to give it another moment of my life." Oh the irony. "I spent over two years hiding the fact I did the show, worried sick that people would find out, and now that it's in the light, I feel like I was screaming the sky is falling when really it was just a bit of rain."

"I didn't watch the whole thing, but you didn't seem like you wanted to be there."

"Not in the least. The only way I could get through filming was to check out. My body was there but my mind was not. I fell off the stage that day." She patted her hip. "Woke me up, really. Best thing that ever happened to me."

"I assume the chap Matt Biglow was involved."

"Yes, but in the end, John, I walked out on that stage. Leading or being led makes no difference. I surrendered to it." She reached for his hands. "I've learned though. No one will ever force me against my beliefs or values again. I won't do what I know is wrong in my heart."

"That's the woman I know and love." He pulled one hand away, reached in his pocket and slipped a cool band down Gemma's ring finger. A diamond surrounded by gemstones. "When the jeweler brought me this piece, I knew it was the one, except if you don't like it then we can shop for—"

She pressed her full lips to his. "Do you forgive me? For the video and—"

"There's nothing to forgive. I admire you all the more for having the courage to change your life, to walk away from a dream that was dying. For trying to protect me. But Gemma, love, will you marry me?"

"Yes, Prince John, darling, honey—"

His kiss came hard and fast, and with an electric passion. Taking her in his arms, he raised her up and spun her around. Now she was where she was always meant to be. This was the world in which she'd make her mark, leave her peace. It would be for a lifetime.

"THERE'S GOING TO BE A ROYAL WEDDING IN DECEMBER!"

– @LOYALROYALSBLOG

"Prince John says mysterious white feathers played a part in his journey to finding love after the tragedy of losing his wife. Find out more as royal reporter Melissa Faris interviews Prince John and Gemma Stone tonight at 9:00 on LTV-1."

– LTV-1 VOICEOVER

"Gemma Stone will wear a hundred-and-ten-year-old wedding gown for her wedding. She told me the dress was very special. 'It helped me heal from past pain. I know God is with me.'"

– TUPPENCE CORBYN ON TUPPENCE CORBYN & FRIENDS

Prince John and Gemma Stone, to be styled Her Royal Highness Princess Gemma, were married Friday evening, December fourteenth, outside Clouver Abbey by the fountain in the Heart of God. The bride stunned in her antique wedding gown. Prince John dressed in the official military uniform of the House of Blue. Gemma's daughter, Imani Shumaker Stone, wore a Melinda House gown and served as maid of honor. His Royal Highness Prince Gus served as best man.

— THE NEWS LEADER

"The crown prince has officially sworn his oath to be the King of Lauchtenland. The investiture ceremony was performed after he and the newly styled HRH Princess Gemma exchanged vows. She also swore her allegiance to Lauchtenland and the cause of the crown."

— PERRY COPPERFIELD, CABLE NEWS PF

I love Gemma already. She's cool. I know the video thing was weird, but I think she's going to be great for our prince. For us.

— @STEFWITHANF ON INSTAGRAM

"Wow, what a story, Maddy."

"I agree, Hy. From widowhood to a raucous video to a proposal in a barn—I loved those photos—to a wedding outside in December. I think we can safely say Prince John has found his happily ever after. As well as Gemma. And she's stunning. More beautiful in person than in photos. There's a light in her eyes I can't describe. Well, to you Prince John and Princess Gemma, many years of happiness."

— MADELINE & HYACINTH ON THE MADELINE AND HYACINTH LIVE!

"The Chamber Office announced today the queen's daughter, Ms. Scottie O'Shay, will join the family at Hadsby Castle for Christmas and New Year's. 'This is a joyous occasion for us all.'"

"Her Royal Highness Princess Daffodil was delivered safely of a daughter, Tuesday, December fourteenth, at 6:20 in the evening. Mother and child are doing well."

— THE CHAMBER OFFICE

LET'S END HERE...

GEMMA

"Hurry." Her hand clasped her husband's as she led him down Queen's Avenue toward the moving lights of the Heart of God. "The clocks are about to strike."

"Darling, it's almost midnight and freezing. We have a nice suite waiting for us with a crackling fire."

"I know, so get a move on." Gemma put her head down against the chilled breeze and stretched her stride against the skirt of her nineteen-twelve mystical, wonderful, divine wedding gown. "This won't take long."

"Why are we reenacting a fairy tale? I had something else in mind for our wedding night." He reached for her waist, but she twisted beyond his grasp.

"You're the one who believes in fairy tales."

"Yes, and I have my Swan Princess." He caught her this time and pressed a cold, sweet kiss to her lips. "What's this all about?"

As he tapped his forehead to hers, a gust of wind brought a swirl of thick snowflakes. Gemma raised her face to the icy droplets.

Maybe she was making too much of it, but she wanted to return to the place where she'd ended their fairy tale last August. Where she chided him for seeing meaning in a feathered gown.

"The Heart of God," she said, moving through and into the lights. "Where I first turned you down."

"Is that why we're here?" John flipped up his coat collar and followed her farther into the Heart. "Should I expect some sort of apology?"

"You should expect this." She retrieved the long necklace box from her coat pocket, shivering when an icy gust slipped in and around her neck.

John gave her a curious glance. "I don't understand. This is the box I found in Holland's closet. The one with the necklace."

"Open it."

"I'm not going to find a rather large and ostentatious diamond, am I? Are you confessing some insider trading, conspiracy entanglement?"

"John, darling, love, honey, babe, you ask too many questions." They'd grown accustomed to the string of pet names. Like some sort of royal moniker. If a future king had four legal names, why not four terms of endearment? "Just look."

Removing his black leather kid gloves, he raised the lid. Inside was one large white swan feather.

"Darling, you're giving me one of my feathers?"

"I'm giving you *my* feather. I didn't make the connection until I came over before the wedding and saw the two on your bureau. You told me Emmanuel said there were three feathers. I knew I had the third. You see, after Adelaide visited me, that feather was on the mezzanine floor. This fairy tale may not have a glass slipper, but it has three feathers." She brushed her hand over his wild, thick hair. "You rescued me, Prince."

"You rescued me, Princess."

Gemma stepped into her husband's arms. "I promise you here and now, in the Heart of God, I have no secrets. I've no back room deals, and pray God, no more salacious videos. You've seen the worst of my past and loved me anyway. I will always love you and admire you, be honest with you and serve with you."

When she raised her gaze to his, tears brimmed in his eyes. "Emmanuel saved us both."

"God with us." She'd heard the story from the queen, from Prince Gus and Princess Daffodil, from the Belly of the Beast proprietor, Ernst. From Prince John. Even from Adelaide.

"Today we had a grand wedding with all of Lauchtenland celebrating but—"

"Music, dancing, confetti in the streets." A long strand of blue and red paper twisted past them.

"The Lauchtens have embraced you, my love."

"I'm not sure I can grasp it all." She gripped her white-gloved hands in his. "The last two months have left me a bit breathless, but you, my prince, you fill me."

A fast-tracked wedding in combination with the investiture meant there was no time for nitpicking or detailed traditions. Two families had to merge.

Mama and the queen bonded over a love of books. Daddy and the king consort took long walks over the palace grounds. Imani tiptoed into her new life with wide, beautiful eyes, Justin and Penny serving as her "people in waiting."

Even Scottie used the wedding to find her place in the royal family.

"But you and me," John said. "We'll always be the couple who tripped in a three-legged race then fell in love over a passel of pups while sleeping on a barn floor bed of hay."

"Best summer of my life," she said. "All those years in Hollywood, spinning my wheels, trying to make it, when Emmanuel knew all along, He'd send Adelaide to help me find my way. That sense of purpose I longed to fulfill was found in Him. I'd have saved myself a lot of heartache if I'd known that sooner."

"Our trials refine us, darling." The snow began to collect at the base of the fountain, but she wasn't cold. Her husband and the lights of the Heart of God kept her warm. "Looking back, Mum asked her son to extend an olive branch to the daughter she never knew and I, not wanting to go, decided to be an do it anyway and look at all the good. Above all, I found you."

At the midnight hour, the cathedral clocks began to chime, and John held Gemma as the sound of each stroke confirmed every vow they'd made today, every whisper of love. And that tonight their fairy tale wasn't ending, it was just beginning.

THE END

ACKNOWLEDGMENTS

As I write these closing remarks to you, I'm battling COVID. My biggest battle is fatigue. I pray I didn't infect Prince John and Gemma!

The weirdest part is no taste or smell. Kind of rude of COVID to do that to a writer on deadline. We need our sense of smell to help us emotionally! We also need our snacks!

As I was going through the last pages again and again, I felt a need to connect with Gemma more. I went outside, sat in the grass and turned my face to the sun. "Talk to me, Gemma."

It was then I realized how much we need our senses to process, to think, feel, and create.

All the while, I was asking God to restore my lost taste and smell. After I was off isolation protocol my brother's family arrived for a few days. Not long after I walked past my sister-in-law and caught a whiff of her body wash. "Hey, I can smell! I can smell!"

I grabbed a tortilla chip to see if taste had also returned. Yep. It was all so instant. There was much rejoicing.

SPECIAL THANKS TO...

Madeline and Hyacinth from Brighton Kingdom for visiting us via your lively show, *Madeline & Hyacinth Live!*

Beth Vogt for taking my calls and brainstorming various parts of the story with me. Also for giving her time to proof reading. Thank you, friend!

Susie Warren, as always, for helping me hash out the story's high-level concept last summer. And for our Saturday morning breakfasts.

Erin Healey for first round edits. Your insights are always spot on.

Barbara Curtis for her tremendous insight and help with two rounds of line edits.

Kristen Ingebretson for the amazing cover.

Darren Plummer who started as a reader and became a friend. Thanks for your help with Imani's character.

Kelly Franklin for her research and help with Queen Catherine's disease. Thank you!

Keith Carroll for his real estate advice.

The *Title Company Guy from Tennessee.* I know, you all need more than the *Title Company Guy from Tennessee,* but I cannot find his information. (Hand to the forehead.) I owe him a debt of gratitude for helping me with Gemma's property dilemma. Thank you!

Denise Harmer and Lianne March for proofreading.

The Advance Readers. The HRH's! I appreciate you all and your support for each story. You cannot know how much it means but it's the world!

My agent, Chip MacGregor for friendship and encouragement.

My family and friends. Thank you!

My dear husband, who is forever patient with this writer chick. Every writer's spouse deserves a gold medal. "Love you always and forever, Hubs!"

Jesus, thank you for every whisper, every touch, every moment of light in my life. I just want the world to know how truly wonderful, marvelous and beautiful You are!

RACHEL HAUCK is an award winning, *New York Times, USA Today,* and *Wall Street Journal* bestselling author.

Her book *The Wedding Dress* was named Inspirational Novel of the Year by *Romantic Times Book Reviews.* She is a double RITA finalist and a Christy and Carol Award Winner.

Her book *Once Upon A Prince,* first in the Royal Wedding Series, was filmed for an Original Hallmark movie.

Rachel has been awarded the prestigious Career Achievement Award for her body of original work by *Romantic Times Book Reviews.*

A retired member of the Executive Board for American Christian Fiction Writers, she teaches workshops and leads worship at the annual conference. She is a past Mentor of the Year.

At home, she's a wife, writer, worship leader, and a semi-enthusiastic runner and weight lifter.

A graduate of Ohio State University (Go, Bucks!) with a degree in Journalism, she's a former sorority girl and a devoted Ohio State football fan. Her bucket list is to stand on the sidelines with Ryan Day.

She lives in sunny central Florida with her husband and ornery cat.

For exclusive content and to *Stay Inspired,* sign up for her monthly update at www.rachelhauck.com.

Made in the USA
Monee, IL
14 June 2021